Praise for the gory, sexy, funny, fierce, and totally

unforgettable series from

J. F. LEWIS

CROSSED

"Eric is back and cruder than ever in J. F. Lewis's epically awesome Void City series.... *Crossed* is yet another tantalizingly abhorrent installment.... J. F. Lewis keeps getting better and better, and Eric keeps getting nastier and nastier."

—Alphareader.blogspot.com

REVAMPED

"J. F. Lewis has delivered an explosively written vampire tale!"
—Sherrilyn Kenyon, #1 *New York Times* bestselling author of the Dark Hunter series

"Vampire fans who like their blood and gore leavened with humor should enjoy this campy sequel to *Staked*."

—*Publishers Weekly*

"J. F. Lewis has a fresh and unique voice. If you haven't read *Staked*, pick it up as well and read them together—you will be glad you did."

—SciFiGuy

Burned is also available as an eBook

"*ReVamped* is hugely entertaining . . . written with twisted humor. . . . [It] meets all of the requirements for even the most demanding urban fantasy fan."

—LoveVampires.com

"Suh-*weet*. Finally, my long dry spell of so-so reads is over. *ReVamped* successfully banished my book blues."

—DirtySexyBooks.com

STAKED

"*Staked* will probably appeal to most readers who like Jim Butcher's Harry Dresden but wish that Harry would stop being so damn nice all the time."

—LoveVampires.com

"A pedal-to-the-metal demolition derby of sex and violence. Werewolves and vampires were never so much fun."

—Mario Acevedo, author of *X-Rated Bloodsuckers*

"A fast-paced story with a heady mixture of humor, violence, and sex."

—*Library Journal*

"Impressive. . . . Reminiscent of the early, and best, of the Anita Blake novels."

—Don D'Ammassa

"From the start I could tell this book would be something special. By page 8, I was proclaiming it a winner to my friends. I'm happy to report that I was correct."

—BestFantasyStories.com

"Eric is the bloodsucking equivalent of a *Spinal Tap* song: he goes all the way to eleven. . . . An entertaining story that stands out from the more generic vampire fare. With a fast-paced plot, a variety of interesting characters, and a certain cheesy eagerness, *Staked* makes for great reading."

—*Green Man Review*

"Uncovering the mystery surrounding our rebel hero is a reward in itself, while the action scenes in this raucous, raunchy blood-opera make for a very satisfying crunch."

—*Dark Realms* magazine

"From the moment you step into Eric's world, you are rocketing from one high-tension situation to another. . . . The exciting conclusion will definitely leave you breathless and wanting more."

—RomanceJunkies.com

"Serious yet funny, gory yet tender, magical and still down-to-earth. . . . In other words, a must-read!"

—*A Bookworm's Diary*

"Once you get caught up in the world of *Staked*, you're stuck in its thrall. . . . *Staked* walks a great balance between suspense and gore . . . a balance one rarely sees in first novels."

—*Our Gaggle of Girls*

Also available from Pocket

Staked
ReVamped
Crossed

BURNED

A Void City Novel

J. F. LEWIS

Pocket Books

New York   London   Toronto   Sydney   New Delhi

Pocket Books
A Division of Simon & Schuster, Inc.
1230 Avenue of the Americas
New York, NY 10020

This book is a work of fiction. Names, characters, places, and incidents either are products of the author's imagination or are used fictitiously. Any resemblance to actual events or locales or persons, living or dead, is entirely coincidental.

Copyright © 2012 by Jeremy F. Lewis

All rights reserved, including the right to reproduce this book or portions thereof in any form whatsoever. For information, address Pocket Books Subsidiary Rights Department, 1230 Avenue of the Americas, New York, NY 10020.

First Pocket Books paperback edition February 2012

POCKET and colophon are registered trademarks of Simon & Schuster, Inc.

For information about special discounts for bulk purchases, please contact Simon & Schuster Special Sales at 1-866-506-1949 or business@simonandschuster.com.

The Simon & Schuster Speakers Bureau can bring authors to your live event. For more information or to book an event, contact the Simon & Schuster Speakers Bureau at 1-866-248-3049 or visit our website at www.simonspeakers.com.

Manufactured in the United States of America

10 9 8 7 6 5 4 3 2 1

ISBN 978-1-4516-5186-7
ISBN 978-1-4516-5187-4 (ebook)

To the readers:

For buying my books, reading the words,
getting the jokes, and enjoying the ride.

ACKNOWLEDGMENTS

This book, like all of the others, had a lot of help. To everyone who pitched in, cheered me on, caught typos, misspellings, and made me rewrite until I'd written what I meant to say instead of something else . . . Thanks!

1

ERIC

ALL A PART OF THE PLAN

Vampires burn.

It's a rule.

A blanket hit me from behind, smothering the flames, and I felt strong arms around me, patting out the more stubborn patches around my neck and shoulders. I pushed Talbot away and rubbed at the smoldering remnants of the sun's wrath the same way a mortal man might dry himself after a shower.

"You could have just turned into a mouse," Talbot said. "I would have carried you in from the car."

Talbot's a mouser. He'd probably tell you that I'm his vampire. A pet of sorts. Mousers are basically cats that can be humans when they feel like it. Talbot has been with me since El Segundo, when the world went crazy and I had to play the hero. He believes I have hidden depths. I think he's deluded.

I tossed the blanket on the floor and stared up at him. Talbot is bigger than me, over six feet tall, and he has better taste in clothes. He's almost always wearing a bespoke suit, with well-tailored silks and satins setting off the dark color of his skin, the bright green of his eyes, and his bald head. I, on the other hand, have all my hair and prefer jeans and a T-shirt.

Smoke rose off my T-shirt as I seated myself calmly in a metal folding chair, waiting for my burns to heal.

"I forgot the sun was out," I said with a shrug.

I've never been too good at keeping track of whether it's day or night outside . . . which may sound funny coming from a person who catches fire if he gets it wrong, but it's the way I am. When I died (okay, if we're being picky, I was murdered), it was daytime when I rose as a vampire, so at least it's not a new development or anything.

I needed to keep it together. This was going to be The Big Day.

With an exasperated sigh, I stopped worrying about having forgotten the sun and decided to blame it on the sunproof glass they have in the back of the squad cars in Void City. One of the perks I get is cop-chauffeur service; I'll explain why later. If I ride around in a squad car too long, though, I forget why it's so bright outside.

Bright.

It was bright inside the warehouse, too. The place was old, but the lights worked well. I closed my eyes, waiting for the last trace of pain to vanish with the burns. My mind doesn't always work properly. It works better at night, but I still have good days and bad days. I needed today to be a good one. This was it. Day number one of my Big Plan.

When I closed my eyes, my other senses kicked into overdrive on instinct. The sound of heartbeats came first. I'm always aware of them on some level, the heartbeats of those who have them. It's worse when I'm hungry. I hadn't fed yet, and there were a lot of heartbeats to hear. Talbot's heart—a strong steady thumping; Magbidion's—a fluttering weak sound; and all the cops who were in on at least this portion of my Big Plan . . . their hearts beat in different ways: harder, softer, faster, slower . . . as unique to me as a face or a voice.

After the heartbeats, other sounds came into play. Outside the warehouse, I knew Sal was still sitting in the front seat of the squad car that had driven me here, wearing a portable radio, with one earbud tucked into the collar of his uniform and the other snaked up into his right ear. He and Little Carl have never been able to agree on a station, so he listens to an earbud and Carl listens to silence. Vampire hearing is good enough that I heard Sal's favorite station as well as he could. Better, even.

I don't know how the station does it yet, but when the Veil of Scrythax, the mystical artifact that used to prevent mundane citizens from seeing or remembering encounters with the supernatural, got ripped to shreds last year, 100.6 FM (WVCT—Void City Talk Radio) kept broadcasting the same as it always has. Mundane listeners seem to hear Christian or sports talk programming, but the rest of us hear the never-ending jabber of Sly Imp: Void City's demonic voice of the airwaves. The damned shock jock is distracting enough to make me forget about the sun, although apparently, that doesn't take much. I'd been thinking about something he said, kind of a tagline of sorts: "In Void City, the vampires run the town, the cops are on the take, and the werewolves have found religion."

Sly Imp's voice caught my attention, and I focused in for a moment. If I recognized the background music, Denis Leary's "Asshole," correctly, Sly was about to discuss me.

"And what do we think of our new Lord and Master, the great and powerful raging erection that is Eric Courtney?"

"Cue laugh track," I mumbled. And as if on my cue, the laugh track sounded. *Who the hell still uses a laugh track?*

"I mean, is it just me, or if our fearless leader is going to fly around in his combat form killing things left, right, and sideways, does he really have to do it with his 'staff of office' swinging in the breeze? We know it's big, pal. You don't have to wave it around out in the open like that. Save that thrill for the little woman back home. Am I right? Oh, oh, and speaking of the little woman . . ."

I really need to put some pants on the über vamp. A pair of shorts. Something. The über vamp is my "big bad combat" mode: all leather wings and ebony claws. Real balls-out vampire badass mojo. Quite literally balls out in my case. I don't know why I can shape-change into a mouse and back while keeping my clothes, but I always wind up naked when I'm the über vamp.

I tuned out Sly's ongoing roast and concentrated on the task at hand. Lord Phillip, the former vampiric ruler of Void City, never had the kind of trouble I was having. Killing him had set loose such a world of shit that I was still dealing with it almost a year later. In my own defense, I hadn't intended to take over.

Lord Phillip had been a twisted freak, which was fine with me—or would have been, provided he kept out of my way. I'm not the sort of guy who runs around righting wrongs and slaying dragons. But Phil messed with Greta, my daughter. She's adopted, one hell of a vampire, and can generally take care of herself, but if you mess with her, I'll kill you, knock your ivory tower down, set it on fire, and slaughter all your friends. It's a rule.

Unfortunately, the act of following said rule put me in charge.

I don't like responsibility, but it's not something I shirk, which is why my singed sorry ass was seated on but not sticking to (thanks to my blue jeans) the aforementioned folding chair, watching Captain Stacey in his office on the other side of town, through the eyes of one of my thralls.

It had been almost a year since I'd knocked down Lord Phil's Highland Towers and taken over, and this was a part of The Plan I couldn't put off any longer. Like I said before, I had a plan. If you know me, you know the idea of me with a plan should scare the hell out of you.

Maybe sometimes in the past I've been willfully ignorant, but I'm not stupid. Remember that bit about not shirking my duty? Keep it in mind. Step one of The Big Plan involved just that: doing my duty. It also involved Captain Stacey of the VCPD.

Captain Stacey had been in charge of the VCPD since the late sixties. Well, mid- to late sixties. Shortly after my death, let's say. He surely must have felt safe, protected, sitting there in his office. No mortal man would be a threat to him. His door wasn't locked. His gun wasn't even on his desk or at his side. I'm sure a being like him doesn't feel the need for such things the way a mortal might. As a mouser, like Talbot, Stacey was nigh immortal, incredibly hard to kill, and his morals were, to say the least, mutable and open to negotiation. I mean, mousers basically have the same morals a cat has. Even so, there are good cats and bad cats.

Stacey was a bad cat. The VCPD badge with his name on it meant he was part of the biggest gang in Void City. Every last cop was either crooked or kept under his mystic control by an ages-old deal with the Mages Guild. A thing like Stacey made the perfect public servant for Vampire High Society. For years I had no interest in him at all, even when he was hired to help capture me a few years ago. I've been historically willing to ignore all kinds of heinous crap as long as the other denizens of Void City stayed out of my way or were willing to offer a simple apology.

That changed when I walked the Paths of the Dead to get my daughter back. Ever since, I'd been remembering some things. Things I was finding it harder and harder to ignore. Too many things, maybe. As a result, I'd been making plans and recruiting allies.

Through the eyes of one of my newest allies, I watched

6 J. F. LEWIS

Captain Stacey sitting at that desk. And I remembered it. It was a classic steel tanker desk. It brought with it flashes of memory: eating lunch with Marilyn, being intimate with her, looking at crime scene photos, drinking with Sal and Little Carl . . . Stacey couldn't see me, of course, because I was in a warehouse all the way across town.

How could I see him?

Interesting question.

Vampires can create a bond with humans, share a little of their power: The human generally does the vampire's bidding and, in exchange, gets increased longevity and some measure of vampiric resilience and strength. They're called thralls. As a rule, I don't like having any because the whole "master" thing makes me uncomfortable.

Now that I have a bunch of them, I've been trying to think of them as little helpers. *Not just for Santa anymore. Heb.* Like it or not, I needed them for the plan to work. And at least they'd all been willing volunteers. While it is possible for a vampire to enslave a human, make a living person into an unwilling thrall, I've never done it, nor will I. My ex-buddy Roger did that to Marilyn (the love of my mortal life), and for that reason alone, I'm glad I killed him. And speaking of killing . . .

Refocusing on my own surroundings, I glanced around the warehouse. It was basically empty except for an abandoned set of old metal folding chairs. Magbidion—I guess you could call him my personal mage, another of my little helpers—was leaning against the wall. Talbot took a seat next to me in one of the empty chairs. A two-way radio indicated in glowing red numbers that it was on the right channel.

Talbot coughed. "Well?"

I closed my eyes and checked in with each of my little helpers. "Everything's ready. Do a quick look around to see if you spot anything?"

"Sure." Talbot stood, smoothing out his slacks. The sunlight outside made him seem bigger, more imposing, than he actually is. Maybe it was the way it reflected off the ebony skin of his bald head or the way he filled up the space. Could just be that he's that much bigger than I am.

Magbidion slumped into the vacant chair. His hands were shaky, his long greasy black hair swept back out of his face. He'd been overdoing it for almost a year. It's hard to keep spells running for long stretches of time, and Mags had been hiding so many of my dirty little secrets for so long, it was no surprise the strain was showing.

At night, I'm not what I used to be . . . and thanks to Magbidion, the number of people who know that can be counted on one hand. He's hiding my thralls, too. Normally, other vampires can sense them, can tell who's a thrall and who isn't. For the time being, all my new thralls are secret. That takes a lot of magic mojo.

"You sure you're up to this?" I asked him.

"When the demon who owns my soul comes for it, will you really feed him to Talbot?" Eating demons is one of Talbot's talents. I don't know how he fits the whole thing inside, but I've seen him slurp up a demon twice his size without so much as an untamed burp or excess bowel movement. That's not a typical mouser trick, though. It seems to be unique to Talbot. Maybe he got it from his mom. I met her in the underworld, a cute little bloodred kitty cat that could probably tear me and a whole army of me's to shreds. Name's Sekhmet.

I realized Magbidion was still waiting for my answer. "Yeah. Of course. Demons are assholes."

"Then I'll manage," he said. The tired smile on his face was born of a long time without hope followed by a sudden change that might make everything right again. I was familiar with that feeling. I had it then. I still do. When I'd gone to the underworld, I'd gotten back more than just my daughter. I'd found hope, too.

Talbot leaned back in through the warehouse door. "I'd have the SWAT team and the uniforms pull back another fifty yards, but other than that, you're good."

"Even the squad car?"

"Yeah. Stacey knows you've been using it, and he'll wonder why they didn't call this in."

I gave those mental orders, listened as the extra yardage piped Sly Imp's yammering down low enough that I couldn't really make out the words anymore, then pulled my smartphone out of my jeans pocket. I dialed in Stacey's desk number and, through the eyes of his deputy, watched him watch it ring. He took a sip of coffee, swallowed slowly, then answered the call on speaker. I hate being on speaker.

"Stacey."

"This is Eric." I looked at Talbot while I spoke, wanting him to give me a look or something if things sounded off. "I need a favor."

"Been a while since I heard from you, Mr. Courtney."

I laughed at that. He almost sounded respectful. I guess killing Lord Phil had bought me a little bonus respect in Stacey's eyes.

"Yeah, well, I haven't been sloppy lately, but I need you now."

"I'll send a few—"

"No. I need *you* out here," I cut him off, "and I need it kept quiet. Not a word in any log or a call ahead to the Mages Guild. I can't even write you a check for it. Everything has to be off the books and under the table." The Mages Guild had worked hard to fill in the gaps that the Veil of Scrythax didn't cover or didn't handle well enough. Now they were handling the whole ball of wax, and the strain on their resources was showing.

"You've never asked that before . . ." There was an implied question there.

"Can you do it or not, Stacey?" I grabbed one of the metal folding chairs next to me and hurled it straight down at the concrete floor. It came apart, scarring the concrete, the pieces clattering to the floor.

"Of course I can, Mr. Courtney." I watched him smile at what he took to be my little display of anger. "With Lord Phillip gone, you're the boss."

"Good." I gave him directions. "Get your ass out here. I already have Magbidion here to help with the cleanup, but I need to walk you through what happened, and then I need some advice."

"What the hell did you do, Courtney?"

"Get out here and you'll know," I said, thumbing the call to an end.

Talbot whistled. "What's he doing?"

"Disregarding my instructions and heading this way." Through borrowed eyes, I watched Stacey tell his deputy, one of my newest thralls, that the Mages Guild should be called if he didn't check back in about half an hour. Stacey walked out into the sunlight, and I watched until he was out of sight.

I clicked on the radio. "Melvin?"

"There's no Melvin here," Melvin said testily.

"Half-n-half calling Mother Goose," I said with a sigh. "Come in, Mother Goose."

"Half-n-half, this is Mother Goose. Come in."

"How's our kitty kat? Over."

"I'm watching his GPS now. He looks to be heading straight your way. He also called the on-duty mage and reported himself en route to a vampire call. Over."

"And, just to clarify, you are the on-duty mage, Mother Goose? Over."

"That I am, Half-n-half. Over."

"Rockstar asks that you remember the favor. Over."

"Will do, Half-n-half. Mother Goose over and out."

"Half-n-half?" Talbot asked with a low, velvety chuckle.

"Ebon Winter's way of keeping me in my place. Or something."

"I don't like that vampire," Talbot said, more to himself than to me.

"Me, either." I stood and started stripping down to my jeans and belt. Then I called in the next part of the plan. The large loading doors of the warehouse opened, and thirty men and women dressed in casual clothes entered. The afternoon sun cast additional illumination across a swath of empty warehouse. It had been abandoned for years, and graffiti covered parts of the floor as well as the walls.

"You're all volunteers," I said as my claws slid out with a familiar creepy nail-bed crawling sensation. Twinges of pain sprouted in my gums as my fangs came out to play, too. "If you want to back out, do it now. I won't hold it against any of you. This is dangerous as hell and there's every chance some of you—maybe all of you—could die. I'll do my best to make sure that doesn't happen, but once we get going, it won't be up to me anymore. Talbot will not step in to stop me."

Some of them said no. Others simply shook their heads.

"Then let's make this look good, shall we?"

I charged into their midst, and the blood that flowed was as real as it gets. So was the pain.

By the time Captain Stacey walked in, the sun outside filled the warehouse to the midway point, picking out the mangled bodies strewn from one end of the warehouse to the other, highlighting the remains of a slaughter that caked the concrete with blood, urine, excrement, and fear. Magbidion and Talbot stood off to one side, letting Stacey see the whole thing in one glance. His gaze lingered longest on a body near the west side of the warehouse: a woman named Katherine Marx—Officer Katherine Marx.

Stacey had always been able to control the good cops and

compel them to do things they wouldn't normally do, make them forget what he wanted them to forget. I wasn't supposed to know it, no one was supposed to know it, but Stacey had been using the same ability that he used to wipe the minds of his subordinates to have his way with Katherine and a few of the other lady cops.

Katherine had been his favorite recently, and she was the granddaughter of a friend of mine, a friend who'd been a cop back when I was alive . . . Thanks to Magbidion's assistance and the peculiarities of my new nighttime circumstances, I was remembering all kinds of things from those days . . . back when . . . when I'd come home from Korea and Marilyn had convinced me to apply for captain of the VCPD. Katherine wasn't the only cop in the pile; in fact, they'd all been cops at one time or another, but she was the one who would distract him. You can't look at a dead lover and feel nothing. Not unless you're dead inside.

"Some of them are cops," I said.

Stacey looked up at me blankly, his eyes taking a few seconds to focus. Where Talbot was impressive and smooth, Stacey seemed a petty creature, his belly showing signs of trained muscle going to fat. His eyes, normally cold and emotionless—mercenary—now showed a broken warmth, a wet edge.

"What the fuck happened?" Stacey shouted, discarding the grief and giving in to rage. It was a move I'd made myself many times. It feels good, but it makes you stupid. Stupid was not a part of The Plan. Stacey saw the blood on my hands, coating my bare chest, my jeans, slicking my face like a gruesome moisturizer mask, and then he was in my face, shoving me back. "What the fuck did you do to my cops?"

"Curiosity," I said. *Killed the cat.*

"What?" He shoved me again. Hard. Hard enough to knock me back against a row of folding chairs. "What?"

Of course, the word wasn't meant for him. It was The Signal, a part of The Plan. With Stacey focused on me, Magbidion dropped one of the spells he'd been maintaining, the subtle one that kept the thirty men and women I'd fought (every last one of them another new thrall) from regenerating. He kept the other spells, including the massive one concealing their thralldom, up and running.

"Nobody preys on my cops, asshole!" Stacey transformed. I have to admit that I dig the way mousers change. They get to skip the snap, crackle, and ouch of a werewolf transformation and the aching discomfort of a vampiric one. A slow glow of golden light suffused his skin, flowing over him. As it faded, the man with the paunch was replaced by a seven-foot-tall, massively muscled feline beast with metallic gold claws and fangs, fur in patches of white and orange, and glowing star-sapphire eyes: the all-cat version of a well-done werewolf special effect.

Stacey yowled, swatting me to the ground with one massive paw. My chest sizzled where his claws punctured my skin, but the pain felt nice. The truth is, I deserve to hurt. I've killed thousands of humans over the years. I can't bring myself to feel bad about it, because becoming a vampire was never my decision—Scrythax, the demon with a wacky sense of redemption who created the Courtney Family Curse, is to blame for that. For years I tried to minimize the number of people I killed by running a club and feeding off my employees as much as possible. If animal blood worked for me, that would have been great, but it doesn't.

"Don't make me go über vamp on you, Stacey," I spat through gritted teeth.

He responded by disemboweling me and hurling me up into the rafters, where I clanged against the ceiling. When I came back down, he was even bigger and more muscular, standing about ten feet tall. His fangs and claws glowed to match his eyes, and I fought to hide my grin. Mousers are different from other supernatural creatures in a whole lot of ways, but one of those differences is stranger than the rest. They exist on more than one plane of existence at once (the physical world, the world of dreams, and something Talbot calls the Akasha), so . . . to kill one, you have to get him all on the same plane with you or be able to affect him on those other planes of reality, too. I glanced over at Talbot. Yep. The way Stacey looked now was his whole being all in one place.

I think he expected me to transform, to become the über vamp, but this wasn't my fight. It wasn't Talbot's, either. I boxed Stacey's pointy cat ears as he seized me in his paws, but if I hadn't started his ears ringing, the gunfire surely would have. The VCPD SWAT team rolled in wearing full supernatural suppression gear and carrying weapons made for taking down monsters. Holy symbols, Elder Signs, and other marks of magical protection bedecked their body armor. Not one of them looked the least bit friendly. And every single one of them was one of my thralls.

The opening volley, twelve shotguns loaded with the VCPD's specialized flechette rounds (twenty tiny flechettes in one cartridge—fourteen steel, four silver, one hardened wood, and a single gold one), blasted Stacey mercilessly, followed almost immediately by two cops with flamethrowers lighting the dirty bastard up as he turned. The VCPD was usually more concerned with protecting society from knowledge of the supernatural than taking the supernatural on head-to-head, but the previous management had equipped them for any eventuality, and this was their fight. Stacey had made them do unspeakable things, had corrupted everything that police were supposed to be, had raped their minds and some of their bodies . . . and now they all knew it.

"Hard to shift part of yourself elsewhere when you're pumped full of metal, isn't it?" I asked as I rose to my feet.

Stacey didn't answer. He'd gone straight into that wounded-animal place mammals go when they're scared, confused, angry, and in pain.

Mousers are not easy to kill. It's a messy business. I wasn't staying for all of it. I had to get cleaned up anyway, because for once I had a bigger plan . . . and if somebody was going to screw it up by letting the cat out of the bag (okay, bad pun), it was not going to be me.

I walked over to where Talbot stood, grimly watching the men and women of the VCPD as they worked with hunting knives and machetes, skinning Stacey alive while others struggled to hold him down. Two officers with spears took turns jabbing him in the spine to keep him mostly paralyzed despite his mystical regenerative properties. Katherine was one of them. She had the slightest twist of a smile on her lips, though her cheeks were wet with tears. Other officers carried in twenty-pound bags of sand and huge bags of salt they must have gotten from a pool supply store. I hoped it would be enough.

"You going to get in trouble over this?" I asked Talbot.

"I didn't tell you anything Greta hadn't already figured out, so no." He frowned. "I can't share any information gleaned strictly from the Akasha, Eric, but as long as I can demonstrate that you could have reasonably had access to the knowledge yourself, the other mousers won't be adding any additional time to my exile. That and I hate this son of a bitch." His frown became a grin as he said the last few words. Talbot doesn't curse often, and I was willing to bet that "SOB" was a much stronger insult for mousers. "But it's flattering that you care."

"You mind taking me to the car?" I turned into a mouse. Talbot tucked me in his breast pocket to protect me from the sun, and off we went. He walked us over to the squad car in which I had arrived and dropped me off in back, then, after a pause for me to change back to normal, Talbot climbed in as well.

"He dead?" Sal asked.

"Yep, or will be soon enough."

"Wish I could have been in on that."

"Yeah," I said. "Sorry. Only room enough for so many."

"Don't apologize, boss," Sal said, the gratitude in his voice making me uncomfortable. "I'm just glad you're back."

The gratitude . . . I didn't know what to do with that or how to react, so I patted the back of his seat and ignored the rest, giving my attention to Talbot.

"You really coming with?" I asked.

"Yes. I want to watch you get haunted. I haven't seen that yet." Talbot folded his arms. "Are they here? When will they get here?"

I shook my head. "Sometimes it takes a while. Don't worry, Talbot, you'll get to see me tortured soon enough."

"That's why I hang around," Talbot said. "You're better than a ball of yarn."

2

ERIC

VAMPIRES NEVER LIVE ANYTHING DOWN

I woke with a start to the familiar sound of crying. A quick glance at my watch revealed that I wasn't wearing one. The sun was still up, but the car had moved. The Artiste Unknown, or rather, the burned-out remains of the Artiste Unknown, which had once been one of Void City's premier vampire hangouts, loomed outside the driver's-side window. Yellow police tape still marked the entrances, and the front windows had been boarded up.

I couldn't remember why I was here. Obviously, I'd been driven, but hadn't Talbot been with me?

"How long have I been asleep?"

"You could try your cell phone, jackass." I knew the voice, had known it since I was nine. Talbot had left me alone in the backseat of the squad car, and now he was going to miss the haunting. Served him right.

My cell phone wasn't in my pocket, but I found it in the floorboard, pressed up against my combat boots. The network claimed it was 3:16 P.M., which meant I'd been asleep for at least an hour. As a vampire, I've always slept in tiny little slices. Usually no more than four hours, often closer to one or two, but in the past I could always feel it coming on. Now sometimes it just happens, as if I'm narcoleptic.

"What, no thank you from the goddamn king of the vampires?" the voice snarked. I still couldn't see him. "Is the golden boy too lofty to pass the time with an old murdered friend?"

"Fuck you very much, Roger." Roger used to be my bestest-ever pal, until he started sleeping with my fiancée, had me killed, and found someone to turn him into a vampire. Not necessarily in that order. When I surprised him by coming back as a vampire, and a more powerful one than he was, he pretended to still be my friend. The whole thing got all melodramatic and shit. He forcibly enthralled my fiancée and used her soul as a bargaining chip to come back from the dead. Then he even tried to steal my soul. I prefer to simply think of him as an asshole who didn't stay dead properly. I waited for him to talk again, listening for directionality.

He stayed quiet, but I knew he was there, and he wasn't alone. The other three had to be somewhere nearby. When the knock on the window came, I was surprised that it wasn't one of my ghosts. It was somebody else's. John Hawkes knocked on my window, peering through his glasses at me with eyes such a startling shade of blue that it always takes me a moment to process them. Some people think they're contacts, but they aren't. He wore a LET THEM EAT SOYLENT GREEN T-shirt underneath a rainbow-tie-dyed Hawaiian shirt. Tan cargo shorts and a pair of multicolored Crocs, the summery kind with holes in them, completed his ensemble. Picture the most handsome guy in the world, with golden-blond hair and a David Bowie–like elfishness, and you'll be picturing John Hawkes.

"We're across the street." He pointed at a trendy little coffee shop that bore the name Hawkes Coffee Jam. Talbot and the two officers who belonged with the squad car were having beignets and café au lait. Now that I saw it, I registered the smell, and the odor brought my fangs out. Though vampires can't eat, we crave food. Most of us try to make our thralls or friends eat food we crave so we can watch them. Polite vampires call it voyeuristic eating. I call it food porn.

Talbot waved at me. "You being haunted yet?"

"Yes, but I don't see them."

Talbot dropped his beignet, sending out a tiny cloud of powdered sugar that would have hit his suit if he hadn't used his catlike reflexes to vault backward out of the chair. His eyes glowed green as they transformed from human to slit pupils and on to luminescent star emeralds. I didn't like the frown I saw on his face. It was two parts "damn" and one part "I don't like the look of this."

"Mauvais le chat," came a woman's voice.

"Bad kitty?" I said aloud.

"What?" Talbot raised an eyebrow.

"The French chick just called you *mauvais le chat.* That's 'bad kitty,' right?"

"Close," Talbot answered. "Since when do you speak French, though?"

"Just shout right past me," John said with no sign of the slight having impacted his good mood, "it doesn't bother me at all."

"Sorry, John."

"Scoot back?"

I did and he opened the car door, offering a cardboard pastry box as my chariot for crossing the street unbarbecued. Taking the hint, I went all mousy, trying to ignore the weirdo balls-receding-from-the-cold sensation that comes with turning into something way smaller than I actually am.

Cars passed by on the street outside my box, and after waiting a few minutes for a lull, John hurried across the street and took me inside his coffee shop. Which is kind of like hell. For all that it's a coffee shop first, John always has the best pastries, confections, and chocolate-dipped anything (ranging from pretzels to strawberries to dried apricots). To put it mildly, the scents, though pleasant, make one hungry for the taste.

"My windows are sun-safe," he said, tossing me onto a small two-top inside. He opened the box and I crawled out, hopping off the table and transforming back to my more human shape. At least that came with the bonus of a little warmth. Vampires don't hold body temperature well, so we're almost always cold. For those of us who can bring our clothes with us when we transform, the transformation leaves our clothes clean, repaired, and fresh-out-of-the-dryer hot. If I concentrate, I can keep whatever outfit I'm wearing, but if I don't actively think about it, I wind up in combat boots, black socks, tightie-whities, jeans, my favorite brown belt, and a black WELCOME TO THE VOID T-shirt. It saves a lot on clothing costs, but the process doesn't come free. It tends to deplete my blood supply, especially when I do it more than once or twice in a day . . . unless, of course, I've eaten thirty police officers' worth of blood first.

I didn't ask John why he had sun-safe windows, and he didn't offer an explanation, but I had a pretty good idea.

"Winter," John said, "wants you to know that she will come tonight to give you the first task." Winter would have been most High Society vamps' first choice to replace Lord Phillip, if I hadn't come along. Since my rise to power, Winter had gone from master manipulator to terrorist. He revealed himself as a total anti-vampire activist and killed half the city's vampires in one glorious death trap of an extravaganza last year. Winter is the most attractive man I've ever met, and he's got more musical talent than your average high-end orchestra shoved together in a bathroom with Elvis. When he isn't singing or playing, he's gambling, but not at cards or in a casino; he bets on outcomes, social interactions, weird stuff—and he always wins. He and John Hawkes bear a striking resemblance to each other, and I've never seen the two of them in the same room together, which doesn't exactly mean Clark Kent is Superman, but I have my suspicions.

"She?" I said. "She as in Lady Scrytha, she?"

The young woman behind the register giggled at that. She was cute. Early twenties. Brunette. Eyes the color of milk chocolate. She had at least three cats at home, one gerbil, and some sort of bird. She didn't smoke anymore, but I could smell the nicotine in her system. Her name tag dubbed her April. I guessed she was trying the gum route to quitting. I wanted to rip out her throat and drink her dry. Not because I disliked her, but because that's how I feel about most humans when I'm hungry.

What?

Vampire, remember?

John put his hand on my arm. "April, why don't you fix Mr. Courtney a whole-fat nukeless venti red blend?"

"I wasn't going to eat her," I said churlishly.

He ignored that with a charming smile and didn't let go of my arm. "Not Lady Scrytha," he said, jumping back to the other conversation.

I blinked, trying to remember what we'd been talking about. "Oh. Right. My first task. So, does he know who it's going to be? Am I right?"

"Winter thinks you are." He steered me to the window, where I could see Talbot gathering his small plate of beignets and coffee, preparing to carry them inside to join us.

"Anything else?"

"He says 'The War' will start tonight when you go to accomplish the task. So be ready for that. He says that I'm to say if your task is what you both suspect it will be, he won't allow it to happen, not the way Scrytha will want it to happen."

"So I'm right about that, too." April handed me a fancy coffee cup with the special sip cap on top, just like everyone else's. The blood in the cup was warm, just a hair under ninety-eight degrees. I hesitated, but given that I was already being haunted, feeding probably wasn't going to bring on anything new. I gave it a tentative sip. It was a mixture of blood types, I guessed from the name, but it isn't like they taste different. I drank it down and felt more civilized and less civilized at the same time. "Damn."

"What?" Talbot asked as he came in.

"I don't like being right," I said, smiling despite myself. "If I'm right too often, it's a sign of the apocalypse."

Everyone laughed. Even April. My own laughter died down when I heard three voices join in from throats I couldn't see. Somewhere off in the distance, a fourth voice I recognized was crying. I hate ghosts. I used to be haunted by an ancestor of mine: John Paul Courtney. I hated that at the time, but given the chance, I'd take him over my four new ghosts any day. These were the ghosts of souls I'd effectively eaten when I was a revenant.

Clearing my throat, I asked Talbot to finish his food so we could head back to my place. If I was lucky, I'd have time to get in some sword practice and a shower before I had any visitors. If I was even more lucky, my ghosts would let me do it in peace.

3

ERIC

HAPPY IN HELL

The infernal deliverer of my presumably never-ending demonic honey-do list stood in a rapidly dissipating puff of red smoke, filling my bedroom with her signature scent. A sulfurous stench would have made sense, would have matched the tiny twin black horns peeking out between her triple-toned blond hair and gone well with the black leather dominatrix dress, nine-inch spike heels, and choker she wore. But the odor wasn't sulfur. Instead, as in life, Rachel had a very distinct aroma: cinnamon.

I looked up from my seat on the edge of my bed and smirked. Rachel. Of course she would be the one they would send to be my boss. How original. I'd been right. I put down the washcloth I'd been using to wipe down my sword, not caring if it got the bedsheets a little wet. "I thought the devil wore a blue dress."

"Get up. You've got a job to do." Rachel eyed the steel long sword in my hand. As she watched, a coat of ice surrounded the metal. It's a great sword, magic and everything, though I think in the long run, a fiery sword would be more useful than an icy one. I'd taken it away from a demon some time ago and pretty much left it in the refrigerator. Now, given the limitations of my powers at night, I was taking time to learn how to use the damn thing. There's more to it than meets the eye, kind of like with Transformers, and well . . . me. What can I say? Boys love their toys.

"Well?" Hands on her hips. Rachel's body language spoke volumes. She was perturbed by my lack of reaction. I'm not sure what she expected. A hug? A curse? A death threat? Before I'd had Greta kill her, she'd been a human, one of my thralls, and my sister-in-law . . . and my lover . . . and things had gotten messy.

"Well what?" I asked.

"Aren't you glad to see me?" She winked. "Or surprised?"

"Nope."

I got up and walked across the bedroom, sword still in hand. Back in my bachelor days, I'd made do with little more than a bed and a sink, but when I got married to Tabitha (Rachel's older sister), Ebon Winter repaired, refurbished, and redesigned the Pollux, the old-school movie palace I call home, as a wedding present.

In my bedroom, he'd knocked out a wall and extended the space. The old queen-size bed had been replaced with a California king. A proper bathroom had been installed. I had a fifty-two-inch widescreen LCD on one wall and a fridge with a specialized holder for my ice sword. Winter is one helluva interior decorator, even though he's also one of the scariest vampires I know. And that's saying a lot, given that when most folks in Void City think Scary Vampire, they picture me. Or my daughter, Greta.

I opened the chrome door of the refrigerator and put the sword away, which isn't to say that I put it in the fridge, necessarily, but that's what I meant it to look like. I assumed I'd have more time to practice with it later. *Too many secrets*.

"Not even a little surprised?" Rachel pouted. "A little glad?"

"I figured it was going to be you," I said over my shoulder, perusing the contents of the fridge. It made sense, particularly the cruelly ironic sort of sense that demons prefer. I'd once been Rachel's boss, and now she was mine. With that said, take a little advice from a being who knows: When dealing with demons (whatever the breed), never use the phrase "Whatever it is, I'll do it." No matter what they offer, no matter how great the need, a smart person—a rational person—will pull a Nancy Reagan and "just say no." I guess that makes me a romantic, because in order to get Marilyn back from hell, I took that deal, and now there was quite literally hell to pay.

Hell isn't what I'd call a nonprofit organization, either. Demons don't take Visa or American Express (I haven't tried MasterCard or Discover, but I'm guessing they're out, too). Not that I'd expected Marilyn's resurrection to come cheaply. Quite the opposite. But what I'd found out since then was that I'd made a deal (an obnoxiously open-ended deal, I might add) with an Infernatti. Infernatti are the demonic elite (a capo, in mobster terms), and I'd made my deal with Lady Scrytha, one of the Infernattiest of them all. She expects a lot of bang for her spiritual buck. And she does love irony.

"When Magbidion gave me the appointment time and location"—I kept my eyes on the fridge—"well, who else but Scrytha's new cathouse hall monitor would want to have the meeting in my bedroom?" In the fridge, a six-pack of Coke (one missing) in real glass bottles (bottled in Mexico with real sugar, not corn syrup) stood side by side with the remains of a BBQ pizza from Carl's down the street. Atop the white cardboard pizza box was a bowl of ranch dip and a plate of curled daikon chips, both covered in plastic wrap. Stacked next to all of that, up against the wall of the fridge, were six full blood bags, each tagged with a sticky note bearing my name: Eric Courtney. "Do you want a Coke?"

"Do I want a Coke?" Rachel scoffed.

"If you're hungry, I have some cold pizza." I smirked again when I said it, but I don't think Rachel noticed.

"Do you want to watch me eat something for you, baby?" Rachel sidled up next to me, her expression tipping toward the lascivious. Rachel knew all about food porn. "For old times?" She licked her lips.

Rachel had been the best and worst thrall I ever had. She'd been an enabler, pushing me to be more and more monstrous, to kill anyone I wanted when I wanted, and to use my powers to their fullest. She'd screwed up in the end, not by doing bad things so much as by letting me find out about them.

I'm the poster boy for blissful ignorance, but once I know something, once I can't ignore it, I have to act. Hoping my brief reverie had been convincingly long, I closed the fridge, wondering if Rachel had gotten a good look inside. Hoping she hadn't.

"No." I snagged a small wooden box from the top of the fridge, opened it, and drew out the steel chain necklace within. A large pendant hung from one end, an unpolished black stone set in its center.

Dropping the empty box, I slid past Rachel, our bodies brushing against each other. Back when she'd been alive and my thrall, our bodies had done more than that. The last time I'd touched her, it had been one last orgiastic good-bye fuck. The sex had been followed almost immediately—once I found out everything Rachel had done (which amounted to mindwiping me so that I forgot about my marriage to her sister, Tabitha)—by me asking Greta to kill her. I wasn't sure I actually would have killed her, but I knew Greta sure as hell had. Rachel seemed to have taken it all pretty well. Better to rule in hell and all that jazz, I suppose. *You think you won*, I thought. *Your boss thinks she won, too. But you're wrong. I saved Marilyn. I won.*

And I'm going to keep on winning.

"Somebody just fed." Rachel puffed up her chest, and I

let my eyes go where she wanted them to go, straight to her breasts. "You're all warm on the outside." She'd been a beautiful woman, and despite her newfound demonhood, her blond hair was still perfect. Her body was perfect, too, frozen at approximately nineteen forever.

I missed the butterfly tattoo she used to have on her cheek, but its absence aside, she'd always be gorgeous. I missed being with her in a remember-how-fun-it-was-that-time-when-we-jumped-out-of-an-airplane-without-parachutes-and-were-saved-by-a-freak-tornadic-microburst-only-to-be-caught-naked-together-in-our-hotel-room-later-and-have-our-lives-destroyed-by-the-relationship-fallout-but-what-a-rush-that-was sort of way.

"Everybody does," I said.

"Does what?" she asked.

"Feeds. So . . . what's my first Herculean task? Are there some stables in hell that need cleaning? Want me to blow up an orphanage?"

Rachel sighed. "All business, huh?"

I took a long deep breath and let it out. "Pretty much."

"Okay. Fine." Rachel clapped her hands together. "But this could be fun for us, Eric. Lady Scrytha sends me to you with your assignment . . . we screw each other's brains out. You feed on me, complete your assignment, and report back. Then we—"

"What's the job?" I wrapped the chain of the necklace around my finger. Cold metal on warm skin. Light not catching on the stone's reflective surface. I caught sight of my warped reflection in the chrome of the refrigerator, and my smile broadened. If people were going to keep meeting me in my bedroom at night, I was going to have to do something about that shiny surface. But the truth was, I liked it despite the risk of someone noticing.

"Would you stop smiling?" She stomped her foot, and a brief flash of flame punctuated the motion.

"I don't think so." I made a deal with a demon and I got screwed . . . those are the rules, right? I thought I was agreeing to do any one single thing, and then that "one thing," from Scrytha's point of view, was apparently "be my bitch for all eternity." Typical demon screw job.

So how come I felt like I won? It's a fair question, but I won't answer it yet. Even when I found out who was going to be giving me orders, the smile on my face just wouldn't go away. It was like being the Joker or something. The grin wouldn't fade. I was the only one who got the joke, and my joy wouldn't die. Even though Marilyn still wouldn't have anything to do with me, not romantically, even though Tabitha (who still thought of herself as my vampiric bride) was furious . . . none of it mattered, because Marilyn, the woman I'd loved most of my adult life and all of my undeath, was alive. As the cliché goes, where there's life, there's hope. And it had been a long, long time since I'd had a strong dose of hope, going way back to before I died and came back as a mass murderer.

I still remember the moment I got hope back. Scrytha was standing onstage at the Pollux, and she offered to give Marilyn back, new and improved—a true immortal. My answer? The insanely stupid one I warned you about. "Whatever it is, I'll do it." Yeah, I know. Not so smart. But since Marilyn was alive, okay, nearby, and even young again . . . Why should I care about the bad things that happen in the world as long as they don't happen to her? I'd seen her die with my own eyes, watched her soul get sucked into hell, and then . . . in spite of everything . . . I got her back.

I won. I won. I fucking won! I still wanted to shout it from the rooftops.

"What if I told you that you had to kill someone?" Rachel's

voice snapped me out of my literal reverie. What can I say? I have a tendency to wander off mentally. Maybe I need Ritalin?

"Unless the target is a member of what I consider my family," I answered, "I'll do it."

"It's an old friend."

"Talbot counts as part of my family," I reminded her.

"Older than that."

"Roger's already dead." *And haunting my happy ass every time I feed*, I added silently. Not that I understand exactly what the link between the feeding and the haunting is . . . or if I'd figured it out, I couldn't remember. Hell, I couldn't remember exactly how Roger died the last time, either, but I knew I was responsible. My memory is better at night now, but it's far from perfect and very hit or miss. Then again, I guess expecting my Alzheimer's to act up only when it's convenient is a little unrealistic. I used to think the memory problems had something to do with being embalmed before I rose as a vampire. Now I knew better. "Isn't he?"

"You ate his soul, Eric." Rachel rolled her eyes. "This time he's dead."

Soul eating. I shuddered. *Right. I remember now. That ability, I don't miss.* "Then I don't see a proble—"

"It's Father Ike." Rachel's gaze went to the hardwood floor. "Lady Scrytha wants you to kill him as proof that you'll keep your part of the bargain."

Bingo! Of course it was Ike.

"No."

"I knew it." She snapped her fingers and pointed at me as she spoke. "You're going to break the deal. Marilyn is going straight back to—"

I donned the necklace and crossed to Rachel in one smooth motion. My right hand closed around Rachel's throat. Her eyes went wide, confused.

"Nothing happens to Marilyn, even if I break the deal."

Rachel winced away from my shout. She squinted, trying to see me, but thanks to my nice new necklace, her demonic upgrade prevented it. "That is the rule I do remember. If I break the deal, I get punished. Other people get punished. But not her. Besides"—I stroked Rachel's hair with my left hand, and she leaned into it—"I didn't say I was breaking the deal."

"Why can't I see you?" she choked out. "What is that necklace?"

"I call it the Blind Eye."

Rachel turned her head, brushing my hand with her cheek as I let her go. Good Lord, we have a strange relationship. I went on, "One half of the Eye of Scrythax. It broke when I went to hell to get Greta back. It's blind now. Magbidion rigged up the necklace for me. When I wear it . . ."

"Demons can't see you." She chewed her lip. "Give it to me."

"Sure," I said.

I'd had help planning for this ever since we'd figured out who my handler was going to be. One great thing about having Magbidion—a thrall who has actually signed a demonic contract before, sold his soul, and had years to sweat about the details—is that guy knows the rules inside and out; information gleaned from hours and hours spent searching for loopholes. I unfolded a little sheet of paper from my pocket and read the words Magbidion had scrawled on a Post-it note for me: "'As long as that is Lady Scrytha's request and she understands that it changes the nature of our transaction.'"

"You have to do anything she wants." Rachel spoke to the room, doing her best to approximate my location. "If she says hand me the necklace—"

"Then it's an exchange of goods, not services," I said, moving closer to her. She tried not to flinch when my breath hit her cheek. "I agreed to *do* anything, not *give* anything. She could make me buy her a hot dog. She could order me to steal something for her but not to give her what's mine. Apparently, in demonic contract law, there is a distinct difference. You said she wanted me to kill him as proof." I shook my head. "The deal doesn't require me to prove anything. If, on the other hand, killing Father Ike is an order made in accordance with the terms of our pact . . ."

"Semantics." Rachel laughed. "You have to do whatever I say."

"And I will as long as you, as her duly authorized agent, say the orders are from Lady Scrytha and you make it a command."

"Fine." Rachel ran a hand through her hair. "Lady Scrytha orders you to kill Father Ike."

My gut tightened as I felt the compulsion of my oath: an itch between my eyes, fleeting but unmistakable. "When?"

"Tonight."

"Kill Ike." The sensation grew from itch to phantom pain, as if a talon hung just above my forehead. "Got it."

I served with Ike in Korea, before I left the military and took the job as captain of the VCPD. He was the company priest. He knew about my troubles when I'd been alive, the problems I had after World War II. Ike knew me inside and out. Even after my decades as a vampire, all the people I'd killed, the stupid things I'd done, Ike still had faith in me. I picked up my iPhone from the nightstand and sent a quick text, then looked up Ike's name in the contact list and made the call.

Rachel saw the iPhone move, then vanish, and started. "Will you take that stupid necklace off?" she growled.

"Is that an order from Lady Scrytha?" I mocked.

She stomped her foot again and made an exasperated noise, but I wasn't paying much attention. The iPhone had my full focus. It stopped ringing.

"Eric," said a sleepy voice on the other end, "when will you remember that not all of God's creatures are nocturnal?"

"Hey, Father." I spoke into the phone, watching Rachel's

confusion play across her face. "I made a deal to get Marilyn back."

"Get her back?" He paused. "How? When?" Another pause. "What did you have to do, Eric?"

"About a year ago. And I agreed to do whatever Lady Scrytha asked."

"Eric!" He was wide awake, with shock and outrage clear in his voice. That one word rang like the slap Marilyn had given me the minute Scrytha brought her back. Idiot, she'd called me. Father Ike was too polite to say it, but he was thinking the same thing. "Surely you understand—"

"They want me to kill you," I said matter-of-factly. "But due to recent . . . political changes . . . if you leave town, they probably won't want me to follow you."

"I'm not going anywhere, my friend."

"Up to you, Ike," I said after a pause. "But I'm taking a five-minute shower, putting on a change of clothes, and then I'm heading over there to wrap my hands around your neck and choke the life out of you. Afterward, to finish the job, I'm going to burn down your church, because let's face it, that building is a part of you."

"So be it," Ike said softly, "and may God forgive you."

As he hung up, I got a text reply to the one I'd sent. Three words: *I win again.*

I laughed and thumbed off the phone. Believe it or not, everything was going according to The Plan.

"You warned him," Rachel spat.

"Was I not supposed to?" I stripped out of my clothes (except for the necklace), went into the bathroom, and started up the shower. "You should have clarified."

"Want a little company?" Rachel asked.

"Why?" I stepped into the shower, even though the water was still a little cold, and put my head under the torrent of water. "Do you think Marilyn would join me?"

Rachel vanished in a puff of cinnamon and I whistled, letting the warm water rush over me. *You can do this,* I told myself. *It's for Marilyn. You can do anything for Marilyn.* I hoped I was right. I had a very big secret, one I'd been hiding almost a year, and I would have to keep it as long as I could. My heart pounded in my chest, but it made no sound. One of Magbidion's enchantments was busy making sure of that.

Yeah. Yeah.

I know.

Sneaky. Sneaky.

4

ERIC

I LIKE IKE

A 1964½ Mustang convertible pulled up in front of the Pollux. Light from the marquee reflected in the red paint of the car's long blunt hood. If I hadn't been smiling already, the rumble of the 271-horsepower V8 engine would have brought a grin to my lips as I pushed open the glass double doors and stepped out onto the sidewalk. Beatrice, her storm-cloud-colored eyes sparking and long fiery tresses windblown but beautiful, waved at me from the driver's seat, having obviously enjoyed her turn as Fang's human "cover."

There's a long story behind Fang, but the short version is this: He's around 3,100 pounds of all-American Ford automobile. He's undead and we're linked. To destroy me, you have to destroy Fang. In Emperor vampire terms, that makes him my memento mori, which, for vampiric purposes, is Latin for "remember that you are mortal." He has a mind of his own, but it's based on mine. Oh, and he eats people.

An Emperor has to store a portion of his might in an object, a memento mori, and mine is in Fang. Through his memento mori, an Emperor also becomes vulnerable to true destruction.

My sire, Lisette, had been an Emperor. She'd risen as a zombie and a vampire at the same time. To end an Emperor, you have to destroy her memento mori, kill her vampire self, and then destroy her other undead form (or vice versa). Fang ate Lisette's memento mori. My daughter, Greta, destroyed her zombie nature, and me . . . I ate her soul. Soul sucking is what revenants do. Once upon a time I rose as the ghost of a murdered man and a vampire simultaneously, courtesy of the now-defunct Courtney Family Curse. You won't see me sucking any more souls, though. And whether I still count as an Emperor is an open question. With Marilyn back, I'm a new man.

Yay, me.

Ever since the Veil of Scrythax was destroyed, the mages had been working like crazy to keep the genie in the bottle. It was running them, and me, a little ragged . . . and don't get me started on the price tag. Fang has been able to do a little influencing on his own ever since he ate my sire's memento mori, but doing it drains him and makes him hungry, so it's best to let one of my thralls cruise around with him when he's out and about without me or Greta. I think Beatrice enjoys it more than the others.

"Hungry?" Beatrice asked me as she climbed out of the car. She was wearing a forest-green V-neck swoop top and a leather miniskirt that had risen to scandalous heights from her time behind the wheel. She patted her inner thigh, the flesh exposed by her miniskirt. The femoral artery used to be my favorite feeding spot. In previous years, my fangs would have come out at the suggestion, but given everything that was going on . . . it was the wrong time. Of all my thralls, Beatrice was the only one who used to serve another vampire. She was the most knowledgeable, and to be honest, she was the one most likely to suddenly figure out the whole "vampire by day, true immortal by night" thing that I was trying to keep under wraps. Maybe if the Eye of Scrythax hadn't split, I'd have ended up a true immortal all the time, but that's not the way it happened.

"No." I shook my head. "I'm fine."

Beatrice put a hand on my chest. "You're still warm. They can't have gotten too far." She scanned our surroundings and saw no one special. "Who is it?"

"Who is what?"

"Who are you feeding on, Eric? You haven't fed on me in a month." A gust of wind caught her red hair and tossed it about her shoulders. "Or on any of the other girls, as far as I can tell."

"Tomorrow," I said. "Or maybe later tonight, but definitely tomorrow morning . . . or afternoon."

"Really?" She perked up. "It won't make her mad, will it?"

"Who?"

"Marilyn." She leaned in close, breath warming my skin. "We all think you've been feeding on her when—"

"No." It came out harsh—angry—my smile faltering. "I don't feed on Marilyn. I never feed on Marilyn." My voice got louder, adrenaline pumping. "No one does! Ever!"

I stopped shouting. Stupidity had no place in The Plan.

"Sorry." I maneuvered past Beatrice and sank down into the still-warm driver's seat. "We'll talk about it later. I have to go kill an old friend."

Fang pulled away, leaving Beatrice yelling questions after us, but I couldn't make out what she was saying.

"Kill Father Ike." I covered my eyes with my hands. "Right."

Being a monster makes killing easier. Having had to do it for so long to survive had taken the edge off of the guilt, formed a scar where that portion of my conscience was. Ike had been warned. Fang went for a semi-oldie and played Alien Ant Farm's cover of "Smooth Criminal."

"No, Fang, I'm not okay, and my name's not Annie." We drove down back streets, cutting across town to Ike's church. I parked in front of the brick rectory and stepped out of the car. The old brown church loomed over me, a potential avalanche of guilt, and I fancied I could hear the church bell tolling out midnight even though it was only a quarter past eleven. The doors had been propped open, candles lit, all the lights ablaze. The welcome mat was out. Literally.

"Damn." I almost forgot to take off the necklace, but I leaned back in and hung it from Fang's rearview mirror.

"What do you think you're playing at?" The voice was Ebon Winter's, and the vampire himself swirled, an angry mist in the shape of a man in leather rock-star pants.

"I don't have time for this, Winter."

"You're here for Isaac?" he snarled, fangs out, blocking my path. "He performed your marriage ceremony in this church. I played the organ. And I sang!"

I caught sight of Rachel out of the corner of my eye, watching the exchange from the shadows of the alley across the street. She'd turned up to keep an eye on me. Good. That was part of The Plan, too.

"It was a lovely service." I stepped through his mist form. Winter looked like he'd run halfway across town after having jumped directly offstage mid-performance to intercept me. "But I have a job to do."

A line of pain scratched across my back from an inch or so below my right shoulder to high on my left.

"Ow. Fuck." I wasn't used to having pain last. Before the Eye of Scrythax split while it was lodged in my heart, I had felt pain like most vampires—the initial sensation and then nothing else unless the wound got worse or I moved wrong and aggravated it. Now—at night, anyway, when I was a true immortal—pain lasted until the wound healed, though that wasn't long. By the time I turned to face Winter, the wound was nothing more than a thin line of blood at my back and a tear in my WELCOME TO THE VOID T-shirt.

I took a swing at Winter, and he dodged it easily.

"Powers acting up?" He smirked. "No vampire speed?"

He sliced me again, his silver razor gleaming in the moonlight, opening a slash on my cheek, another on my chest, and a third one across my forehead. *Huh. I'd never noticed that Winter had no claws. Fighting with a razor. How very Jack the Ripper.*

"I don't need powers to take care of you, queer boy."

Winter's eyes sparkled. "I hope you mean *strange*, darling, because I find the implication that I even possess sexuality, regardless of gender specificity, grossly insulting."

My next punch went straight through Winter's chest, his body misting before I made contact, curls of vapor trailing after my knuckles.

"Coward." I dashed through him, trying to make my way through the open doors of the Gothic church. A kung-fu-movie *swoosh* broke the air as Winter hamstrung me. My Achilles tendons rolled up to the back of my knees, splitting the skin and etching twin lines of agony along my legs. I cursed, nearly blacking out, the edges of my vision blurring. Another slash opened my throat, severing the jugular and sending a gout of crimson across the steps.

"Fang!" I tried to gasp the word, managing nothing more than a gurgle, but Fang understood. His engine roared, and my undead Mustang came into play, grille angling for Winter, mist or no mist. Winter did as expected, and the bumper never touched him, but Fang didn't slow. Winter had never been the real target.

Fang's grille cut into my back; the kinetic force of the impact sent me toward the church doors. Back broken, legs useless, I lay flat on my face and let the wounds knit. The healing of my Achilles tendons hurt more than the initial injury; the sound of my vertebrae realigning was like a bone xylophone to my ears.

Winter shouted, "No!" as I rose to my knees, head still

spinning, eyes unfocused, and Fang slid into reverse, seeming to catch him by surprise, rolling over him and giving him the old chomperoo. Winter's skin came off with the sound of shucking corn, but he didn't stop talking.

"This will be war, Eric, not just with me—" The rest of his sentence vanished as Fang stripped the muscle layer and Winter's bones landed in the trunk. A little blood and he'd be good as new. Angry as hell but okay. After all, Winter's a Vlad. Practically top-tier vampire stock.

If you're new to Void City, you may not know that vampires come in four basic levels: Drones, Soldiers, Masters, and Vlads. In cinematic terms, Drones might be instructional videos you watched in high school (better than nothing but not much entertainment value); Soldiers would be the cartoon before the movie (fun but not really worth the price of admission, if it's all you're going to get); Masters would be black-and-white movies (some real classics, but most don't stand the test of time); and Vlads . . . would be modern classics or remastered greats (they might go out of fashion, but they're impressive as hell and keep coming to theaters again and again).

There's another tier, kind of a best of the worst, in which two kinds of undeath happen to someone at the same time. Most people would still count me as one of those—a damn near unkillable Emperor-level vampire. In movie terms, an Emperor would be like the hybrids you see at high-end theme parks where the special effects encompass 3-D, physical effects, live actors, and damn roller-coaster motion, updated with all the new gadgets. The kind of movie you never forget. An Emperor is the kind of vampire who can walk into a church . . . if he has to.

Father Ike was waiting for me in front of the altar, a short, fat, wonderful man with a heart so pure, I don't think he needed Clorox to keep his whites white. He wore a priest's alb and preaching scarf over a single-breasted cassock, and he clutched his Bible in both hands.

"Vampire hunters are already making their way into Void City now that Lord Phillip has been dethroned," Ike said softly. "Kill me, and the last barrier between them and you will be gone."

"You sure know how to brighten a murderer's day, Padre."

"If you do this, Eric," Ike began—his voice, not pleading, sounded more concerned for me than for himself—"where will it stop? How many tasks will you have to perform before you are free? Have you thought of that, my friend?"

I had, actually. It was all part of The Plan, but I couldn't share that information with Ike or nearly anyone else, even the folks who knew part of it: Talbot, Magbidion . . . every new person was a risk. Hell, I hadn't even told Greta.

Fang crashed through the doors of the church behind me, and Ike winced as the pews pulled out of the floor.

"I have a plan," I said.

Ike laughed bitterly.

"I'm not stupid, Ike," I told him. "I may have early-onset Alzheimer's, and I may have spent a lot of years trying to ignore what was happening around me, trying to let the world spin by until Marilyn died and I went crazy, but that's not what's happening now. I got her back. She's immortal. If I'm lucky, she might even learn to love me again. I just have to show her I'm worthy and that she's worthy, too."

"And killing me is step number one?" He spread his arms wide and knelt before me. "I can't understand your logic, my friend. Not a bit. But I won't fight you."

"Think of it this way, Father . . ." I put my hands around his throat and began to squeeze.

Ike's flesh didn't burn me. I'd thought that it would have, even with the whole immortal-by-night thing going on. I tightened my grip and waited for his breathing to stop. When it did, I dashed out to Fang, grabbed the Blind Eye necklace, and returned to wrap it around the dead priest's neck, arranging him neatly so that he stared up at the ceiling, his head tilted back to show the bruises still forming around his neck.

"Kill Father Ike," I said aloud. "Done."

"Good job, baby," Rachel called from the broken church entrance. "I know it was hard." She held her arms out to me. "But if there's anything I can do to make you feel better . . ."

"Get away from me," I snarled. "It's done, and so is your job, so fuck off to wherever you fuck off to or I swear to God I'll kill you and lay you out right next to him."

"You're so cute when you're tough," she said, but before I could charge, *poof*, she was gone. The compulsion to complete my task faded, and I went on with the next step of The Plan.

5

GRETA

MY TWO MOMS

Marilyn . . . No, that wasn't right . . . And neither was "Old Mom," now that she was back from the dead, young again, and apparently immortal. Mommortal?

No.

Mom.

Mom looked lost behind the counter at the Demon Heart. She'd been used to serving drinks and tending bar, not spraying disinfectant into used shoes and selling lane time. Her fingers twitched, eager for a cigarette, something to do with her hands, but the Demon Heart is nonsmoking. It smells better that way. I don't really care about people's health, but to a vampire's nose, cigarettes smell extra bad. Cigars are nice, though; cigarillos, too. The aroma wakes up a really old memory in my head of some old guy who was very nice to me. *I think I'll eat a cigar smoker tonight.*

Despite Mom's discomfort, I was glad to see her. She was younger than when I'd first met her (and I'd known her since I was nine) and as pretty as the picture of her that Dad keeps in his wallet. The red and black of the Demon Heart Lanes bowling shirt suited her, even though she wore it unbuttoned like a jacket, the white T-shirt and tight jeans underneath showing her hourglass figure in a way that would have driven Dad crazy if he wasn't out doing . . . stuff. Secret stuff. My problem with that was I didn't know if it was supposed to be a secret from me, too, or if it only seemed secret because I was supposed to have figured it out on my own.

I sat on the burgundy felt of my favorite pool table in the Demon Heart, idly rolling a cue ball around and around. Blood dripped off my fingernails, marking the off-white of the ball with bright unclotted red.

A troll wearing a big gray hoodie bowled on lane twelve, keeping to himself. He was small for a troll, only about seven feet, but his mottled green skin and gnarled knuckles would have thrown up a big warning flare to anyone paying close attention. Or it would have if he hadn't been paying some guild mage to cover the entire bowling alley with a spell to keep norms ignorant. His presence gave Magbidion time to go running off with Mags's new friend, the midget bitch, to talk bad about me.

"Hey, uh, Greta," one of Dad's thralls—a mousy little blonde—said to me as she walked past with a big order of fried mushrooms for the troll. I smelled fear on her skin, beneath the smell of grease, hair spray, and deep-fried veggies. Then her name came to me.

"Hey, uh, Erin," I said back. "Does my hair smell like smoke?"

She leaned forward instantly to sniff it. "No," she answered. "Should it?"

I didn't answer, and she hurried on her way with the tray. I like Daddy's thralls. On the other hand, I've seen the way they watch Mom when they think she isn't looking, like she's a threat to them. No one was rude, but I could hear it in their breath, their heartbeats.

Dad would do a lot for any one of them, protect them, feed them, take care of them, even; but he wouldn't go to hell for them like he had for me and for Marilyn.

I sensed New Mom's . . . Tabitha's . . . no, *Stepmom's* approach and compared her style of dress. She was still outfitting herself like she worked in a strip club or burlesque. Tonight's over-the-top-sexy attire resembled the collision of a Victoria's Secret and a Calvin Klein catalog. I could dress that way, too, if I wanted, and be more impressive than she was. I'm taller than her, just over six feet, my breasts are bigger (and perkier), and I was in better shape when Dad turned me at twenty-one. My long blond hair stood out in contrast to the short cropped look she was sporting again. But I prefer to wear jeans and a T-shirt when I'm hunting, like Dad.

Stepmom saw Mom and stifled a sneer, walking in a wide arc to avoid her yet still approach my perch. I shifted my view from Mom to Stepmom slowly, rolling balls around the table with my hands.

"Where is he?" Stepmom asked.

"Beatrice said he took off in Fang an hour or so ago." I picked up the eight ball and fought the urge to throw it, not because I felt like I shouldn't but more because I couldn't decide whom I wanted to hit with it. Who was married to Dad? Who was going to be married to Dad? And could I eat the other one to cut down on confusion?

"That's just great." Tabitha adjusted her bustier. "We were supposed to talk over . . . dinner."

"He probably forgot." I rolled the eight ball into the corner pocket and settled on the fourteen ball, spinning it on the table as if it were a top.

"He didn't forget." Stepmom looked at the clock.

"Maybe"—I stood up, my nail beds crawling with sensation as my claws slid out—"he *did* forget." My eyes went red. "Or maybe *you* got the time wrong!" My jaw popped as my fangs tore through my gums and locked into place.

Or maybe—Dad popped into both of our heads as he got close enough for us to sense his presence—*he got sent on his first little demonic errand and had to kill an old friend.*

Who? Stepmom thought at him.

Ike, Dad thought back. *And now there are representatives from Sable Oaks, the Shifters, and the Mages Guild to talk to me about more City Council shit. Can I get a rain check on our chat?*

Oh, baby, Tabitha thought, *they made you kill Father Ike?*

But Dad had already cut her off.

Oh, get down, Stepmom said to me irritably. *Eric wouldn't let us kill each other anyway.*

Not that you even know how to end me, I thought to myself. *While I keep what it takes to end you in Fang's trunk—and a duplicate set in my room in the panel hidden under my recliner.* I jumped off the pool table just the same.

"I don't see what the big deal is," I said. My claws retracted, fangs receded. "I took my shoes off first."

"Sorry." Stepmom rubbed her eyes, glancing over at the troll and his mage. "You know what? You're right. Sit on the pool table all night. It's fine."

"Thanks," I said. *Not that I need your permission.* Unless she was really going to be Mom instead of Stepmom. Then maybe I did need her permission.

"Will you tell your father I went to my apartment?" Stepmom asked.

"Why don't you just stay with Dad?" I slid my sneakers on without bothering to untie them. "You could stay in my room until he's done with his meeting," I added hopefully. "I cleaned it up."

"Not yet," Stepmom said. "Your dad and I need a little time apart."

I'd heard that before. It wasn't as though Dad hadn't had plenty of girlfriends before; he just hadn't married any of them before Tabitha.

"Okay."

She turned to walk away, then stopped, turned back around, and lightly touched my arm. "You know this has nothing to do with you, right?"

"Yeah," I answered. I'd heard that before, too. It came before bad times and foster homes. Her fingers tightened around my arm incrementally—a gentle squeeze—and then she left. Mom watched her go without a word.

Mom came up to me next. She still smelled like smoke, but not like sickness or old age. A slight tang of disinfectant and sweaty feet hovered around her forearms, but her heartbeat . . .

"Can I?" I asked.

Mom let out a single braying "ha," following it up with "Knock yourself out, kiddo."

I rested my head against her chest, feeling the drive of her healthy circulatory system, blood coursing through her veins without the slow buildup of plaque she'd had when she'd been old. Her lifeblood flowed smoothly, the rhythm of her heart: pristine and good.

"You're so healthy." I hugged her around the waist and lifted her into the air. "Dad did good."

"I wasn't worth it." It was a lie; her heartbeat betrayed her.

"Fibber." I put her down again. "You're glad to be back."

"I'm glad to be back," she admitted. "But it wasn't worth the cost. I know he hasn't had to do anything yet—"

"Sure he has." I pointed to the television in the game room. "We were just talking about it." Above the caption BREAKING NEWS, a blond newscaster blabbed on about the scene behind her. Father Ike's church was in flames.

"My God." Marilyn gripped the edge of the pool table. "He had to burn down the church? Why?"

"No, silly. He had to kill Father Ike, and then he burned the church down for free. Nothing big or horrible. The fire smelled nice. It must have been the incense or something . . ."

I was surprised when she threw up. *I hope she's not catching that stomach bug that's been going around.*

✦ 6 ✦

ERIC

PUTTING OUT OLD FLAMES

A vampire, an Alpha werewolf, and two mages were waiting for me in the Pollux lobby. Sounds like the beginning of a joke, but it wasn't. The vampire, Lady Gabriella, represented the Sable Oaks contingent, the surviving group of High Society vamps who'd escaped my attack on the Highland Towers and the subsequent attack by "unknown individuals" on Winter's club, the Artiste Unknown.

I sensed Gabby on the way in. Her recently dyed black hair hung loose and long, as unfamiliar as her modern apparel. She was one of those vamps who preferred old-style clothes, real Renaissance stuff, fancy brocade gowns and the like, but given recent developments, she—like most of the remaining supernatural citizens—was finally having to learn how to blend in. For her, that meant designer slacks and a matching silk blouse. She looked uncomfortable wearing pants in mixed company.

"Lord Eric." She inclined her head, offering her neck.

"Don't start with that shit, Gabby." I waved off the formality.

The Alpha was William, the occasionally overzealous

leader and reverend of the local werewolf pack that claimed the Orchard Lake area. His hair had begun to go a little gray around the edges, but he was a big guy, a good half a foot taller than my five-ten. He held a Bible in his hand, and every time he shifted his grip on the book, Gabby surreptitiously checked its potential trajectory.

William nodded. "Good evening, Eric."

"Hey, Bill."

One of the mages belonged to me: Magbidion, one of my thralls. His immediately apparent nervousness bothered me more than the presence of the other mage.

"This is Paula Mallory?" Magbidion indicated the four-foot-tall woman next to him, making it a question, like he wasn't sure.

"She's a fuck'n midget," I said. "Sorry. Shit. What's the term now? Little person."

The young dark-haired woman raised an eyebrow. "Aw. How sweet. Someone's been watching *Little People, Big World.*"

"No. I just got the last season of *Boston Legal.* You look like . . . what's her face? She played the short lawyer . . ."

"Candice Bergen?" Paula smiled sweetly, batting her eyelashes.

"Candice Bergen's not a midget." I let myself wince slightly after the fact. I wasn't trying to offend her, but people have to remember, I'm effectively in my eighties, and the "correct" words have changed a lot over the years.

She laughed. "Meredith Eaton, then?"

"I guess."

"I'll take that as a compliment," Paula said. "She's hot."

So was Paula. She wore a red pantsuit that must have been altered to show as much cleavage as it did. A single ruby on a platinum chain hung around her neck. Long dark hair with subtle red highlights framed her face, and her makeup was warmer than I expected from a gal wearing that type of business suit. A golden rune was etched into each painted red fingernail, and a single gold piercing glittered between her chin and lower lip. She felt like magic all over, exuded it. Warmth, too . . . more than a fever. Like she was her own little space heater.

"So are you." My face twitched. "That's not a hit, by the way," I added quickly, "observation only. No flirting intended." Then it struck. "Wait. Paula? Shouldn't you have an M name?" *Don't all mages have M names?*

"Shouldn't you be named Varney or Vladimir or something?"

"I didn't know we were actually *trying* to be rude." I winked. "Do I get to break out the C word now, or do I have to start with the B word and work up to it?"

"Okay." She chuckled. "Okay. A mage traditionally picks a working name that matches the first letter of her specialty. A garden-variety multipurpose mage gets an M name. A specialist can go with an M or with the letter signifying her area of expertise."

"P." I added it up. "Pyromancer?"

Her runes flared. The inside of her mouth glowed a fiery orange—a jack-o'-lantern effect I could see right through her skin as well as through her open smile—and her irises lit up in a matching shade. "That's me."

"Burn down my building, and I'm killing every mage in the city except for Melvin and Magbidion."

She laughed again, a single brightly accented squeal. "Oh, please, I think we both know I'd toast you."

"Try it and I'll sic my car on you."

"Steel frame?" Paula narrowed one eye, bobbing her head slightly from side to side as she weighed the options, her hands mimicking the movements of a scale. "Steel vaporizes at about fifty-five hundred degrees Fahrenheit . . . I can get that hot, but it's a pain in the butt, and it does horrible things to my hair. Wouldn't have to vaporize it, though. Steel melts at what? Twenty-five hundred degrees Fahrenheit? I think it's a safe bet you'd both be nice and melty before you ever laid a hand on me. You might come back, of course, but if there's one thing I'm not short on, it's BTUs."

"That wasn't some sort of weird come-on, was it?" I asked.

They all stared at me. I stared back. Paula shook her head, a definite no. *Whew*.

"So . . ." I let the vowel sound linger on until it became an inquiry. "You guys are all cluttering up my movie theater because . . . ?"

"I believe we're still waiting on Captain Stacey?" Gabby said.

I'd opened my mouth to make his excuses when Katherine Marx walked in. I'm sure it looked like I was checking her out when I glanced down at her chest, but I was really just making sure Magbidion's spell was still in place. When a vampire makes a thrall, the thrall gets a blood tattoo. To a vampire who has made a thrall, that tattoo can show up even through clothing. Katherine asked me to put hers right over her heart. I couldn't sense her thralldom, and since that was a power I had all the time—even at night—probably because of Fang, I hoped the others wouldn't be able to sense it, either.

Katherine had cleaned up so well that I didn't think anyone present would smell Stacey's blood on her. I couldn't, but that wasn't a sure sign, given how different my daytime vampire powers are from my nighttime true immortal powers.

Katherine wore the dark blue uniform of a VCPD police officer; the only sign of her different status was the SWAT patch on her shoulder. She was model-pretty when you got past the cop aura, though most people wouldn't. I thought the shotgun she was carrying might be a little over-the-top, but she was a human among the supernatural, and if it made her feel safer, who was I to object to a tiny equalizer?

"Sorry I'm late," she said to all of us, then directed the last to me as if mine were the only opinion that mattered. "Mr. Courtney."

"Is Captain Stacey okay?" William asked.

"He was a pussy, and I fired him," I said curtly. "Marx is handling things now, and she's better than Stacey because she has a pussy but isn't one." Gabby looked offended. Paula cracked a smile. Marx was cold as ice and twice as frosty. "So what the hell are we here to talk about?"

"Eric," William began, "you know what this is about."

"You promised to consider it," Gabby added. "And we've brought in the Mages Guild, as requested."

My heart sank as I realized what it was about. "Greta again?"

They nodded. Paula spoke up. "Without the Veil of Scrythax, we simply don't have the mage-power to cover every supernatural citizen. The . . . culling . . . of the vampire population has certainly helped, but the Supernatural Citizens—the SCs—absolutely have to help us help them. Most understand this. But your daughter is still hunting as if it's the good old days. Her actions alone require up to six interventions a night—she's a staffing nightmare!"

"I'll talk to her again."

"That's not enough, Eric." Gabriella was faking a light French accent. "As we have told you before, you need to stake her until the new Veil or a sufficient substitute is in place, or—"

"Like that's gonna happen," Paula cut in. "You stake his daughter, or try to make him stake his daughter, and he'll respond by killing or staking whatever number of other vampires is required to bring the feeding requirements down to acceptable levels so that we can cover Greta."

I like Paula. She's smart.

"We all know that, don't we?" Paula continued.

"If we kill all the Drones and Soldiers . . ." I let that sentence hang there.

William nodded. "Obviously the therianthrope community is okay with the destruction of as many vampires as Eric *and* the Sable Oaks contingent"—he gave a brief nod to Gabriella—"will agree to, but there is still the problem of the demons."

"Triple-T Waste Disposal," Paula joined in. "Tiko, Timbo, and Tombo are Oni. As Japanese Ogres, they've helped the SCs in Void City with body disposal for years, but they're also big monsters with a nonstandard number of eyes or horns and an obviously avant-garde skin color. It's taking twenty-four-hour magical coverage because Triple-T is also a legitimate waste disposal service with mundane clients and without the Veil—"

I held up a finger. "Did I or did I not bequeath half of Phil's surviving assets—a sum with more zeroes than I like to count—to the Mages Guild in exchange for you guys taking care of this shit for me?"

"Money can only do so much, Eric," Paula said. "I'm not asking for more money. What we need is more time, more mage-power, and more cooperation from the SCs. Yes, Greta, but not only her. The Fae largely police themselves, and the mouser population isn't an issue, but the more outré SCs have to take up some of the slack."

"Then it's a rotating curfew." They all stared at me like I'd grown an extra head. All of them were used to cursing, enchanted, drunk, or fatalistic Eric. I'm not unintelligent or uneducated, though it's true I've had a penchant for taking the easy way or letting things go on too long. It's simple and thoughtless and . . . fun. But it wouldn't get me out of this contract, and it wasn't going to win Marilyn back.

"No more than one problem population out past sundown on a given night. Vampires get Mondays, Wednesdays, and Fridays. Demons get Tuesdays, Thursdays, and Saturdays."

"What about Sundays?" Gabriella asked.

"The Mages Guild gets to work a skeleton crew on

Sundays." Paula brightened, literally, when I said that, letting me know that at least one person in the room liked the idea.

"And therianthropes?" William asked.

"Don't get seen," I said. "If you do, you pay a double-sized Fang fee and wind up on my shit list."

"What happens to curfew breakers?" Magbidion asked.

"I happen." I snapped my fingers and grinned.

"That's nice, Eric," Paula cut in, "but most of the infractions will take place at night."

Did she know? I tried to cover my concern with bravado. "I suppose you have a better suggestion?"

"Than you?" Paula chirped. "Almost always." She held out a small sachet of leather, a medicine bag. It smelled like ashes, demon, and magic. "The council and I got together and whipped this up using the remaining ashes of the Veil of Scrythax. It basically does what the Veil did, but for the bearer and his—or her—immediate vicinity only."

"And I don't get it because?"

"Oh, you can have it." Paula's smile widened, and her eyes flickered from within. "But why don't we kill two birds with one stone? We'll give it to Greta—"

"I object," Lady Gabriella spoke up. "As the senior vampire—"

Marx casually shifted her shotgun so that it was aimed (and yet somehow not quite aimed) at Gabby's chest. It was the first time she'd done more than breathe since entering the room and being introduced.

"And," Paula continued, "we'll let her play sheriff. If the SCs won't play nice, then she gets to eat them. She'll love it!" She waggled the sachet, then tossed it to me. "What do you say, Tall-dark-and-scary? Based on what Greta did to Lisette when she came to Void City, there's a sizable portion of the population who's a hell of a lot more terrified of *her* coming for them than they are of you."

"With me, they could probably talk their way out of it." I sighed. I'd followed similar logic when sending Greta to kill Rachel. "Can the VCPD work with her?" I asked Marx.

"As long as you make it very clear to her that she's not allowed to hurt us," Marx said, shifting her shotgun back to a more neutral position.

"Can do," I said. "Gabby?"

Gabriella nodded, not even bothering to disguise her displeasure. "As much as I'd like to make an argument for the sachet coming to me, Paula's right. Eric, you're a threat with whom one can reason, but Greta . . ."

I held the sachet in my hand and frowned. It was a good plan. I didn't like it, but the little mage had it right. Greta would be happy to play sheriff, and it would keep her out of trouble—or at least out of trouble she wasn't supposed to be in.

"Is everyone agreed?" I asked after a few seconds. They were. "Then look out, Void City, there's a new sheriff in town."

As we broke up, Gabriella pulled me off to the side with a subtle nod. Hoping this wasn't some weird try-to-bang-the-new-top-dog thing, I dismissed Marx and joined Gabriella on the mezzanine. "You come-hithered me?" I said.

"I didn't want to bring it up in front of the others, because I'm not entirely sure how much they understand about how the city really works . . ."

"Uh-huh," I prompted.

"But I'm surprised that you haven't made a move toward vampire repopulation. Our numbers were cut by more than half in Winter's strike against us, artistic though it may have been, and . . ."

"And?"

She looked me straight in the eye. "And are you sure Population Control can handle all this?"

"Population Control?" I had no fucking clue what she was talking about.

"Yes," she said. "You've spoken with him?"

"It's covered," I said abruptly. What the hell was she talking about?

"Oh, good." She breathed a sigh of relief that was more for effect than anything else and kissed me on the cheek before taking her leave. "I was afraid you didn't know. I wouldn't want him to start bringing in more chupacabras."

I watched her go, then called Talbot's cell. "You ever heard of some guy with Population Control?"

"No." He sounded genuinely confused. "Why?"

"No reason, " I said after a moment. *Chupacabras aren't real. That's UFO-nut bullshit.* I was this close to asking Talbot about it, but I couldn't do it. I shook my head, still holding the phone. *I mean, if chupacabras were real, I'd know about it, right? Gabby was just having you on, dude. Got to be.* I hung up and stared at the phone for a minute before heading off to explain Greta's new job to her.

"Chupacabras, my ass."

7

GRETA

HAVE FANGS, WILL TRAVEL

D o I get a badge?"

Daddy stared at me without comprehension from his spot at the doorway to my room in the Pollux. He didn't come in because it's pretty small for two people, even with everything unboxed and half of it thrown away or put into storage. I used to sleep on top of all my stuff before I got used to bunking in Fang's trunk. Now that I'd converted the space into what basically amounted to a huge live-in closet, there was room to stand in. The space had hanging racks on either side of the room, the comfy recliner from my old apartment, a wall-mounted smartboard (which doubled as a TV), and my skull collection (each skull mounted to the cornicework and wearing a different hat). I took the black Stetson off of Telly's skull and donned it, adjusting the brim to a rakish angle.

"A star," I tried again. "You know, like a badge, but an Old Westy one?" I tipped my hat.

He smiled, which was good, because I'd come close to saying "badge" again instead of "star," but I thought a sheriff's star would be more endearing. I know I'm his number one and only daughter, but Daddy's fickle, or he can be, or it seems like he is sometimes. A frown thinned my lips and pulled at the corners of my mouth. Being critical of Dad is bad unless it's with my out-loud voice and I'm teasing. *Bad, Greta!*

"What are you frowning about?" Eric's brow furrowed. "I haven't said no yet. Of course you can have a star. I'm sure we can order—"

"Thanks, Dad!" I wanted to hug him but settled for a kiss on the cheek instead. Dad wasn't smiling, and I needed him to smile, needed to see it, to know he was okay. "So . . . I can eat anybody I want as long as I can make them break curfew first?"

"No. They have to break curfew all on their own." As he spoke, I got my smile. "If you have any questions about whether somebody broke curfew or not, you need to ask me, Paula, or Talbot."

"Okay." Now for my real question. "What about Mom?"

"Marilyn?" He crossed his arms. "Yeah. Yeah. Okay, but try not to bother her too much about it—"

"Marilyn, right?" My teeth clamped together, cutting my sentences short, jaw tensing as I spoke, stomach churning. "Marilyn is Mom. Not Tabitha. Right?"

"That's your thing, Greta, I—"

"No!" The shout surprised us both, even though I was the one shouting. "You have to say who Mom is, because you're Dad." Unconsciously balled into a fist, my hand tapped his chest. "Who is more important? It's Mom . . . Marilyn Mom, not Tabitha Mom, right? Marilyn is . . ." I looked around for words and found skulls instead. Telly's skull couldn't tell me anything. He was just a skull with a bullet hole. Unless the answer was zero, circle, or the letter O, he was useless.

"It's Marilyn," Dad said finally, his tone soft. He hugged me and I felt his warmth, ignoring what he seemed not to want me to know. He kissed me on the forehead. "Always Marilyn."

"So Tabitha is just—"

"I don't know what Tabitha is, sweetheart. Why don't you go ahead and end her just to keep things simple?"

Or . . . that's what I wanted to ask, what I wanted him to answer. Instead, Dad said it was my thing, and that was the end of it. Instead of challenging him, like I was dying to do, I said one meek little word, "Okay," and smiled sweetly as Dad kissed me on the forehead.

"Oh, and Dad?"

"Yes?"

"If I'm going to be sheriff, are there any things, you know, that I should know about?"

"Know about?" He played it cool, but my line of questioning clearly worried him.

"Secret stuff," I said. "Because I know there is some strange . . . stuff going on, and I don't know if it's okay to investigate it or not. I want to check it out, but . . ."

"Just use your best judgment," Dad told me, and walked out like everything was settled.

But that doesn't answer my question, Dad! If I'm sheriff, what does that mean? Am I really just a big bogeyman scaring everyone into line like John Paul Courtney did when he was alive? Do I arrest people if I don't want to kill them? I mean, I'll probably want to kill them, but what if I think you don't want me to kill them? Are there crimes for which I don't kill? Do I hand out Fang fees for those? If so, is there a chart? Is this a real job? Do I get paid?

I came back to the mom question again just then, grabbed one of my pet skulls, and smashed it on the floor. I realized too late that I'd grabbed Telly's skull, so I sent another down to join him in a shattered pile of splintered bone.

Dad's just really stressed right now, I told myself. *I need to be more understanding. I can work this out. I can.*

"Maybe if I killed both of them . . ."

Public Safety Tip #1: Perpetrators will be eaten.

8

ERIC

HOME TO ROOST

Used to be there was a time when dawn surprised me. Not anymore. I know it's coming. It starts with a burning in my gums, nagging and insistent. More painful than having popcorn stuck between my teeth but just shy of the ripping sensation I get when I pop my fangs. Greta wanted to talk more. I knew she did; even an hour from dawn, I felt it. The pain spread to my throat, like acid reflux or heartburn, then down to my belly, which churned and roiled like a cauldron of witches' brew or battery acid.

My nail beds started to crawl (toes and fingers). I tore down the hallway to my room as fast as I could. Mags stood in the center of the room, runes set up and glowing. Waiting.

"A little early, aren't you?" he asked, but I couldn't answer—my fangs extended, painfully so, to their maximum über vamp size and length, but in a human-sized mouth, uppers and lowers gouging holes in the roof of my mouth and piercing my lower jaw. My eyes quivered, vision blurring. Etched in red, like blood poisoning chased with lava, my veins stood out raw and angry.

I blame Scrythax.

The door to the hallway closed behind me. I felt the ear-popping *Zot!* of Mags's ward going live, then I dashed into the bathroom and got it over with. No one heard me scream. Mags warded up the bathroom door, too, a second layer of protection for my secret. Maybe it was getting worse. Maybe it wasn't. I wondered what would have happened if I hadn't broken the Eye of Scrythax—or if the other half had broken. Would it have mattered? Would I be a vampire by night and a true immortal by day instead of the other way around? Would the sun and I have been on friendly terms again? I like to pretend it wouldn't have made any difference, but deep down, I suspect it would have made all the difference in the world.

An hour later, the sun outside was bright and shining in the sky. Not that I could go out and take a look without bursting into flames, but she was there. I could feel her laughing at me. Sitting on the bed in a pair of tan slacks, a white undershirt, and a button-down blue dress shirt, I slipped on my new brown belt, dress socks, and the loafers I'd had Talbot pick up for me, while forcing myself to keep taking hits off a blood bag fresh from the fridge.

The first blood bag always goes down easy, no matter what, but tonight the second one was tough to stomach. My brain was playing games with me, more than usual. I didn't want blood. If I had to drink something hot and red, I preferred a Bloody Mary. So far none of my thralls had figured out the whole taste-enhancement side of what Rachel used to do when I fed on her.

I finished the second bag anyway and headed down to the garage to check on Greta. Fang's trunk popped open as I approached. My little girl slept amid the bones of Fang's victims and her own. She'd started taking a skull to bed with her a few months ago; her favorite one had a large bullet hole in the forehead. She'd apparently forgotten it today. About the same time she started cuddling up with a skull, I stopped having to do as much when I tucked her in. She still needs a little cleanup now and again, but mainly, I lay out new clothes for her and clear away any random bone fragments she's fallen asleep on.

Talbot walked into the parking deck from the street, his footsteps as recognizable as his breath, his heartbeat, his smell, or his laugh.

"So this is what you used to dress like, huh?"

I looked up at him and smiled. Wearing a custom suit, as usual, he looked better than I did. Ladies really go for the whole big, black, and confident thing he has going on. Even being bald works for him.

"I'm not the one in the suit," I muttered, closing Fang's trunk. "Where'd Tabitha sleep?"

"Back at her apartment," Talbot said. "She said to tell you to drive over and force her awake if you want to talk or hang out."

I shook my head. "That's not happening."

"Eric—"

"Follow The Plan, Talbot." I looked at him. Did he seem a little older now? A touch softer around the middle than he had when I met him? A few more laugh lines? "Can you do that?"

"Sure." He broke into a wide grin. "Mom says you should come around more often. She liked chatting with you."

"She could always visit," I offered. Talbot's mom had helped me through the afterlife when I chased after Greta. She was nice, as far as ancient Egyptian deities in whom I don't want to believe go.

"No," Talbot answered. "She's too mythic for the real world now. She can affect things here, but showing up in person takes a lot of power and leaves beings like her too exposed."

"Where's Marilyn?"

"Over at the bowling alley."

"Did you talk things over with the Iversonian?" Talbot

winced when I said the name. The Iversonian is Void City's senior true immortal, not that we have many. He and Talbot have some kind of history I don't want to know too much about.

"I did, and he'll do it, but I think you'd be better off sending her to Europe to study with . . . what was it you called him?"

"Fuckup Courtney?" I spat on the concrete deck, leaving a splatter of blood on the ground. "Dumbass the First?" Jean-Paul was my oh-so-bright ancestor who got the family cursed in the first place. He was turned into a vampire when Scrythax decided to impersonate a god, respond to his plight, and turn him into a true immortal rather than a vampire. Instead of killing Lisette (the vampire who'd turned him) and ending the curse before things got weird, Dumbass the First ignored her completely and let generation after generation of Courtney take it up the rear for his stupidity. Let that idiot teach Marilyn how to use her powers? I spat again. "No. Maybe the German chick, but she's probably busy. Anyone else would just screw Marilyn up. The Iversonian, I can keep an eye on."

"You're the boss." Talbot spread his arms and dipped his head in a mock bow.

I shrank into mouse form, feeling like too much person in too small a package, and let Talbot pick me up by the tail.

"Take me over to the bowling alley and quit screwing around," I squeaked as he dangled me over his open smile. "If you eat me, I'll turn into an über vamp in your stomach."

"If I ate you"—his fangs slid out, his eyes shining a brilliant emerald green—"you'd be dead. Mine is the power to devour. Remember."

"You want to give it a shot, T?" I squeaked at him. "You wanna take the old man out? Bring it."

He laughed a rich velvety laugh and slipped me into the front pocket of his suit coat. "I'll pass."

"Coward," I squeaked.

Waiting in Talbot's pocket for a safe second to cross the road, I panicked. It's one thing to make a plan and another to pull it off. I had no doubt Marilyn would have stayed with me, working in the bowling alley until the end of time, watching me sleep with other women and refusing to have anything to do with me, just like she had when the Demon Heart was a strip club. But the status quo wasn't good enough. At least the Stacey thing was over. Marx could handle herself, and she was on my team.

"Don't have a little mousy heart attack in there," Talbot purred.

"Fuck you, cat."

"Hey!" Talbot darted out between cars, and I shifted around in his pocket. "No need to be insulting."

"Fuck you, mouser, then."

A horn beeped at us, blurred by the Doppler effect. "Much better," Talbot answered with a chuckle. "None of that cat stuff. Not from you. You know better."

He lifted me out of his pocket, and I concentrated on re-forming with my new clothes intact. This early in the morning, Marilyn and Erin were the only two up and about. Erin looked down when she saw my clothes, blond bangs falling over her eyes. "I'll go check . . ." She headed down to the lane without clarifying what, exactly, she meant to check.

"I'll go check, too," Talbot said wryly, heading back out the front door.

"Hey," I said, walking toward Marilyn. She was behind the counter next to the register, double-counting the till. She used to do the same thing at the original Demon Heart, twice when she counted down the drawer before running the deposit and twice more in the morning checking for payouts from me or what's-his-face (Edgar, maybe? some vampire I used to run the club with) in case she needed to run to the bank for more cash or change.

"Greta's stealing money out of the till again." Marilyn set her jaw. "You need to speak with her."

"How do you know Greta took it?" I put my hand on the counter, resisting the urge to pull myself up on it, slide across the intervening space, and pull Marilyn into my arms.

"Well, gee, Eric," Marilyn snapped. "Who else do you know who would steal all the quarters, spend them on bouncy balls and capsule toys from the vending machines, and then leave all the plastic capsules sitting on the floor around the machines?"

Heh. I smirked. "She can have it." I waved the crime away. "I—"

"I know she can have the money." Marilyn slammed the drawer closed, still holding a red Void City Metro Bank bag in her hand. She'd written out her change order on a purple Post-it and had it stuck to a fifty-dollar bill. She slid the bill into the bag. "But you have to get her to do the paid-outs right so I don't have to recount the drawer and figure out how much she took."

"Fine." God, she looked beautiful. The smell of her, and not just the low-down feminine scent but her hair, the toothpaste on her breath, her detergent . . . her youth . . . it was so much worse during the day, so much harder to ignore. "Listen—"

"It's not fine, Eric!"

I blinked, recoiling instinctively. Why was she yelling?

"Greta only does this kind of thing when she's seriously upset." Marilyn dropped the bank bag on the counter.

"I'll talk to her about it." I leaned against the counter, trying to ignore the furnace-like glow of her body heat. Feeding on cold blood lowers a vampire's internal thermostat below room temperature, and despite the warmth of my newly re-formed clothing, my skin was hypersensitive. My fingers unconsciously tapped out her heartbeat on the countertop before I noticed and forced my hand to be still.

Marilyn didn't seem convinced.

"I will," I insisted. "But she's down for the day and we need to talk about something else."

"Where's your wife?"

"Technically, I don't have one," I said. "Tab's and my vows were—quote—until one of us departed this world—end quote—and I did. I ran through the Paths of the Dead. I was judged—"

"You came back."

"True, but it still counts, *and* she was brain-whammied by Rachel when we made our vows, so the ceremony was bullshit to start with—"

"Tabitha doesn't feel that way about it." Marilyn's tone was measured and sure. She'd been waiting for this talk; she'd had time to think it all through. "I asked her the week I came back from the dead. She loves you, and you married her."

Oh . . . gut shot! But one I'd expected all along.

"But I love you," I said.

Marilyn smiled, a tear in the corner of her eye. "Of course you think that, Eric." She touched my hand. "I love you, too—I always have—but that doesn't make it right."

"What do I need to do to make it right?" I knew the answer to that one, too, or thought I did. I couldn't make it right. Not really. Even if Tabitha stepped aside, Marilyn would suspect I'd used my Sire abilities to force Tabitha to be a good little offspring and get out of my libido's way. Which I'd never do, of course, but the doubt would be there, and it would poison everything. So I had to eradicate the doubt.

She laughed that single braying "ha" with which I was so familiar. "Eric, even if you could make it right, if we got married right now . . . would it really change anything?"

"Yes."

"And you'd still want me after I cheated on you?"

"With whom?" I asked. "When?" There are things I decide to forget. Marilyn's infidelity was one of them. I didn't care, and I didn't want to know, and if I don't think about something for long enough, whatever's wrong with my brain, whether it really is early-onset Alzheimer's or something else, it takes the memory and eats it. When it comes back to haunt me, then I ignore it, and if I pretend long enough, eventually, I forget for real. I remembered that she'd cheated, but in my head, there were extenuating circumstances, and it had happened after I was a vampire. That wasn't quite true, but I wanted it to be, so I had every intention of acting like it was.

My memory was working . . . and I knew Marilyn had slept with Roger. I killed and ate Roger. If it was a question of revenge, I think that counts as handled.

She searched my eyes with her gaze. "You really don't remember?"

"I know some bad stuff happened, and the guy who did it is dead now," I answered. "Anything that happened between you two, I don't hold against you."

A tear ran down her cheek. "If we walked down the aisle right now, what song would you pick for the first dance after?" she asked.

"'We've Only Just Begun' by the Carpenters."

"Why that instead of 'Stardust'?"

"Because we have forever now, or we can have it." *And weird things happen when I play and sing "Stardust."*

"Damn."

A car pulled up and parked in the back. V8 engine but not Fang's. Two more parked next to it. Car doors opened.

"What?" I asked, trying not to notice the sound of booted feet on concrete and asphalt.

"That's a good answer."

"I guess that's love, then." I smelled gun oil, too, and kerosene. I listened for heartbeats. Talbot was no longer within hearing distance, but there were a dozen humans behind the club. I also heard a mechanical whine cutting through things. A winch? I started rounding the counter, not to get closer to her but to make sure I was between her and the back door.

Fang, I thought as loudly as I could. There was half a reply, a disembodied engine rev, and then—

"Eric, we never really loved each other."

"Bullshit." A stabbing pain punched through my chest. I balled my hands into fists, trying to cover up the pain and hold in a yelp. Somebody had just staked Fang. I could sense it, but I was finally having The Talk with Marilyn, and . . .

"Don't be mad, I—"

"Oh, I'm not mad, I just recognize bullshit when I hear it." I clutched my chest over my heart, the sensation of sharp, intense agony still clear and present. "If we weren't in love with each other, or . . . if I wasn't in love with you . . . then it's like that poem I learned for our wedding."

"What poem?"

"Shakespeare's." In my mind's eye, I could almost see the group of men around Fang. One of them reached for the trunk release, but another man stopped him. "Sonnet 116."

We'll count the bones of the victims later, the man seemed to say.

"You were going to recite a poem?"

I nodded. Gun oil filled my nostrils. *Maybe I have enough time,* I thought. As they formed up at the rear door, the whining stopped, and I heard what sounded like rubber wheels on the concrete—a wheelchair?

"I thought it would be romantic. It goes like this: 'Let me not to the marriage of true minds / Admit impediments.'" I felt for the power of the über vamp and couldn't touch it. "'Love is not love / Which alters when it alteration finds,'" I closed with Marilyn as I recited the verses, and she didn't fight me when

I put my hand on her arm. "'Or bends with the remover to remove: / O no! it is an ever-fixed mark.'"

More heartbeats approached the front of the building, but I didn't stop reciting. "'That looks on tempests and is never shaken; / It is the star to every wandering bark, / Whose worth's unknown.'" My eyes locked with hers and I felt her soften. The key to Marilyn's heart was and always would be in revealing within myself the man she once loved, the man who went to war and came back broken. A man she fixed and sent off to war again. "'Although his height be taken. / Love's not Time's fool . . .'" But I was Time's fool. There's a sound of metal on metal when a lock is being picked. I heard that sound. ". . . 'though rosy lips and cheeks / Within his bending sickle's compass come . . .'"

Walkie-talkies beeped from the front and back of the Demon Heart, audible only to me. The attack was coming, but I was almost through. My chest tightened. If I'd been human, I wouldn't have been able to breathe, but I was almost through. If I could only kiss her . . . "'Love alters not with his brief hours and weeks, / But bears it out even to the edge of doom.'" I pulled her tightly to me, crushing her against my chest, her breasts against me. Even through our clothes, the sensation brought out my fangs, but I forced them back in. "'If this be error and upon me proved, / I never writ, nor no man ever loved.'"

I leaned in to kiss her, and her eyes closed. Maybe I hadn't won her back, but it was going to happen . . . she would allow something that had been off limits to me for almost fifty years: a simple kiss. Our lips almost touched . . . and of course that's when they opened fire.

9

ERIC

IT'S ALL ABOUT TIMING WITH SOME PEOPLE

I hate bullets, especially when some jackass has blessed the damn things and started shooting me with them. Why can't all vampire hunters be like that dumbass in El Segundo who tried etching crosses onto the shell casings—you know, the part that doesn't actually hit the vampire? Heh. That was classic.

All sounds except for a high-pitched whine went away as I shoved Marilyn to the ground. These guys couldn't kill her, but bullets hurt. They lit me up from both sides, the rapid jerk of automatic-weapons fire making me dance like a squirrel under high voltage. I counted a dozen assailants, including one in a wheelchair. At night, the wounds would've kept burning, but not during the day. During the day, my powers work close to normal, which should be taken as a sign of how screwed up they've gotten.

Spirals of smoke wafted up from my wounds and in my best Southern drawl, I said, "That ain't the way my momma taught *me* to say hello." No claws. No snarls. Not glowing eyes. Not yet. This was all part of The Plan, too, not the Win Back Marilyn Plan but the other one . . . or maybe it's a subsection of the Marilyn Plan. I'm calling it Operation Let's All Get Drunk and Screw, but that's mainly because I want to confuse anybody who can read my mind. I may have already said that. Very prone to the fuzzy is my brain.

"I don't want to fight any of you guys."

They continued to fire, so I closed my eyes and concentrated. Turning to mist is like walking out into a freezing winter rain. You feel cold, soaked to the bone. Everything goes hazy, like there's gauze over the camera lens, or there would be if I opened my eyes. Misting makes me motion sick if I move too quickly or look around too much. I don't know how Winter does it without throwing up all over the place.

Once I felt soaked to the core, I opened my eyes. The weapons fire had stopped, but the vampire hunters were still there. I closed my eyes again and focused on pulling myself back together, becoming whole. The bullets made it harder. I wanted to be whole and healthy when I rematerialized, but the bullets wanted to be inside me, burning my undead flesh and generally showing their disapproval.

Being water vapor sucks. Resuming my physical form felt great, almost as good as jumping into a swimming pool on a warm summer day. Even though I lost my courting clothes, reverting to a WELCOME TO THE VOID T-shirt, jeans, belt, and combat boots, it seemed to have done the trick.

"That was mist," said the man in the wheelchair.

"Yes, it was." I turned to face him slowly, palms up, hands at shoulder level. "I don't want to fight you guys."

"My research says you turn into a ghost."

"I used to," I agreed. "You're about one version behind in my development cycle."

"How?" he asked. His crew smelled of fear, hate, and resolve, but not him; his scent was neutral.

"I close my eyes really, really tightly and try to turn to

mist. It feels similar to the way turning into a ghost did, but I don't glow blue, and the world doesn't go all screwy watercolor-painting."

"No." He met my eyes without fear. "How did they change? A vampire's powers, even an Emperor's, don't usually change so abruptly."

"My powers change more often than a stripper swaps outfits on a Saturday night," I said. "It's from all the powerful muckety-mucks who keep messing with me. Now here's the deal. I . . ." And then I forgot the deal. It went right out of my head. Told you I was addled. Fortunately, I had an app for that. "Crap. Hold on."

I pulled out my cell and pressed the question-mark symbol I'm supposed to use if I utterly blank.

My screen displayed a tiny rolling smiley face and:

CONNECTING . . .

DAYTIME SUPPORT: *What happened?*

ME: *Vampire hunters just shot me up in the Demon Heart.*

DAYTIME SUPPORT: *Did you kiss her first?*

ME: *No time. They were too fast.*

DAYTIME SUPPORT: *No worries. That will work out sooner or later.*

ME: *I think I'm not supposed to fight the vampire hunters. Right?*

One of the vampire hunters cleared his throat. Marilyn brushed herself off and got to her feet. "What are you doing, Eric?" she asked.

"Sorry. Just a second."

I looked back at the phone and frowned. I understood what I read, but even seeing it didn't make it ring a bell.

ME: *I don't remember that part.*

DAYTIME SUPPORT: *N_CASE_OF_HUNTERS1.*

ME: *Seriously?*

DAYTIME SUPPORT: *Do it or don't, but it's the next step in The Plan, and you do want The Plan to succeed, right?*

ME: *I'm doing it now.*

I thumbed through the contact list, and sure enough, there it was, just like Daytime Support had typed: N_CASE_OF_HUNTERS1. I thumbed the contact and let the call connect. The voice on the other end of the phone was one that always made me smile, even if it did sound a bit more hoarse than usual.

"I got vampire hunters, and they staked my car," I said. I could only imagine how strange it must have looked to the people in the bowling alley. This is not how fights with me work. I'm usually all bull and no china shop, but that was back when I had little to lose and nothing to gain.

"Mr. Courtney," said the man in the wheelchair, "if you're calling in mage support—"

"I swear on Marilyn's life that I'm not calling in any kind of air strike or hit squad."

The man swallowed hard, looked more confused, and nodded. His unease was hard to miss.

"Do I send her in yet?" one of his men called in on the walkie-talkie.

"Give us another minute or two," wheelchair boy said calmly.

"She won't wait much longer," the voice on the walkie said.

"Understood, but the situation is not as expected."

"What's your name?" I asked, interrupting.

"Um . . . Pythagoras."

"Here." I thrust my cell at him. "He wants to talk to you."

"Who wants—"

When he didn't take the phone immediately, I held it up to his ear. Vampire hearing let me get both sides of the conversation just fine, but I'm keeping one side of it to myself 'cause I'm all sneaky and shit.

"Eric?" Marilyn tried to catch my eye, but I was too busy watching Pythagoras. He had the look of a guy who wasn't often surprised, was unsure how to react when he was, and definitely was now.

"Even if I did believe that I—" Pythagoras found himself cut off by the person on the other end. His eyes widened. "But surely. Ah. Yes. Are you certain? Can— No, that's true." An exasperated sigh. "No. Yes. Well, obviously, that's accurate, but . . . No. No. I agree that he would be quite valuable in that role." One last long look at me. "But . . . he's a vampire! What? No. I was unaware of that. Very well. Out of respect for you, then. Seventy-two hours. Yes, you have my word."

He pulled his head away from the phone, and I put it up to my ear, but the call had already been terminated. I said "Thanks" to the empty air and clicked back over to the app represented by the smiley-face icon.

DAYTIME SUPPORT: *Do you remember step seven of the M protocol?*

My heart sank. How could I ever forget step seven of the M protocol? I had nightmares about it, even though I'm the one who came up with that part.

ME: *Yes.*

DAYTIME SUPPORT: *Do it after the fight.*

ME: *What fight?*

CONNECTION TERMINATED.

It kicked me back out to the main menu, and I frowned. Pythagoras and his men were arguing, but I could tell they were going to comply. There was a halfheartedness to the objections. Deep down they trusted him, and he trusted N_CASE_OF_HUNTERS1.

Pythogoras held out a hand, and I shook it.

"I can't believe I'm saying this, Mr. Courtney, but I wish you the best of luck." He spoke into the walkie-talkie. "We're pulling out. Password: Golden Triangle." He took his finger off the button and said, "This may not go well with one of our allies, but my men will all follow orders."

"Which ally?" I asked. If I'd waited a few seconds, I could have spared myself the breath, because my front door slammed open so hard, it came off of its hinges. Standing in the doorway was a woman who looked vaguely familiar. She stood out on the sidewalk, blond hair illuminated by the sun, eyes awash with glowing red fury, nails extended into claws, fangs bared. She wore a pair of tight blue jeans with decorative lacing up the sides, brown boots, a red leather belt, and a cream-colored silk blouse. A red scarf around her neck and the matching pair of fingerless gloves completed the odd ensemble.

"There is no way in hell we're calling off this attack!"

Normally, vampires can sense each other at a distance. Vamps we're used to sensing barely register if we're busy. Greta and Tabitha, for example. I sense them all the time, so if I'm distracted, I won't get a full contact; I kind of dismiss it instinctively without paying attention, like hitting the snooze button on an alarm clock. But this woman—why I didn't sense her until we locked eyes, I can't say.

Now that I sensed her, she felt like a Motörhead album, one of the newer ones. Her name was Evelyn Courtney-Barnes. I guessed she'd been made a vampire no more than three to five years ago, and where I'd normally get a sense of a vampire's power level, from her all I sensed was: KILL ERIC COURTNEY.

Never a good sign. I had time to ask, "Do I know you from somewhere?" and then she was heading toward me at top vampire speed, and the fight was under way.

❖ 10 ❖

ERIC

WHY *NUKEKUBI* SHOULDN'T FIGHT IN BOWLING ALLEYS

She wasn't expecting me to block. It's not something I do, but one can't start learning more about fighting smart without having some of it stick, even with a memory like mine. Evelyn aimed two claw rakes at my neck. I batted them both aside and tried to sweep her legs. The fight would have gone faster, but thanks to my newest batch of power issues, I can't go über vamp without help from Fang, and with Fang staked . . . Is it still staking if it involves a tire iron and an engine instead of a piece of wood and an undead heart?

I was wondering that when a knee to the crotch filled my world with pain and nausea. It was only luck that I saw the stake and misted right before it would have struck home. Misting made the nausea worse, and I vomited, a cloud of pinkish mist puffing off my main "cloud," which turned solid (or, well, liquid) and splattered the floor once it was clear of me and the magic keeping it mist. One good thing about having all your bodily fluids replaced with blood is that when you hurl, at least it doesn't stink. True, there's blood everywhere, but . . .

It's not always easy for me to stay mist. If I get distracted, I can go physical again without meaning to do so. The rush of transformation is unmistakable, though, so the moment I was solid again, I knew I was. Score one for Team Alzheimer's.

"Look. I've pissed off a lot of women, but—" I ducked another angry volley of claws, rolling backward, then leaping over the seats bracketing lane six. I landed with the squeal of rubber soles on wood, wincing as they left skid marks near the approach, the cool solidity of the ball return against my calves. Momentum sucks.

"Bastard!" Evelyn snarled.

"My parents were married, but if you want to try 'asshole' or 'motherfucker'—"

We clashed, hands locked in more of a push-and-pull than a fight. She was strong, if not as strong as me, then close.

"You murdered me!"

"It obviously didn't take, so that's a bonus."

To the left of the angry woman with the claws and accusations, I saw Marilyn heading toward the door. Being a true immortal doesn't exactly come with superstrength, as far as I can tell. There are ways to make yourself stronger and faster, but most of them are visible to other supernatural types, and I didn't think Marilyn had taken the time to learn anything about them yet. All the same, I knew she was headed to get the tire iron out of Fang.

Marilyn Amanda Robinson, I love you so much, I can't stand it.

Full names.

Evelyn Courtney-Barnes.

I'd heard it as Evelyn Courtney Barnes in my head, but when I'd seen it, it'd had a hyphen like a bra burner's last name. My family name is Courtney. Another knee to the crotch nearly broke my train of thought, but I found it again pretty damn quick. When I was murdered, it was the Courtney Family Curse that brought me back as a vampire. The curse turned any

Courtney who died while not following the usual family path
of religion into a vampire or something else it thought suitable.
John Paul Courtney, my great-great-(great?)-grandfather, had
been turned into a ghost and attached to his magic revolver,
El Alma Perdida. I'd broken the curse and lost the revolver a
year ago, but unlike in the fairy tales, breaking the curse hadn't
suddenly made me human again.

"Wait!" I shoved her away. Regardless of our almost equal
strength, I had at least fifty pounds on her. "Your maiden name
was Courtney? As in related to me?"

She growled, charged, and went for a tackle. We tumbled
together out onto the approach and slid halfway down the
lane, the mixture of mineral oils on the polished wood letting
us slide farther than normal. She rode atop me, growling and
lunging. Typical vampire move to go for a bite when in close.
She snapped once, twice, then smiled. "You think you're so
damn smart." Her fangs grew a little longer and turned up,
more tusklike. "Can you mist while I have a grip on you? Can
you do it, asshole?"

I tried, but "no" seemed to be the answer. "Look, if you're
my relative, I understand why you might be mad at me. Maybe
you wish I'd broken the Courtney Family Curse earlier on, and
then you wouldn't be a vampire, but—"

"Screw the curse!" Evelyn snarled. "You think I give a shit
about some damn curse? You murdered me, asshole! I was
heading to my goddamn bachelorette party, and you swooped
down out of nowhere, snatched me away to a rooftop, and
beat the hell out of me before tearing off my clothes like I was
some damn Christmas present."

"I—I don't rememb—" But then I did remember . . .
maybe. I've killed a lot of people, well over ten thousand, but
I've never done much dragging off to rooftops. I don't know
why, but there's usually a more convenient place, and— "Wait.
Rooftop?"

"I parked my Jag across from Starbucks and ran in to load up on coffee, because I hadn't been sleeping much and I wanted to be awake enough to enjoy the party, but I never made it there. You killed me, ripped off my fucking head, dropped it down a sewer drain, and left my body on the roof." She hissed, then let loose with a catlike yowl, a frustrated mixture of rage and regret. "You probably don't even remember it, you useless—"

I did remember. It all came back: the smell of her expensive perfume, the smoothness of her newly shaved legs . . ." You were wearing purple lingerie, right?"

"How sweet," she said sarcastically. "You remember."

"If I ripped your head off, then how?"

"How did I come back?" She grinned a wicked self-satisfied grin. "Oh, the Courtney Family Curse was one insistent bit of magic, I'll give it that. It always found a way. Have you ever heard of a *nukekubi*?"

"A what?"

I felt her claws dig deep and lock; her legs were rigid, gripping mine. Her grin broadened, and then her head came off, letting the scarf fall loose to reveal a line of glowing red *kanji*-like symbols. They looked Japanese, but they could have been any Asian language. My vampire sense tingled again, and KILL ERIC COURTNEY was replaced with a feeling of power levels and might. It felt strange and ephemeral, not like normal, but she was definitely Vlad-level, at least. Was she an Emperor? I had no clue. She was a vampire whose fucking head could pop off and fly around. How the hell was I supposed to know? That never happened to me when my head got ripped off.

"That's convenient." I struggled against her grip, but locked in one place, her strength seemed to have increased. "An undead chick with a detachable head: the blow-job potential alone . . ."

Never underestimate the capacity unrestrained lewdness has when it comes to deliberately pissing off a female opponent. Just ask my almost-hopefully-soon-to-be-ex-wife, Tabitha. Free of her body, Evelyn's head was transfigured. Long blond hair floated about her as if only tangentially affected by gravity, as if she were floating on her back in a pool. Her skin took on a porcelain pallor, and the fangs receded to a more normal length. I watched the whites of her eyes go crimson, as if they'd been injected with red food coloring. When she spoke, her voice, though clear and comprehensible, sounded like it came not from her mouth but from all directions at once.

"Pig." She spat the word, then buried her fangs in my throat.

I don't like to get bitten. It's a whole thing. But there are few times a vampire is more vulnerable or more distracted than when he's feeding. I felt my strength begin to fade, my hunger grow. My thoughts went cloudy, and then . . . then I felt an engine turn over, felt it deep in my chest, in the very core of me. Fang revved his engine, pegging out the RPMs while staying in one spot, tires squealing and throwing up smoke. And I . . . well, I went über vamp.

I halfway expected Evelyn's legs and arms to snap, but they gave way instead, like the spring-loaded arms of a life-size doll. Evelyn tried to disengage her fangs from my rapidly expanding throat, but my hand was already there, locking her into place. A gruesome *crack-snap* made me wince as one of her fangs broke, snapping midway down the tooth. My skin flushed black, a wave of jet staining me obsidian. Leathery bat wings erupted from my back with a sound like sailcloth catching the wind.

"Okay." My claws sank into the approach, and I winced again, wondering how much it would cost to fix it or if I'd have to replace the flooring. "Nobody bites me." I pulled her free, my long black claws glistening against her blond hair. "It's a whole thing—a rule—don't fucking do it."

"I'll kill you!"

"Already dead, cousin. It is 'cousin,' isn't it?" I held up her head so I could see her expression, careful not meet her gaze, because I didn't want to get into some weird mental battle and find out the hard way that she had more going on upstairs than me. Most people do. "Are we like first cousins? Second cousins? Once removed? I'm guessing at least once or twice removed, no matter what, because of that whole generational thing, yeah?"

Beatrice caught my attention from behind the computer controlling the lanes. She held up a crossbow, and I gave a slight shake of my head. Marilyn could have made the shot, but I doubted Beatrice could. With my off hand, I made a little circle in the air with my forefinger. Bea smiled and shook her head, not a "no" but more of an "I can't believe he's going to do this."

Evelyn had answered my question while my mind was on Beatrice, so I had no idea what she'd said, but frankly, I didn't care. I knew I'd been an asshole. Even with the new plan, that wasn't going to change. It's how I am. It's in my DNA or something. I try to play nice, give folks a chance to back down, but it never works out. When it doesn't, I wind up looking like even more of an asshole after I take drastic actions, like I had with . . . cat guy . . . orange and white fur . . . evil police dude . . . Whatever his name was. Stacey.

The fog effect from Cosmic Bowling kicked in along with disco lights and the Scissor Sisters' cover of "Dancing Queen." Behind me, I heard the lane resetting. Pins setting up.

"Can you drink animal blood?" I asked over the music.

"Of course," she spat. "Unlike you, I make it a habit never to feed on humans. I—"

"Yeah?"

I'm a monster. I'm trying to be a kinder gentler monster, but like the asshole thing, that will always be there. And the monster doesn't like it when people who have it easier than me piss and moan. The monster doesn't even like it when I piss and moan.

"Well, fuck you, then." I held her head up closer and snarled. "Animal blood makes me hungrier instead of nourishing me, and trust me, I've fucking tried it all. Bats. Cats. Mice. Rats. Cow blood. Pig blood. Mouse blood. Snake. Birds. Fish." The light from my eyes turned purple, and where it struck her face, it canceled out the disco lights. "I even tried this really damn complicated mosquito idea once, and all it proved was that I have to drink the blood of sentient beings to feel full. When it's real bad, I can't control it, and I know that if I feed, I'm going to kill, so I hunt far away from my friends and my business to try and make certain I only kill people I don't know."

"You murdered me! I'm not going to feel sorry for you. You should have just committed suicide, greeted the sun, or—"

I gave her a head butt to cut her off. "I'm not complaining. I just want you to understand why I think you're a spoiled little bitch. I could have saved myself a whole lot of aggravation by staying in the seminary and never going to World War Two, but I didn't. As a result, I died on the wrong side of the holy whoever, and you know what? So did you, or the family curse wouldn't have done shit to you when you kicked it."

She flinched at that.

"As for the sun thing? Been there. Done that. Early on. Add a little blood to my ashes, and presto change-o: instant vampire." We locked eyes for a moment, the idea of avoiding mental contact having flown out of my head. "I've been staked, beheaded, blown to smithereens, and had a demon try to steal my soul. Shit. I even walked the Paths of the Dead and let Osiris judge my soul, and do you know what he told me?"

The look on her face said she didn't want to believe me but did. "I saved the world once back in the eighties, so it's all good. Water under the fucking bridge. I guess if you save a few billion people, the Powers That Be are willing to overlook

it if you have to murder a few thousand of them to survive."
I waited until she opened her mouth to respond, and then I
turned and bowled her at the waiting pins.

She made a piss-poor bowling ball.

No proper spin, and she left me with a terrible split. The
seven and ten pins sat there mocking me as the lane reset. The
seven pin wobbled, but it wasn't going to fall. I eyed the ball
return, wondering if Evelyn would make it through, like on
that episode of *CSI*, or get stuck under the lane. She did have
kind of a roundish head, and it was on the smallish side. Who
the hell do you call to get a decapitated head out of the ball
return? Surely someone at the Mages Guild would have an
idea. Maybe Melvin . . .

A cacophony of thudding, screeching, and cursing came
from the ball return. Leaning over, I shouted down the hole,
"Try to roll with it."

Leaving that be, I walked back to her headless body and
yelled, "Stake!"

Bea slid across the counter, crossbow bolt in hand, which
she tossed to me when she thought she was close enough. I
caught the bolt and rammed it through the heart of Evelyn's
headless Barbie-doll-stiff body. No whooshy dusty end
of undead existence, but then again, I hadn't expected it to
kill her. A stake through the heart usually only does that
for Masters and below. Hmmm . . ."See if you can Google
'nuk' . . . 'knuck' . . . 'headless vampires,' and see how I kill one,"
I shouted.

"Bastard!" Cousin Evie's head shot out of the ball return.
"You don't even have the decency to feel guilty."

"Oh." I stood between the head and the body. "I'm guilty as
a motherfucker, and it tears me up inside sometimes, but you
won't hear me whining about it, and I'm not sorry."

"There's a difference?" She circled me, trying to get an
opening to reconnect with her body.

"Between guilt and regret?" I laughed. "A big one. I'm guilty because I know a lot of what I've done is wrong, but to be sorry, I'd have to regret doing it, and the only thing I'm really sorry about"—her head darted in, thinking she had me, but I was too fast and caught her by the hair, slinging her around and letting go as she rocketed back toward my lane—"is that horrible first frame split."

"You son of a—" The ball return cut her off again.

"Hey," I yelled, "here's an idea. If your head comes off, don't start a fight in a goddamn bowling alley."

By the time she came back up a second time, Bea had Googled *nukekubi*, and I had ripped the metal plate off Evelyn's headless neck and jammed two pens and a pencil in its place, like ungainly spikes. There was nothing on the net about the metal plate; then again, the net is not the end-all, be-all of human knowledge. The copper plate was shaped exactly to the dimensions of her neck and about a centimeter thick, with a hole matching the dimension of her throat and inch-long spikes countersunk to help keep the thing in place. Where her neck had a simple line of *kanji*, the plate was covered in finely engraved patterns of the stuff.

"No!" Evie's head flew straight for her body, and I let her past me. "I can't stay detached from my body for long without the copper plate. Not during the day." She bit down on one of the pencils and started working it loose, ignoring the way the pen gouged at her cheek when she did so. Blood ran down her cheek, and all at once, the memory of feeding on her rushed back at me hard. Her blood hadn't tasted special, but all blood is best straight from the vein. Feeding thoughts can also get all wrapped up in other urges—lower ones, sexy ones.

The über vamp's arousal was obvious. The urge to feed . . . and do that other thing . . . was almost overwhelming. I had to do one or the other or I was going to do both. And I was certainly not going to rape my cousin or anyone else.

"Beatrice," I said. "I—"

I didn't even need to finish the sentence. She knew from the sound of my voice—the twinge of desperation—that I needed blood. I've been trying to avoid feeding on live humans, even my thralls, because while feeding in general brings out the souls that are haunting me, live feeding tends to make the haunting worse. It had to happen eventually; I'd be nuts to believe I could get away with it forever. Maybe it was less nuts to think I could go a whole day, but . . . this is me.

"Whatever you need, Eric." Beatrice bared her neck, but I lifted her into the air, sinking my fangs straight through her jeans to get at her femoral artery. That was a mistake, too. I've always thought of Beatrice as safe, since she didn't become a thrall because she was some vampire groupie; she did it because she wants to live forever and thinks getting bitten whenever her "Master" needs to feed is a small price to pay. It's not like vampire bites feel good or anything. They hurt like crazy, but based on the scent of arousal that filled my nostrils, it's a pain some begin to enjoy.

Blood and warmth flowed through me. No matter how warm I stay, there's nothing like that feeling—not warm clothes, not a sauna. Nothing. It was only the third time I'd fed live since I got Marilyn back, and I wasn't ready. The world beyond Beatrice and me fell away.

"Oh. Master. Don't. Stop." Beatrice pulled my head to the right. "Just let me get these—"

Thank goodness she said "Master." Vampires subconsciously emit a signal to their thralls. I don't know if it's a pheromone or magic or what, but if we concentrate, we can negate the effect. Most vampires don't give a shit and treat their thralls like little fuck-bunny slaves. Not me. I don't like having thralls at all. The reason I have Erin, Gladys, and Cheryl is because I'd rescued them from their Masters on Sweet Heart Row, who had them working as blood whores. I'd have let them go, except that

Gladys was so old that resuming her natural age would mean nigh-instant death; Erin needed protecting and didn't want to leave; and Cheryl . . . she didn't want to go any more than Beatrice did. My mage Magbidion is with me because he sold his soul to a demon to gain magical powers and because his term is coming up and he wants my protection from the demon coming to call in his marker and drag him to hell.

The short version is: They all know not to call me "Master." So when they do, it's a sure sign that I'm influencing them accidentally. I concentrated on making Beatrice not want me, but that didn't work either, though from the look on my face, she seemed to understand what I was doing.

"It's not that," Beatrice said. "I . . . I can't describe it. You haven't bitten me in months, but it wasn't like this before. Your bite hurt at first, but then . . . I . . . I felt this rush of warmth and safety, like there was no place on earth I'd rather be than wherever you are and with your fangs inside me. I was . . . I felt so . . . grateful that when I saw how excited you were, I thought, *What the hell, let's do this. Whatever he wants.*"

"Oh, fuck you, you goddamn asshole piece of shit," came a familiar voice. Told you the haunting comes on fast when I drink live. "That's my fucking special ability! Some best friend you are."

I flinched, ignoring the voice and knowing damn well I was the only one who could hear it.

Evelyn had gotten the first pencil out of her neck and was working on the second one, but I'd jammed them in well.

Beatrice gestured at my groin. "I'm feeling normal again, but if you do need to take care of that, I could manage something . . . um . . . it's a little large for . . . um, traditional—"

I looked down. I'd forgotten I was the über vamp. The more I purposefully change into it, the more comfortable it feels. In the back of my head, I worry that one day I might be the über vamp all day, looking human only at night, when

I'm a true immortal. "I think I need to put some pants on the über vamp," I interrupted. "Go steal some of Talbot's workout shorts. The black ones. That shouldn't look too stupid."

"Sure!" said the voice in my head again. "Steal my special gift. Steal the fucking cat's pants. Why not? Now, while she's gone, why don't you go for the triptych and ass-rape your cousin over there? She's in the right position for it."

"Shut up, Roger." I looked around and found him leaning against the ball return, smoking a cigarette. I didn't smell the cigarette smoke until I saw it. In Talbot's absence, my ghosts were happy to come out and play. Nice. I wondered what they were hiding from him.

"Come now, my boy," another voice began. "Though I admit the language is certainly of the low quality one might expect from a person whose name means 'famous with the spear' and has become slang for 'having sex.'" I looked at the new speaker and found a short, fat, balding man with an evil smile, standing, arms crossed, near the register. He wore the same open robe he'd had on when I ate his soul. "Still." He crossed the room to eye Evelyn's rump appraisingly. "I must admit that I see little reason why you should deny yourself."

"Because it would be rape, Phil. Um . . . I know I kill people, but that's 'cause I have to eat." I grasped for a comparison with my left hand, as if I might be able to snatch the perfect analogy out of the air. "Hunting just to kill things is evil. Rape is evil. And evil is something I try not to be."

"'Pleasure *is* the greatest incentive to evil,' or that's what Plato claimed." Phillip moved closer, and I caught the hint of blood and sex on his breath. "Of course, I prefer to side with Oscar Wilde in that regard. 'An inordinate passion for pleasure is the secret of remaining young.'"

"Wow, are you ever a pompous jackass," Roger quipped. "You almost make me forget how much I hate this asshole." He gestured at me with his cigarette.

Lisette didn't say anything when she appeared, but she was dressed in the freaky Victorian bordello outfit she'd been wearing when I ate her soul. The worst was the crying. It came last, though it was fainter now. I spotted Suzie in the corner of the Demon Heart, hugging her knees to her chest and rocking. Hers was the first soul out of four that I'd ever eaten on purpose. When I'd been a revenant *and* a vampire, before the whole breaking of the Eye of Scrythax thing that made me undead part of the time and ever-living the other half, I could do stuff like that, eat souls, but apparently, when I lost that side of my supernatural self, it stopped the digestive process. Or that was my theory at the time. I was wrong, but it was a good theory.

Beatrice came back with the shorts, and I slid them on the über vamp before transforming back into my more human size and shape.

"Are you all right, Eric?" Beatrice held up her hand so I could see the purple light hitting it. "Your eyes are glowing purple."

I held on to the sensation of warmth, from both her blood and my newly re-created clothes, before I answered. "They'll fade after a while." I was looking at my mind-fucked menagerie of the mostly-but-still-annoyingly-not-quite-totally-dead assholes. "They always do."

"C'mon, Eric, that's cold. Even for you."

Evelyn had gotten the second pencil out by then and was working on the pen when I walked over, pulled the pen out, and tapped the small metal plate back down where it had been.

"What are you doing?" Evelyn snapped.

"I just wanted you to know that I can kill you." I put one knee on her back and yanked the crossbow bolt out of her heart. "I know how to do it, and I can do it anytime I want."

"Oh." Phillip closed his eyes rapturously. "Oh, I see. How marvelous. This might be equally entertaining. I never thought you had it in you, my boy. The luscious thirst for adequate enemies. Humiliate her. Show her how powerless she is and then . . ."

"This isn't about you." I aimed the comment at both of them, a skill I learned when I was haunted by my great-great-great-grandfather John Paul Courtney.

She and Phillip responded at the same time. "No?" Evelyn sneered. "Then who do you think it's about? You?"

"Come now, Eric. *Fas est et ab hoste doceri!*"

I translated what Phillip had said and used it as my answer to Evelyn, ignoring Phil completely. I even remembered where the quote came from. "There was this guy, Ovid, from back in the day, and he said, 'It's proper to learn even from an enemy.' He also said . . ." I paused, looking directly at Phillip.

"You expect me to give you the quote?"

I kept staring.

"Did you forget it?" Evelyn tried to slip past me to reattach her head, and I let her by.

I didn't answer, but suddenly the answer came to me, like Phillip was thinking it, and purposefully not saying it, but I could hear his thoughts. Interesting.

"The Latin is *Perfer et obdura; dolor hic tibi proderit olim.* It means 'Be patient and tough; someday this pain will be useful to you.' He wrote this story about a mom who kills her own children to get back at their dad. An asshole I used to know would quote shit like that at me all the time. Usually right before he did something nasty."

"You!" Phillip jabbed his finger at me. "You stole that out of my mind!" When his finger touched me, we both blinked in surprise. Phillip took two steps back, his mouth opening and shutting like a fish's, before he vanished. *If they can touch me,* I thought, *then I . . .*

I glanced at Roger, but he and Lisette had already fled, and though Suzie was still in the corner, I wasn't interested in messing with her. I felt bad for her. *Phil seemed as shocked as I was. Hmmm . . .*

"Sounds like a real bastard." Evelyn stood, adjusting her scarf so that it covered the thin line of copper separating her head and her neck.

"He was. He killed my daughter, so I ate his soul and knocked his building down before charging into hell after her."

"Bullshit!"

"It happened." We turned to look at Marilyn, who'd come walking in the front door. She held a crossbow and had a cigarette sticking out of the corner of her mouth. "Because I was down there, too, and then this moron cut a deal to get me back. A deal with a demon."

"You were in hell?" Disbelief sounded loud and clear in Evelyn's voice.

"It wasn't all that bad," Marilyn said. "They were too afraid of him"—she gestured at me with her chin but kept the crossbow trained on Evelyn—"to actually torture me. But it's not a place you'd want to visit."

"Why does he get to be so special?" Evie's voice was angry and tinged with something else. Envy, maybe. I saw the welling of bloodred tears at the corners of her eyes. "Do you know how hard it was to convince those vampire hunters to trust me? And he . . . he puts them on the phone with someone with a raspy voice and . . . and they just call everything off!"

"You want to kill me?" I asked matter-of-factly. "Then come work for me. I'll let you try a new method once a year, starting with today. I'll even cooperate, but in the intervening time, you work with me and with my daughter to keep the vampires and other supernaturals of this city in line."

"What?" she scoffed. "Like if I said, 'I want to stake you and leave you in the sun,' you'd say okay."

"On your one day a year, if that was your one attempt, sure."

"Eric, no!" That one came from Beatrice.

Marilyn just let loose one braying "ha!" and lowered her crossbow.

"And if it doesn't work and I break my word?" Evelyn asked.

I gave her my most charming smile and bared my fangs. "Then I'll drag you back here and bowl ten frames with that detachable head of yours. Or worse: I'll sic my daughter on you."

Well, I thought as I let Evelyn stake me and drag me out into the sun, *that's one way to avoid killing your cousin.*

I'm not sure I can recommend it.

♦ 11 ♦

ERIC

NIGHTTIME IS THE RIGHT TIME

Sunset brought me back like a bad penny or gum on the shoe sole of the world. One moment I'd felt the fire raging over my body as that big old Southern sun wiped me off the face of her favorite planet, and then snap, crackle, pop, the setting of the sun brought me back. No blood required. I arrived without clothes, which might have been a clue to someone who knew me well, but Cousin Evie was not that person. I drew in two sweet draughts of night air before opening my eyes.

Evelyn stared at me with a slack jaw and furious eyes.

"Okay," I said as I stood up, wiping parking-deck grit off my butt, "so obviously, that didn't work." A quick look around told me we were on the top of the parking deck adjoining the Pollux. Convenient.

"You . . . you just re-formed." Evelyn poked me with a foreclaw. "You're even warm!"

"That's how it works." I glanced toward the stairs, trying to resist the urge to bolt to my bathroom and let Magbidion do his daily maintenance to hide all the things he's hiding for me: the true immortality at night, all the new thralls . . . I have to admit that in some ways, being burned to ash was less painful than what's been happening to me each morning since my trip to the Paths of the Dead.

Making the transition from ever-living true immortal to undead vampire feels like going through the transition from human to vampire every morning, like dying over and over again: body emptying of all fluids but blood, purging itself of any human waste, heart growing still, warmth draining away. Burning is less complicated. I'm not saying it's a good alternative, but it's a more familiar pain. Hmmm. Note to self: *Eric Courtney, you have spent way too much time on fire.*

Sunset is way better. Going from undead back to ever-living—anything I could say to describe it seems inadequate. It's like waking up after a car crash to find out you're Captain America. I just wish I were as powerful an immortal as I am a vampire. A vampire's power is tied to the strength of personality, willpower, drive, creativity, and force of character. No problem. A true immortal's power comes from age and the number of other immortals who owe fealty to you. As a true immortal, I come up short in both areas.

"Your heart is even beating."

"Look." I headed for the stairs. "I have some things to take care of real quick. You wait here. Greta's not supposed to be up for an hour or so, but she can be erratic when she feels me in pain. Talbot should have been standing by to inform Greta about our arrangement, but she's likely to be a little . . . put out with you for wanting me dead, much less having a go at it. Whether I was willing to allow it probably won't enter into the equation for her."

"I can hold my own." Evelyn crossed her arms over her chest.

"Not against—" I began.

A shadow passed between Evelyn and me, and then her body was falling backward, headless, to the concrete. A sound

like a steam whistle was all I heard of Evelyn's scream before
I saw Greta's silhouette on the edge of the concrete wall of
the parking deck. She held Evelyn's head firmly in her hands,
her own eyes bright with crimson sparks. "Me," she whispered.
She was far enough away that I couldn't hear her words, not
without my vampiric hearing, but I knew what she'd said.

"Let me go!"

"Your head really does come off," Greta continued,
oblivious to Evelyn's objections, "kind of like LEGO."

Talbot arrived via the stairs moments later. "Greta! I told
you. Your dad said—"

"Don't hurt her, Greta." I spoke softly, trying not to sound
proud of her overprotectiveness. "She's your new deputy, and
I'm fine."

"Okay, Dad." Greta shifted Evelyn's head to one side and
cradled it under her right arm like a football helmet. "We'll
just . . . talk . . . a little."

"Promise?" I asked.

"Pinkie swear," Greta said with a nod. She was wearing
pajamas (pink bottoms with a Void City Howlers hockey
jersey as the top), and someone had put her hair in pigtails.
When she nodded, they flounced in a way that was far too
cutesy.

"Fine." I headed down the stairwell, ignoring my cousin's
muffled protests as the door cut them off. On the way into the
Pollux, Gladys greeted me with a leer and a whistle. Her hair
was purple, though she'd been playing around with hairstyles.
She currently had it done in sort of an updo held in place with
a black lacquered chopstick. Two long, purposefully errant
strands framed her face, and her makeup had been done in
smoky bluish-purple. She wore a tight white baby-doll T-shirt
under an unbuttoned Demon Heart Lanes bowling shirt, the
thinness of the material making it clear to everyone that she

was wearing a very lacy purple bra. Daisy Dukes and high heels finished off the ensemble.

Without the benefits of my thralldom, Gladys is older than me by at least a decade or two, but her spirit has to be mid-twenties, tops. Back in my day, women would have called her a "bad girl" or a "whore," while men would have used terms like a "real sport" or a "good-time girl."

"I think I have the taste thing Rachel used to do figured out," she said as I walked past her toward the stairwell that led up to the mezzanine and back around to my office and bedroom if one took a left at the top. "Want to give it a try?"

"Not tonight." I stopped at the bottom of the stairs. "Maybe tomorrow morning. I appreciate it, though."

"Magbidion's already up there," she offered, taking my refusal in stride.

"Good." I started up the stairs.

"So's your wife."

"Fuck!" I slammed my fist down on the wooden railing and was surprised when it hurt.

"Beatrice said I should give you a heads-up."

"She was right." I rubbed the heel of my hand. "Thanks again."

She whistled again. "You're thanking me enough just by walkin' up those stairs in the altogether, darlin'."

I laughed, which I think was all Gladys really wanted out of the exchange, and continued up the stairs. When I hit the top, I felt the familiar tingle of Magbidion's magic and spotted a hastily drawn mage circle scribed in chalk on the hardwood. *Clever boy, Magbidion,* I thought, *you deserve a raise.*

Standing in the portal, I suppressed the nausea that usually accompanies this particular set of spells and shivered as magic, like a cold washcloth, slid across and then within my chest. My skin lightened, and I fought the urge to scratch as my skin went dry. My lips felt chapped and rough when it was over, and my entire body felt as if it were raw with razor burn. Hunger bit deep in my belly, but I ignored it. First things first.

Tabitha was sitting on my California king, reading something on her e-reader, when I opened my bedroom door. I have to admit that she's a beautiful woman. She wore an Asian-style floral halter dress that came down to about three inches above her knees. Long black ties cinched it tight around the waist, going up over her shoulders to hold it up. The dress accentuated her wasplike figure. She'd left her long raven-black hair down (the way I like it). Hadn't it been short yesterday? I didn't remember. I didn't see her shoes, either, which was unusual, because Tabitha is the kind of gal who tends to leave whatever clothes she takes off wherever they happen to land, often putting shoes right out in the middle of the floor.

"Hi." She lowered the e-reader and gave me a smile meant to convey a message somewhere between "Hello, stranger" and "What the hell have you been up to?" I couldn't decide which one.

"Nice dress," I said, looking around for Magbidion. "You look pretty."

"Thanks." Her eyes brightened. "I asked him to give us some privacy," Tabitha offered when she realized I was looking for Mags. "He said he had some rituals to perform for you in the bathroom anyway. Do I even want to know what that's about?"

"No." I headed for the bathroom door, but she beat me to it with vampire speed.

"What? You're just going to walk past me?" She put a hand on my chest and shuddered at the bit of warmth the magic hadn't washed away. "You already fed."

"Something like that." I gently pushed her hand back. "Look, I have parking-deck grit all over my butt. I want a shower and some clean clothes."

"Why don't you just turn into a bat and change back?" She tried to make it seem like a casual question, but there was venom, too.

"When I do that, it wastes blood."

"You used to do it all the time."

"I was showing off." I looked past her impatiently. "Look, can I please go take my shower now? I was staked through the heart and burned to ash in the sun. It was not the best start to my evening."

"Fine," she said, meaning it wasn't. She did step out of the way, though. "Do you want some company?"

I fought off the sigh. I may be a murderer, but I'm an honorable man. I truly love Marilyn, but I guess I might be actually married to Tabitha, even though I think I shouldn't be. As long as Tabitha insists we're married . . . gah. When I married her, I didn't think there was any way to get Marilyn back, and I still left myself all kinds of loopholes in the ceremony. I told Tabitha I'd cheat on her. I told her I was marrying her only because I wanted to keep fucking her. Instead of saying "I do," I'd said "I'll do what I can." Our vows had definitely ended when I left this world and came back, but I couldn't just ditch her because Marilyn wouldn't like it. Sometimes being a man of my word sucks.

"If you really want to join me," I said after a minute. "But I'll warn you, I'm tired and—"

"Do you want me to seem human for you, baby?" Tabitha's green eyes sparkled. Seeming human is her special gift. All Vlads seem to have one, and some lesser vampires do as well. When Tabitha used her gift, her heart beat, she breathed instinctively (and quite convincingly), she could even eat and drink (though apparently, her taste buds didn't work). It's a rare gift. Vampires who possess it are called Living Dolls. It even gets their bodily fluids going again. Normal vampires have all their bodily fluids replaced with blood: saliva, tears, other things. But Living Dolls can turn that stuff back on. Which meant if Tabitha did that, she would almost certainly notice that where I was supposed to get bloody, I wouldn't. At night, I sweat real sweat and have real saliva, and all the downstairs plumbing works, too.

Damn.

"Whichever you want, Tabitha." I let my forehead rest against the door frame. "I feel like a heel asking you to jump through hoops for me. I don't deserve it."

"Oh, Eric."

Well, that was the wrong fucking thing to say. I felt her breasts against my back, cold at first but warming as she concentrated on bringing her body to a deceptive semblance of life. On the other hand, since doing so dulled her vampirically enhanced senses and totally killed her taste buds, maybe I could pull it off.

Sometimes I do the wrong thing. Have I mentioned that?

Case in point: Tabitha joined me in the shower. She slid out of her dress and followed me in, handing the garment to Magbidion as she walked past him. Mags looked more drained than normal, his eyes half open and underscored with purple bruising. He tried to hide the two empty, unused blood bags he had with him, but he needn't have bothered. Tabitha wasn't paying attention.

"Should I . . . ?" Magbidion looked toward the door.

Neither of us answered him. He sank down onto the toilet seat (lid down) and let his head rest on the counter. My new shower is impressive. Winter went all out when he put it in. I'm not a big sauna guy, but the ceiling shower system (with central and outer ring rain), combined with three wall sprays, rubbed brass fittings, heated shower bench . . . even at night I was a true believer. Hot water rained down, steam rising up around us. I'd wondered if I'd need to use a blindfold for Tabitha to hide the lack of the blood that usually accompanies vampire sex, but I didn't.

Tabitha rubbed the grime from my back, soaped up the loofah, and slowly scrubbed all traces of parking-deck grit and grime from my back.

"Want me to wash your hair?" Tabitha wrapped her arms around me from behind again, breasts pressing against my back. I love that feeling. She kissed the nape of my neck and let the tip of her tongue touch my skin following each kiss. Where she got that from, I don't know, but it gets to me.

"Tabitha," I protested softly.

"We're married, Eric. It's okay for me to turn you on."

"Maybe."

She reached past me to grab my shampoo, and a little squeal of a laugh escaped her lips. "When did you start using Garnier?"

"Paris."

Tabitha guided me to the shower seat and poured a small amount of shampoo into her palm before rubbing it in my hair, leaning my head forward to rest below her breasts as she worked the shampoo into a lather, the fruity smell mixing with her clean odor. *What is it with me and showers?*

I remembered a time before I died when Marilyn briefly considered a change from tending bar to beauty school. A warm towel on my face as her fingernails worked across my scalp, waking it up, making my skin tingle and my senses flare to life. The smell of her cigarettes banished by the fragrance of the shampoo. She used to love to shave me, too. Her hands soft and loving on my skin just before she brushed on the lather and starting shaving with careful strokes of the straight razor against the grain for a closer shave.

As the warm false rain washed the shampoo from my hair, I felt Tabitha's hand questing low, between my legs. "There you are," she said as that part of me decided it was ready for more than just a shower. Our lips met, and there was no turning back. She kissed her way down my chest, and I pulled her head back up, not wanting to risk her noticing the lack of blood down there if things went on too long and I climaxed.

Instead, I kissed her again, hungrily. Call it lust or whatever you want, but I do care for Tabitha; it's just not the same emotion I have for Marilyn.

"Do you want—" she started as I stood, pushing her against the wall and reaching down to grasp her sex, finding purchase there, warmth and access, first with one finger and then a second. We knew each other's bodies well, even if I sometimes felt like we were strangers as people. What is there to know about a person as young as she is? Which isn't fair, but it felt true. There's a rhythm she likes, a pattern of thumb, index finger, and forefinger, a rocking that's all in the wrist.

She cried out, not my name, but a nonsense noise of passion, and my lips found one breast as my left hand found the other. Her climax built, harder to detect with my senses dulled down to almost human, but unmistakable. A twitch at the corner of her lips, sharp animal breaths, and the sense of tightening centered in an area ranging between her knees and belly button.

"You're so beautiful," I said.

She didn't answer with words but with the rapid movement of her hand, a series of milking strokes followed by an urgent pull at my thigh.

"Now," she said, and then the slick tile squeaked as I moved her up, then let her drop, joining us at the groin. "I love you," she said, and I didn't return it, not with the same words.

"You're beautiful," I said again. I guess it was enough, because she smiled, biting her bottom lip as I moved inside her, my hands gripping her breasts for purchase. When she climaxed once more, I pulled her toward the shower seat and sat down, pulling her onto my lap, my chest against hers. I missed the mark and she reached back, guiding me into position, her gasp matching mine as we were joined again.

When I finally found completion, she did as well, our peaks overlapping, close enough to simultaneous that it may have been.

Panting, she let her full weight rest on my thighs and leaned back as I cupped her breasts, rubbing her nipples between my fingers the way she likes right after sex. Sighing, she touched my hands after a minute or so had passed, and I ceased my digital manipulations. "I needed that," she said.

I opened my mouth to reply in kind, but instead, I said, "I want a divorce."

Yeah . . . I could have picked a better time.

✦ 12 ✦

DEPUTIZED

W e should have special cop names," I said to my new deputy. She'd finally stopped struggling under my arm, but I didn't think she was happy about her positioning, like maybe she wanted me to reattach her head to her body, which was fine and dandy, really, but it's important to make sure that your subordinates understand who's in charge.

"What," she asked, "like Holmes and Watson?"

"You're very good at conveying incredulousness." I let go of her head so I could watch it not fall. This time she didn't try to float back to her body, simply spinning in place to face me. "No, I meant more like Batman and Robin."

"Pinky and the Brain is more like it," she grumbled, letting her head drift higher so we were almost looking each other in the eye.

"Hmmm." I thought that over. "I don't know that it fits." I narrowed my eyes at her, flashing them red for a brief moment. "Try saying 'Narf.'"

"Narf," she said without enthusiasm.

"Nah." I waved my hand under the clean smooth base of her neck. "It's so cool that there are no bits of spine or anything dangling down."

"I agree."

"Does it hurt?"

"You already asked that."

My eyes flashed red. "I'm checking again."

"No. It doesn't hurt."

"And you can walk around in the daytime?"

"Yes."

"Do your powers work any differently then? During the day, I mean."

"Not especially, but apparently I'm a very powerful *nukekubi*. The equivalent of a Vlad or something."

I nodded to her body. She paused, waiting to see if I was going to play more Charlie Brown and Lucy games with her, then floated back over and reattached herself. When she was all together, the glowing red symbols on her neck faded quickly, first to a dark black, giving them the appearance of tattoos, and then to a light pinkish-white, like faint scars.

"And you're Dad's cousin?" I asked.

"Yes. Second cousin twice removed."

"Interesting. So . . . technically, you could get married."

"No chance."

"Your loss." Dad's soundproofing has been improved by Magbidion, but I heard something loud from the Pollux and cocked my head in that direction like Superman or Lassie. "I wonder how many of Dad's other relatives are running around as weird funky undead things."

"Not many, I'd guess." Evie stood, rubbing at the thin line of copper separating her head from her body by the width of a penny. She wrapped a scarf around it. "At the last family reunion, the hyper-religiousness almost made me vomit. Then again, I guess they're all right. If I'd been going to church and saying my prayers at night, I'd probably be in heaven now instead of being undead."

"I went to hell once," I said in as chipper a tone as I could manage. "Well, to the gates. Dad wouldn't let me go inside."

There was another loud noise from the Pollux: sort of a *thoom*. Was that Dad's *oof* I heard?

"Do you hear that?" I asked.

Evie shook her head, and it didn't come off. "My senses evidently aren't as keen as they are in other types of vampires." I was already walking for the stairs. At the last second, I changed my mind and hopped off the roof of the parking deck.

". . . son of a bitch!" I heard Tabitha shouting as I got closer. Hitting the street would have hurt if I let myself feel it, but for vampires who know, who understand what they really are, the body is just an interface, a tool, and if I'm expecting the pain, I can prepare myself not to feel it. I hit the sidewalk feet-first, knees loose to ablate some of the damage from the fall. Things broke and fractured in my legs and, as I fell backward and caught myself, my hands and arms. Rolling backward with the fall, I came up, claws out and fangs down, already healing.

"I should have just moved to Hawaii," Evie said as she stared down at me from the top of the parking deck. "What the hell are you doing?"

"Sheriff," I corrected. Flexing my arms and legs as the bones snapped, crackled, and popped back into place, I twisted my neck and my back to loosen up. "I'm pretty sure you should call me Sheriff. Or Sheriff Courtney." My back gave another deep pop, and I was all done healing. There was barely any blood on the sidewalk.

"Fine! What the hell are you doing, Sheriff?"

"I think I'm about to kill someone." I looked at the doors and decided outside would be fine. Dad was doing another summer series, and the movie poster from *Mr. Blandings Builds*

His Dream House was illuminated brightly in the window of the box office, with Cary Grant looking angry, Myrna Loy looking wry, and Melvyn Douglas in a state of disapproving bemusement. I wanted to watch *The Shining* instead (I like the cute little girls), but Dad's not into horror movies.

"Tabitha." I heard Dad's voice more clearly from down on the street than I had eight levels up. "Would you fucking stop? I don't want to fi—" There was another *thoom*, and Dad came right out through the wall of the building, brick and insulation raining down around him. I would have caught him if I'd thought he needed me to, but he's tough, and I don't want to insult him. Instead, when Tabitha poked her head out of the hole, I shouted, "Fang, it's time!" and leaped.

Tabitha swore, ducking back inside. Like Dad, she wore no proper clothing but was covered in his blood. It wet her fangs and gloved her claws and fingers. It left a trail from the broken exterior wall of the building, through the hall, into the bedroom, and back to the shower, where Magbidion lay unconscious on the tile. Where Tabitha ran out of room to run.

"What did I tell you I'd do?" I shouted.

"What are you talking about, Greta?" Tabitha did a quick change from humanoid to sparrow and back. When she re-formed, her default outfit came with her, though the blood was still there. "You ought to be on my side. Do you know what he said to me?"

"I don't care, Tabitha."

"He—"

"I! DON'T! CARE! what he said or did, Tabitha." I took her hand and turned it back and forth, examining the blood. "That's not your blood, Tabitha. I didn't see any of your blood on Dad either, Tabitha. Why is that, Tabitha?"

She tried to jerk her hand away, but I didn't let her.

"Why do you keep saying my name?"

"Because you need to understand something." I released

her and sniffed the air. Scent reveals so much. Chalk loomed underneath the blood, which meant magic. Filtered water. Tabitha's sexual excretions. Dad's semen. I hadn't smelled that since the wedding. The very faint odor of cinnamon (which kind of explained the semen to me, though to be honest, I was not that interested in how Rachel had or had not been involved with what Dad and Tabitha had been doing in the bedroom). Magbidion's cigarettes. Urine from where Magbidion had fouled himself. Adrenaline. Anger. Dad's sweat. "You are not my mom. And no matter what happened, this is your fault. Dad is never at fault."

"Bullshit!" Tabitha's eyes flared as red as mine. "He said he wanted a—"

"Never." My slap sent her backward into the bedroom, where she clipped the wall and came to a stop. "At." Tabitha rolled back to a ready position, but I was already behind her. "Fault." Her skull cracked as I rammed her into the doorpost, increasing the damage she'd already done to it with Dad. Not that anyone would be able to tell. They'd wrecked the room and torn both the bathroom and bedroom doors off their hinges. Holes dotted the walls, and it looked like Tabitha had purposefully put Dad's head through his television.

"You bitch!" Her claws caught the meat of my thigh, but who cared? There wasn't any blood. I refused to bleed for her.

"If Daddy confuses us, it's because we're supposed to be confused, or we've been too stupid and have failed him by not understanding." Tackling her was easy. She clawed great rents in my face and stomach as I wrestled her into position. "If he makes us sad, then we're supposed to be sad, or we've failed him by reacting inappropriately to his actions."

Ripping off an arm isn't easy. The required strength isn't the problem. It's the leverage. But I've practiced. Ripping off a hand or a forearm isn't so hard, but getting the whole thing off cleanly requires a special two-part twist and tug. You have to dislocate the shoulder, then tear the muscles without losing any of the arm. It seems to hurt a lot, too. Tabitha screamed a wounded-animal scream and went from fighting to trying to get away. Typical. It's astonishing how much other vampires whine about pain.

"Greta!" Dad yelled my name, but I didn't answer.

"I told you," I hissed in her ear. "Do you remember?" I grabbed her cheeks with my left hand and forced her to look me in the eye, then I made contact and brought her into my head. With vampire telepathy, someone always has the upper hand. Whoever has the strongest will, the most agile mind, usually wins. I'm quite insane, so that gives me an edge. I took her to my special place of remembering, front row, center stage, at the Pollux. I wasn't in my pajamas anymore, having clothed the mental me in jeans, a pink baby-doll WELCOME TO THE VOID shirt, and Skechers.

I kept Tabitha the way she was in the real world and pointed at the movie screen with her dismembered limb. "Right there!"

Public Safety Tip #2: Ignorance of the law may be a reasonable excuse, so I will educate you immediately before your sentence is carried out.

Darkness fell as the theater lights went down and my memory lit up the screen like a film.

We were in the hallway of the Pollux, right outside my room. It was shortly after we (by which I mean all Dad's allies except Tabitha) found a way to regenerate Dad's body after he'd been blown up in the first Demon Heart, back when it was a strip club. Tabitha had been nosing around the dressing rooms while drying off after a shower.

My hands slid across the surface of my door, making sure I'd closed it properly by giving it a gentle nudge.

"This is my room and my stuff," I said, baring my fangs.

"I don't want any of your junk."

"You want my dad."

"Maybe," Tabitha said, rubbing her privates with the towel as she spoke. "I guess I do. I'm really not sure."

"Cut off your head, stuff your mouth with garlic, stake you through the heart with any kind of hard wood"—I narrowed my eyes—"then bury your head and your body in two different plots on consecrated ground. That's all it would take."

"What?" Tabitha pulled her hands away from the towel as if that could conceal that she was so hot for my dad, she'd started touching herself at the mere mention of him.

"You're so unimaginative." I watched her hands, making sure she wouldn't try to go for a claw. I hadn't had the chance to fight her, so I couldn't be sure how fast or slow she might be. "I know vampire hunters who would try that method first thing, and then you'd be gone forever."

Her fingernails stretched into claws, but too slowly to be a real threat. Either that or she was trying to undersell her abilities. "Is that a threat?"

"No." I poured on the speed, sliding around behind her and shoving her head at the floor. I sort of thought she'd catch herself, but she was so darn slow. She hit the floor face-first, breaking her nose, and started crying. It was hard not to feed on her then and there. Any vampires displaying that much weakness make me want to end them. By the time I realized what I was doing, I'd twisted her arms behind her back and broken them, and my fangs were at her neck. I almost forgot the rest of my sentence, what we'd been talking about . . . So I decided to make sure she understood how serious I am about protecting Dad. "This is."

I zoomed around in front of her, and I could see a trace of a reflection in her blood on the floor. When I knelt on the ground to get a better look at it, the reflection was gone. Then I gave her my warning. She looked so pitiful that I had to fight not to pop her chest and tear out her heart. I mean, come on. She was crying! "Hurt my daddy," I said, "and I'll kill you."

Tabitha, the one with me in her head, not the one on the screen, winced as the memory faded and the lights came back up. I blinked and broke the telepathic contact. "Do you remember now?"

"I never forgot." Tabitha stared at me coolly, the pain in her shoulder obviously having subsided. "Eric wouldn't, either. If you killed me, he'd remember it forever, and you'd see it in the way he—"

My laughter cut her off. "This is Dad we're talking about, you moron. He forgets *everything* eventually!" I blinked away tears of blood, uncertain why I was shedding them. "Given long enough, he'd forget you, me, everyone. Everyone except her!"

Out in the street, Dad was trying to get to the front door. He'd had no way of knowing Fang was going to stop him. Fang and I had already talked this through. Fang knew what to do. It wouldn't hurt Dad to land in the trunk with the bones. He'd be angry, but it was for his own good.

Tabitha took that moment to try to surprise me with her remaining arm, so I tore it off at the elbow. It wasn't as elegant as taking off the whole arm, but she screamed. I growled.

"I keep what it takes to kill you in my bedroom, Tabitha, all the time . . . just in case." I grabbed her by the neck, hauling her along behind me like a struggling cat. "Let's go give Daddy the divorce he wants."

"Hiya, slut." I smelled the cinnamon and heard the voice in unison. Then I was on fire. "How ya been?"

I hate Auntie Rachel.

✦ 13 ✦

ERIC

MY CAR HAS A MIND OF ITS OWN

Only in Void City can a man wind up naked in the street, cornered by his undead car while trying to stop his daughter from murdering the wife he wants to divorce. Fang's engine revved, and "Tubthumping" started playing over his stereo.

"Chumbawamba?" I shook my head. "Really?"

Fang revved his engine again.

"Really?" I said again. A plume of fire spat out the hole in the side of the Pollux, and I tried to use the distraction to go up and over Fang's hood, but he was too fast, rocketing into reverse with such alacrity that I wound up on my ass. Fang took the opening and rolled over me. Whatever magic he uses to pull things against his undercarriage and eat them slammed me against him. To be honest, it looked sort of like a mass of purple glowing tentacles, but even with my true immortal nighttime powers, I could only see the energy in a very out-of-focus way.

"Dammit, Fang!"

Greta screamed, and Fang let go of me at once, rolling off as quickly as he could, replacing Chumbawamba with Sam

& Dave's "Hold On, I'm Coming." I jumped to my feet and ran for the building, letting myself tap in to a little speed. It felt different than vampire speed, and doing it ran the risk of lighting me up spiritually, tipping my hand.

Greta is my little girl, and if saving her fucks up The Plan, then I'll just get a new plan. I tapped in to the strength for a split second as I hit the sidewalk and jumped for the hole. My heart pounded in my chest, not the too-fast pounding of an out-of-shape human but a steady and efficient thump. Small strands of blue sparked between me and surrounding objects, then faded as I was airborne and released the strength.

"Greta?" I yelled. "Tabitha?"

Greta rolled on the floor in my bedroom, singed and yowling. Tabitha didn't have pyrokinetic powers, which meant . . . I spotted Rachel, arms folded across her chest, in the bathroom doorway. She was wearing a blue dress this time, and if Greta hadn't been hurt, I might have laughed. Tabitha stood behind her sister, feeding on Magbidion as her arms grew back. One arm seemed to be making more progress than the other.

"Hellfire doesn't just burn the flesh, Greta." Rachel's voice was edged with menace. "I don't want to burn you again . . . okay, well, I actually do, because you killed me in a very unpleasant fashion the last time I was alive, but your dad would be really pissed at me if I did, so please stay back."

Greta wasn't healing.

I opened the fridge and pulled out two of the bags labeled ERIC COURTNEY (only two more left, I noted) and handed them to Greta as I walked past. "Demon fire can be as slow to heal as holy wounds for vamps with that problem." Greta snatched the first bag and bit into it.

"This is yours," she said with her mouth full of blood, wounds healing readily now.

"Yup." I stood between her and Rachel. "That's enough, Tabitha."

She reluctantly pulled her mouth from Magbidion's throat. "I didn't take too much," she said defensively, "and your psycho bitch of a daughter tore my freakin' arms off."

"Oh, shut up," Greta snarled, my blood dripping from her lips. "I didn't even have enough time to end you."

"You." I pointed at Greta. "Are you okay?"

"I'll be fine now, Dad." Her wounds were already fading.

"Good. Go get dressed and patrol with Evelyn."

"But I have to kill Tabitha!" Greta was on her feet in a blink. "She created a disturbance that could have drawn attention to everything, and I get to kill people who—"

I cut her off. "I'll handle the matter, Sheriff. Go." She stood up to leave. "And be careful out there. You're my girl."

Greta smiled a smile designed to let me know I'd set the world to rights, but I suspected she was angry underneath. I watched her go, then walked over to my wardrobe and pulled out clean socks and underwear before crossing to my closet to dress.

Rachel whistled at me, and I blushed. "You shut up." I pulled on my undies and jeans. "Why are you here, anyway?"

"I have a new task for you from Lady Scrytha."

"Lovely." I shrugged into a clean WELCOME TO THE VOID T-shirt and sat down on the edge of the bed to put on a pair of thick black socks. "Tabitha, are you rearmed over there?"

"Yes." Her voice was sulky. "I'm still hungry, though."

"I told you, you should have stuck them back on and healed that way." Rachel crossed the room and pointed to what I assumed were Tabitha's dismembered limbs. "It would have been a lot less draining."

"That's stupid." Tabitha stalked out of the bathroom.

"No," I corrected as I pulled on my combat boots, "it *sounds* stupid, but it's pretty good advice. I've tried it both ways, and putting the severed limb back on feels weird but works better."

"Well, pardon me." Tabitha looked away. "It's my first time having parts ripped off."

I gave a noncommittal grunt and tied my shoes. "So, here's the thing." I grabbed a new black leather belt from my top drawer and slid it on, missed a loop, and got it right the second time. "I get that you're mad at me."

Tabitha scoffed. "You GET it, huh?"

"Yes," I said calmly, "I do, but I can't have you causing shit like this to happen in my home."

"I didn't cause anything, you fucking prick!" Tabitha's eyes blazed red. "You wait until after we have some of the most tender, romantic sex we've ever had, and in the afterglow, you tell me you want a divorce . . . and I caused it?"

"I gave the most unromantically truthful and pessimistic warning to you during our wedding. I promised I would fail you eventually and that I'd try to be faithful but would not succeed. I wouldn't even say 'I do' to the vows. I said, 'I'll do what I can,' and you married me anyway."

"I was being mind-controlled!" Tabitha spat.

"Exactly my point."

"Not controlled," Rachel corrected. "Heavily influenced but not strictly controlled."

We both glared at Rachel.

"In demonic terms, it's a very important technicality," Rachel said with a shrug.

"I don't think our ceremony counts. And if it did, the vows would have ended when I went to the underworld. But obviously, you think differently, so I offered to let you out of the marriage. You said no." I walked back over to the fridge and pulled out the last two bags of my blood. "Look, I'm not going to argue with you while you're still hungry. Here." I handed her the bags, and she smirked.

"I didn't know you'd taken to labeling them."

"Ever since someone spiked them and no one noticed." I pulled off the label, and the writing faded. "Magbidion made them for me. They identify the donor and detect most major contaminants or spells that affect vampires. I have twelve hundred of the things."

"That's clever," Rachel said, squinting at the Post-it. "Simple but very hard to fool. Elegant, even." She looked at Magbidion lying unconscious on the bathroom tiles. "You got a good deal when you enthralled him. Diaxicrotioush'nar has been scared shitless to come to collect on his debt because he saw what you did to the last demon you took down. Magbidion has a real flair for the sort of work you want him to do." She smiled. "He uses magic so efficiently, too. His enchantments are nigh invisible, not a speck of magic wasted."

Tabitha cleared her throat. "If you guys start making out in front of me, I'm attacking you both." She'd downed the first bag of blood and was sipping on the next.

"So . . ." We waited in uncomfortable silence for Tabitha to finish the second bag.

"Okay." Tabitha sat the empty bags in the sink. "That's better."

"Good," I said. "Now fuck off."

"What?" Tabitha snarled, and Rachel laughed.

"You're a beautiful and intelligent woman, Tabitha," I said softly. "You deserve someone who will love you. You won't get him, 'cause your taste in men is shit, but I want you to be happy. You'll never be happy with me. You need to figure out what you want to do with the rest of eternity and do it. The reason I insisted all the strippers who worked at the Demon Heart go to college was because you need that scrap of paper in this world for people to take you seriously. You've traded on your looks and men's desire to get in your pants for so long that you think about that first and foremost: finding the right man and keeping him."

I touched her cheek gently, almost afraid she'd bite me. "The right man won't need to be kept, Tabitha. He'll be too damn busy trying to keep *you*. I'm not that guy."

"So . . ." Tabitha took a deep breath. "So what? You're going to go back to screwing Rachel?"

"Been there." I held up my hands as if warding off the thought. "Done that. It was a blast, but I wouldn't go back in with a borrowed dick."

"Oh, sure," Rachel said, "you say that *now*, but—"

Tabitha and I both shushed her.

"Marilyn, then?" Tabitha asked.

"Probably not." That seemed to take them by surprise. "Oh, I love her more than any woman I've ever known or ever will know. But unless something changes, that ship has sailed. Roger sabotaged it beyond all reasonable hope of repair."

"Do I have to leave Void City?" Tabitha's voice sounded distant, like it was just clicking that things were really over.

"Of course not." I sighed. "You know, I think the worst thing about us as a couple is that maybe we were never meant to be more than friends. If I'd been my right age when I first met you, I'd have been too old for you. I could have been the dirty old man who steered you clear of the wrong guys and set you on the path to a great career in classical dance or psychology or some shit. We're too much alike to make it as a couple."

"You're really not that much alike," Rachel butted in.

"Really?" I asked, enumerating points on my fingers. "We're both smarter than we look. We both have serious anger issues." I grinned. "True, I've never learned to tie a cherry stem into a knot with my tongue, but . . ." I looked to Tabitha, hoping for something like a laugh.

"You're giving me the 'Let's be friends' speech?" Tabitha frowned, her eyes rimmed with anger. At least she wasn't crying. "Fuck that!"

"I don't want to have some ongoing war with you, Tabitha.

I'll give you a nice and official divorce settlement. Money. Your apartment. I'll make sure Greta knows she doesn't get to kill you."

"Fine." Tabitha's face was torn between resentment, hatred, and maybe a glimmer of some positive emotion. "You're right. My life can't be about you."

"Friends?" I held out my arms, offering a hug but fully expecting Tabitha to attack me again. Instead, she gave me the briefest of hugs.

"Go fuck yourself." She pulled away. Her claws extended, but she didn't seem to realize it. She wiped at her eyes, blinked, sniffed, and gave an irritated grunt, throwing her arms down by her sides. "Send my money and my shit to my apartment, asshole."

Brushing past me, she transformed into a cat (probably to mess with her sister, who was always afraid of them) and sauntered off. She didn't look back, and despite myself, I almost went after her. That was not part of any plan, though, so I stuck by my guns and stared out the hole in the Pollux. *What a mess.*

"I could have sworn she was going to attack you." Rachel put an arm around my waist.

"Me, too." I smelled cinnamon, but I let it pass without comment. She really is God's gift to cock, but the baggage is too extreme to mention, and I have my Plan. A Plan she's not in . . . at least not in a knocking-boots way. I extricated myself from her grasp and asked a question. "Why did you save her?"

"She's my sister." Rachel gestured, and a reflective surface wavered into existence, hovering in the air. She touched up her lipstick and her eye shadow with a touch of her fingertips, then straightened out her low-cut blue dress. She looked over her shoulder at me and wrinkled her nose mischievously. "No one gets to murder her but me."

◆ 14 ◆

ERIC

DO I OR DON'T I ACTUALLY HAVE TO DO WHAT I DONE DID?

After that, we had work to do. As commands go, my second one, helping to install an artificial locus point in the middle of the street between the Pollux and the Demon Heart, wasn't a hardship. Certainly not compared to strangling Father Ike. Demons have to use locus points if they want to travel quickly from the Pit (some kind of staging area for hell) and the material world. Talbot and I had been forced to chase a demon all over Void City a few years back, trying to kill him and succeeding before he made it to one of the locus points around town to make good his escape.

My deal with Scrytha apparently allowed her "rightful representative" to appear in my vicinity or near my places of power without one (which was how Rachel got to *bamf* back and forth so darn easy), but that wasn't enough for Scrytha. The whole locus-point thing can only be installed by powerful supernatural beings . . . I couldn't decide whether I should be flattered, but I didn't much care.

VCPD officers manned roadblocks at either end of the street with flashing squad car lights, Mages Guild representatives, and the whole spiel. It was a lot more impressive than the job Melvin had done back when I was obliterated and reduced to a ghost, but strangely, it cost about the same in man-hours and overtime. Maybe that was because my new "man" in charge of the VCPD side of such things, Katherine Marx, was an evil mercenary bastard like the old one.

Melvin, the member of the Void City Mages Guild most likely to be mistaken for one of the Blues Brothers, was overseeing the operation on behalf of the city and the Mages Guild, but the magic was being done by Rachel and me. Yeah, I'm so multitalented. Watch me pull a rabbit out of my ass.

So far, my involvement had involved ripping a goat into thirds and waving the pieces about in whatever direction I was told.

"So is this thing safe to leave out here in the middle of the street?" I asked.

"Yes," Rachel instructed. "No demon would mess with it, because breaking an artificial locus point would blow all the natural ones for most of a day and piss off every last Infernatti something fierce. Now hold out your hand and agree to allow this area within your power to be used as a locus point."

"Say it," I said.

"Say what?"

"Say it's a command from Lady Scrytha."

Rachel narrowed her eyes at me. "On Lady Scrytha's behalf, I command you to hold out your hand and agree to allow this area within your power to be used as a locus point."

"How do I do that?" I asked while waving a goat head in a small spiral with my left hand. I waited for a painful twinge like the one I'd gotten when I'd been ordered to kill Father Ike, but as I suspected, it wasn't there. I kept my face frozen. No sign of expression.

"You just say it."

"It," I said with a smirk. Melvin chuckled but didn't lose his concentration. He stared between a frame composed of his right and left hands, like a director trying to frame a movie in his head, his attention on Rachel.

"Dammit, Eric!" Rachel flared her nostrils at me.

I frowned because I was supposed to, and asked the question that interested me. "So what are these locus points for again?"

"We already went over this."

"Go over it again," I said calmly. "Maybe I'm finally getting curious about magic."

"Why?" Rachel asked with a wink. "Thinking of taking it up? I might be available to tutor you. We could take it out in trade."

"I want to know."

Rachel reached down and lifted a golden pentacle roughly the size and heft of a manhole cover out of the now-shimmering air. She lowered it over the two thirds of the goat I'd already spent time rotating in little circles. "Time really is of the essence here."

"Then talk fast," I said, not budging. Still no ache.

"It focuses power. So Magbidion and any other mages you have around will get a boost out of it, too, and any true immortal in the area could more easily draw soul energy, but Scrytha wants it here because there aren't any convenient ones on your side of town, and it makes scrying easier."

"Soul energy?"

"That's what they call it. They get most of theirs from each other, humans, or in duels or other crap, but it's basically spiritual power. It flows through most living things. Plants. Even the planet."

"Fine." I swung the goat and gave my mental permission for the locus point to be installed. I knew this was part of The Plan without having to check in with my app, which I considered a bonus. "But do I need to post a guard or . . . ?" I asked.

"Nah," Rachel said, as if the reason for my questions suddenly made sense to her. "No extra work for you. Mundanes couldn't hurt it with anything less than a nuclear bomb. It takes a powerful supernatural force. Something like you or another Emperor. One of the Infernatti. No need to babysit it."

"Good." I let the questions drop after that.

An hour later, I was showering again despite the large plastic sheets billowing in the wind that blocked the large hole Tabitha had made in my building. Talbot stood guard while playing the part of goat-stench detector.

"Well?" I asked.

Talbot leaned into the bathroom and sniffed the air. "Yes"—he sounded relieved—"that's got it. You don't smell a thing like goat now. Or, well, I think it's mainly the shower now, not you."

"How's Magbidion?"

"Weak." Talbot leaned back out. "You've been overtaxing him."

"He'll be okay, though. Right?" I turned off the shower and grabbed for my towel. "The locus point will help?"

"I think so."

Yeah, I told myself. *Let's hope so.*

Showered and dressed, I left Talbot milling about and walked back over to the Demon Heart. We'd had to "officially" close for the evening, what with the work Rachel wanted done in the street out front, but Marilyn had thoughtfully arranged to offer discounted lane time to the Mages Guild as a thank-you for all the good work, so the place was crawling with magic freaks who didn't go by their real first name. A couple of mages were being difficult with Erin about the discount, wanting a better one. Still, it looked like most of the bowlers were drinking pretty heavily, and Cheryl, over at the concession stand, was doing brisk business in pizza, burgers, and popcorn. The smell of burnt popcorn was there, too . . . I think.

I've always loved bowling.

I walked up to the counter and said hi to Gracie, the cute little brunette behind the counter. I don't know why, but it felt like forever since I'd seen her. Which was weird, because she was almost always behind the counter when it was League Night. Glancing around the place, I didn't see my bag. My car was back at the station, so the bag couldn't have been there. I remembered walking over, the cool night air blowing away the smell of popcorn burning on a stove. It had to be all in my head, but the odor clung.

"Gracie," I said, feeling a little embarrassed, "I must have left my bag back at the station. Could I get some size tens?"

"Are you feeling okay, Eric?" Gracie had done something with her hair. It looked different in some way I couldn't put my finger on. She had it pulled back into a simple brown ponytail. Hmmm . . .

"Yeah. Sure." I gave her a friendly smile. "Maybe I'm coming down with something. Nothing to worry your pretty little head about, though. It's just a bowling bag. I'm sure it's back at the station."

"Ummm . . ." Gracie chewed her lip. "If you're sure."

"Yeah," I said, staying friendly but getting a bit impatient. "You got those size tens?"

She got the shoes and came back with them, skirt swishing as she walked. "Here you go, Eric."

"How much do I owe you?" I asked. I'd had my own bowling shoes for years and couldn't remember how much the rental was.

"Don't worry about it."

"Hey." I smiled. "Thanks. You're a pip. You seen Marilyn? Usually she beats me here."

"I'll go check." Gracie ran off like a cat with her tail on fire.

If I didn't have Marilyn, I might have to . . . No, best to put that thought out of my head. I walked down to lane three and sat down next to the guys to put on my shoes.

"Hey, boys. I feel like a real heel. I must have left my bag, ball, league shirt, and everything back at the station. I hope you don't mind having an unmatched sock bowling with you tonight."

Steve, Little Carl, Jones, and Bill all stared at me like I was a raving lunatic or some drunk they'd hauled back into the station to sleep off the one too many he'd had after work. Sal took a different approach. "What the fuck are you talking about, man?"

"Hey." I looked around warily, my voice hushed. "Sal, watch the colorful commentary, buddy. You want Carol or Marilyn to hear you swearing like a sailor? They'll think you flipped. Is it about the Murcheson case? I know how tough it is to respond to a crime scene like that one. Anytime a kid gets . . ."

The scene flooded back to me. Those two little girls. Standing over their remains. It came in snapshots. Blood. Two little bodies. Blood-soaked clothes torn to tatters. Sal staring at me. "I can't find the heads, Cap. I looked everywhere, and I just can't find them." The sound of vomit hitting linoleum in the kitchen as Little Carl found the heads. The popcorn burning on the stove. Taking it off before it started a fire. The thing that charged out at us. My brain telling me that it was only a wolf, but . . . but . . .

"I didn't do this," the wolf had yelled. "That fat bastard wants us out of the city! He did this! Can you even hear me? He did this!"

Opening fire to stop the thing from howling. Me, Sal, but not Little Carl. Little Carl just stood there in the kitchen, screaming and vomiting and . . . that weird stray thought. How much must it cost for us to be packing these silver bullets?

What is it with the VCPD; are we each supposed to be the Lone Ranger? I've always—

"Eric?" Marilyn stood over me, flanked by Gracie and another girl I didn't recognize. "What's going on?"

"I left my bag at the station," I said numbly. "It's nothing big, angel."

"What kind of bag, Eric?" Marilyn seemed genuinely perplexed.

"What do you mean what bag? My bowling bag."

"Guy's freaking out," Sal said derisively.

"You watch it, Sal." I raised my voice. "You aren't the only one who had a rough day today. I'll cut you some slack. Sure. Yards of it, but don't forget, I'm still your captain."

"Oh, fuck." Marilyn barely breathed the words, but they hit me like ice water. She wasn't one to curse, not out in public. Not until . . . not . . .

I went limp, sliding out of the chair like a sack of potatoes. Marilyn and the strange woman grabbed me to keep me from hitting the floor.

"What the hell?" said the mage with the dagger tattoos on his face. One minute I'd been sure Sal was standing there, and the next some guy with so much metal in his face I could mine him for gold was staring at me. Marilyn, Beatrice, and Erin stood over me.

"Eric," Talbot said as he burst through the doors of the Demon Heart, "I was standing out front when I smelled them. I tried to call Greta, but . . ."

"Smelled what?" I said weakly.

"For lack of a better word: a chupacabra hit squad. I've heard of them taking over towns near Texas, but . . ."

"You're shitting me." I watched closely for any crack of a smile that might tell me it was a joke. "Chupacabras are real?"

I looked around me at the assembled mages. They seemed to believe him, too. *Damn*, I thought, *here it is*. I always screw up over something dumb, and here's what it is this time: lame-ass Scooby-Doo monsters that— Suddenly, I knew what to do. "I'll pay fifty grand per dead chupacabra, but only for the next two hours."

Half the mages dropped their shit and ran for the front door as if someone outside had shouted, "Free beer!"

Talbot opened his mouth and started saying something else, but I couldn't hear him because my world was going fuzzy and dropping away. For the record, I'm fairly certain that hallucinating and then passing out was not part of The Plan.

✦ 15 ✦

CLUE CLUB

W hat are you hiding, Dad?" I mouthed the words from under the bed as soon as Marilyn left him. When the Demon Heart had been redone as a bowling alley, Dad had them put in a bedroom, like the one he'd had at the original Demon Heart. I think it was there in case the Pollux got messed up (which had just happened, so good planning, Dad) or in case someone needed a place to crash or canoodle. It was small, but it had a king-size bed, even if the shower/bathroom area was tiny and utilitarian. Marilyn left the television playing reruns of some old black-and-white show.

"Does this mean she's Mom again?" I asked, but Dad didn't answer. Marilyn's footsteps clicked down the hall, and I heard her talking to Talbot, their voices hushed, urgent.

"I don't want them near him, Talbot."

"Someone has to check him out, Marilyn."

"Magbidion can do it as soon as he's well, but I don't trust those guild mages any farther than I can pee standing up."

They went on arguing, and I locked the door, sneaking back to Dad's bed. He was warm to the touch, and not just warm: fed-hot or alive-hot. Fever-hot! Marilyn had stripped him down and rubbed cold washcloths across his skin. I can't see magic or ghosts, but this seemed like it to me. Laying my head on his chest, I listened but could neither hear nor feel a heartbeat. His smell, though—it was muted but different—

Jumping clear of him, I retreated to the bathroom and hid behind the door, staring through the crack at his chest. It rose and fell, though there was no sound.

"Sneaky Daddy," I mouthed, not wanting to make actual words lest Talbot hear them. They'd told me to stay outside, to patrol, but they aren't the boss of me. Only Dad and Mom get to tell me what to do. Right now Mom's identity was vague and mysterious, scary even. Who was Mom? Only Daddy could know, and until he gave me enough information, I couldn't deduce it on my own. Still, Marilyn seemed to be in the running again. Which is a good thing. I love Marilyn. When Dad wasn't raising me, growing up, she was. The back-and-forth of who was my mom confused me, but not as much as Daddy's chest. I watched it rise and fall and got an idea.

Approaching him carefully, like a bomb that might go off or a frightened child I wanted to grab before he could scream, I laid my head on Dad's chest and thumped him with my finger, softly once, then harder when I heard no sound. Oh, I heard the sound of flesh on flesh, but no resounding noise from within. With no sound to go on, I watched the vein at his neck. My mouth made an O as I discovered part of Daddy's secret in that gently moving vein.

Thump-thump.
Thump-thump.
Thump-thump.

Under everyone's nose, Dad's heart was beating. I straddled him in the bed, eyeing him for more signs, rubbing one finger across his lips, then daring to explore his mouth with it, to touch his tongue. My finger came away wet but not bloody.

Extending the nail of my forefinger into a claw, I carefully opened a line on his side, watching blood well up and run, catching it with my tongue, feeling the strange sensation of the wound closing as I licked it.

"Seeming human, Daddy?" I said, licking his blood from my claw. "Is that what you're doing? Why you don't want Tabitha anymore? And you don't want me to kill her because it's something she taught you and you're grateful?"

I rolled off the bed, smiling when Dad's manhood responded to the motion. *Silly penis,* I thought, *I'm not Mom.*

Unlocking the door, I slid back under the bed to smell Dad's shoes. *Where has he been?* An odor clung to them. A hospital smell but not quite. Slipping out from under the bed, I rearranged Dad's covers and kissed him lightly on the cheek before vanishing down the hall past Marilyn and Talbot.

"Greta," Talbot called, but I didn't listen. A law unto myself, I slammed the door behind me and rejoined Fang and my deputy one block over.

"Dust-bunny central," Evelyn said when she saw me.

"Oh." I looked down at my shirt and touched my hair. "Sorry, I had to hide under the bed. Can you?" I turned around, and Evelyn brushed the dust bunnies off as best she could.

"Why did you hide under a bed?"

"Because they would have thought to check the ceiling."

That gave her pause. "You know you're screwed in the head, right?"

"You're the one who wants to kill my dad." I vaulted into the driver's seat, and Fang started up without giving me time to touch the keys.

"He killed me first." She stressed the words in the same way a child might complain that the other kid started it.

"Look!" I snapped. "Dad says it's okay for you to try and kill him once a year, so I'll go along with it because he says I have to and because it is officially impossible to kill him."

Fang revved his engine, and I swatted the steering wheel. "Start taking me places that Dad drove to over the last few days, Fang. Do I have to spell out everything?"

"What do you mean, impossible to kill?"

"I arranged it." Fang drove around the block twice, as if deciding where he wanted to go, almost as if he had instructions not to take me someplace. On the third loop, he took a right, taking us farther into the east side.

"You arranged for Eric to be unkillable?"

"Yup." A burned-out warehouse loomed on our right across from the worn redbrick of the Alexander Greyson Mission. I sniffed the air, trying to capture familiar scents and traces of Dad. A homeless man lay on the sidewalk at the mouth of an alley, so Fang and I detoured, not even slowing as the man vanished underneath the Mustang's front bumper and was consumed with a brief scream silenced by a wet ripping and the tinkle of bones landing in the trunk.

"Motherfucker!" Evelyn shouted, her hands gripping the door and the dash. "What the hell?" She glanced back as if Fang might be messy enough to leave a scrap behind. "You just—"

"He was sick and homeless." I looked askance at my deputy. "Some sort of cancer, it smelled like. He wasn't going to last long."

"But—"

"But what?" I reached for the glove box, and it fell open before I touched the latch. Inside, I grabbed the gold-rimmed glasses that Uncle Percy had given Dad. I put them on and glared at Evelyn as the lenses tinted. I wanted Uncle to get a good look at her. Uncle Percy used to live in a glass box with a plaque on it, back when Uncle Phil was still around. Everyone thought he was Phil's prisoner until he revealed himself to be an Emperor whose special ability was immunity to the effects of being staked. Instead of hurting him, staking him made him not need to feed and concealed his mind from the sort of mental detection experienced between Masters, Vlads, and Emperors.

He's a creepy-kinky voyeur, but he helped Dad onto the Paths of the Dead to come find me, and he agreed to live in a glass case in my old apartment to make it up to me. Plus, he's fun to talk to.

She's going to try and kill me, isn't she, Uncle? I thought.

Oh, you dear thing. The words formed before my eyes so that only I could see or read them. *You knew I'd want to get a good look at her.* I knew Uncle Percy could have spoken to me directly, mind to mind, but after what has happened to others who mess with me telepathically, I think he's too chicken to risk it himself. Silly Uncle. Just because I might decide to play with him a little . . . It's not like I'd do much permanent damage. Not much. He could hear me think, though, when I wore the glasses.

Answer me or I'll feed your memento mori to Fang, and you can just be a dried-up old mummy.

Yes, I think she will, but she may surprise you. Where are you going? May I please watch? The words appeared on the lenses.

Why don't you put one of your little spies on me, like that so-called bum?

You keep eating them yourself or feeding them to Fang.

So?

Please, Greta, I thought Phillip was a monster, but you, you're so . . . fresh, so unique. I just want to—

Evelyn was saying something plaintive, but I'd tuned her out while reading what Uncle had to say, so I answered them both aloud. "Some vampires you are."

"You killed him without even blinking or thinking about it. I'm surprised you didn't giggle."

"So?" I knocked her head off and floored the gas pedal. Fang accelerated so fast that Evelyn's head couldn't keep up with the car. She cursed almost as well as Dad, though. A familiar mediciney odor hit my nostrils, and I stomped on the brakes to make Fang slow down.

Okay, you can watch for a bit, Uncle, I thought. *But if you notice something and don't tell me, I'll leave your glasses in the glove compartment for a month. A very interesting month.*

As you wish, my dear.

"Did you take him somewhere near here, Fang?" I demanded. "Where? Which building?"

We slammed to a halt in front of a series of shotgun houses that looked older than Void City. I scanned the area, sniffing. A glass-strewn parking lot held a general store with a busted neon sign and one gas pump. There was a pharmacy next to it that looked clean even though the burglar bars and the partially lowered steel shutter over the front door made it look more like a fortress than a pharmacy. Fang crept forward reluctantly and turned in to the driveway of a small apartment building. He stopped in the driveway and turned off his engine as Evelyn's head caught up with us.

"Will you stop goofing around?" I said absently. "Help me figure out why Dad would come here."

"Please stop knocking my head off," Evelyn said as she reattached herself.

"Why does it pop off and on if I'm not supposed to play with it?" I asked. "What is this place?"

There was magic here, but of a very subtle sort. I can't tell whose, but I'd guess Magbidion's, Percy spelled in my glasses. *That mage hoards his magic like a miser. I guess it comes from feeling its cost more and more dearly with each moment past his contract's collection date.*

Evelyn opened and closed her mouth like a fish a few times before she could answer. "Agh. This place smells like an old folks' home. Just like the one Nana went to before I got bumped up to anchor and moved her to Westside."

"It smells like death, pee, Clorox, and licorice." I walked

up the gravel drive, expecting to see a few old geezers sitting around in folding chairs or nurses carrying bedpans. A small tarnished plaque at the front walkway read: VOID CITY MUNICIPAL RETIREMENT COMPLEX FOR LAW ENFORCEMENT OFFICERS.

"Void City has a retirement home strictly for police officers?" Evelyn asked. "You'd think I would have heard of that before."

Inside, the place was abandoned. "I don't hear any heartbeats," I said. "You check that side, and I'll check this one."

"It's locked," Evelyn said, trying the knob.

I kicked mine in, looking back at her to make sure she got the idea, but she was already kicking in hers. Each small living area told the same story: bed, bathroom, sitting area, and kitchenette. The appliances were old but well maintained, and each unit was spotlessly clean. Some units had a copy of the Void City *Echo*, our local paper, folded up on the bar or on the table in the sitting area. The papers were only about a week old. When I met Evelyn back out front, she'd found the same thing. One thing that concerned me was the scent of blood. Dad's blood. It would have been too faint for most to catch it or identify, but I know Dad's smells by heart, and the scent of his blood was in each apartment. Sometimes in the kitchen or the bedroom, but in all thirty units of the three-story complex, it was there.

"Did he kill them all?" Evelyn asked as we walked back to the car.

"I don't think so." I watched Evelyn walk a wide arc around Fang's hood. I think if I'd told her that his simulated knockoff hubs could become spinning blades of death, she'd have believed me (I wonder if they can). "The blood I smelled was from Dad, not a bunch of old police officers."

Evelyn jumped into Fang the same way I'd seen children do when I looked in their windows at night, leaping into bed from a distance to make sure nothing underneath could reach out and snag them, dragging them under to be eaten or worse.

"Then what?" Evelyn asked.

"Not sure." I scanned the street. "Did you see an office building or anything?"

We looked past it twice before noticing the square of newer gravel. Kicking at it with my shoes, I found a concrete slab. Evelyn located two shorn connections: one for power and the other for phones or something with similar cables.

"They tore down the whole building?" Evelyn squatted next to the wires, a vampiric Nancy Drew.

"Dad did it." Closing my eyes, I sniffed slowly, mouth open so I could breathe out that way. I don't know why, but it helps. Faintly, under the smell of shifted dirt, the raw primal odor of the über vamp clung to the slab. "And . . ." I knelt low, gravel digging into my jeans and my palms. "Something . . . else."

"What are you? A drug dog?"

"I'm better." Waving a claw in her direction, I worked my way from one corner of the slab to the other. Then I got it. Fire was the missing element. "He was here during the day," I muttered. "The über vamp was sizzling. Come on." I hopped up. On the way back to the car, Evelyn touched my shoulder, and I realized that I really must like having Deputy LEGO-Noggin, because I hadn't clawed out her heart or even growled.

"If we're going to work together, Greta—"

"Sheriff," I corrected.

"Sheriff," Evelyn conceded, "then you're going to have to stop killing people in front of me."

"Where would you prefer I kill them?"

She sighed and started saying something else, but I didn't care what it was. My thoughts were all on Dad. Maybe if I tried repeating his experiment from yesterday, it would all make sense. *I will know your secret, Dad, and then you'll be proud of me for figuring it out all on my own, and as a reward, you'll tell me who Mom is.*

"Uh-huh," I said, because I had to say something to cut

Evelyn off. "Let's go down to the old Bitemore Hotel and check for curfew breakers. We can eat them while I think this over. Then I need to go to church."

We climbed back inside, and Fang's engine purred to life. Strains of Jan Hammer's "*Miami Vice* Theme" filled the air. "Why church?" Evelyn asked, but I was already on to my next train of thought.

"Maybe we should buy an alligator."

✦ 16 ✦

GRETA

NATURE ABHORS A VACUUM

They aren't vampires." Evelyn sat next to me on the edge of the fire escape, overlooking what used to be called Sweet Heart Row. "What are they?"

Chupacabra, Percy spelled in my glasses. I think he would have written more, but he knows I don't like lectures. I wasn't thinking about other monsters anyway; I was remembering the three children I'd rescued, turned, and let loose here: Petey, Darla, and Spanky. I couldn't remember their real names, only the ones I'd given them because they reminded me of the Little Rascals. I considered the memory of their rescue and decided it might be fun to throw at Evelyn when she eventually tried to mess with me. A dark basement. Pain. Tears. Blood. And then me. Dark. Furious. And vengeful. The hero. I shook off the thought and focused on the new monsters.

Seven curious creatures sniffed around the edge of the hotel, yipping to one another in a series of hisses and barks that might have been a language. Cracked gray skin hung from their muscular forms, with patches of fur turned greenish-gray by the presence of what smelled like moss or lichen. A ridge of giant porcupine-like spines ran down each one's back, growing longer and sharper at the end of their kangaroo-like tails. Broad boarlike muzzles ruined the puppy-dog look of their faces, and forked black tongues tasted the air. Claws tipped the fingers of their obviously functional hands, but even bigger talons curved raptor-like at the ends of each massively splayed five-digited hind paw.

Their scent, equal parts sulfur, iguana, and dog, with just a hint of lime, rolled about my nostrils and was cataloged, not to be forgotten. The stink of human fear coated the air, too, but not in equal measure.

"Look how they herd that hooker and her john." I elbowed Evelyn. "They're good. Watch how the big one is deliberately leaving an opening for one of the food to bolt."

"That's on purpose?"

"Sure." I stood. "They could tear the two of them to pieces, but they're careful. I think I like."

The hooker, a bedraggled blonde in hot pants, opened her mouth to scream, but when she did, the creatures hissed, tongues vibrating and extended. Her face twisted in confusion, and she tried to scream louder, but nothing made it to my ears except the hissing. "Noise cancellation." I stepped up onto the steel rail and leaned out for a better vantage. "How cool is that? I didn't know chupacabras could do that."

"Chupacabras?" Evelyn wrinkled her nose. "I thought those weren't real. Didn't they prove those were all just diseased hyenas or weird dog hybrids spotted by drunken hunters, farmers off their nut, and UFO wackos?"

"What else could they be?" I grinned. "I've heard about them, but I've never gotten to eat one."

"You want to feed on them?"

"I want to feed on everything." I licked my lips. "What do you taste like?"

"Ugh." Evelyn shook her head. "Can we at least save the humans first—"

I frowned. "I want to see what their bite marks look like."

"Please," Evelyn touched my shoulder gently, "Sheriff?"

"Oh." I grinned again, "That's either assault or sexual harassment. Thank goodness you weren't fat when you died, or I'd be offended." I rocketed down the fire escape at top speed, halting only when I reached the bottom. Knowing Evelyn was sitting where I left her, I waved up at her with impatience. "Move your ass, Deputy!"

Evelyn stepped off the ledge. Instead of plummeting to the ground, she glided to the pavement with all the grace of a wire-fu martial artist. "I thought chupacabras fed on livestock."

"Humans count as livestock, don't they?" I asked rhetorically.

Evelyn rolled her eyes.

"I wonder how easily they die." Darting into their midst brought me a wall of near noiselessness, nothing making it through to my ears except the hissing. The seven chupacabras swapped off hissing, rotating their noise cancellation, keeping out all sound. I struck at the one closest to me, avoiding his spines and going for the throat, only to find my hand full of quills from its tail. I sat there staring at my palm, trying to fathom how it had been fast enough to swat me, when I realized it hadn't. The one I'd struck at hadn't even moved. The attack had come from the one next to it.

I tried to block out the pain, shut it down, but it grew brighter, more insistent. Just because I couldn't block it out didn't mean I couldn't take it. Attempting to yell a warning to Deputy LEGO-Head, I smirked when hissing from the chupacabra nearest me swallowed the sound. We fought in silence broken only by that hiss. It caught up everything: the sounds of claws on pavement, screams from the humans, and grunts from me. None of it escaped.

Greta, Percy thought at me concisely, so as not to obscure my vision with words, clearly trusting I wouldn't leave myself open to attack to thwack him with my brain, *maybe you should withdraw.*

Why don't you shut the fuck up and watch? I sent back. *It's what you're good at.*

As you wish.

On my right, a chupacabra struck out with its tail. I rolled left to avoid it, only to discover that was a feint and catch a savage hindclaw from the chupacabra to my left side, opening up four long gashes from the back of my neck down to my mid-back, ripping my shirt and cutting my bra strap. Hissing noiselessly against the pain, I leaped up and back as hard and high as I could, reaching for the gun in my thigh holster. Red and hungry, the tearing pain from my wounds hit a crescendo and leveled out, intense, unbearable for a human, but I haven't been human since the eighties. I hate wounds that cheat. Holy ones. Demonic fire. And now whatever was up with chupacabra-inflicted injuries.

Normally, I carry my 9mm (it's a Glock 17) when I hunt vampires, to inflict pain at range (most vampires aren't as good as shutting out pain as I am), but there was no rule that said I had to use it only to kneecap vamps or shoot them in the eye. Speaking of eyes, I shot the chupacabra that had slashed my back in the eye, following it up with a potshot at the one who'd feinted me into the attack. Two shots. My clips hold seventeen, but I couldn't remember if I'd reloaded after I went hunting the other night. I thought I'd fired three shots then. Three is my average: eye shot, knee shot, crotch shot. So, possibly only twelve shots left . . .

At top speed, I got ahead of wound perception, and was forced to wait several beats to see the impact of ranged attacks. Counting off beats in my head to keep from pulling the trigger too fast, I got to three before firing at the next monster in my sights. Turns out their sights were on me, too.

A barrage of quills struck my gun hand, one quill

penetrating the chamber of the gun itself, the other pinning my hand to the pistol grip. But the ones I'd shot went down. Laughing soundlessly, I rolled as I landed, dodging another group of quills. That time I saw how they shot, snapping the tips of their tails like whips, hurling the quills free like wicked slingshots from hell. I tried shouting for Fang, but the hisses caught that, too, and he can't hear my thoughts like he can hear Dad's.

Where the hell was—?

Evelyn's head came shooting past me. Fangs curled like tusks at the corners of her mouth. I didn't see how she could bite anything, but as it turned out, she didn't have to. Droplets of blood poured out of the mouth and eyes of one of the chupacabra, flowing into Evelyn's open mouth. The chupacabra sank to its forepaws, struggling in a battle that it had already lost. My "How cool is that?" didn't make it past the hissing, but another volley of quills lit up my side in pinpoint spots of ragged agony.

I cursed, pulling quills from my hand, and hurled my Glock at the nearest chupacabra. The gun struck it in the forehead, caving in its skull. I guess maybe guns do kill if you throw them hard enough. The fight turned for me when I flinched. The three remaining beasts honed in on me, moving wide and trying to herd me, letting the humans, their former prey, escape in the process. My left hand snagged the man as he tried to shoot past me out of the alley. I snatched him off his feet, pulling him upside down so I could get at his femoral artery. His neck snapped as I rammed it into the ground, dropping to a crouch. As it turns out, the other way is better: grabbing a human by the throat and sinking my fangs into his neck while using him as a shield. I'd wondered if a leg over each of my shoulders might work out, but no. Too awkward.

The chupacabra on the left flexed its tail at me, and I flinched. I never flinch! My rage isn't like Dad's, there's no über vamp, no massive swinging phallus (he really does need to put some pants on that thing), but it's berserkery enough. Tearing my human into two unequal pieces, I roared silently, hurling the part of a leg that came loose in my left hand at the chupacabra on the right and the bulk of the corpse at the creature on the left. I'd like to say I was smart, using the larger portion of corpse as a shield, chasing it to that chupacabra. Instead, I charged right down the middle. They lit me up with quills. Magnificent plumes of pain, like barbed holy arrows, pincushioned me, but I would not surrender to it.

My target stayed in place, waiting for its companions to intervene: a neat tactic, but they needed bigger numbers for it to work on me. Plunging my claws through its chest, I grabbed the spine and pulled out a chunk of it, my hand covered in foul-smelling blood as I hurled the vertebrae at the chupacabra to my right.

"Kill you!" My voice rang out in my ears. "Kill you! Kill you!" I hadn't even realized I'd been shouting. My ears had become so accustomed to the hissing and the absence of other sound that the sudden return of my own voice made me dizzy. Then sound went away again as I saw the others. Not just seven—three times as many, filling the street from the east end. They approached slowly. Hissing.

"You can't kill me," I screamed without sound, "only I can kill me!" My right hand wouldn't unclench, for some reason, and my neck tensed and relaxed with a pulse not unlike a heartbeat, but I didn't stop. I didn't care what they thought they could do to me. So they could make me feel pain. So what? I fell onto my left side, my leg unresponsive, and then the human blood I'd gulped down from my temporary hostage came violently back up, splattering the road. It smelled sour and sick.

Vampires don't get sick.

"Vampires don't get sick!"

I don't change shape often, because I can't bring my clothes with me and I only have two forms. When I do change, I usually use my nonsecret form, my favorite bat—a golden flying fox—but I have another one. A better one.

The way I figure it, most vampires who aren't Dad have a certain number of slots, and each time they transform into a type of animal, that animal gets programmed into a slot. The more specific or unique the animal, the more slots it takes up. Vlads get a lot of slots, and my secret form used up all the rest of mine, every last one. My arms began to lengthen, as did my fingers and claws. My jaw unhinged and elongated as my teeth stretched and additional ones thrust up out of my expanding jawbone.

My flesh burned and bubbled as I grew, like I was a skin balloon being pumped full of acid. I felt stretched and overfull, painfully so, until the pain of the transformation overran the pain of the chupacabra wounds. A tail burst out at my butt, and it felt somehow like I was defecating the massive muscular thing. Skin thickened and turned reptilian. *You think you're the monsters,* I thought at them. *I'm the motherfucking monster here. Nobody but Dad is allowed to be scarier than me! NO ONE!*

The frames of Percy's glasses stretched, and as they were dragged away from my eyes by my expanding muzzle (or is it "snout"?), I saw *Bravo, my girl* appear in gold script on the lenses. Best of all, my transformation forced the quills out of my body. I still felt sick and trembly, but it was nowhere near as bad. Then I roared. Crimson light from my glowing massive eyes filled the street like twin spotlights in some crazily lit zombie movie. All twenty-three chupacabras pulled back and bolted as if they'd heard their master's voice and had to run home. I'm embarrassed to say it, but I let them go. I didn't even swipe at the two closest to me when they ran past.

Sound came back, and it was nice to hear the background noises of my city. LEGO-Head reattached herself, but I stood there roaring over and over again until Fang pulled into the alley. I lumbered in a circle, the red light of my anger reflecting off of windows, daring something to jump out at me so I could chew it up in my fanged maw and spit out the pulped flesh and bone, the unneeded solids. No challengers arose.

Changing back felt like being a blimp punctured by a giant spear. All my mass collapsed in around me, and I deflated and plummeted toward the ground. With the impact, the pain from my wounds returned, though the quills were long gone.

Evelyn caught my arm as I sagged, though I did manage a weak smile when I noticed Fang was playing Blue Öyster Cult's "Godzilla."

"Holy shit!" Evelyn said breathlessly. "You turn into a goddamn T. rex?"

"Don't be stupid." I swung, trying to knock off her head but failing. "T. rexes are scavengers, and they had tiny little arms. No way I'd turn into one of those pussy dinosaurs. Appalachiosaurus is way cooler. It was a predator. It would have eaten"—I slumped to my knees as Evelyn failed to completely hold me up—"T. rex for lunch and shat on the corpse."

"But . . . a dinosaur?"

"Nobody said I couldn't try something extinct."

"But . . ."

I growled, and that shut her up. Naked, cold, and shivering, I made it back to Fang, where I had a set of clean warm clothes in the trunk. I always let him eat a few changes of clothing, just in case I need them, since Dad says he doesn't want me walking down the street naked and covered in gore unless it's absolutely necessary.

"So the only clothes you keep when you transform are your sunglasses and your . . . what is that hanging around your neck? A gris-gris bag?"

"No, it's . . ." I started to explain about the whole Veil of Scrythax getting pulped by Dad and then turned into a personal veil for me by the Mages Guild, but I let my sentence trail off. Let her figure it out herself.

Once I was dressed and leaning up against the car, I noticed the weirdness. I wasn't hungry. In its place was nausea. I knew I needed to feed, but the thought of it made the sick feeling worse.

The queasiness didn't keep me from sensing the cloaked figure that entered the alleyway. Evelyn saw him, too. He moved with a limp, and there was something wrong with his face: It was diseased, and though covered in flesh, it was skeletal, with sunken eyes and a gaping cavity where his nose should have been. What skin there was seemed scabrous and discolored.

"We need to talk, Sheriff," he said in a voice that sounded all business despite the slight lisp and the accent I couldn't place.

"Who the hell are you?" I snapped.

"Most people refer to me simply as Pop C or Poppa C. It's more of a title than a name, though it's close to the same with me."

"Popsie, huh?"

He moved closer, so that Fang's brights (which snapped on as if on cue) lit him up. The cloak was a very expensive-looking black number, and his suit was an Italian bespoke custom job that I bet would have impressed even Talbot, if the damn cat had been here to see this. Two fingers were missing from Popsie's left hand, and the others curled uselessly.

"It's short for Population Control." His voice was hoarse, as if speaking was an effort. "Or did you think that a city in which vampires kill, on average, 4,239.7 humans per year maintains a steady population rate and a burgeoning economy without someone at the reins?"

"No?"

"No," he agreed. "Phillipus and I had an understanding, but

your father has not yet met with me, and his current goals are a mystery to me. Mr. Courtney cannot simply allow the vampire population to dwindle as it has. The machinations that support the harvesting of humans cannot be turned on a dime. I plan decades in advance. He cannot curtail the killing so extremely and expect me to be able to readily adjust without substantial advance warning."

"He can do whatever he wants," I barked.

"To a degree, I concede," Popsie purred, "but I must cull the humans somehow while Mr. Courtney makes up his mind. From what I've seen, you appear to object to chupacabra. So I'm here to ask you, Ms. Courtney, as his sheriff . . . how would you prefer that I proceed?"

✦ 17 ✦

POPSIE

So if I kill four people every night, that puts us at . . ." My wounds still burned and had yet to heal, but I had sheriff work to do; I wanted to make Dad proud. I'd just sneak in and steal some of his blood before bed. Surely that would make me feel better.

"Fourteen hundred and sixty." Pop C sat across the desk from my deputy and me in a well-worn office chair that might have been quite expensive once. We had folding chairs, though he had offered to clear a chaise longue for us. His office was on the top floor of the Lovett Building, which made perfect sense. Demons tended to keep offices there, as did many of the larger supernatural movers and shakers. Now that the Highland Towers were no more, plenty of vamps had moved into the place. What didn't make sense was the decor.

I'd expected something well outfitted and impressive. Instead, his desk was a plain wooden affair with a central strut held up by a box of printer paper. Boxes of paper covered the place. And where there wasn't paper, I saw tech. A row of laptops, tablet computers, and smartphones were plugged in to a bank of chargers and lined up on an old folding table. Other workers moved swiftly and efficiently through other similarly outfitted offices, and I don't think I passed a room that didn't hold at least three doggie beds with snoozing mange-ridden mongrels.

"You have the entire floor?" I asked, distracted by a rumbling in my belly.

"Indeed," he answered casually, as if the topic change didn't frustrate him.

"How many people work up here?"

"Several hundred."

"Are they all—?" I chewed over the word. "Do they all wear the weird cloaks and stuff?"

"Most of them choose to, yes, but I don't enforce a strict dress code unless they are in a customer-facing role."

"So why are you so fucked-up-looking?"

"Greta!" Evelyn objected.

"What?" I had no clue what she was pissy about. The dude had almost no face. He was alive, and he didn't have that weird spicy smell Uncle Percy has, so I assumed he and his crew weren't mummies. Zombies look even worse, and the scent of rot is hard to hide, so these guys couldn't be zombies, either. I was curious. Besides, it wasn't as if I'd asked him whether his dick was as scabbed up and grody as his face. Probably was, though.

"Leprosy is unkind," Popsie answered.

Evelyn wrinkled her nose. I don't know why. It's not like either of us could catch it. "Don't they have a cure for that?" I asked.

"Let us say simply that they didn't when I contracted it, and now my condition is beyond what mortal science can arrest or repair."

"Sucks to be you, then, Mr. Scaly Pants." I fought the urge to claw at my hand, where the quill wounds laid my flesh open to the world. The world didn't have any business seeing it, but what could I do? Wear gloves? That certainly wouldn't take care of the wounds to my face, back, neck, and side. Popsie didn't seem to mind. I guess from his point of view, I was pretty hot. "So . . . wait. Can't the Mages Guild help?"

"They help keep the supernatural a secret and adjust the memories of survivors when absolutely necessary, and they work with me in other ways, though I doubt they're cognizant of that fact. My plans are far-reaching, dipping into many different realms: the mundane, the supernatural, the legal, the economical, and the political."

"Sounds boring as hell to me." I stood up, wincing against the pain I'd known would be coming when I stood. *That's not a good sign.* "I'll talk to Dad about it. I don't see why he'd have a problem. We'll just have to set up some sort of hunting trips to cull the humans like they do deer. And you can get rid of the chupacabra or whatever."

He started to say something else, then thought better of it.

Evelyn cleared her throat. "Actually, I have a few questions, too." She looked at me. "Sheriff. If that's all right?"

"Fine." I leaned against the doorway. Percy started to write something on my glasses, so I took them off and put them in my pocket.

"You implied that you're older than you look, Mr. C. Do you mind if I ask how old?" Evelyn asked.

"I'm afraid it's none of your concern, Miss . . . ?"

"LEGO-Head," I blurted. "She's my deputy. Deputy LEGO-Head—or Bobblehead." I blinked, fighting off the urge to vomit. I wanted to lie down. To go home or . . .

"I'm Evelyn," she said, correcting me, and offered Popsie her hand. He shook it, firm but brief. Power lurked behind it, not only political power but physical strength beyond his outward appearance. It didn't take Evie by surprise, either. She'd expected it, and maybe I should have.

"Evelyn . . . ?" Popsie drew out the word, turning it into a question.

"Courtney-Barnes," she added. She didn't like giving up that information. I don't know why, but it seemed to give Popsie the upper hand in a way that didn't tend to work with me. It's hard to bargain with someone who might eat you at any second. That's why, or I think that's why, Dad chooses to be so unpredictable. There is power in madness. Makes people fear you and respect you. Let them believe they can placate you. Barely. Makes placating you hard but the cost for not doing so even harder. No, that's not what Dad does. I . . . couldn't think about it properly. My head hurt and my wounds hurt and I . . .

Someone was growling. That someone was me.

"Sheriff?" Evie said my name like it was a wuh-wuh word: a question. Who, what, where, when, or why.

I growled louder.

"I think your sheriff is succumbing to her injuries, Ms. Courtney-Barnes," Popsie commented. "Or do you truly prefer to be called Deputy LEGO-Head?"

"What?" Evie was thinking about Dad. She liked me and wanted another shot at killing him. I confused her. Dad confused her more. Popsie confused her, and she wasn't the sort who liked being confused. "Can we help her?"

"I can, but only if you're willing to—"

"No!" I wasn't sure about anything else, but I was sure Dad wouldn't have let Scaly Pants dictate how things worked. I yowled again, spines, new ones, growing, poking out of my skin. "I'm the boss, applesauce."

Evelyn opened her mouth to say something, and I hissed, my tongue splitting into twin vibrating tines. Like a tuning fork, my mouth shook, vibrations blurring my vision as my hiss blocked out her sound. Popsie's sound.

Popsie smiled. His mind pressed in on mine, even without

eye contact, as if he slid in through my wounds. My mind was breached. Laid open. He walked inside. Then he stopped smiling. In my own mind, I fear no one. *Big mistake,* I thought at him. *You're in my house now.*

"What issss thissss, Popsssie?" The forked tongue made it hard to speak, even in my own head. The pain was there, too. My skin split open, spines bursting through the open gashes. My mouth stretched into a muzzle.

"But you're infected." Popsie took a step back. We were in the desert, somewhere like Mexico, and I didn't like it there, so I dug down deep and willed us into a memory, the one I'd prepped for Evie. I'd let Popsie have it. My deputy wouldn't mind. I'd find her another one. I have plenty.

The ground split open, sand blowing away, drowning the sun until the day became night as the sand-choked sun surrendered, becoming the moon. Popsie stepped away from me, but I didn't care. Where could he run inside my head where I couldn't find him? It was like swimming farther into the ocean to hide from the sea. You're in it. There's no place to go.

Lightpoles erupted from the street revealed by the sand's absence, and buildings, too. It was a bad part of town. Not sort of bad, like the area around the original Demon Heart, but really bad. The part of the city where piss stained the streets and lay beaded like dew on the walls of unused car parks. I didn't remember the address. I always found the place by smell. Despair has its own odor, and that's what this place was.

I'd been here before. Watched three children. Listened to their fears and the evil of their foster parents. Watched and waited. This memory was of the night I needed to wait no longer. Intercession time. Rescue time . . . hero time . . . Greta time was at hand.

Still changing, I leaped onto a skyward-rocketing fire escape, rusted red and creaking where I touched it.

Inside, Petey, small and fightless, crouched in the corner

while men took turns with Darla. She was younger than I was when I had my first time, and this wasn't her first. She made more noise than I had, but then again, there was more than one of the men. Bad men. It was the work of an instant to break their arms and legs so they'd be more manageable. They weren't like Dad. None of them were good men, like him.

Dad doesn't hurt children. He rescued me from my foster dad at the age of nine. I'm always trying to understand why. The window was open, so I stepped inside. I don't know how many men there were, but it felt like seven or so. I didn't count the bodies, and there was no need to count them before the fight. Humans are no threat to me. They die too easily. Not that I killed them. I just hurt them. One of them, the biggest, fell to his knees before Petey and I tore open the man's chest; I pulled out his sternum to show Petey how to find the heart. Petey didn't smile and lap at the blood or bite the heart. He hadn't been turned yet. He screamed and screamed.

"Why did he scream?" I shouted at Popsie.

Daddy made me strong, so I tried to do the same for them. I thought Petey was defective, so I took a different approach. They'd hurt Darla more directly, more intimately, than Petey, so I tried to help her hurt them back. She was so weak and small. Her black hair lay matted with sweat and baser excretions, so I lifted her like a doll and held her to the neck of the man who'd sold her body. Darla didn't want to bite through his veins at first. Maybe it was because I hadn't turned her yet, but I wanted her to be prepared, to know what to do.

Finally, with help, she managed it. I don't know why she cried.

"Why did she cry?" I screamed at Popsie. He trembled as if he didn't know how to react. He tried to block the noise. His tongue split and began to vibrate, so I tore it out. "This is something special I'm sharing with you," I growled. "It is knowledge and insight and—" He covered his ears, so I dragged him into the next room. There was still the fat boy, Spanky, left to go.

I found the boy playing video games in another part of the rambling squatter's hovel. Ozzy Osbourne's "Mr. Crowley" played from the speakers of the entertainment center. He cried worse than Darla. "I'm making you strong now!" I shouted at him as I showed him how to use claws to get to veins blocked by fat or muscle. "Don't you understand? Strong!"

He didn't.

None of them did.

I dragged them out kicking and screaming under the stars to the rooftop so they could be free. The moon shone brightly for them, but they failed me. Still, I wasn't angry. They cried and mewled when I drained them. They turned away from the blood when I offered them mine, tried not to drink it, but I forced them to be saved. I took their little bodies, dragging them behind me to Sweet Heart Row, and hid them in the sewer access so they'd be safe from the sun. Popsie wanted to run away, but no matter where he ran, I was in front of him with Petey, Darla, and Spanky.

"I don't understand what I did differently," I shouted at Popsie. "If you're so fucking old, explain it to me!"

He withered before me. "I can't. You're insane. You—"

"Then make me feel better." I leaned in close. We were back in the desert. "Make me feel better, or you can see it again and again until we both understand why they didn't turn out like me."

I took us to another night. Popsie and I watched as the me from only a few years ago wandered Sweet Heart Row, trying to catch a glimpse of my children. We watched the remembrance of me torturing the vampires I discovered until I found one who knew what had happened.

"The Big Guy killed them. The Eric guy. Him and that car of his."

The other me tore the vampire into little pieces while I stared at Popsie, watching his expression. He'd considered himself scary. He'd considered himself better than me, superior. Now he knew. He was never going to make it out of my head unless I let him go.

"I can cure you," Popsie whispered. "I can undo the chupacabra infection. We can work together. Population Control and the Courtneys. I—"

I let him go.

He fell backward out of my head, and I stared across the room at him. Evelyn was surround by chupacabras, but they withdrew at a gesture from Popsie. "No. No. We have an accord. They are the new masters of Void City." The chupacabra transformed, some becoming leprous humans in their tatty robes and others mangy dogs scampering back to their warm doggie beds. *So that's how that works*, I thought. *Sneaky. Sneaky.*

"Drink." Popsie held out his wrist. "The blood will taste foul, but I'm the Prime Contagion. My blood can cure you."

I drank and grinned. I hadn't even needed to bother Dad.

I'm a good sheriff. Look how scared my citizens are!

◆ 18 ◆

ERIC

WAKEY-WAKEY

At dawn, my eyes snapped open. If I'd been a rooster, I would have crowed. Farmers would have shouted at me to shut the hell up, which would've done as much good as the voices of those around me. Words filled my ears, but they had no meaning. Crimson tinted my sight, lending reality an ink wash of blood. Heartbeats throbbed about me, blood coursing through veins so loudly that it hurt all the way to my hair. Sounds I knew well. Figures leaned over me, their features obscured by my need; a desire for blood screamed in my mind, blocking out other thoughts with near-complete success.

What the hell? I don't usually let the hunger get this bad.

A vampire's thirst is never weak, but this was different. It was the thirst that comes on after several nights of not feeding: a killing thirst. The kind where one drop of blood can send me over the edge and I'll kill anybody . . . well, almost anybody. I heard Marilyn's heartbeat and howled. I didn't want her blood, have never had the slightest desire to drink from her, not even when I first rose. But there were other things I did want to do, and I didn't have permission to do them.

Hands touched me, bringing with them the scent of jungle cats and sacred waters. Talbot. Blood filled my mouth, cold, from a bag. It was human blood, but my body didn't want it cold; it wanted fresh blood. Strong blood. The blood in my mouth was straight human, and I swallowed, but my body rejected it, violent heaves sending it all back up, like the first time I tried to drink animal blood. I don't know why animal blood doesn't work for me, but it never has. Human blood, though—unless some idiot had microwaved it—had always done the job, warm or cold.

"Not working," I panted.

Other voices were trying to make themselves heard, but they made no sense, as if the part of my brain that spent time decoding such things didn't consider that function important until after I fed. Out. My wings flapped involuntarily, sending two sources of blood with heartbeats against the wall, my first sign that I'd gone über vamp as I woke. I wanted—no—needed out of the room to hunt, needed to hunt far away from the people I knew. I couldn't remember all their names, but I could feel them near me, willing to be drunk from, marked with my blood and my essence, but not perhaps as deeply as I feared I would drink.

Why does all the really fucked-up shit keep happening to me?

"At least you still have a body," said a weak female voice from nearby. The soul of Suzie Hu, caught in a state of undress from being eaten on my vampiric wedding night, sat on the ground next to me, rocking back and forth as she hugged her knees. No, not next to me. Her form intermingled with the über vamp's, her rear end overlapping with my taloned foot. At least the über vamp was wearing pants.

The inner part of me that senses prey assessed her and, discounting her as a source of blood or a potential threat, howled again. I felt Talbot's claws sink into my skin, and he yowled, releasing me. Singed cat filled my nostrils. For the second time ever, the nature of the über vamp overwhelmed Talbot's holy blood, burning him where his claws normally burned the undead or demonic creatures of the world. Beneath my talons, something trembled, not the ground, not even a physical thing, an undercurrent of magic, the turning of the world. At the edge of perception, I sensed Fang, not heading for me but coiled steel, ready to pounce if I summoned him.

Next to him, distant but not far removed, I felt my thralls, my army of little helpers. The über vamp howled one long note, and they all responded, some nearby . . . mine for years . . . familiar, others new and yet in some ways older, but all answering my call with one of their own. Farther still, beneath the wave of contact, I sensed animals gathering to act. A single thought could call down a plague of rats, a horde of bats, and other creatures. Above it all, I felt my offspring in their various states of wakefulness or slumber. All of them said "Master" except one:

I love you, Dad. Greta rolled over in her sleep and smiled. *I took care of the chupacabra and Mr. Scaly Pants.*

I had no idea what she was talking about, but I was proud of her all the same. *Good girl,* I sent.

My oldest, Lisa, squirmed in her sleep, long blond hair cascading over her breasts. She'd fallen asleep with her jeans on, as usual. She was staying as Lady Gabriella's guest out in Sable Oaks. This close, my presence forced her awake. "Master?" It was a question.

Not yet, I sent.

She waved a hand in the darkness, and a human, not the one I'd sensed a few years ago, a new one—a girl—began playing the cello. Lisa drifted back into death's temporary embrace.

Not in the same house but in the same neighborhood, Nancy, my second offspring, slept in a coffin with dirt in the bottom, the interior lit with black lightbulbs. She'd always been superstitious. Nancy wore a red silk nightie, her supple chestnut-colored skin standing out in sensuous contrast, as it always seemed to do. We shared the same exchange I'd shared with Lisa, and she hit play on her iPod, sounds of a podcast starting up. *Drunken Roundtable* scrolled past before the backlight winked out. The host, Kate, sounded like she might be a fun person to know.

Irene twitched in her sleep. Of the first three girlfriends I'd turned into monsters, she was physically the closest, safely ensconced in the uppermost suite of the Void City Hilton. Her eyes snapped open, closed, then open again. In my mind's eye, she slept naked with two anemic or soon to be anemic young human men sharing the bed to keep her warm. "Master?" she asked, anger flashing across her face, replaced quickly by fear, then neutrality.

Not yet, I assured her.

She bit the bicep of the sleeping man on her right, playfully but penetrating, and fell asleep once more as the human yelped in pain and surprise. Being bitten doesn't feel good.

"Master?" Tabitha woke fully, grimacing against the word. "Fuck off!" she said, rolling out of bed in her apartment. "I'm tired of your shit." She faded from view, still angry. She wasn't in on The Plan.

I can't count the times I've stood on the edge of, well, not the edge of becoming a monster, because I am one, but on the edge of losing who I am to the monster I've become. Giving in, letting myself . . . A quote came to mind, one I hadn't thought about in years, and then Phillip, or the apparition of Lord Phillip, coalesced next to me, a wry expression on his face as he gave voice to the quote: "'Be sober, be vigilant.'" He said it mockingly, phrasing it as a question. "'Because your adversary the devil, as a roaring lion, walketh about, seeking whom he may devour.'" He laughed. "You aren't the devil, my boy."

"Then you haven't heard 'Devil Inside' by INXS." I thought

I said it, but I didn't. The über vamp was quiet. On the precipice of power, my form was frozen, my might summoned. I could use it or not. Part of me wanted to, but not the part with The Plan. The hungry part that didn't care.

Phil's form quivered as the über vamp roared again. It wanted to rage, like some werewolf without an Alpha to rein it in come full moon. Heartbeats retreated from me, all except for Marilyn's. I couldn't see her, but I didn't have to see her to know her. A succubus made that mistake once in El Segundo, back when I first met Talbot. She took Marilyn's shape, trying to seduce me. I didn't even notice the resemblance. Like I said, I always know Marilyn.

And she knows me.

"Looks like she's sending the children to bed, hoss." Roger bloomed into being at my back. "When you feed, she'll really want it. You won't have to try any poetry or flower nonsense. Just take her." Roger cut his eyes to Phillip, and the fat little bastard gave the barest of nods. "Try her ass," Roger continued. "I did. She makes the weirdest little faces."

Roger wanted to make me angry. I don't know why. It worked, though. My sense of connection snapped off like a light, and all my attention rested on the oily little man who'd been my best friend—or played the part.

My hand closed around Phillip's neck, and he felt solid to my touch. He choked, gargling as I broke his neck, but I couldn't kill him. Not now. Phillip laughed as if that were all he'd wanted to determine. Roger flailed at my forearm, but his hands passed right through me. I could touch him, but he couldn't touch me.

"Joke," he choked. "It was a joke."

I sank my fangs into his arm, but those veins held nothing for me, nothing I could drink.

"What happened to you?" he asked as I pummeled him

with my free fist. "Why don't you just digest our souls? Why keep us like this?" His eyes widened as he reached the same conclusion Phil had reached moments before. "You can't."

I opened my mouth to answer and felt soft skin at my lips. I forced my mouth wide to avoid the bite, but then Marilyn pressed her flesh against my fangs, literally impaling herself on them. Her blood was in my mouth, and all other thoughts fell away.

Blood doesn't have much of a taste—I've described it as sucking on a copper penny—but this wasn't about taste. It was about longing and proximity, about physical contact and warmth and the woman I love. Memories flooded back to me on a tide of sense memory as she wrapped her arms around me and her blood drove the red from my vision and filled in the gaps, draping veins in flesh once more, lending meaning to words that had been meaningless noise.

"I've got you, Eric," she said.

I collapsed to my knees, shrinking back to human size, but there was no pain or discomfort. For the first time in a long while, I felt at home in my own skin. This was the Marilyn who'd held me when I came back from World War II, who'd held me when I was drunk on both alcohol and the horrors of war, who'd held me but stopped me from going too far that night, and the Marilyn whom I didn't stop from going too far the next night in Fang's backseat, before I was an undead monster.

It was the same Marilyn who'd disagreed with my decision to reenlist for Korea and who'd talked me into changing careers after that war, convinced me to do something good or try it. If we hadn't lived in Void City, I think she would have fixed me, and I would have died an old man after church one Sunday. Maybe I would have tried preaching again eventually. But in Void City those things don't work out. Neither one of us had any idea vampires were real back then and that the cops, even the good ones or the ones who were trying to be good, all worked for Lord Phillip, whether of their own free will or with a little magical coercion to ensure acquiescence and memory adjustment to avoid any troublesome issues of conscience. Some might call it destiny, but it wasn't. It was just bad luck.

Until my Plan, it had been decades since I'd thought about my time as Captain Courtney of the VCPD. It had been Halloween, when Magbidion shot a mage with my service revolver, that had brought it back to mind. Until things started coming back to me recently, I didn't have many memories of my time as a cop at all. In this town, I guess, more than anything, that's a sign that I was an honest cop. I've always been honest.

I was about to be honest again, but in a very bad way. It was part of The Plan, but I'd been having trouble managing it, because I can't fool Marilyn. It had to happen naturally. She had to give me a reason first, any reason.

I pulled away from her and realized we were already on the bed, my shirt was off, my belt undone, and for reasons unbeknownst to me, the pair of jeans I'd come back wearing were old-school button-flys. My hands cupped her breasts, one over the bra, the other underneath. Our mouths were rimmed with Marilyn's blood, like strawberry jam on children's faces. She undid the first button and I stopped her, calling myself an idiot the entire time. I could have had her again, but I didn't want an easy tumble with my girl. Something she and I could both question. Even if that meant she was never mine again. When we were together, at the end of The Plan, it would not be like this.

"You stupid jackass." Marilyn laughed. "After all this time, I finally—"

I rolled off the bed, buckling my belt. "You're fired."

"Ha!" Marilyn let loose one of her trademark braying laughs. "Okay, let me hear it."

"Hear what?"

"Whatever this is." The line between angry and amused with Marilyn is like oil on water. You can see them both together, but the only way to separate them is to burn off the film and see which one there's more of. Her shirt was going back on, too. Wounds at her neck, thigh, and wrists where I had apparently fed sealed as I watched. True immortals heal with impressive alacrity. Marilyn was no exception.

"I'm not sleeping with you like this." I wiped at the blood on my lips and held it out, tacky on my fingertips. "Not in some vamp feeding-frenzy afterglow."

"But you would have screwed my brains out if the vampire hunters hadn't interrupted us yesterday at the bowling alley?"

As her clothes went on, it got easier.

"I told you and everyone else to let me go so I could fly off and feed somewhere."

"You would have rather murdered some stranger than drink my blood?" She gestured wildly with her hands. "That doesn't even make sense!"

"I don't drink from you, Marilyn. It's a rule."

"Eric." She slapped her sides. "I don't believe this. I really don't. I'm a true immortal. I was the obvious choice. You couldn't kill me, and I can regenerate blood faster than your most talented thrall. Even if you'd torn me in half, I'd have been fine in ten minutes. Less, even. It's the least—" She caught herself, but it was too late.

"The least you could do?" I dug around in my pants for my wallet and found it under the edge of the bed.

"Eric." She wouldn't hold her hands out to me, like Tabitha might have; nor would she put a hand on my shoulder and try to calm me down, like Nancy. "You know what I meant." Marilyn's hands were on her hips.

"Yeah." I fumbled for an envelope inside the wallet and unfolded it. "Yeah, I do. You think you owe me."

"You brought me back from the dead, Eric. Rescued me from hell and—"

"And you don't owe me shit!" My voice was hard-edged and sharp, like I wanted it to be. "I won't take a pity fuck, M. Maybe I should. Maybe that's the best I can expect after all that's happened. And maybe that doesn't make any sense." The envelope had Marilyn's name printed on it in my handwriting. "But I'm good at not making sense. It's my superpower." I handed her the envelope.

"What's this?" She tore it open. "A Dear John letter? You shouldn't have."

"It's a check for two million, four hundred sixty-nine thousand, nine hundred forty-two dollars and sixty-three cents." The note line on the check read "back salary."

She stared at the check and then at me. "What is this?"

"Magbidion and Beatrice helped me pull the numbers based on the files you had in your old apartment before you died." I looked at her feet, not able to meet her gaze. "It should be right. According to the records, Roger never paid you, so this is what you're owed, plus six months of termination pay."

"Explain it to me slowly, Eric." The set of her mouth made it clear that I'd gone past any thin veneer of amusement. She was angry. "Pretend you're trying to explain it to some really dumb animal, like . . . I don't know . . . a man."

"You need time," I said. "Whether you know it or not. You do. If we get together again now, after this, it will never work. If you feel like you owe me because I got you out of hell or if, I don't know, if you feel responsible for the stuff I'm having to do to pay that off." Our eyes met, but it was her turn to look away. I could see what she saw. She saw me strangling Father

Ike in her name, and it was a wall between us. It needn't have been, but she didn't know that. "You didn't get to lead the rest of your life, Marilyn. I ate it up with my bullshit, and then Roger stole what was left. You used to want to go to college. Business or something.

"Do it.

"You have forever to figure out what it is you want to do with your life, and then you have forever to do it. I've made arrangements with the Iversonian . . . or rather, Talbot did. He's going to teach you how to use your powers and about how true immortal society works without letting you wind up in some of the weird soul-bondage serfdom crap that tends to happen to newbie immortals."

"Eric," she interrupted, but I barreled on.

"The girls will help you pack your stuff and get settled in a new place."

"Eric," she broke in again.

"If you think I owe you more money . . ." I kept on talking. If I stopped, I'd never get it out, and I'd never be strong enough to say it all again. "I'll give you whatever you want, but I knew you'd probably be offended if it seemed like I was just trying to thoughtlessly throw cash at you."

"Eric," Marilyn tried a third time, her voice growing louder.

"There's a bigger mix of supernatural types hanging out at the Iversonian, so if you want to work there for a while to get exposure, I've made sure you can do that, too."

"Eric!" The fourth time, she slapped me, but I barely felt it. "What?"

"I love you." She said the words plaintively, like an excuse, an accusation, or the answer to a riddle. I needed it to be true. It was true.

"I know that, dumbass. I love you, too." I turned around

and grabbed my shirt off the floor on my way into the bowling alley proper. "But for this to work, it has to be about that and only that. You can't be with me out of guilt or habit or because you think it's expected of you. I love you, and you're the only woman I've ever said that to in a romantic way."

I looked over my shoulder at her, from my position in the doorway. She wasn't listening anymore. Like mine, her anger is prone to take hold and block out reason. My girl has a will like the edge of a samurai sword. You could cut steel with it.

"Fine." Her fingers curled around the check.

"Once you've lived some and had a chance to be who you want to be . . ." I trailed off. "Then maybe you can come back, but until then, I can't look at you every day, do what I have to do to pay my debt, and smell your vomit from how sick what I've done has made you. I can't look at the pity in your eyes."

Her will softened and I almost caved. I caught a twitch of movement from her hand. She'd almost reached out for me. If she had, it would have all been over.

"Get the hell out of my bowling alley." I was halfway down the hall when she threw the brick at my head, but it was daytime, so I caught it easy. "I left you a present parked outside."

Well, I told myself, *there's step seven of the Marilyn portion of The Plan. Better late than never.*

My cell phone chirped. When I unlocked it, it opened directly to my Plan app.

DAYTIME SUPPORT: *That went well.*

If you say so.

DAYTIME SUPPORT: *I'm supposed to tell you that Code name Garnier is in play.*

Yeah. That's good, I guess.

DAYTIME SUPPORT: *Shock and awe.*

"Shock and awe." I thumbed the app closed. "Time was, when supernatural folks in Void City said those words, they'd be talking about the über vamp."

✦ 19 ✦

EVELYN

A BRIEF INTERLUDE, 1 OF 3

The sheriff was fast asleep and tucked into the trunk of her dad's car when the woman she'd called Mom walked out of the bowling alley and into the sun, all red hair, curves, and the kind of smolder most women have to work hard for. I could see why Eric found her so attractive. She was very much his era, transplanted into the modern age. She wasn't a vampire, but she was something magic. When I focused on her, a tinge of blue flared around the edges, soul magic of some kind. Maybe a sign of immortality. Hard to know from this far away. Following her would be easier if I could use the car, but it doesn't seem to like me. On the rooftop of the parking garage, a thrall with binoculars watched everything but the birds. Specifically, he was watching the woman, too.

She strode up to a classic bike, an old Harley-Davidson Duo-Glide, a 1963, if I recalled correctly. I did a story on classic bikes once, and it seemed familiar, not one of the bikes from the story but the same family. I forget what the difference is between a hog and a normal motorcycle.

Eric didn't come outside with her, and I felt torn between

my two goals. I wanted to kill the son of a bitch so badly, I felt like a tightly strung cello whose metal strings might snap at the lightest touch of the bow. But I liked the sheriff. I couldn't say why, but when she did the whole monster thing, it wasn't as shocking as it should have been. It seemed natural when she did it.

Okay. Maybe this is just something that happens once you're a vampire. One day you're all hot for revenge, and the next, people start to look like menu options.

The woman carried only one bag, an army duffel. She wore an old leather jacket that had been well maintained. A scent of Old Spice and sweat, beer, and good times clung to it. She walked around the bike one time and snorted in either derision or amusement before climbing on and riding off. There was an energy to the bike, and I wondered if that was what caused her reaction. I could wait for Eric, but my instincts told me she was the real story, so I followed her.

Even without the magic in the city, no one stared up at the rooftops, checking for *nukekubi* gliding from roof to roof. Her trail led to the Void City Trust. While she did her thing inside, I dug out my e-reader and tried to settle back into my book. I'd been rereading *Don Quixote* back at Pythagoras's hideout, before the attack on Eric, before they all pulled out, but the section where I'd stopped reading vexed me:

> *"And do the enchanted eat?" said the cousin.*
>
> *"They neither eat," said Don Quixote; "nor are they subject to the greater excrements, though it is thought that their nails, beards, and hair grow."*

After my fifth time rereading the line, I scrolled through my books and found the next Rob Thurman book on my list and bought it. It had just finished downloading when my target came back out. Her gait was lighter, less concerned. Either she'd just paid something off or deposited a large sum of money she wasn't comfortable carrying around. I slid the e-reader back into my bag and slung it onto my back. Backpacks may be out of style, but nothing beats them for roof hopping. I can scarcely imagine trying it with a normal purse in tow.

Marilyn drove over to the Iversonian club, the magic there so obvious it would be hard not to notice it. I don't do spells, but I've seen enough of them over the last few years to know that those were there to say, "Hello! I'm a magic freaking ward, and if you mess with me, you will have no way to claim you didn't know about me because I have a giant backlit sign declaring MAGIC FREAKING WARD in forty-point type. So don't make me tell on you. Capiche?"

I wished she'd move again, because gliding from rooftop to rooftop tailing her had been the best fun I'd had in a long time. She didn't, though. The mnemonic device I used to remember her name and her face ran through my head over and over until I was sorry I thought it up: Marilyn was marry'n the man I want to kill. / Once I've gone and murdered him, she'll be his lover still.

It's a habit I picked up as a reporter, before I got in front of the camera. It's amazing how much leverage remembering a name can get you. I tried everything. Mentally spelling out a name in my head in all sorts of different ways . . . picturing a face on a name tag next to a name . . . but the silly rhyme thing is what works for me, even if it does have a few disadvantages.

Marilyn went through half a pack of Marlboro Reds before she walked up to the front door of the club and knocked. A troll with mottled gray-green skin, rootlike fingers, and a suit I might have admired if there hadn't been a troll in it let her inside the bar. *Huh. Trolls. It doesn't seem real.* I took a moment to text my location to the sheriff, even though I knew she wouldn't get it until dark, then settled back into my book. Or tried to. My brain kept screwing with me, taking me back to that section of *Don Quixote*, those next few lines, before Sancho decides that Don Quixote is insane:

"And do the enchanted sleep, now, señor?" asked Sancho.

"Certainly not," replied Don Quixote; "at least during those three days I was with them not one of them closed an eye, nor did I either."

I quoted the proverb that was Sancho's reply to that from memory—"Tell me what company thou keepest and I'll tell thee what thou art"—and sighed.

My dad quoted it at me when I told him I was going into journalism and moving to Void City. He'd been a high school English teacher before he retired, but he was a preacher off and on for my entire life and most of his. When quoting the Bible didn't work on me, he quoted the classics.

Being a vampire gives you a world of time to play the what-if game: "if" I hadn't left home, "if" I hadn't stopped to get coffee, "if" I'd worn different perfume.

Dad was right, though. It had been so easy for Eric to lure me in. He hadn't even been trying. It took no effort on his part at all, and bam, he had the upper hand. It seemed like such a good idea, too. When he told me he'd let me try and kill him, I'd thought, *This idiot will stand still for it? Sure. Whatever. I agree.*

There'd been a nobility in the way he let himself burn. The pain must have been incredible. But when it was over, he hadn't snapped at me, or yelled, or laughed . . . He hadn't even bragged. He'd said, "That's your shot at killing me this year, okay? Now go help my little girl."

And so I was keeping company with vampires. According to the classics, that made me just like them—just like any other vampire. I didn't like the proverb, but when I tried to disagree, I had no words to make a liar of them. No logical words. My little brother would always counter Dad's quotes with references from cartoons. Old ones. New ones. It could come from anywhere, but his favorites were lines from Looney Tunes characters. I knew what he would have said in response to Sancho or to my dad: "Well, you know what they say: If you can't beat 'em, join 'em."

Maybe there was something more to this guy and the people who followed him than I first suspected. My instincts seemed to think so. I let my head detach from my body, the tattoos on my neck stinging like blue blazes as they lit up, the copper plate at my neck cold against me as I levitated. My senses are better when I'm just a head. Inside the club, I sensed power. It felt blue, electric, and alive. I heard a man with a stern voice saying, "Again. I cannot train you if you cannot perform the simplest step of spiritual empowerment."

Marilyn made a noise that sounded like anything but defeat, and I let myself be whole again, felt the shock of reconnection, a jolt of electricity up and down my spine, one to which I'd never become accustomed. My e-reader was still clutched in the viselike grip that my body takes on when I'm not one with it. The gnawing thirst of bloodlust curled more in my teeth than in my belly, a desire to coat my tongue and slosh the precious red liquid across my gums, swirl it around in my mouth. I took a thermos of goat's blood and milk from my backpack, poured myself a full cup, and slugged it down, pretending I was on assignment in some Arab country where this was what they drank crossing the desert.

The blood tasted better than the milk. That's something I didn't like to admit to myself. Not like Greta. Greta loved the blood and didn't care who knew it. I was still pretending that I didn't, that I was something more than a monster.

I dropped my e-reader and the empty thermos lid to the concrete rooftop, scarcely caring that the e-reader didn't break and not jumping in surprise when the fans from the building's rooftop ventilation system kicked on. It didn't matter what I told myself or what my brother might have said to make me feel better. Sancho was right. The quote was right. Had I run back to the vampire hunters? No. I'd cut a deal with the vampires and started making friends.

"Jesus Christ." I ground my fist into my forehead, eyes closed tightly, teeth clenched. "I'm a damned vampire."

With perfect timing, my cell went off. The caller ID listed the number as Pythagoras, the wheelchair-bound vampire hunter who headed up the Pythagorean Theorem, a group of vampire hunters hell-bent on destroying vampires, demons, and whatever other supernatural monsters they encountered that couldn't prove themselves friendly to humankind. They knew what they were, and I wasn't one of them. Never had been. I thought of Greta, eyes blazing red, fangs out, reveling in her monstrosity. Were those the only two choices? Monster or hero?

I answered the phone. "What?"

"You're working with Courtney's daughter now?"

"You're the asshole who bailed in the middle of a fight, Pythagoras," I snapped. "What the hell was that?" The anger felt good.

"My attack orders were countermanded by a higher power."

"Who?"

"I'm not at liberty to say."

"Of all the—"

"I'm sorry about that." In the background on his end, people were doing combat drills, their shouts making the signal warble. "What I am at liberty to say is that we owe you a debt. Don't let them suck you in. Courtney and his daughter are monsters. The daughter more so than the father."

"No shit, Sherlock."

"If you need us, call us. We owe you a debt. If you need

information or if you feel lost and need us to end you"—his voice dropped low, intense—"you know where to find us."

I ended the call and stared back over at the club and watched the cars go by. All those people going about their lives, not knowing that at any moment, a monster could sweep down and tear their world to ribbons.

"I am not a monster," I said under my breath. "I am not a monster."

✦ 20 ✦

MARILYN

MY UNFAIR LADY—
A BRIEF INTERLUDE, 2 OF 3

Can you really not sense it all?" the angry bald man asked.

"You suck at this." I fished a cigarette out of my purse and lit up. As much as I hate the damn things, I'm addicted. When I was a thrall, each one was a victory over Roger. Each step took me closer to death and escape. It was the same way with alcohol and anything that did long-term damage in subtle ways. With faster methods unavailable to me, I didn't care what killed me first. I wanted out. With me gone, I thought Roger would screw up, try to take someone Eric cared about and be caught at it, or cross Greta, try to force his way into her pants . . . and then either Eric or Greta would put an end to his evil ass.

"You can't smoke in here," the Iversonian snapped.

I answered him with two careful rings of smoke, one inside the other, both of them aimed at his face. "I can smoke where I damn well please."

"Do not test me, Marilyn." The Iversonian gestured as if

drawing a sword from midair, and *bam*, there it was in his hand. It would have been more impressive if I hadn't seen it several times already. I'd been here, what, an hour? The man sure liked to whip it out.

"What are you going to do?" I asked. "Kill me?"

"No." He spun the sword in a practiced arc. "But you are wrong if you think death is beyond you."

"So the 'true' part of 'true immortal' is a load of crap?" To be honest, it was the first interesting thing the man had said since I walked in. He was a guy, but not in the same way as Eric. The Iversonian liked to have his way, and he liked to be a big man. Showing off was so important to him that he collected things and people, not because he cared about them but because he wanted to keep others from possessing them. A trophy hound. A trophy hound who thought the fighting part was important. Inside, I was too busy alternately mooning over and being pissed at Eric to care about boys and their toys.

"As a true immortal, your energy may never be destroyed, but that does not mean it can't be absorbed and repurposed by another."

"I already told you, I'm not going to suck it." I was this close to stubbing my cigarette out on his nice dance floor, but he wasn't doing anything wrong, so I ground it out on my palm instead. The pain was disappointing and brief. Probably like the Iversonian in bed. Not that I knew for sure, but it was an educated guess. For the first time in many years, the smell of cigarette smoke didn't smell so sweet. *Maybe I should try those darned electronic cigarettes.* I looked up to see the Iversonian staring at me. "Okay. Sorry. Tell me again."

"Close your eyes and concentrate," the Iversonian said without missing a beat.

"Do you know how hard it is to take a man seriously when he expects to be addressed with a definite article in front of his name?"

"Then call me Iver," he snapped. "Now concentrate."

I closed my eyes but not all the way. Not in the presence of any man I don't trust. He closed his eyes and started talking about breathing and breath control. I didn't have the heart to tell him that yoga hadn't worked for me when I was alive, either. I'm strong as an ox, and I can work all day long and still have plenty of fire left in my tank to—

Right. Enough of that, Marilyn. A younger body came with a libido I hadn't gotten used to having back yet.

"Anything?" asked Iver.

"No." My mind was too busy. I was looking at the second floor and wondering why there wasn't a satellite bar up there. When this place was busy, it had to be a pain in the ass to get to the club's lone bar. It was a waste of space. He could probably get away with only stocking more expensive liquor at the upstairs bar, forcing clientele to choose between the long trek down to the main bar or spending a few bucks extra.

It was an otherwise impressive club. High-end lighting and sound system. Oval central bar. The decor was a bit mod, but in a good way. I caught myself wondering how much he pulled down on Friday and Saturday nights.

"So how does that work, then?"

"What?" he asked.

I was thinking more about the staffing but decided I'd antagonized him enough and made it about something he thought of import. "The dying-but-not-dying thing."

"True immortals may kill other true immortals," he began, "by bringing their souls or life forces into direct opposition. They extend their personal spirit into their weapons and use them to sever the connection between an immortal and his or her body; then they clash, soul against soul, the stronger soul defeating the weaker and assimilating it into his or her own energy."

"How do you know who wins?"

"It can be a game of inches." He smiled, and for the first time since I'd met him, he looked vaguely attractive. I think it was the humility. He knew all too well. I didn't know how, but there was loss in his eyes, things he could never get back. Not possessions but something else. "The largest factor is will, force of personality, but experience plays into it also." He dismissed his sword, a short utilitarian blade that I thought looked Roman or Greek. It vanished in a swirl of blue that sank into the Iversonian, merging with the subtle yet ever-present glow he seemed to have lurking just under his skin.

"The most intriguing part of any immortal conflict is the Soul Battle. There's no telling what it's going to be like until the combatants are truly committed."

"The winner gets the loser's energy?"

"Something like that, but it's more complex." He gestured for me to follow him, and we walked toward the back office. All the shallowness fell away from him, leaving behind a gravity that got my full attention. "Take me, for example."

"No, thanks," I mouthed to myself.

His office was impressive, if a bit tacky. I don't know what it is with guys in this town and having living quarters in their offices, but his was basically a two-room apartment with a bathroom and kitchenette. It was shelves to hell and back, with various antique-looking knickknacks (some labeled, others not) covering every inch. The lone exception was a painting against the far wall that seemed to depict a Roman general with Timothy Dalton's eyes, Pierce Brosnan's hair, and Daniel Craig's rugged good looks.

"Who's the guy?"

"Me," he said softly. "As I was when I first became immortal."

"I thought immortals were changeless."

"We are." He stood in front of the painting so I could compare. "After a fashion. When the Soul Battle is close . . .

well, the closer the battle is, the greater the influence the loser's energy may have over the victor."

"What sort of influence?" It wasn't a good likeness. The nose was wrong; Iver's nose was too rounded and pronounced. The jawline was wrong. Even the skin tone was wrong.

"Oh, anything, likes . . . dislikes . . . even, as you no doubt noticed, physical changes. I"—he paused as if he found that "I" ironic—"lost my hair in a battle with an immortal known only as the Old Man in the Monastery." He chuckled. "He even stayed around for a bit, haunting me, as it were, until his energy could be processed . . . absorbed. If I'd been smart, I would have put up with his presence, let him erode over time, taking only the pieces of his knowledge that I wanted, but it's a long process. There are those we hate with such passion that we must eradicate them from existence."

"I don't understand why you wouldn't always do that. Just put up with the haunting, I mean."

He sighed. "Well, self-control is usually hard to maintain when the one you hate is forever at your side, nattering in your ear, ready to take up the fight again. And haunting isn't always all there is to it. Sometimes the weight of an enemy spirit is enough to cause other problems: hallucinations, fever, confusion, the sense of being unstuck in time."

"Remind me to never kill another true immortal," I said.

"It's not all bad," he continued. "I gained an unrivaled knowledge of wines from Emile, the bastard, and it's not uncommon to learn languages that your opponent speaks, or to gain other tidbits of knowledge."

"You get an unwanted face-lift in the bargain?"

He nodded. "From time to time. There is a reason true immortals rarely risk . . . confrontations of such . . . finality."

"That's the first intelligent thing I've heard you say all night."

"Of course it is." Iver winked. "You have the wrong impression of me."

"I do?"

"Of course you do." He closed his eyes, a slow smile spreading across his lips, warming his features. "It is to be expected in one so young."

"Young? I'm—" I caught myself.

"Under a century, yes?"

I nodded.

"To someone your age, a woman in particular, I would believe you think me a . . . trophy hound. You think I care about possessing . . . people and things . . . to an extent that is . . ." He touched his chin thoughtfully. "You are probably right. But you should not let that keep you from learning what I have to teach you. After all, despite what you may have heard, my obsession with collecting is relatively recent and . . . not entirely of my own making, if you follow?"

"No, I don't. Oh, you mean it was part of a Soul Burn?"

"Yes." He shook his head again. "Or maybe no."

"Well, which is it?"

"It is hard to quantify." He held up a hand, warding off further comment. "I have slain other immortals over the years. Many, actually—don't take that as bragging, it simply is. As a result, a true immortal can reach a sort of tipping point where cumulative Soul Burns begin to add up, and each additional Burn, despite the insignificance to the whole being, can make a tremendous difference when weighed against the original whole."

"The core becomes . . . what? Diluted?"

"There are certain special talents some possess to minimize the effect or limit it, but"—and he seemed proud of this—"I possess none of them."

"You had one too many?"

"You could say that." He looked at the painting again and

smiled vacantly as if momentarily somewhere else, then led me over to a tablet computer framed on the wall. The resolution was so high that at first I mistook it for an actual painting, until the image changed. Old photos appeared on the large surface. He touched it and typed in a code on the keypad that appeared. A few folders later, and a new slide show ran across the screen. The Iversonian wasn't in all of the pictures, but the ones in which he featured showed him as very much the same man physically as the man with whom I now spoke. He looked dapper and happy and—

"Is that Talbot?"" I reached out tentatively, pausing the stream of captured images.

Talbot, looking very much the same as modern-day Talbot, stood smiling next to the Iversonian. They were linked arm in arm with another man, a man with sullen eyes and thin severe lips who smiled as well, though the smile didn't reach his eyes. They stood in front of a building—

"Is that the Lovett Building?"

"Yes and yes," he answered. "The other man is Isaiah Emmanuel Lovett."

"You and Talbot look pretty chummy for a white and a black during Prohibition."

"There are very few things in true immortal society that have progressed so far in advance of mortal society as have race relations. Another . . . ah . . . benefit of absorbing the ones you kill as literally as we do.

"There are exceptions," he continued, "among those of us whose talent or will is so strong that the effects of Soul Burning are negligible . . . or, as I mentioned before, those who allow themselves to be haunted by their victims long enough for each persona to surrender to the inevitable slow ebb. Though I think you have mistaken me again."

"Really?"

"Yes." He pointed to the figure who resembled him. "That

man is Lovett. He and Talbot were very fond of each other, and I am the one who came between them. I killed Lovett, and the Burn was so shocking, so intense, that Talbot thought I'd been completely overwhelmed and that I was Lovett. And we were happy for a while."

"You . . . and Talbot? But I thought he was strictly a skirt chaser."

"Talbot chases whatever interests him, Marilyn." Iver looked at the picture again. "The parts attached to the individual rarely enter the equation once his interest is piqued. Though I believe his wife would say he's just being eccentric."

"Talbot's married?"

"Indeed he is." Iver touched my shoulder. "Dezbah is an impressive creature, as, I suspect, are you." He pulled me to him and forced me into an embrace, his mouth on mine.

The explosion of power came instinctively. I needed to be stronger, and I was. *He* flew across the room before I realized I intended to throw him. I charged after him, but the expression on his face—a knowing amusement—and the laughter caught me short. "You did that on purpose to make me tap in to my power!"

"Of course." And then I saw his power. Flowing around him and through him like a billowing cloud of azure blue, his soul roiled about him, tendrils reaching out in all directions, extending out of sight through the floor, the walls, the ceiling. "I had to find out how to reach you, and the more I stood here and read your mind, the clearer it became: You are a fighter. I never intended to hurt you, so your essence never felt the need to respond."

"You can read my mind?"

"Why else would I have agreed to train you?" Iver did a standing kip-up like you see in the movies. "The man you love has taken the attention of the mouser who was once mine. Through you, I can get a sense of the man and perhaps understand what fascinates my blackbird so utterly. Is this going to be a problem?"

"Are you going to stop reading my mind?"

"Of course not. You will stop me from reading it when you are able." The blue cloud of energy rolled around him again, leaving some sort of Roman legionnaire's armor in its wake. I knew the sword was next, and I didn't like the idea of him being armed and me defenseless. Running might have been smarter, but I've never liked to run. I charged in and grabbed at the energy, the part that felt like a sword to me, and that gladius was in my hand instead of his.

"Excellent." He slapped his hands together. "Now give it back or I shall be forced to take it back."

"Stop reading my mind," I repeated.

"No," he said softly.

"Then I think I'll hang on to the sword."

He gestured again, drawing a spear out of his cloud of energy.

"How many weapons do you have in there?" I asked.

"Only the ones I cherish." He lunged, and I barely managed to bat the spear away. "Defend yourself."

I should have simply handed his sword back, but let's face it. I'm too damn stubborn.

✦ 21 ✦

TABITHA

A BRIEF INTERLUDE, 3 OF 3

Just as I was thinking there was nothing more pathetic than a vampire browsing through a course catalog for her local college, *TMZ* came on. I had no intention of listening to celeb babble, so I shut it off with the remote. The course catalog glared up at me from my little glass table, and I snatched it up again.

Go to college. Me. Why on earth would I ever want to do that? That was one response. The other made me feel even worse. *Maybe,* the other part of me thought, *maybe if I go to college and get a degree in something really impressive, he'll want me back.* There was another thought, though, so I guess there were three. *What if I? I mean . . . Grrr . . .*

"Stupid." I banged my palm against my forehead. "Stupid!" And again. "Stupid!" The third time, I hit myself hard enough that I saw sparks in front of my eyes.

Why the hell did what he said matter so much?

"Eric Courtney is a no-good, lying, cheating piece of shit."

On the coffee table, my cell vibrated as it received a text. I got up out of my chair, dropping the course catalog on the glass table in my breakfast nook. I won't say this apartment was better than the suite of rooms I had at the Highland Towers before Eric totaled the building, but it was nice.

I was still downtown, so hunting was easy, and there was plenty of space for one. The kitchen I rarely used had all-new stainless-steel appliances and opened onto a breakfast nook, which was where I liked to read. Even now my e-reader was plugged in to charge. I wasn't sure whether I liked it enough to do most of my reading on it, but Talbot had given it to me (he called it a late wedding present), so I was trying to deal with it.

Rounding my couch to reach the cell, I caught sight of the city outside my window and sighed, wishing I had a deck or a balcony. Instead, there was a ledge running around the outside of each floor of the complex. Pigeons seemed to like it, but I don't know that anyone else got any use out of it.

He's certainly a cheater, but I disagree about the rest.

It was from Talbot. I looked around the room, listening hard for the sound of his breath or his heartbeat.

Where R U?

Close

What do U wnt?

I brought the rest of your things.

What things?

I'd had a lot of clothes, but that had basically been it. I hadn't even owned a computer, though I bought one when I got my cable and Internet hooked up. The laptop was in my bedroom. Eric owned a PC, so I went with a Mac just to annoy him, even though, in retrospect, I'm not sure how something he didn't and wouldn't know about could accomplish that.

Can I come in?

I saw him waving at me from the ledge outside my window, and I smiled. We'd had a thing, Talbot and me. It had been short but fun and had demonstrated why mousers make bad boyfriends. Everything went along just swimmingly until he decided he had somewhere else to be.

"These windows don't open," I said, raising my voice to make sure he could hear me.

I can't come in through the door, Greta's sitting out there waiting to kill you.

"You've got to be kidding me."

Nope. Never mind. I'll just leave it out here.

Reaching into the pocket of his charcoal-gray suit, Talbot withdrew a sock, a thong, and a piece of paper. The wind picked up, momentarily causing the items to flutter and flap. When it died back down, he reached into his other pocket and pulled out a metallic paperweight in the likeness of a cat. Gingerly crouching on the narrow ledge, he placed the cat atop the thong, sock, and . . . was that a check?

It's a check. Best of luck with Her Slaughterness.

Pausing only long enough to give me a wink, he leaped upward, vanishing into the night. God, that mouser is a great lay! Check. Check. Check. A check from Eric, no doubt. The so-called divorce settlement. I walked across to the window to peek down at the rectangular promissory note and counted the zeroes I could see. How much did Eric think our time together had been worth? What price did he put on our—

I must have read that wrong.

Four.

Zero.

Zero.

Zero.

Zero.

Zero.

Zero.

Decimal point.

Zero.

One.

Four million dollars and one cent.

Vampire speed has its drawbacks. One of them is how easy it can be to punch through a window to grab something you want. You decide you want it. You think about it. And you do it. Sometimes before you've even realized that maybe it would be just as effective to turn into a bird or cat, sneak out through the ventilation ducts, and then (in bird form) fly down to get the check.

In the "for" space, Eric had written simply *The Only Apology You Get.*

It was over. Really over. In the absence of Eric, of the hope of Eric, the real problem that had been haunting me came through loud and clear. It wasn't a fear of Greta but of . . . I looked back at the course catalog for Void City University. What if I was too dumb to go to college? High school seemed so far away. And what the hell use was a degree in dance? I . . .

"Crap."

The wind blew as I gathered up the thong, sock, check, and paperweight. I carried them into my bedroom, down the short hall, past the economy washer and dryer concealed in the hall closet—devices I doubted I'd ever personally use.

Lying on the king-size bed, what's-his-name looked peaceful. His breath came in light shallow puffs. His skin was pale but not vampire pale. I wanted a thrall, someone to force me awake in the morning so I didn't waste my days, someone like Eric's whores, who cared even if it wasn't a romantic thing. This guy wasn't it. He was nice in bed, and his abs were fine, as was the rest of him, but— I walked back down the hall and looked out the spy hole in my front door. There was Greta, sitting patiently next to a headless body.

"Greta," I called through the door, "what's the penalty for a vampire killing a human in the comfort of the vampire's own lair?"

"That's not a lair," Greta grumbled. "It's more an abode."

"Okay." I scoffed. "Abode, then."

"You're not spooky enough to have a lair."

"Fine. Abode."

"Dracula would have a lair."

"For Christ's sake, Greta." My hands clenched into fists involuntarily. "I agree with you. It's not a lair. My apartment counts as a fucking abode."

Then I sensed the other vampire. The power level felt squirrelly, and instead of my usual sensation, kind of a 3-D hologram effect, all I saw was a floating head and the name "Evelyn." She felt like she hadn't been a vampire much longer than I had.

"What the—?" I turned in time to see the floating head with blond hair coast in through the window.

"So you're Tabitha," Evelyn said after a moment. "We sensed each other earlier, near the Demon Heart, but you were preoccupied."

"What?" I asked. "Are you the new mom now?"

"I don't even know what you're talking about."

"You haven't heard her do the 'One Mom, Two Mom, Red Mom, Blue Mom' crap?"

"Shut up, Tabitha," Greta growled through the door. "I sent her to pick up your crap up off the ledge, but then you already did that, and instead of coming back, like a good deputy, LEGO-Head took it upon herself to investigate."

"LEGO-head?" I asked.

"Because my head comes off," Evelyn explained. "It's a whole thing."

"I want to talk to you about something," Greta called. "Let me in."

"You're here to kill me?"

"No." She sounded disappointed. "Dad told me not to kill you. I just want to talk."

"And you didn't just kick in the door?" That seemed incredibly polite for Greta. Maybe she really did want to talk.

"Do you want me to kick the door in?"

"No," I said quickly. I let her in, and Evelyn flew out past me to reconnect to her body.

Greta surveyed the room as if cataloging possible weapons before she walked over to my sofa and plopped down on it. Her "deputy" came in a few moments later, glowing marks on her neck fading from red to black, then pale, as she wrapped a black scarf around it to cover the marks and what looked like a thin line of copper. Then she walked over to the window and stood in the breeze.

"Call the window people and have them fix the window, Evie," Greta said imperiously.

Evelyn rolled her eyes but whipped out her smartphone and began scrolling through listings.

"Bill it to My Dad Killed Your Dad Web Designs," Greta continued. "I have an account with almost everybody in town."

"Web design?" Evelyn and I asked.

Greta scowled. "What, did you think I sponged off my dad

for money?" She eyed my check. "Jobs are like humans: stupid but necessary. I picked one that let me work really hard up-front and in spurts but could be set on autopilot if something came up."

No one knew what to say to that, so we all stared at one another uncomfortably. "I didn't know that," I said, more to break the silence than anything else.

"So now you know." Greta put her feet up on my coffee table. "Now I want to know. Did you teach Dad anything?"

"Yeah," I said, "I taught him what a clitoris was. All those women before"—I clucked my tongue—"and he'd never figured it out."

Evelyn snorted, but Greta vanished from her position on the couch, reappearing in front of me. I expected glowing eyes and fangs, but instead, she smiled her bright, happy little-girl smile, and the fear that hadn't quite managed to rear its ugly head when I'd found out she was waiting outside my door came in waves so fierce that I felt sick to my stomach.

"How's the arm?" Her hand touched my shoulder, and it took all my self-control reserves not to jump out the window and run away or pop my claws and attack. Neither was the right move. Me snarking at Greta hadn't been the right move, either. I've never met another being like Greta; not even Eric's hose-bag ex—sex bomb Irene was close. Greta's particular brand of crazy was rarefied and fierce.

"It's fine now." I rolled my shoulder as if to demonstrate.

"Good." Greta sat back down. "I'll ask again. Did you teach Dad anything and"—she held up a finger—"I don't mean sexual. Something with his powers? Something unique?"

"What? You mean my special power?" I started to sit down but caught myself. I didn't want to sit that close to her. I needed to be able to move and react. She may be faster than me, but I'm no slouch. I wouldn't go down without a fight. "My seeming human?"

"Okay," Greta said. "Yeah. Sure. That. Or anything else, really."

I thought back on our time together. Had I ever taught Eric anything? I didn't think I had. What was it he'd said about my powers that time? I opened my mouth, hesitating before speaking.

"He once told me that any power I had, he—" The memory washed over me. I had just been turned into a vampire, and Eric was being such an asshat about everything. I know now why he did that. He did it to push me away because he was afraid of hurting me any more than he already had. It's how he operates. "He was yelling at me shortly after I turned. He said something about being the biggest, baddest motherfucker on the planet and that any vampire power I had, he either had it and could use it better or he didn't need to use it, because he had a stronger power or a better way of doing the same thing."

"Did you ever see him do it?" Greta asked. "Seem human better than you?"

"No," I answered, "no, I think he was just talking big and trying to keep me in line. When he found out I was a Living Doll, it seemed to impress him, and he never said anything about the power thing again. Why?"

"No reason." Greta got up, joining Evelyn at the window. "I think that's everything. You can kill the guy in your bedroom as long as you dispose of the body or pay someone to do it for you."

"One more question," Evelyn said, "if you don't mind."

"Sure." I shrugged. "Why would I mind a little more interrogation in my evening?"

"Have you noticed anything different about the way you sense Eric at night recently?"

"What do you mean?" Greta asked.

"You do the same thing," Evelyn said. "Sometimes I can detect you, like I do other vampires, and sometimes not. I assume that's a special power you have, but Eric . . . during the day, I sense him just as I would any other Vlad, but at night"—she shook her head—"not once."

"I didn't notice," I told her. "He's spoken in my head, but it might have been different. I don't remember."

"I'm going to see if I can get out the same way Talbot did," Greta said, directing her statement more to Evelyn than to me. With her questions answered and no permission to kill me, I was little more than furniture to Greta. "I'll meet you back at Fang."

We watched as Greta crept out on to the ledge, following Talbot's method of egress.

Evelyn stayed long enough to arrange for my window to be repaired, pausing to confirm when would be a good time. Before she left, she offered her hand, and I shook it.

"Sorry about the circumstances," she said with a smile, "but it was nice meeting you."

"Yeah." I thought that over and realized it actually had been nice to meet her. "Nice meeting you, too. Are you sure you're not Eric's new girl?"

"I'm his cousin," Evelyn said. "He murdered me a few years ago, and the Courtney Family Curse brought me back." She touched the scarf with her hand. "Like this."

"Did"—I paused again—"did you used to be on television or something? You look familiar."

"Guilty as charged," she said. "Former news anchor."

"Hard to do that as a . . . what did you say you are?"

"*Nukekubi*," she said. "Not really. We still show up in mirrors and on camera. It's the whole having-been-very-publicly-murdered thing that's the real problem." Evelyn looked over at my course catalog and weighed whether or not she should say anything. "You want a little free advice?"

"Why not?"

"If you're thinking about it, going to college, then go.

List yourself as undecided and take classes that interest you until you figure out what you want to do." She picked up the catalog and tapped biology and chemistry, some of the hard sciences. "And try some of the stuff you assume you won't be any good at. I had no idea journalism was my thing until I took a course on a whim. I thought I was going to be a computer programmer. I have a niece who didn't realize how good at biology she was until she took a freshman-level course. Now she's a research scientist."

"Seriously?"

She nodded. "You're in a world where all the older male vampires are going to assume that all you're good for is what's below your neck and above your knees. It's up to you to remember that's your least important aspect."

"Thanks, Mom."

"You're welcome, dear." Evelyn patted my shoulder. "Do we need to talk about tampons next?"

"Ugh, no."

Evelyn laughed. "Good." She picked up my cell and started keying something in. "My cell is programmed into your cell now. If you need to talk, call me." She stepped backward out the window, and my jaw dropped open when she hovered there.

"That," I said, "is so unfucking fair."

✦ 22 ✦

ERIC

HARD TASKS

The hardest thing for me was waiting a week. I'd never gone without Marilyn for so long, not since the Courtney Family Curse (and a healthy dose of stubbornness) had brought me back from the dead as a vampire/revenant. Not while she was alive.

When she died the first time, it was hard, so hard I almost blocked it out. I got busy, and I had things to do. I had stuff to do now, too, but the plans I'd made, I wished I could go over with her. I wanted her advice and her approval. I needed her to hate my plans or love them, or slap me in the face, or laugh. I wanted her to blow smoke in my face and tell me to go to hell. Instead, I tried to keep everything going according to The Plan without her. I made myself stick to the regimen Magbidion had helped me work out. He still looked bad, but the artificial locus point did seem to help. It brought in the customers, too.

Supernatural types liked being around it, like freezing Boy Scouts crowding around a bonfire on a cold camping trip. We had to keep them out of the street, they loved the damn thing so much. That was part of the plan, too. N_CASE_ OF_HUNTERS1 called to let me know the face-to-face with

Pythagoras and his loonies had gone well. They were all on board. All I had to do was not screw it up. That can be hard to do when screwing up is your single greatest talent.

By Friday, though, it was either go see Marilyn (which would royally screw up The Plan) or follow up with "Popsie" and find out exactly what Greta had agreed to with regard to the Population Control issue. After her few sentences the night of the chupacabra, I'd done some asking around. Turned out Talbot wasn't the right being to ask about Population Control. Magbidion knew all about it. At Mags's insistence, I made my visit during the day, when things were easier on him.

It wasn't the first time I'd been to the Lovett Building, but I hoped this time I'd get out without punching through walls or getting shot. The last time I'd been there was to visit a demon who'd had Marilyn's soul. It had been a trap, but then again, isn't it always?

This time, rather than riding in a purse, I came in via Beatrice's ample bosom. Nestled there, I was warm and could easily poke my mousy noggin out to see or smell better what was going on. Bea wore a woman's business suit with a blue suit jacket, matching skirt, and a cream-colored silk blouse.

"It's fine." She pushed open one of the multiple glass doors in the lobby. "You're warming up now."

She sounded awfully chipper for a woman with a dead mouse down her blouse. Her hair was in an attractive updo with ringlets to straddle the line between businesslike and sexy. Jewelry-wise, she wore two golden ear studs and a tiny golden padlock on a short gold chain around her neck—it had become a sign, to those who knew to look for it, of a thrall going about her vampire's business.

I smelled melons, strawberries, oranges, and lemons, each mixed with water but in a separate carafe. "The fruit wasn't here last time," I squeaked.

"They've redone the lobby," she said softly. "Higher

security. It looks like a hotel lobby, and now you have to walk past two guards to get into the complex proper. I think they're demons. And there's something like a metal detector, but it feels . . . off."

"What about the glass?"

"I don't know if it's safe for vampires or not." She chewed her lip. "It wasn't last time."

I thought I'd be fine going through the detectors, but I couldn't be certain without Magbidion or Talbot there to verify what they detected. Daytime should have been relatively safe, but—

"Lord Eric?" I heard the shuffle of robes accompanied by the arrival of someone who smelled of sulfur and lime. Whoever it was, he moved wrong, and the heartbeat was thready at best.

"I bear Lord Eric." Beatrice's breasts swelled (maybe with pride, maybe with something else) when she said that. Her high-heeled shoes clicked against the floor as she walked across the room to meet the new arrival.

"This way, please." Soft but firm, the voice sounded of confidence tainted by obedience.

"No." Beatrice shifted.

Glancing toward the detectors, I guessed.

"Ma'am?"

"Lord Eric doesn't walk through any mystical detection system without a Mages Guild rep or his own personal mage on hand to verify the purpose and extent of the scrying capacity. It's a rule."

He hesitated.

"Fine." Beatrice's heels clacked firmly on the floor. She was heading for the door. "Tell Popsie that he is to report to Lord Eric at the Demon Heart within the hour, and arrange to have yourself punished appropriately."

"That's a little much, don't you think?" I squeaked.

"Lord Eric says an hour is too much time," Beatrice said,

deliberately misunderstanding me. "He would like Popsie to be waiting at the Demon Heart when we arrive."

"It's . . . it's okay, ma'am. Please." I expected fear, but this guy was more angry than afraid; the stammer came not from hesitance but a restrained desire to commit violence. "Please bear the Lord Eric this way. Around the detectors."

Beatrice paused but didn't turn. Her head cocked to one side, like she was listening to instructions.

"Please," the lime-and-sulfur-scented man added. That "please" hurt him deep down, and I knew instantly he'd never like me. He'd do as he was told, maybe, but not because he wanted to do it. I hated that. He hadn't even met me.

"Very well." Beatrice allowed herself a reluctant reverse course. This part, the High Society bullshit, she knew how to do quite well. She'd done it before she'd been my thrall, back when Lady Gabriella had been her vampire. With Rachel gone, Bea was my most experienced thrall. All the stuff other vampires do to prove to each other whose penis truly is the longest . . . I hate that stuff, too, as surely as I despise the idea of anyone's being forced to obey me for no better reason than that I can kill him. I felt like a monster. Monster mouse.

We made it to the bay of elevators. If I recalled correctly, there were eight, four on each side of the corridor. The *click-clack* of Beatrice's heels acted almost like sonar (which only gives me a headache when, as a bat, I try to use it) but even when I was a mouse, it revealed certain things about my surroundings. The corridor sounded the same shape and size. The soft metallic click of a panel being opened and gloved fingers punching in numbers on a keypad. Up above us, the drive motors began moving immediately. In the food court, farther into the interior area of the lobby than the bank of elevators, someone ordered Szechuan beef with double fried rice and a spring roll instead of an egg roll.

People laughed, conversed, ate, and watched the news and

weather scroll by on what sounded like five or six different televisions. Even farther inside, it sounded like a book fair of sorts was under way. Normal people in an abnormal building. I flashed back to my memory, the one that had messed me up earlier, about the Murcheson case. The wolf had said: "That fat bastard." It had all felt wrong. Gritting my tiny mouse teeth, I closed my eyes.

I like to bury my head in the sand, to ignore things that are going on around me. If my girlfriend is cheating on me, I'd rather not know. If my best friend is robbing me blind, I'd rather not know that, either. I prefer the lie. But once I know, once I can't ignore it any longer, then I act, with finality.

Back then, the magic that was used to control more honest members of the police force had erased my memory and made me forget about the talking wolf. I snorted as the elevator doors opened and we went inside.

"If you don't mind my asking—" said the man.

"Yes?" Beatrice said quickly, to trip the guy up and put him off guard.

"Where is Lord Eric?"

Beatrice laughed at that. It was the same laugh you give someone who's just asked you an impertinent personal question that you have no intention of answering.

"Sorry." His voice, more muffled than usual, told me he'd looked down and away, so I used the opportunity to mist free of Beatrice's blouse, my eyes closed against the vertigo that such a transformation normally induced. Not staying mist for long seemed to help. Beatrice breathed out loudly as I coalesced in front of her, making it look like I'd been hiding within her and had erupted as mist rather than being a mouse and jumping out of her bra. Hot-out-of-the-dryer warmth wrapped itself around me, and my clothes re-formed . . . only this time I'd manifested not just in a WELCOME TO THE VOID shirt, jeans, combat boots, etc., but with three Swatches on my left arm and sand on my boots. WTF?

The night I turned Greta rolled back over me, and I shuddered, the smell of the sea air near the beach where I'd done the deed and turned her on her twenty-first birthday filling my nostrils. What was going on with my brain? Well, okay, Alzheimer's, true, but still . . .

"What's the sunlight situation upstairs?" I asked Beatrice instead of leper boy because apparently, that was how this worked.

"Lady Greta informed me that it was quite safe." She looked at hooded-robe guy.

"Yes, there is no danger of sunlight exposure," he said.

"What's your name?" I asked.

"I'm Todd."

"Todd?" I raised an eyebrow.

"Yes."

"And you're a chupacabra, Todd?"

He nodded.

"I didn't think you guys were real." The doors opened, unleashing the scents of sulfur and lime, and vanilla-scented candles meant to mask more unpleasant odors. Things smelled old and sick. Dried blood odors weren't immediately recognizable, because the blood was filled with taint. "Being a vampire may have its drawbacks, but being a chupacabra must really suck."

Heartbeats came from all directions, each with a thready beat similar to Todd's. Hundreds of heartbeats but no voices other than mine. I walked down a row of ledger-covered tables. Cracked and drying wallpaper covered the walls, the burgundy color of the paper faded, adding to the appearance of decay. Mange-ridden canines rested in dilapidated doggie beds, opening their eyes long enough to view and dismiss me as I passed. Robed figures, like Todd, moved about the place, creating a susurrus of swishing cloaks. Yes, susurrus. Remember, I was educated long before No Child Left Behind. Hell, I even know what "opprobrious" means.

"You guys must hate noise." I watched for signs of flinching when I spoke and caught a few robed dudes doing it.

"Our hearing is very sensitive," Popsie said as Todd broke away from us. I don't know how I knew it was Popsie, but he was obviously the guy. Face blackened and skull-like, he reminded me of the "Masque of the Red Death" outfit the Phantom wore in Andrew Lloyd Webber's *Phantom of the Opera*. His clothes and surroundings showed fewer signs of wear, tear, and decay.

I held out my hand, and he shook it with a firm (if brief) grip. As he released my hand, the air grew stale and oppressive. The back of my throat tickled. Popsie watched me with steely, sunken eyes. So I announced myself, forcing my mystical presence out into the surrounding area: a mental roar. I don't do it a lot, but it's a way to demonstrate one's level of power to other vampires. I'd learned that there are other supernaturals who feel it, too. Popsie and his ilk counted among them.

The oppression faded only slightly, so I roared again, pushing my mental shout farther and louder, again and again, until Popsie took a step back and the dogs in the hall whined in their sleep.

"You screwing with me, Popsie?" I growled the words, fangs out, eyes flashing red, their light turning his robes the color of blood. Outside, I felt a patrol car stop. *It's okay, Sal*, I said mentally, and the car rolled on.

"I'm the Prime Contagion, Lord Eric." He bowed stiffly. "I must make the challenge, and you must answer it, so that my outbreak understands that you are exactly what we fear you are. That we may accept you as our better, as stronger than we."

"Well, whoopty-doo." I touched Beatrice on the arm and pulled her a little closer to stave off the cold. "Looks like I'm the biggest badass at the Ugly Motherfuckers Convention. Are we good now?"

"I concede your power and authority." He spoke like he was transferring command of the *Enterprise* to me, all formal and brisk. "We must, however, still discuss the matter of the culling of the humans. I had not planned for such a marked decrease in the death rate, Lord Eric."

"Just Eric," I corrected.

"Very well, then . . . Eric. What would you have us do about the population? I can run you through the bulk-population-increase plans we have slated for the next few decades—"

"Nope." I shoved a pile of papers to one side and leaned on the table. "First, tell me this. Do chupacabra have to feed from humans?"

"We prefer livestock, as a general rule." Popsie cleared his throat. "Cows, goats, large mammals. Feeding . . ." He trailed off, averting his gaze in a look I'd seen on Greta's face when she had something to confess that she didn't want to tell.

"Feeding?" I prompted.

"Feeding." He crossed to sit in a large overstuffed chair upholstered in crushed velvet, but stopped himself as if he were loath to sit while I was still standing. "It's a communal thing for us. We still live, so we don't require as large a quantity of liquid sustenance as do vampires. Also, feeding on livestock keeps us out of the way of the more aggressive predators. We can fight them, but we prefer not to do so."

"Good." I nodded. "Go ahead and sit if you want. I don't care."

Popsie gathered his robes, lifting them slightly, and sat.

"What happens if we don't increase the culling to previous levels?"

"Then the population of the city would rise by as much as

ten thousand mortals a year." He gripped the arms of the chair. "A disaster."

"Why exactly is this a disaster?"

"It would violate our treaties with the surrounding territories."

One of the benefits of being as powerful as I've been in the past is what I call the eight-hundred-pound-gorilla syndrome. Like that old joke: Where does an eight-hundred-pound gorilla sit? Anywhere he wants. It's the same with Emperor vampires. Where do Emperor vampires go? Wherever the Emperor vampires want to go. That's mostly true with Vlads, too. As a result, there were lots of rules I'd never had to learn, systems of checks and balances, because nobody wanted to come by and try to enforce them on me. I've been all over the country, and no vampire has ever shown up to ask me to leave or check in with someone or follow guidelines. I did get assessed the occasional Fang fee, but that made a lot more sense now that I remembered more of my life. Even that was only in or around Void City.

Elsewhere, vampires tended to stay the hell out of my way.

"What treaties?" I sat down on Popsie's desk. Eight-hundred-pound-gorilla syndrome.

Popsie laughed. "The nonaggression pacts with our surrounding territories." He waved his hand absently in the air as if I should have seen a mental chart or a map.

"Okay." I nodded. "What territories?"

Even Beatrice scoffed at that one, but she covered it well, pretending she'd swallowed wrong.

"Surely you know about—"

"Pretend I don't," I interrupted.

"The United States of America and most of Canada and Mexico are divided into territories of various sizes and shapes."

"What, like Balkanized states or something?" I asked.

"Exactly. Each one is ruled by a supernatural group or individual, some by vampires, some by Shifters, others by immortals; it varies. Void City is one of the smaller ones, but it has historically been one of the most stable, too."

"So what do these treaties have to do with the population?" I rubbed my eyes and took a deep breath just to feel my lungs expand. This wasn't part of The Plan—how could it be when I hadn't seen it coming?—but I knew what I was going to do. My cell vibrated in my pocket, but I ignored it.

Places like the former Soviet Union and Czechoslovakia were broken up into squabbling little states, but not my country. My country was one people. We disagreed. We fought. We acted stupid together, and we were a political nightmare, but the United States, in my day, when I was alive, when I fought in World War II and Korea, we were the best damn country on the planet. Human, revenant, vampire, immortal, half-n-half . . . whatever else I am, I'm proud as hell to be an American.

"We keep the size of our territory within certain pre-agreed-upon parameters. Our neighbors do the same, and we all agree not to encroach on one another," Popsie said.

"Fuck that." I got off the desk. "Are you in the mood for a change?"

"Perhaps." Popsie leaned forward, the light of my glowing eyes casting his face in bronze.

"You make this the best city you can." I slapped the top of the desk, and everyone jumped. "I want this place to be prosperous and growing. I want Void City to be a place where the American dream comes true."

"That will surely antagonize—"

"Yeah." I nodded. "Let's do that. Let's antagonize the fuck out of them."

"But it will cause a new blood war."

"Good." I looked him in the eye. "Then let's do that. I

fought in two wars when I was alive. My side won both. Let's act like the good old U.S. of A. and throw our weight around."

"But the humans," Popsie said, rising to his feet. "They might notice."

"Good." I turned, taking Beatrice's hand and heading for the elevator. All the chupacabras stared at me as I passed. "It's about damn time."

◆ 23 ◆

ERIC

CRAZY THEY CALL ME

By the end of the next month, it was clear people thought I'd lost my mind. And maybe they were right. Magbidion sat on my bed at the Pollux, eyes closed but still talking. I'd stopped listening a while ago, though he wasn't trying to convince me of anything. It was all venting, and if it made him feel better, I saw no reason to shut him down. My tie had my full attention, anyway.

Since turning into a vampire, I'd been unable to tie my own tie. I've always had to watch myself in a mirror to do it correctly. As a result, for the few occasions I've had to wear one, one of the girls (or Marilyn) has tied the darn thing for me, but not at night. Then I tie it myself, looking at my reflection in the mirror. If I'm not careful, I find myself staring in the mirror each evening after I change. Since I haven't seen myself in so many years, my mental self-image has degraded, colored by years of killing. I expect to see a hideous beast when I look in the mirror. When I don't, it surprises me.

The suit was a shock, too. I looked good in it. The suit was for the annual Master/Thrall Social at the Irons Club. I'd never heard of the damn thing before, but Beatrice had informed me that, as head honcho of Void City, I absolutely had to show up, and I had to bring the thrall I wanted others to view as my "most valuable and important thrall." Doing so would announce that person as my majordomo or chief executive assistant or number one slave, allowing the thrall to deliver instructions to other vampires on my behalf and marking the thrall as inviolate, for the purposes of vampiric political games and attacks.

What it reminded me of was the prom.

The door opened, and the scents of lilac and honeysuckle filled the room. "Why, don't you look all dolled up and ready for prom."

I looked away from the mirror in the restroom at Dad's five-and-dime, then shook my head when I saw Betty Lou. She wasn't even dressed yet. Hadn't started. "And you know what happens after the prom, right?" Betty Lou said with a smile, and I blushed. I felt indecent with her standing next to me as I tried to tie my tie. The restroom wasn't a place for women, well, not women and men together. Unmarried men and women.

"Could you please wait outside, Betty?"

"So I'm Betty now, huh?" She moved in close, her hands teasing the tie out of mine. "Okay, sugar. I can be Betty if you want. Do you want to try that taste thing I've been working on?" She licked her lips and patted the inside of her thigh.

"It wouldn't be right," I said, trying to keep my eyes off of her legs. She was wearing a pair of really tight pants, and I wondered why her mother had let her out of the house in them. Then again, maybe she'd sewed them herself and her mother didn't know. "Even if I weren't leaving tomorrow—"

"Leaving? Where you going to, honey? Ain't nobody said a word to me about you going on a trip."

Roger sat up from where he'd been lying down on some old piece of furniture, a bed or something. I couldn't understand why a bed would be back here, but maybe Dad thought he could sell it. Or maybe it was a special order . . .

I rubbed my eyes. When had Betty and I walked out into the stockroom? It was more appropriate, but I didn't remember moving . . .

"Yes," Roger said shakily, "where are you going tomorrow, Eric?"

"Come on, Betty." She snugged up my tie even though she wasn't paying attention to it anymore. I went on, "We've talked about this. I'm going to enlist. Fight the Nazis and the Japs. I have to do it. I can't hide behind the seminary while brave men are out there fighting! I can't do it, I tell ya. My country needs me, and I can't turn a deaf ear to her call."

"Oh, fuck me running," Betty Lou said. "He's doing it again."

"Betty." My chest hurt, and I looked at Roger, not for help but for things I couldn't think of, so I turned back to Betty Lou. "What's gotten into you? You shouldn't be talking like that, not in front of Roger. Or at all." I took her hands in mine. They felt cold to the touch. "And I told you, we can't. We just . . ." Sweat, real sweat, I don't know why, but in the back of my head, it seemed wrong. Shouldn't it have been red?

"You can't be Betty Lou," I said, squeezing her hands. "Where are we, really?"

"The Pollux." Betty Lou frowned. "You're getting ready for the vampire/thrall dance."

"That doesn't make any sense to me." I pulled her close, clinging to her like I had the real Betty Lou that night after the prom, when both of us had let things go too far. Betty Lou had been the first woman I'd slept with, though I definitely hadn't been her first . . . and . . . the memory of the two of us awkwardly fumbling at each other flushed through me. Betty's voice, when I was spent: "That was nice."

"Which part felt best to you?" I'd asked.

"I can't talk about that, I—"

But she had talked, and after a little experimentation, we'd managed better than nice.

Then I was elsewhere, elsewhen, a letter in my pocket from Betty. She was pregnant, and I was in a war zone. I looked up at my buddy Carmichael and knew he wouldn't make it through the war, because he hadn't, and as if following a thread, I remembered another letter, bittersweet, from Betty, letting me know that she'd lost the baby, that everything was okay. She hadn't said anything to anyone, and no one needed to know.

I remembered writing a letter back home to Marilyn and asking her to check on Betty Lou. Marilyn, eternally ten years my senior. I had never kept secrets from her. Marilyn would know what to say. If my emotions were anywhere close to as complicated as Betty Lou's . . .

"I'm sorry about the baby, Betty Lou," I said now. "You know I would have done right by you. But by the time I got back, you'd already married Roger and—"

Time marched on. Fast. Painful. And it took me with it.

I was outside on a beautiful summer day, standing at Betty Lou's funeral. I'd been dating Sheila at the time. She stood next to me all in black, her blond hair in a perfect wave. It was over and done. Marilyn stood to the side, comforting Betty Lou's mother, and Roger stood off by himself. I remembered seeing him smile and wondering what he had to smile about. It was later than that when I finally started dating Marilyn.

"It's so tragic," Sheila whispered in my ear. "Things like this are exactly why women shouldn't be allowed to drive. How are we supposed to know when the brakes—?"

"Roger killed Betty Lou." I whispered the words. "How did I never realize it?"

And then I was somewhere else again, in Fang before he was Fang, going off the cliff. But that wasn't right, because I hadn't been driving Fang the first time. I'd been driving Roger's car. I'd relived my death inside Fang, later . . . The inconsistency didn't matter. The memory swept me on, and I remembered the instant I knew I was going to die. The freedom I felt. I gunned the gas one last time and smiled to hear the engine roar. I'd been so happy in that moment. I . . .

I died and came back. Another memory come to life, and I remembered tears. Hearing them from a long way off, somewhere far below me, like someone crying underwater. In this last memory, there was no visual component other than whiteness and the sound. I remember knowing that I shouldn't go toward the tears but not being able to stop myself.

"Eric," said a voice, "for what are you waiting?" At the time, I don't know to whom I'd thought that voice belonged . . . God? Saint Peter? But now I recognized it all too well. It was the voice that had let me through the wards at the Highland Towers when I went to steal the Stone of Aeternum from Lord Phil. Later, in Paris, I'd heard it when I entered Le Château de Vincennes and set eyes on the alien-looking decapitated head of the demon Scrythax.

"That's Marilyn," I remembered saying. "Something's wrong. I gotta make sure she's okay."

"Eric," Scrythax said again, "for what are you waiting?"

"Will she be okay if I don't go to her?"

"No," Scrythax told the newly dead me.

"And if I do?"

"Eventually." Scrythax laughed when he said that, because I was already on my way back to her. Was he laughing because I'd almost gotten away, escaped the Courtney curse? Was it because he was looking forward to playing games with me? I don't know. Maybe one day I'll ask him.

Next came pain and fire and a grave. I'd never remembered it clearly, my return from the dead, but now I did. The memory of a true immortal, though fouled up by my Alzheimer's, finally brought it back. I knew what was happening to me then. I think I could have stopped the flow and regained control, but I wanted to know. I wanted to see. To feel. To remember after all these years.

The stink of rotted flesh in my nose and chemicals beneath that smell. The scrape of wood against my fingernails. Pain as my fingernails lengthened into claws. Dirt filling my mouth as I fought my way toward the sound and scent of Marilyn. Hearing her heartbeat, her lungs gasping those little gasps between sobs.

"I'm coming," I tried to say, but the dirt stopped my words, and then the sun set me on fire. I ran to the cemetery chapel for cover, and sizzling in the shade, I asked one question before passing out. "Am I late for something?" The clock struck two. I was late for something, all right. My wedding day.

I closed my eyes, and when they opened again, I was lying in the middle of the road in front of the Demon Heart, the hard metal of the artificial locus point jabbing into my back. Cheryl, Erin, Magbidion, Beatrice, Talbot, and Greta were all standing over me.

"Can I be Claude Rains?" Greta asked.

"What?" My skin felt cool again. The moon was high, full and orange in the sky.

"If you're going to hallucinate some more," Greta clarified. "Let's do *Casablanca*. You be Humphrey Bogart and I'll be Claude Rains and we can do the part where they're sitting out front and I say, 'Waters? What waters? We're in the desert.' And you say—"

"'I was misinformed,'" I quoted. And I was, fundamentally. My information about how I came back from the dead had always been from Marilyn's point of view. She'd seen it firsthand, and she'd thought she knew what she'd seen. It didn't change a thing about the last half a century, but in a way it changed everything. I didn't come back as an angry ghost—a revenant—because I was murdered and I wanted revenge. I hadn't even known it was murder at the time.

I came back as an angry ghost because Marilyn was crying over my grave. She needed me, so I came back . . . and then the Courtney Family Curse (administered by freaky demon head) had its way with me and made me a vampire as well . . . the two-for-one-undead deal making me an Emperor-level vampire in the process.

Fumbling for my cell, I brought up my special app and typed in what I'd just figured out. The only response:

NIGHTTIME SUPPORT: *I'm aware.*

Which just goes to show you, even when I'm being a sneaky son of a bitch, I'm always the last to know.

✦ 24 ✦

GRETA

VAMPIRE BUDDY COP MOVIE?

A re you sure it's Friday?" The vampire I held aloft was too scared to comment sensibly. I wasn't asking him anyway. He's one of those vampires I hate. Chicken vampires (fraidycats, not vampires who are chickens, cuz that would be cool) piss me off. Pudgy ones piss me off more. Fat boy wore belted gray slacks with a white dress shirt and a plaid sweater vest. He smelled like Old Spice and pig blood. Worse, his BMI had to be at least twenty-five.

"I—I—I—" he babbled.

"Shut it, fat ass!" We stood on the edge of a butcher shop's rooftop. He was dangling over the side. I don't know why he let that scare him. Maybe he sucked at flying. "Evelyn?" I asked.

"It's Friday, Sheriff." Evelyn stood off to the side, holding up a digital tablet with the calendar app open.

"And vampires are immune to curfew on Mondays, Wednesdays, and Fridays?" I asked, even though I already knew.

"I'm pretty sure."

"Oh." I looked back to Fat Ass and frowned. "Then you can

go." I opened my hand and let him fall. Flailing, he grabbed for me, but I slapped him instead, the sharp blow carrying enough strength to knock him farther past the edge of the rooftop. He yelled all the way down, even though it was only a one-story. When he hit the ground, he grunted in pain and fell over.

"Pathetic."

The corner of Evelyn's lips turned down in a grimace. "Was that absolutely necessary?"

"Public Safety Tip number four: The sheriff doesn't like fat vampires." I shrugged.

"Fat?" she mouthed. Evelyn's perceptions of who was and wasn't fat were totally out of whack. Sure, she was skinny, but most people aren't.

"And he took up valuable solving-the-mystery-of-what-Dad-is-hiding-from-me time by breaking curfew."

"Which," Evelyn said pointedly, "he didn't actually do."

"I'm hungry," I said, ignoring her. "Are you?"

"We just ate." This was a conversation Evelyn and I were beginning to have a lot. She tended to eat once a night and then not eat again, treating blood like medicine instead of something to be wallowed in and played with and imbibed at every available opportunity.

"Does that mean you aren't hungry?" I drew my Glock and kneecapped Fat Ass as he ran. He rolled into the street, avoiding being struck by traffic with the judicious application of vampiric speed and reflexes.

Evelyn flinched. "Yes."

"I could always feed off of you, and then you would be hungry, and we could go get someone to eat—"

"I don't think so." Evelyn was already gliding down to street level. It is totally not fair that she can fly—like real Peter Pan flying.

"I still haven't tested that theory I need a church for," I said, looking toward Void City Episcopalian. "We could do it now. Don't they have Friday-night Mass or—"

"Sheriff Courtney?" My cell chirped, interrupting me.

"What?" I replied, clicking and releasing the transmit button.

"We need an SC to assist with a domestic disturbance on Third and Midnight."

"Is this Kat?" I asked.

"Yes, ma'am. This is Captain Marx."

"Does 'SC' stand for 'supernatural citizen'?"

"Yes, ma'am." I liked to keep Marx talking until I could clearly hear agitation in her voice.

"Can we change it to Salacious Crumb?" Evelyn got the *Return of the Jedi* reference, which impressed me, but it was lost on Marx.

"Will that make you respond to the call?"

"I am responding to the call, Kat."

I heard her sigh, but she wasn't quite there yet. "I mean, show up and assist us."

"Oh." I thought for a moment. "Can I call you Kit Kat?"

Evelyn's head shook in perpetual disapproval with my teasing of Captain Marx. I didn't understand. Why shouldn't I tease her? She was the one who dared to speak with me.

"Can I call you Slaughterhouse?" the reply crackled back.

"Nope." *Not bad, Kat.*

"Then no, ma'am." I heard another sigh. The edge to her voice was ragged and worn, tired beyond belief.

"Why do you need help with a domestic disturbance, Kit Kat?" Evelyn rolled her eyes at me, silently disapproving of my continued antics and disrespect.

"Because the domestics involved are both demons, Sheriff, and—"

"Cool!" I jumped off the building, going into a roll as I hit the pavement and came up minimally injured and already healing. I passed Deputy LEGO-Noggin on my way to Fang. He was parked around the corner from the butcher shop, waiting as patiently as a moray eel while a stray cat sniffed at his tire. I wanted to stop and watch, to see if the cat would be dumb enough to crawl under the car, but we didn't have time, so I kicked it underneath. There was only a brief yowl before its bones tinkled down atop the others in Fang's trunk.

"We have a domestic disturbance!" I told the car as I jumped into the driver's seat. Fright Ranger's "Oh Oh Oh Sexy Vampire" began playing over the Mustang's speaker, and I gave his steering wheel a good thump. "Would you stop being silly?"

Fang's left-turn indicator flashed, so I looked that way and caught a glimpse of a chupacabra teen in ratty jeans, gloves, and a gray hoodie, watching me from the shadows of a closed-down bar. He'd positioned himself downwind so I couldn't smell the sulfur-lime mixture. He couldn't have been older than nineteen or twenty, and he had a thin rangy look. The disfigurement wasn't so bad on him, maybe because he was so young: little more than reddish blotches on his skin that could have passed for eczema or maybe acne scars. Our gazes met and he looked away first, but not before I saw longing in those brown eyes.

I tossed him the universal "What?" gesture, and he opened his mouth to speak, then lost his nerve and looked away. Evelyn climbed into the passenger seat. Fang's engine roared to life, but I put my foot on the brake.

"What?" I shouted across the street. "You need something?"

Shoving his gloved hands awkwardly in the pockets of his hoodie, he turned and dashed down the sidewalk, but not before I saw what he'd stenciled on the back of his hoodie in bright red paint:

SHE'S THE BOSS, APPLESAUCE

"Ha," Evelyn snarked, "looks like you have a fan."

"Shut up." I raised my hand to knock her head off, but

something stopped me. It could have been that I didn't want to annoy her, but more likely, I was just tired from holding Fat Ass over the edge of the roof for so long. "Third and Midnight," I instructed Fang as I took my foot off the brake pedal. He pulled away from the curb and let the music change to Megadeth's "Sweating Bullets," but I wasn't in the mood. Folding my arms under my breasts, I slunk down in the seat and closed my eyes.

"Um?" Evelyn said.

"What?"

"Won't people think *Knight Rider*? Oh. Right. Never mind. You have the little bag thingy."

I dug it out of my pocket and held it up. "Yep. Portable short-range Veil of Scrythax and, like Tigger, it's the only one."

"So what do you think the mortals who notice that you aren't driving will see?"

I closed my eyes, putting the gris-gris bag back in my jeans. "Maybe they'll be too busy looking at you?"

"Oh." I could hear her blushing, her hand touching her hair. "I'm not that—"

"Nope." I knocked her head off with an absentminded swat. "You're not."

I didn't even have to hit the gas myself. Fang was in on the joke now and knew exactly what to do. With wind blowing through my hair and the sound of heavy metal (and my deputy's curses) in my ears, I felt better again. Besides, it's not like it took Evelyn's head more than a few blocks to catch up with the car and reattach to her body. Where's the harm in that?

✦ 25 ✦

GRETA

BAD COP/WORSE COP

Third and Midnight took us close to the Episcopal church. I studied the stone architecture, wondering when it had been built and whether I'd catch fire if I walked inside. It smelled, even from a block over, of candles and hopeful people. The flashing red and blue lights of the VCPD squad cars parked in front of a multistory high-rise drew my attention back to the matter at hand as surely as my deputy's hand on my shoulder did.

"We're here."

"I know." I glanced back at the church. The sounds of a hymn cut through the night and reminded me of a thing so long gone and well forgotten that only the ache of its absence was left—the final twinge of remembrance. Long before foster care . . . I think I'd been to church.

"You still aren't thinking of trying out some plan involving a priest, are you?"

"Hmmm?" Dad stood in my mind's eye larger than life, as I remembered watching him strangling Father Ike, standing in the shadows like a child on the stairs eavesdropping on the grown-up conversations she's not supposed to hear. I understood most of it. I knew why he'd strangled Father Ike. He'd been ordered to do it, but the second part . . . that made no sense.

"The priest thing," Evelyn repeated. "You're not thinking about—"

"No." I climbed out of the car and headed for the officer who looked like he was in charge. "Not until after this demon thing."

The SWAT team stood outside looking conspicuous as hell, but passersby weren't paying them much attention. They had the front of the building cordoned off, with less combat-ready cops moving along the few mortals who thought to stop and stare. It was almost like the olden days . . . of several hundred days ago.

"Distraction screen," I said, mildly impressed.

Four mages stood one at each corner of the building. I could see only three of them, but I knew the fourth was there. Properly trained mages could set up a field like the one the Veil of Scrythax used to give off, but only on a smaller scale, and they aren't capable of keeping it going indefinitely. From what I understand, it takes a lot out of a mage to keep any kind of enchantment running long-term.

"I'd say so," Evelyn said. "You see them a lot in Atlanta."

"You spent a lot of time in Atlanta?"

"Sure." She looked down and away, which she'd been doing a lot. I didn't understand quite why. "I did. Yeah. The vampire hunter presence is pretty strong in Georgia, what with the Lycan Diocese being based in Rome."

"You hung out with humans?" I raised an eyebrow and squinched my mouth.

"As a rule, yes. I . . . I hunted vampires."

"Me, too!" I knew I liked Evelyn for some reason. "I mean the vampires, not Atlanta. Though Dad and I went to

Dragon*Con once. We both went as Ghostbusters. How long did it take you to figure out the heart thing?"

"Ghostbusters?" I could see she had trouble picturing that, so she swallowed the mental image and moved on to the next query in the queue. "Heart thing?"

"Sure." One of the cops tried to wave me over, but I was in no hurry. Demons can be fun to fight, but their blood isn't always edible, so I was trying not to get too excited. I gave Evelyn my full attention, turning my back on the cops. "In higher-power vamps, most of the blood is in the heart. There's a spot—"

"Sheriff?" Captain Marx interrupted me, and I was going to snap at her for it, but instead, I stared straight at her chest.

"Holy crap! Your sweater puppies are growing out of control!"

"It's a side effect," she said, flatly meeting my gaze (though I guess it should have been impossible for her to do anything flatly now).

"Of what?" Evelyn asked.

Wait a minute!

I narrowed my gaze, trying to spot whether she was a thrall. I'd never made a thrall, so I couldn't just sense one; it was on my to-do list, though. I'd just never found the right person. Even so, I could usually guess by the evidence—stronger heartbeat, enhanced attributes—but I'd have to see the mark to be sure.

Each thrall bears a mark, a blood tattoo, bestowed upon them by their vampiric "master." Dad uses a butterfly, but it can be anything. Uncle Percy uses an ankh. Lady Gabriella, a rose. Of course, nothing would keep a vampire from changing things up. I think if I make a thrall, I'm going to use a little heart with demon wings. That or an upside-down Mary Poppins silhouette.

"Turn around," I said abruptly. When Captain Marx responded too slowly, I spun her in a circle, eyeing her for traces of a butterfly, but I didn't find anything. Very powerful vampires influence their opposite-gender (or gender of sexual preference) thrall's physical appearance subconsciously. Dad's thralls tend to get very busty and curvy, like, well, like Mom.

"What the—?" Marx said.

"Nope, no blood tattoo," I said. Did I smell Dad on her, though? A trace? Perhaps . . . hmmm. "Sorry, for a minute I wondered if you were Dad's thrall."

Her pulse quickened at that, but she obviously didn't have a tattoo (I should have been able to sense it even if it was some-place out of sight), and the Dad smell was faint enough that it could have been from one of the meetings he'd been having with the reps from the VCPD, the Mages Guild, the Orchard Lake Pack, and the Sable Oaks Vampires. I had a mind to go back and put on Percy's glasses to get his opinion, but I didn't want to read snark and fight a demon at the same time.

"Can you please see what you can do?" Kit Kat gestured at the building. "We've got two Khan Canis tearing the place apart because one of them has apparently been spending way too much time around a Gallus and—"

I held my hand up.

Kit Kat paused. "Yes?"

"Khan Canis?"

"Dog-headed ones with leathery wings." She cracked a smile. "They tend to use melee weapons. Some enchanted. Some not."

"Oh, that's what those are called." I nudged Evelyn. "I didn't know that. Did you know that?"

"I've never fought a demon," Evelyn said softly.

"Really?" I clasped my hands together. "This will be awesome. Big doggies are fun to fight! You basically just hit them over and over again until they stop moving."

"Oh." Her eyes sparkled with inner crimson, the *kanji* on her neck pulsing red to match the glow. "That I can manage. What's a Gallus?"

"Who cares?"

"Do we have a plan?"

"Let me demonstrate." I checked my Glock to make sure I'd reloaded the clip, reholstered it, and looked at the building. "Which floor?"

"Twelve."

I nodded, grinned at Evelyn, reached out, and popped Kit Kat's uniform shirt open just to make sure there wasn't a tattoo hiding under there, and charged.

♦ 26 ♦

ERIC

I'M NOT WEARING A FEZ OR A MOOSE HAT

As far as I could tell, the Irons Club had once been a country club. Maybe it still counted as one. If it had been my club, I've have done something about the roads. We'd driven round and round on a winding road up the non–state park section of Bald Mountain, and it seemed as if the road's planners had gone out of their way to make it seem like Bald Mountain was more of a mountain than it is. It's big enough, but these aren't the damn Smokies.

In Fang, the drive might have been fun, but in the back of a limo, it had me wanting to throw my chauffeur out the window and drive myself (and my chauffeur weighed half a ton). Houses became more and more expensive as we entered the Sanguine Hills area. There were a fair number of for-sale signs posted, the owners having died when I knocked down the Highland Towers (of which Vampire High Society highly approved) or when Winter trapped them in the Artiste Unknown with a glorified death trap (on which Vampire High Society frowned).

Finally, the pricey houses gave way to a long stretch of

well-manicured cherry trees and boxwoods. As we neared the
gates, the bushes took on a topiary aspect: lions, tigers, and
(bears!) other predators rendered in living plants stalked the
massive iron gates. We stopped at the granite-hewn guard
shack where some douche in a burgundy security uniform
looked out. He walked up to the limo, bypassing the chauffeur's
window and heading straight to mine.

"I'm terribly sorry to delay you—" His eyes widened. "Lord
Eric. I—"

Beatrice leaned forward so she could be easily seen around
me. If I thought I looked good in a suit, she put me to shame
in her dress. Green is her color, and she'd worn a strapless
green thing that was all mountains and no molehills. It hugged
everything it ought to hug and flowed and folded where a man
might hope it would. Her red hair was done up, with ringlets
hanging down to accent her cheeks. Those storm-cloud eyes
of hers twinkled with mischief as she spoke for me.

I'd already been warned that even though I didn't give a
damn about propriety, I should do my best not to talk to the
staff. I didn't care about the rules, but apparently, they might
wind up in hot water (real hot water) over it, so I decided to be
a good little Emperor and let her talk.

"These aren't the droids you're looking for," she said,
following his gaze to her chest. If he'd been awestruck by me,
he was even more awestruck by Beatrice.

"I'm . . . I'm sorry, Lady Beatrice."

She smiled, cutting her eyes pointedly at the gate. "Should
I get out and open that myself?"

"Invi—" He almost got out the entire word before deciding
that whether we had my invitation with us or not, he wasn't
going to get in trouble for letting us in. At least not as much
trouble as he might find himself in if he offended me. Stupid
vampire groupies. You gotta love 'em. "Ah. Ahem." He

straightened and bowed so low, he missed hitting the door with his forehead by only a few centimeters. "Welcome. We are honored by the presence of your power."

"Weird," said Magbidion from the front passenger's seat. We'd weighed leaving him close to the artificial locus point against being that far away from him at night and decided it was less of a risk to bring him along.

"What's weird?" I asked.

"I half expected him to offer himself to you on the spot," Mags said.

Beatrice spoke up. "Oh, he wouldn't dare. Not in front of me. It's presumptuous, and I gained a reputation for frowning on that sort of thing when I was with Gabriella, or he might have risked it anyway."

"Mortals," our driver scoffed. Tiko was an Oni, and limo service was just one of the many enterprises that the brothers at Triple-T had gotten into. Normally, he was horned and strangely colored, but tonight he appeared to be a middle-aged Asian man. I'd seen him stick a piece of paper with strange writing on it to his forehead to enact the transformation, but I had no idea how it worked on a mystical mechanics level.

Through the gates, the drive transitioned from asphalt to cobblestone, and the ride got bumpy.

"That'll do wonders for my hairdo," Beatrice complained.

"You weren't getting lucky anyway," I said with a smile. "Besides, it isn't like there will be any pictures."

"You don't understand. It looks old, but it's newly done. Someone, possibly Piotr, wants those of us who weren't expecting it to look bad in front of our vampires." Withdrawing a compact from her tiny green handbag, Beatrice inspected her hair as best she could when we rolled to a stop in the entry circle. A huge building, the Irons Club looked from without as if it were once a small civic center but had gotten a growth spurt designed by someone who would have been cutting-edge however long ago they'd built the place. I had no idea where to park, but Tiko seemed to know, so when a uniformed valet came to the door, Tiko waved him away. Before he could open my door, I'd already done it.

When I opened Beatrice's door for her and offered my hand, she quirked a smile at me and let me help her from the limo. "Now everyone thinks we're sleeping together," she whispered in my ear in as she rose.

"Because I helped you out of the car?"

She nodded. "Welcome to the Lion's Den, Master." She composed herself, and I took her arm in mine. "These people read layers of intent and meaning into the smallest detail."

"Fuck 'em." I failed to suppress a sneer.

"Oh, they'd let you make them airtight and brag about it to all of their friends." She plastered on a smile. "Don't be surprised when we walk in the door."

"What's going to happen?" I did a double take. "Airtight?"

"If you don't know, you don't need to know." Her tone, a mixture of pleasant surprise and condescension, let me know I'd passed one of those pop quizzes that ladies throw at vampires from time to time to see if we really are better than the other men.

"Tiko?" I said softly.

"I'll keep an eye on your mage," he said pleasantly. "I've got three brothers on telepathic speed dial if I need them, and the mouser I wasn't supposed to notice is tailing us on that hot-shit motorcycle. Your mage will be fine."

Magbidion closed his eyes, already asleep. The wear on him worried me. I didn't have any other mage I could trust.

"Good." Beatrice and I were ushered through the grandest of three glass double doors into a hall with a grand chandelier and a boatload of undead assholes and their dates. What got my attention was the full orchestra playing incidental music to an empty room down the end of one long hallway. They were in a small theater that appeared to have been built for just such a purpose, the volume controlled (for our sensitive vampiric ears) by a series of sliding glass panels.

Waiters and waitresses in various states and styles of dress carried platters of food and beverages about the checkered tile. Plenty of room for dancing was unoccupied in the middle of the hall under the chandelier, and tables and chairs had been artfully arranged around the edges. Each had a little placard denoting who was to sit where once the more formal portion got under way. Apparently, there was to be a speaker, your basic socialite verbal masturbation and ego stroke. All of which I had expected. What I hadn't known was that when I walked in, everything would stop.

Everyone turned to face me. It was a High Society thing I'd seen before, reorienting one's self to face the most powerful and/or influential person in the room. Up until that very moment, that person had never been me. It had always been Phil or Winter. Beatrice's hand tightened around my biceps.

"Acknowledge them whenever and however you wish, Master," Beatrice said.

The "Master" thing grated like hell, but I'd been warned about that, too, so I let it slide, knowing that she'd back off as soon as she could without appearing to disrespect me. Maybe that's why I opted to "acknowledge" them all with a middle finger and my general disdain. I scanned the crowd in a 180, then flipped off the people behind me at the door just to make sure I got everybody.

They ate it up. My middle finger was met with applause, catcalls, wolf whistles, and bemused laughter like some bad-boy celebrity showing off at the Oscars. Everyone bowed, and I escorted Beatrice toward the Orchestra Hallway. Each glass pane was controlled by a volume knob set into a lacquered panel on the right side of the hallway.

"Is the music too loud, Lord Eric?" called a thin voice. Truth be told, I could barely hear it, my senses being what they are at night. "Or not loud enough?"

I'd expected a Peter Lorre–looking little sycophant and was surprised to find a very manly-looking guy in the kind of shape actors complain about having to work so hard to get into. He had a disarming smile, and I shook his hand without thinking about it. A lot of thralls seem not to know how to give a good handshake, letting their hand rest in mine like a dead fish. Manly Guy matched the firmness of my grip, smiled, and met my gaze.

"Forgive me for speaking out of turn, Lord Eric, but our music system is unique."

"Just Eric," I said. "And don't read anything into that. I don't like titles."

I didn't expect a thing when Beatrice laid him out. I don't think I'd even seen her throw a punch before, but she opened with a forearm to the jaw, or was it an elbow? Before I could decide, he lay sprawled on the tile, blood dappling his dress shirt, trying his best to dodge a high heel to the crotch. Emphasis on the word "trying." "Back off, Piotr!"

"You seem to have that covered," I said, not knowing what else to say. I reached over and slowly turned the volume higher until, one by one, all the panes of glass between us and the orchestra stood open and I could hear the music. When I looked back, it was to see Piotr catching Bea's leg.

I growled, and the room stopped again.

"I don't know what you did, Handshake." I rubbed my fingers together as if they felt oily. "Probably you shouldn't have shaken hands with me or engaged me in conversation without Bea's permission. I don't know, because I don't care about all the froufrou societal bullcrap you people get up to. But whatever it was, I can tell you this much: You knew, and you knew it would piss Beatrice off, and that's why you did it."

I focused my gaze, and a symbol, something like a V

within a V, although they intersected, appeared plain as day over Piotr's head. I didn't know who belonged to that symbol, so I asked: "Where's your vampire, Piotr?"

He let go of Beatrice's leg. "Each Irons Club is managed by a thrall of Duke Gornsvalt. I—"

I shushed him. That name rang a bell. If I remembered correctly, he specialized in making blood wine and other beverages that could inebriate vampires. Lord Phillip had him do steaks once. Before I killed Phil, of course.

"Oh," I said softly. "I like him."

Beatrice paled. Piotr let a hint of smug grin creep onto his face and he looked like every bully you've ever met. He thought he'd won, and he had his victory speech all ready.

"I was going to destroy him," I continued. "But not just now." I looked around. "Is he here?"

An older gentleman got up from a table in the corner. "Yes, Eric."

I crossed the room in my own time and shook Duke Gornsvalt's hand. This was where Piotr had learned that handshake and the smile. It was pure good-old-boy network. I bet all the thralls he counted as friends were men, and any female thralls he had were for housework, bedroom work, or both. "Release Piotr from your thralldom," I said.

"For what offense?" Duke Gornsvalt asked.

"Annoying my thrall and daring to touch her." Arms spread, I gestured to the room as a whole. "That's how you do things, isn't it? That's the vampire way? Right? You make me mad, and in order to prove I'm head leech, I have to come down on you with hellfire and brimstone and scorch the earth! And if"—I straightened Gornsvalt's tie for effect, even though it wasn't mussed—"if I don't, then you stop respecting me."

My pocket started vibrating, but I couldn't remember why. My hand went out, and Beatrice took it. Handshake's blood had spattered her bare arm, and I plucked the handkerchief out of Gornsvalt's suit jacket to wipe it away. I spat with real saliva and realized my mistake as I made it. They gasped as one. My pocket stopped vibrating and chirped once.

"Impressed?" I laughed. "A parlor trick. I told my last vampiric girlfriend"—I mimed my apologies—"we'll get back to the chewing-out part, but I'm getting old, and I have to tell these little stories when they occur to me, or I won't remember. I told her once that there was no power she possessed that I couldn't do better."

Even Beatrice hadn't seen this; her surprise aided the illusion. "Tabitha's a Living Doll." I held my hand out level, then waggled it from side to side, one side lower, then back up. My pocket vibrated again, but I still had no clue. "It's cute, but she loses her vampiric powers, whereas I"—I tapped in to my strength and felt it flow, hoisted Duke Gornsvalt into the air with one hand, and slowly tucked the bloodstained handkerchief into his mouth—"don't. That's yours."

With my spare hand I beckoned a waiter carrying a plate of appetizers, selected a small hors d'oeuvre, and bit into it. It was a stuffed mushroom, but the meat inside wasn't meat, it was . . . I spat it out. "What the hell is that? Boca burger? That ain't meat, gentlemen. It never was, nor will it ever be."

I looked up at Gornsvalt as if I had forgotten him, and there was another chirp from my pocket. I needed to hold him up there long enough to make sure everyone saw it as a feat of supernatural strength, just in case anyone was putting two and two together and realizing that someone had poured Liquid Paper over the real problem and that their Emperor vampire, the one they all feared because he could go all über vamp and kill them, couldn't do so. Well, at least not at night. Selling them on the idea that I had even more powers than they thought seemed like the best idea for keeping the wool pulled firmly over their beady little eyes.

"I . . ." Real problem. Plan. Phone. Shit!

I looked back up at Gornsvalt and couldn't remember why he was there. I saw Beatrice and couldn't recall why she was important. I knew she was . . . was . . .

"And to think you started without me," called a musical voice from the entryway. I turned. There stood a vampire whose force of character could cut through even my bad memory. Ebon Winter wore a formal kimono in white, blue, and silver, his bleached white hair pulled back in a long ponytail. "I called to ask you all to wait, but no one"—he looked right at me—"answered the phone. How rude."

Was that a samurai sword? He drew it. Tapping in to my power as I was, I could just make out the blue tinge of enchantment on the blade.

"I think," he said, slicing the air with his katana in a downward arc, "that I shall be quite wroth."

✦ 27 ✦

GRETA

FIGHT, DEMON, FIGHT!

How is it that you only bleed hot pink?" I asked the bleeding doggie-headed demon. One wing torn, the other coated in her own gore flapping uselessly against a wall-mounted poster of *Night of the Lepus*. Yowling in unison with its injured mate, the pink-blooded one threw another ax at my head.

"Where do you keep getting those?" Evelyn asked as she snagged it out of the air and slammed the double-bladed ax home in the other doggie-headed demon with a loud *kathwack*.

"And can you throw them faster?" I pointed at Pink Blood's mate. "Because my deputy needs a few more."

A geyser of green blood erupted from the newest ax wound, and I wished someone were running around with us videotaping. True, I wouldn't show up (probably Evelyn wouldn't, either, but who knows with *nukekubi*), but I'd never fought demons who bled rainbow colors. Blood in all colors of the rainbow dripped from the multiple ax wounds, streaming down the demon's lightly furred skin and dyeing the carpet in patches of color that did not mix and blend.

It had been a nice apartment before we started wrecking

it. Very fifties-retro, which made me suspect the two lovebirds would really dig the Sci-Fi Drive-in Café at Disney World. I mean, seriously, *Night of the Lepus*? I like bad movies as much as the next psychopath, but . . .

"Why won't you leave us alone?" Rainbow Blood screeched.

"I don't know," I said, sinking my claws into Pink Blood's biceps. She hurled me against the wall, and I laughed at the crack of my own bones, the twist and tear of muscle and ligament. "Marx called me and I came."

"Marx?" Rainbow Blood howled again. "Marx, you bitch! Marx!"

He turned for the door, heedless of the five axes sprouting from his back, torso, and shoulders. Evelyn backed away, unwilling to follow through.

"Kill it!" I shouted, and when she didn't react, I added, "Bread and butter!"

Jumping over the broken sectional sofa, I rolled past Pink Blood and grabbed her mate by an ax lodged in his back. It popped loose, and I licked the yellow iridescent blood as it oozed from the wound, only to take an ax in my own back, chunking into my spine. The pain roared bright and hot, then dimmed like it ought to dim. Then . . . nothing.

Special though its color may have been, the demon's blood tasted plain and ordinary. Still, there is pleasure in eating funny-colored ice cream, even if it tastes like vanilla. Life has many simple pleasures. Murder is my favorite.

"Where do you get these?" I pulled the ax from my back and decapitated Rainbow with it. His head rose ceiling-ward on a fountain right out of a Skittles commercial. "And how did he do that?"

Pink Blood screamed unintelligibly instead of answering. It may have been a "no." Hard to say.

"What the hell is going on in here?" Kit Kat picked then to intervene. Dressed in full supernatural-suppression gear, she strode in, aghast. "This is how you resolve a domestic dispute?"

"Well, you brought a SWAT team!" I turned to Kit Kat, and Pink Blood grabbed my arm.

"Why?" the doggie demon screamed. "Our blood is a dye. We make clothes. We were only—" Her ax vanished when I tried to chop her with it.

"A clever defense mechanism." I tried to hurl her across the room, but she was bigger than me, the mass more than I could overcome at such a strained angle.

Evelyn mouthed "Oh my God" and stepped back, her shoe slipping in the blood of many hues. She caught herself on the wall-mounted flatscreen.

Pink Blood pulled and wrenched at my left arm in an emotional attempt to pull it off. She did it wrong, so it only came loose at the elbow.

"That's not how you do it!" A few drops of blood leaked from the wound, but not much. My free hand found my Glock, and I fired all seventeen rounds into Pinkie's face. All the sound went away, replaced by the whine of ringing ears and damaged hearing. It's hard to behead a demon one-handed, but you can do it if you get her in a headlock first. A muzzle helps. It makes for a better grip.

Pinkie's headless corpse bled the color of her namesake in such quantities that I thought it might flood the floor. Gallons and gallons flowed out. Her lifeless claw held my dismembered forearm, so I pried it loose, turning to show Kit Kat as I touched the wounds together, skin, bones, and muscle reknitting in seconds.

"Why? You?" Katherine opened her mouth wide to make her ears pop, but she could hear again normally already, like I could. Too fast for a human but just right for a vampire . . . or a thrall. "I—"

"Spit it out, Kit Kat." I knelt in the rainbow-colored blood, which hadn't mixed with the other colors, tasting each color in turn and trying to imagine that each hue bore a minuscule variation in flavor. "I won't hurt you. I'm the sheriff." It had come off during the fight, but I found my old-timey sheriff's star and pinned it back on my shirt.

"Every few months," Kit Kat began carefully, "we get a call to break up a fight between those two. They almost always send a few good VCPD police officers to the hospital. But Captain Stacey would come in after the fight and calm them down and get them to shell out a large Fang fee and . . . I thought if I called you, I could avoid some banged-up cops."

"And you did." All the colors tasted the same. I dipped one finger into yellow, another into blue, and dribbled them together in my palm, but they still wouldn't mix.

"You killed them." Kit Kat breathed in a ragged sigh, reaching out to me as if I could return her wacko sense of outrage. "They run a huge fabric operation, with dyes that never run or bleed together. They employ four hundred people."

"Not anymore." I lapped up the blood in my palm and frowned. *I wonder if the colors mix inside of me . . .*

"Greta—" Evelyn started, but I silenced her with a look.

"Do you have a knife?" Neither woman responded, so I picked my way through to the kitchen and found a set of Shenzhen ceramic knives. Taking the six-inch blade, I rejoined the others. "I found one."

Cutting barely even hurts properly with a sharp enough blade, like getting a shot when you're a kid. "Ouch then over," as Marilyn used to say when she'd take me to get my boosters, vaccinations, and immunizations. Inside me, the blood dye failed, assuming the familiar red of my favorite and only beverage. I flung some of it on Kit Kat, and she flinched.

"Want to be my thrall, Kit Kat?" I dropped the knife. "You might understand me better. My blood's already on you."

"How would your dad feel about you forcing—"

"Forcing?" I barked. "I asked. I made an offer." Red light poured out of my flaring angry eyes, and I wanted to rip open the world and drink it down. "You threaten to tattle on me and lie on me to MY DADDY?"

Evelyn touched my arm. "You just scared her, Greta. She understands now. She won't tattle."

"You won't?" My fangs were out, and I slurred my words, but she understood.

"No." Kit Kat took a deep breath, looking over the damage. "I misunderstood. I . . . when your father said you'd work with us, I assumed you could help fill part of the role Captain Stacey used to fill before your dad got rid of him."

"That's police work." I tapped her badge. "I'm the sheriff." I tapped my badge. "When the bad guys ride into town and they're shooting up the place or harassing the locals, you call me up and I'll do some real sheriff'n." I kicked my foot through the room-wide puddle of blood. "The police'n is up to you."

She nodded. "Understood."

"Good." I was all chipper again. "Then I have to go across the street and strangle a priest."

Cops were chatting on their way up in the elevators, so Evelyn and I took the stairs. When we got to the bottom, there was no sign of Fang.

"Did any of you see what happened to my car?" I asked the uniforms securing the area.

"It drove off," one of them answered.

I frowned. "I wonder where he went," I said to no one in particular, then, "Oh well, Dad must have needed him." Eyes on the prize, I headed across the street for the Episcopal church to finally test my theory.

✦ 28 ✦

ERIC

SAMURAI SHOWDOWN

Nice sword," I told Ebon Winter. His grin deepened unpleasantly, no sense of mirth reflected in his eyes—those demonstrated frustration and concern. For half a second, they reminded me of the look I'd seen in the eyes of any number of women I'd dated . . . right after they'd realized I wasn't just saying that stuff about how I can never love them in order to be dramatic, and that I do truly love Marilyn, and all they are is an enjoyable way to pass the time.

"Does complimenting another man's sword sound queer to you?" I asked Beatrice.

"You really are a card." Winter never took his eyes from mine. He made contact, but it wasn't the mind-to-mind contact of two vampires fighting for supremacy, it was something else, and it contained vital information. I didn't understand it all, but it definitely seemed vital. "Though the leftover-remnant-from-the-Greatest-Generation bit is wearing a trifle thin. Gornsvalt there"—he nodded to the vampire I still held aloft in one hand—"fought in the Crusades, and you don't hear him going on and on about it."

"The Crusades," I said, lowering Gornsvalt. "Those were like the Dark Ages version of Vietnam, right?"

"Bravo." Winter tittered. "For a brain-addled simpleton, you are almost charming in a *Flowers for Algernon* way . . . when you aren't being odious, arrogant, and disrespectful."

"I wasn't aware that anyone in this room deserved my respect. After all, we won the two wars I fought in."

What was the other thing I was supposed to be doing? Fang. Right. If in trouble, try to summon Fang. Concentrating on seeing the world of the magical brought a display of energy strands into view. Some of them were connected to me. Others were connected to the thralls in the room, but not the vampires, except for wavering ones running between thrall and master.

A red line ran between me and Beatrice, so hard to see that I could barely make it out and then only because I'd caught it at the right angle. Trying to find the one between me and Fang was like being at one of those damn Harry Potter movies and trying to spot the golden whosits. Fang had grown more powerful after Greta and he destroyed my pseudo sire Lisette's memento mori by essentially feeding the squidlike golden travesty to Fang. Now, when Fang did his equivalent of my über vamp, gold detailing appeared on the car, even on the knockoff hubs.

Fang's connection to me was also gold. I found it and concentrated on it. Moments later, I felt a sensation as if someone had injected pure adrenaline straight into the old heart box. It shot blood through my veins like a nitro boost.

In my mind's eye, I saw Fang burn rubber out of downtown, right up the side of a high-rise near the old Episcopal church, and launch into the air. To be honest, when Talbot told me Fang could drive up walls and glide now, I thought he'd been fibbing. Apparently, not so much.

"You stole credit for Lord Phillip's death," Winter continued. "I planned for years to execute that fat, twisted mass of fecundity, and you ruined it all." He gestured at the assembled vampires and their dates. "All of you did. The so-called Vampiric Elite failed to comprehend the marvel of my plan and viewed you as a murderer rather than the mere implement of destruction. You"—he leveled his sword at me—"took credit for the kill and left me with no choice but the rather brutish display I delivered at the Artiste Unknown."

I ran my thumb across my middle finger and forefinger in imitation of the world's smallest violin playing the world's saddest song, "My Heart Bleeds for You," and ignored Winter.

"You're being awfully quiet." Duke Gornsvalt had been in my hand for a while, so I gave him my attention and dropped him unceremoniously. "Are you going to withdraw your whatchamajigger from Handshake or what?"

Gornsvalt looked at Winter. "If there were some other way—"

I grabbed Gornsvalt by the chin. "He ain't helping you, asshole. He's whining about how I stole his kill and walked off with his unique drop."

A surprising number of vampires got that joke. Frick'n *World of Warcraft* junkies. Duke Gornsvalt wasn't one of them. "He's been with me centuries, Eric. Please."

"I—" Winter's katana burst through my shoulder at an angle cutting down into my heart. Have I mentioned I heal very quickly? At night it's even faster. Not that it felt great. I sagged against the duke. "Tell me something. Did that prince wannabe just stab me?"

"Lord Winter?" the duke asked.

"Yep." My wounds closed around the blade. "That's the one."

A heart can't beat with a blade in it. If my heart's not beating . . . I'm . . . dead? But a funky little side effect of my condition is: I can't be dead, only ever-living or undead. I wondered which way my condition was going to deal with this one. I suspected Ebon Winter already knew and had bet on it.

A coil of wrongness twined through me, the enchantment on the blade pulling me down to the edge of unconsciousness. Fang's engine roared. I felt myself growing cold. Undead. I guessed Winter had arranged this as a little demonstration. Nice. Painful but nice. If all went well, I'd be able to manage the über vamp.

Fangs tore through the roof of my mouth, uppers and lowers sliding jaggedly into place, but not before they rent the inside of my mouth. My eyes flashed red, then purple. My ghosts came along, too, even though I was the only one who could see them.

"The Master/Thrall Social?" Phillip said with a tut-tut in his glare. "You're shouldn't have." He gestured at his dressing gown. "I'm not even dressed for it."

Roger opened his mouth to say something, but blue light washed him away. I screamed in unison with the phantasms of Lisette and Suzie Hu as the light took them as well.

When it came for Phillip, he responded with a complex gesture that my eyes couldn't follow. The blue light shattered off him in millions of tiny shards, and when it cleared, he wore a WELCOME TO THE VOID T-shirt and blue jeans under his dressing gown.

"How?" I asked.

"You took a thought from me"—his grin grew to Grinchy proportions—"a quote I knew and you wanted to know. That's when I realized we weren't ghosts. When Talbot couldn't see us but we could touch. I don't understand. What have you become, my boy?"

"That," I growled at him mentally, "would be telling!"

"If you can take things from my mind, boy, then I assure you I can read what you're hiding inside yours." He grabbed my head in his hands, and I felt like an open book.

"What is Operation Let's All Get Drunk and Screw?" he snapped.

"As Edmund Burke put it," I said, stealing another quote as Fang crashed through the glass doors, his tires squealing on the marble, "'Reading without reflecting is like eating without digestion.'"

I love my car. Fang always seems to know when to show up and what to do. But I guess there always has to be an exception to the rule. As Fang raced across the marble, I expected him to spin out around me and crash into something important, then eat a vampire or two. He didn't.

Note to self: Sometimes magic vampire convertibles don't roll with changes in the plan. I don't know exactly why Fang did what he did. Maybe he was trying to help hide my secret. But as I opened my mouth to shout, "No. No, stupid car," Fang ran me over, tore the flesh from my bones, and deposited them in his trunk. I heard Phillip say, "Of course." I hate it when evil asswipes figure things out.

Pain wiped out any reply I might have had. Re-forming is something I've done loads of times, but never as an immortal, from just bones, and never after having been eaten by Fang. Blue light washed over my body, coming in from the lines I'd seen all around, and powered my regeneration, converting the energy to matter like a damn *Star Trek* episode.

Through the trunk, Fang's radio blared "This Town Ain't Big Enough for Both of Us" by the Sparks. Cloth moved across my skin. Was Fang dressing me? Could he do that? As if in answer to my question, the trunk sprang open, and an unseen force tossed me out of the back like toast from a toaster, clad in my usual WELCOME TO THE VOID T-shirt and ensemble. The katana stayed in the trunk. I was afraid to mess with it, anyway.

Winter glared at me. "What," I asked, "you gonna stand out here and not kill me some more?"

"Be as glib as you wish, Eric." He waved away my comment, then snatched at the air as to grasp more words out of it. "Yet, I'll remind you of this. I may not have killed Lord Phillip with my own hands, but I arranged his death. Whether you give me credit or not, I marched you down the path and handed you the motive after ensuring that, having already defeated Lisette's memento mori, Fang would have the power to assist you. It took time, but as a vampire, I have plenty of that particular commodity."

"And so you're going to kill me?"

"Oh yes."

"But you're not going to kill my daughter or blow up my business or set fire to my movie palace or kill Marilyn or frame me for murder or wipe my brain with magic, right?" I folded my arms across my chest and watched him bristle. "Because all that's been done already."

Winter remained silent.

"No." My voice told those gathered that I couldn't believe such a thing. "You weren't planning on staging a repeat and calling it an encore?"

"Of course not."

I indicated him with both arms like Vanna White showcasing a brand-new car or a trip for eight to Disneyland. "Not Ebon G. D. Winter, artiste of bullshit and treachery and seven shades of I-told-you-so. Not him."

"I said I wasn't," Winter maintained.

"Good." I turned back to the duke. "Then fuck off, would ya? The big kids are having a dick contest, and we know you don't like to use yours for anything . . ."

Winter stalked from the room and misted through the shattered glass from Fang's arrival off into the night. As he left, I couldn't help but notice that none of the attending vampires shifted to follow his exit. Their attention and their directional disposition were squarely on me. *You win again,* I thought after him, *and they have no idea.*

"Beatrice," I called over the murmur of vampiric congratulations from the suddenly vociferous crowd.

"Yes, Master." She appeared at my side in a flash from wherever she'd run when Fang barged in.

"What was I talking about?"

"You were explaining to Duke Gornsvalt and those assembled that you hate Vampire Politics and hope that we can move toward a new level of civility."

"I was?" I raised an eyebrow.

"I could be wrong, Master. I am merely human, but I thought that's what you were doing." She batted her lashes at me.

"Wait." I pulled her close, as if greedily hoarding her warmth, and continued in a stage whisper. "Is this the thing where I was going to wait until someone pissed me off, act like I was playing hardball, and then be magnanimous to prove a point?"

"That is what you talked about in the car."

I leaned in and kissed her on the cheek. "Well," I said, looking right at Duke Gornsvalt, "if I was already talking about it in the car . . ."

✦ 29 ✦

GRETA

LOSING MY RELIGION
(OR THIS PARTICULAR PRIEST, ANYWAY)

Stained-glass images of scenes from the New Testament framed both sides of the church as Evelyn and I walked in. On my right, Jesus fed the five thousand. On my left, He walked on water. Farther down, He turned water to wine, healed the lame, and made Lazarus rise from the dead. I didn't know what all of them represented, but the ones with Jesus I knew from Sunday school, from a time before foster care and vampire dads.

The pipe organ played, and it was a bigger, better one than Father Ike's church had before Dad burned it down. I wasn't going to burn this one down, not unless I had to do it. No, my business was almost certainly restricted to the priest.

Wisps of smoke curled up from my shoes and off my shoulders as the strength of the beliefs of those present and engaging in active worship tried to force me out and destroy me . . . but not Evelyn. Religion is fickle.

"What are we doing here?" Evelyn whispered a step behind and to the right of me.

"I told you," I whispered back. "I have to strangle a priest and see if I understand why Dad did what he did. Give me your scarf."

"I'm not letting you strangle a priest with my scarf." Her voice got louder, and the ushers at the back moved toward us.

"That's not what I want it for, you goof," I replied, exasperation clear in my tone. "Just give it to me."

Reluctantly, Evelyn unwound the scarf, and I draped it around my own neck. The scant flock seemed to take no notice of us as we walked down the center aisle. The building was laid out like a cross, a long central section with pews on either side, then more pews to the right and left of the altar. Behind the altar, a huge stained-glass image of a resurrected Jesus ruling over the cosmos (or I think that's what He was doing) loomed over the priest and the altar. Atop the altar, a golden cross caught the overhead light shining brightly.

At the podium in front of the altar, a priest in a cassock and purple scarfy thing went through some sort of call-and-response deal with the parishioners. He'd say a long passage, and they would all respond in unison, standing, kneeling, standing, kneeling. It reminded me of an aerobics class, except I think most of it was in Latin.

"Thank you for joining us," the first usher said. He was a tall, pale-skinned food with blond hair. He blanched when he saw my fangs but kept on with his spiel. "There are plenty of seats in the empty pews . . ." He let the words trail off as he noticed the smoke rising off of me.

"Cool," I said, snapping his neck, "I see a spot."

He fell down like they all do, a marionette with cut strings.

"Was that really necessary?" Evelyn hissed. "We can't just murder people."

"Maybe you can't." I caught the other usher, a bald food with dark skin, and hurled him over my shoulder to where the organist sat amid his controls and pipes. "But I can do whatever I want."

"What in God's name?" the priest asked.

"I want to try something with you, Father." I had to shout to be heard over the commotion near the front. Then Evelyn came at me with a stake, one of those customized jobs that had a combat-knife handle. I spun to the right, grabbing the stake, and she nailed me in the side with a second one I hadn't spotted. It missed the mark, though, puncturing my lung and not my heart.

"I won't let you do this," Evelyn said, struggling to drive the stake farther home, to nick my heart. Her fangs sank into my neck, and I twirled free, letting go of her arm but shoving her through the nearest pew in an explosion of wood.

"Don't you be a bad deputy, Evelyn," I chastised her. "I like you, and I don't want to have to kill you."

"I told you, Greta." Evelyn pulled herself up, holding the stake point up, warding me off. "You can't just keep killing people in front of me. I'm not one of you. I can't sit back and—"

"Everyone please, remain calm," the priest was saying, "come this way and get clear of the rogue elephant. If anyone has a cell phone, please dial 911."

"Rogue elephant." I laughed. "I don't think the old Veil ever made anyone think I was a pachyderm. This is awesome!"

"Why are you doing this, Greta?" Evelyn floated over the broken pew, interposing herself between me and the priest, directly in the middle of the center aisle. "You didn't even eat those two men."

"I need to understand." If Evelyn kept this up, she was going to really annoy me.

"Understand what?" Evelyn looked back over her shoulder. "What it's like to kill a priest?"

"No, stupid." I heard two heartbeats behind me in the organ loft. "Besides, I only killed the one whose neck I broke. The other food still has a heartbeat."

"They're not food, Greta." Evelyn drifted back to the ground. "They're people. Humans. Like you and I were before we were turned into vampires by your father."

"Daddy didn't make you." I dropped low, into a crouch, like a linebacker getting ready to sack the other team's quarterback. "Daddy made me. You just happened. I was on purpose." I broke left and charged through the stained-glass depiction of Jesus walking on water, landing in the holly bushes that flanked the building. Slowing as little as possible, I cut back around the entrance and burst back in through the image of Lazarus rising from the dead on the right.

"Damn it, Greta! No!" Evelyn caught me less than a hand's breadth from the priest, my claws closing the gap enough that a single drop of blood rolled off his nose where she made me nick him.

Hands full of me meant she didn't have the stakes anymore. When had she dropped them? Oh. Just before grabbing me. I reached for the floor, snatched up a stake, and stabbed her through the eye. Her scream let me know she felt that more than I would have. I grabbed for my Glock, forgetting that I'd already emptied it into a demon until the lightness of the empty clip reminded me.

I didn't spot the other stake before it was piercing my chest—barely enough time for me to catch Evie's hand and keep her from actually staking me. "If you want to play, we can wrestle later! This is serious!"

"So am I!" she spat. We rolled on the ground, scrabbling for control of the stakes. When Kit Kat and several members of the VCPD hit the door, it brought a smile to my face.

"Thank God," Evelyn said as she struggled to hold me in place.

Kit Kat drew a crossbow and fired.

It *thunk*ed home.

I don't know why Evelyn thought Kit Kat would choose to shoot me. Maybe she thought it would be like the song and that Kit Kat would sing a verse about whom she shot and whom she didn't, but I didn't see how lyrical correctness would get Kit Kat to shoot this sheriff.

"Nice job, Kit Kat," I said, pushing Evelyn off of me. "Now take these nice people outside to safety and leave me alone with the priest." My shoulder caught fire, but I patted it out. I was running out of time.

"I—" Kit Kat opened her mouth.

"Don't make me quote the Incredible Hulk at you." I drew myself up to my full height. "You wouldn't like me when I quote the Incredible Hulk at you."

She nodded before giving orders to the other officers. "Get all the parishioners out of here, but keep the good reverend inside. Our sheriff would like a word with him."

A confused padre sat in the front pew while his flock was escorted out, some sure they'd seen a Bengal tiger, others an elephant or a group of gangbangers. I sat on the carpet patiently, with my staked deputy. It was funny to listen to them babbling about what they'd seen, all having seen something different.

"What about this one?" Kit Kat nudged Evelyn with her boot.

"I want her to see this," I said softly, "but you wait outside."

Kit Kat left without another word.

"Now, I don't know why you're so upset about all this." I detached Evie's head and walked toward the good reverend with my best friend's head under my arm. I wondered why the staking had disabled her whole self, head and body and not just neck and below, like it had when Dad staked her. Was that the effect the church had on her? She couldn't detach naturally? "I don't understand why you have this perverse need to keep me from testing my theory, but I want you to see this, to help me interpret it."

I sat her head on the pew next to the priest, and smoke began to rise from her neck. I looked back to see that the body was doing the same thing. Yep, it had to be all the holiness and stuff messing with her.

"Boo," I said, snatching up the head and thrusting it at the priest, but he didn't react. I set it back down, and he jumped when I let go of it, as if seeing me for the first time.

"What are you?"

"Don't be afraid, Father . . . ?"

"Paul," he said.

"Don't be afraid, Father Paul," I said. "It's true, I'm a vampire, but I don't want to eat you. I need you to help me understand something. Can you do that?" My left shoulder chose that moment to ignite, but patting it out worked again. A red rash was slowly working its way across my skin, a first-degree burn in progress.

"A vampire?" His eyes were unfocused. I'd lost him. All of this was beyond him, not the kind of up-close-and-personal encounter with the supernatural to which he'd been looking forward all of his life.

"Maybe it's better if I show you?" I asked.

He may have nodded slightly, I don't know, but I decided to interpret it that way. I wrapped my hands around his neck, and as slowly and gently as I could, I choked the life out of him. Eyes bulging, face turning purple, he asphyxiated. I eased him to the ground, not letting up even when his priest's alb began to make my skin smolder faster than the belief surrounding the place.

Flutter as it might, his heart could not keep beating without oxygen in his lungs circulating through his bloodstream and on to the brain and back. I listened carefully for the last beat of his heart as he pounded on me with his fists until they fell limply to either side.

I stepped back and watched him for a count of three before wrapping my borrowed scarf around his neck and beginning CPR, just like my dad had done with Father Ike.

"C'mon, you bastard, c'mon," I said, repeating Daddy's words. "I killed you fair and square, but nobody specified how long you had to stay that way." One moment Father Paul was dead, and then he was alive again and coughing on the floor of his church.

"Did that make any sense to you?" I asked the priest. He rolled away from me in fear, and I gathered up Evelyn's head, reattached it to her body, pulled the stake from her eye, then jerked out the crossbow bolt. She stopped smoldering, but I did not, which is a total rip-off, if you ask me.

"I don't think he gets it any more than I did," I told her.

"You wanted to strangle him just so you could resuscitate him?"

Like that wasn't totally frick'n obvious. I scoffed. "Duh!"

We walked past Kit Kat on the way out. "Thanks, Kit Kat. That's all I needed from him."

Evelyn and I stood out in the night air, both of us as befuddled as could be. My skin was bright pink, like a bad sunburn. In places, I had black spots where I'd burst into flames.

"Are you still my deputy?" I asked. "Or do I have to end you?"

"You don't know how," she said. "Keeping my head separated from my body during the day is extremely uncomfortable, and it causes serious damage that takes a long time to heal, but it doesn't end me."

"Trust me," I said, patting her on the back. "With as much

time as we've spent together, I know exactly what it takes to end you, but I'd rather not."

"Thanks," she said.

"Now if we could only get you over this weirdo 'it's bad to kill' thing you have going on . . ."

✦ 30 ✦

GRETA

INSPECTOR GRETA

"A re you sure we're going to learn anything this way?" Evelyn asked. "What if he isn't really hiding anything?"

"He's meeting with Rachel again," I hissed.

"Is that the one who used to be human and was Tabitha's sister?"

"Yes." I pointed at my laptop screen and maximized the feed from the bedroom cam over at the Pollux. Dad appeared on it, though the image of him shook and stuttered. I still hadn't been able to figure out what made the sound so wonky. I had it cranked up to the maximum, and Dad barely came through.

"Another task?" It had been a month since the last one, and that one had come a month after the fiasco at the Irons Club. At least I knew where Fang had run off to. "Have some pictures that need hanging down at the old Demonic Humpatorium?"

"Why is the sound so bad?" Evelyn asked. "Vampires use the phone with no trouble."

"When you figure it out," I snapped, "let me know."

Evelyn wandered around my apartment. It was a

five-bedroom on Eighth Avenue, but I hadn't put much effort into it. Mostly, it was a place to keep stuff that wouldn't fit in my tiny room at the Pollux. I'd had to hock a lot back when Roger had blown up Dad, Marilyn, and the Demon Heart. I'd been desperate for liquidity just to keep Dad's business properties from being bought up and auctioned off. In my new role as sheriff, though, I'd wanted a place to serve as my office, so I'd started stockpiling things in the apartment: stakes, guns, ammo, and computers, though the computers were mainly for my other business. Two of the bedrooms had been turned into server rooms. There was a mattress in one of the others, but no bed frame or box springs.

I tracked my deputy's movements by sound. Ending her had shown up on my mental to-do list immediately after she attacked me at the church, but I'd put it off because I didn't want to do it. She couldn't be Mom, but I'd never had a vampire friend who was a girl, and I enjoyed it. If I was to learn anything from Dad's example, I supposed that what I ought to do was find a same-sex shapeshifter friend. Maybe a wereraven or a weresnake? Could a *nukekubi* count?

I reached down into the bucket of gerbils I had sitting in my extra chair, grabbed one, and drained it, holding the corpse against my cheek to feel the fur and fading warmth. Evelyn didn't seem to like being in the room when I killed one. She was awfully squeamish for a vampire. Then again, maybe that was a side effect of being able to point at blood and have it fly into her mouth. It gave her distance from the act. Even so, she could have sat down and watched with me . . . I would have moved the bucket. I mean, sheesh, I went out and bought a second chair because Evelyn had mentioned it might be nice to have a place to sit down.

"Couldn't you have gotten space at the Lovett Building or police headquarters?" she asked. Another cool thing about being friends with a vampire was that even when we were in different parts of the apartment or out and about, we didn't have to shout. We could talk in normal tones (whispers, even) and carry on a conversation.

"Maybe," I answered, fiddling with the audio filters, "but I don't know how much they know, and I don't want to put him at risk."

"What's in here?"

"The file room?" I thought that's where she was, but I'd been distracted by something Auntie Rachel had said about oral sex, and wasn't Dad curious about something called a Blood Dragon? I looked it up on my tablet and found a reference to something called a White Dragon and sighed at the mental image: Why would any man be stupid enough to hit a woman in the back of the head while she was in a bite-it-off stance . . . and why did she think Dad would want to see blood shoot out her nose? Wasn't that a waste of blood?

"The one with all the boxes?" Evelyn asked.

"Yup, it's from Marilyn's old apartment. I cleaned it out and stored the stuff until I could afford a place to put it. I kept meaning to have Dad go through it to see what he wanted, but . . ."

The screen stole my attention and my words. Auntie Rachel gave Dad the hard sell, sliding his hand beneath her dress to demonstrate her inability to find clean underwear when she got up in the morning. He didn't pull away, but he didn't respond, either. Her eyes half closed, and as she moved his hand, she whispered suggestions about where he might put his Daddy parts and how and with what frequency. Her tail slid down his pants, and my fangs burst through my gums.

"That's new," I said in reference to the tail.

"So," Evelyn said, making me jump, "what do we call this, then? A tail job or a skank wank?"

"A Bill Clinton," I said, "'cause it's not technically sex, but it sooo totally counts."

"What's she doing with her hands?" Evelyn asked. "Oh. Never mind."

I felt a flush throughout my body, the desire to feed rising like a wave. I wanted to grab a man, any man, and ride him like Rachel wanted to ride Dad, and then tear out the stranger's throat as he sullied me, then start over, going through his friends and neighbors one by one. I remembered sex with Telly, the parking attendant who used to watch me hunt vampires, the smell of him, the touch of him. I missed his skull, wanted to cradle it to my chest and think of blood.

The skin at my nipples tightened, and for just a moment, I considered how much easier life would be if I were Mom. My chest heaved, my lungs springing into action as being that in touch with my body's carnal desires stirred them to life.

I sniffed the air and caught the odors of sulfur, lime, and maleness. Had the chupacabra boy in the hoodie who was dedicated to me found my house? Followed me here? If so, I wanted him. I wanted anyone. I . . .

Evelyn.

I kissed her, my tongue exploring her fangs. She returned the kiss hesitantly, the scrapbook she'd held dropping to the floor, but she absolutely wasn't into me. There was no arousal. I would have smelled it. She simply didn't know what would happen if she pushed me away. Her fear tinted my vision red, increasing the lust for blood. I didn't want her . . . or any woman.

Experiment over.

"Sorry," I said before I could remember not to apologize. Daddy doesn't. I shouldn't, but the rules are so hard to remember, and sometimes they change, or maybe I never understood them correctly in the first place. The boy in the hall? His heartbeat sang to me, low and thready, not quite human, because he wasn't. To screw him would be to kill him, but I didn't want to kill him . . . he put my words on a hoodie, wore them like an echo of me, a mark, and I wanted him to be, to exist, not to die.

Frustrated, I turned back to Evelyn. She stood, hands raised at shoulder level, as lost as I was about what to do.

"Um . . . hell-o," she said as I kissed her again, letting my hands find her breasts, cold beneath my touch. I grabbed her groin and she took my wrist, gently pushing me away. "What the fuck, Greta?"

"No," I growled. "You're not. I . . . don't . . . Rrr." I backed away. "Sorry. Sorry. I—" I hate apologies, but I like Evelyn, and she deserved them.

My front door exploded as I went through it. My own mewling hit my ears along with the sound of Dad extricating himself from Rachel's grasp. He had self-control. Dad did, but not me. I was lost somewhere in the confusion of trying to understand his newest set of unspoken rules. Why was his heart beating but his skin cold? Why did he breathe even more than usual? Why was there blood, his blood, in all those apartments for retired cops? What was he doing during the day? How did Kit Kat seem like a thrall without being one? Why did he kill and resuscitate Father Ike, then hide what he had done rather than rubbing those demons' noses in it?

I wanted to ask him, but I wasn't sure whether I was supposed to figure it out myself. I really didn't want to seem stupid for not knowing. Stupid people annoy Dad. He doesn't respect them. He sends them away. And even though he's promised never to send me away again, knowing that he wants to but can't because he promised not to would be even worse.

I kicked in the door of what would have been my next-door neighbors' apartment if I hadn't slowly killed them all and taken over their spaces. Mrs. Rosetti's lonely apartment still looked clean and tidy, like I'd had the Mages Guild leave it.

Throw rugs covered the floor, and my feet tangled in them as I moved too fast, crashing down in front of her old boxy cathode-ray-tube television set.

Shelf after shelf of her Russian stacking dolls stared down at where I lay on the floor, and I leaped to my feet, seizing the television with which to smash them to bits.

"I DON'T UNDERSTAND!" The TV exploded with more smoke and sizzle than flash and bang, and it wasn't enough.

"Tell me what's happening, Greta." Evelyn arrived in the doorway with vampire speed but came no farther.

"Why can't you be Mom?" I asked, blood tears streaming down my cheeks. "If you're Mom, then liking you, being friends with you, makes sense, and then Dad will have someone to fuck and the world will be right." The pain in my hands didn't even register, so I clawed them, each with the other, to make sure they still could. Why was I sobbing?

"If you were Mom, I could ask you to explain Dad, and you would have to do it." I clapped my hands together, rubbing the blood into my skin as the greedy flesh sucked it back in. "He's good in bed. He always makes them come." I nodded at her as if willing her to agree. "Even when he's preoccupied with Marilyn, he's not a selfish lover. And if he's not big enough in human form, the über vamp has a really really big—"

Sulfur. The odor had grown, was closer. It was not alone. It was listening at the wall and at the floor. There was more than one heartbeat now, but only one that I recognized. He was overhead, in the Martinezes' former residence.

I leaped through the Sheetrock between the joists, claws first like a diver, tearing my way through carpet, falling down on the first attempt but making it all the way through on the second. Hoodie boy was halfway out the door when I grabbed him and forced him onto the carpet of the now-sagging floor.

"Why are you following me?" I rolled him over so I could

see his face and pinned his arms down on either side of his head. "What do you want?"

When he spoke, his accent reminded me of Telly's. English was a second language for him. The first sounded like it might have been Spanish. "I want to be yours," he said, eyes alive with passion. "To be near you. My kind, the older ones, they are afraid of the loud . . . of the noise, but I saw you conquer the Prime Contagion with your fury, and I want that. You bring the noise, and I want to bring it, too."

Three other chupacabras: an Asian boy, a Latina, and a heavyset African-American—all young, like him, but all old enough to eat by Daddy's rules—peeked in through the front door from the hall. There were more out there with them. They all wore my words on their clothes: SHE'S THE BOSS, APPLESAUCE.

"I want to have you and then kill you." My fangs were at his throat.

"Do what you want," he whispered. "I don't want to die in silence."

"Make us scream," said the girl. She could have been his sister; her skin was marred by the same eczema-like blotchy patches.

"All we know is quiet," said the heavyset boy. "Life in the plague is about silence. Keeping ours, enforcing it on others."

"You're the opposite," said the girl. "When you rage, you howl and growl and flaunt it. When you hurt, you scream."

"Teach us how," said the boy beneath me, his rigid manhood pressing against me through his jeans, "and we will go where you want during the day, when you can't, and be quiet there and listen and see. If you choose it, we will die for you. Just give us voice."

I sank my teeth into his jugular, and his blood had taste, sour, tart, and bitter, like lime. I kissed him then, his own blood slicking his lips, and if I hadn't taken so much, I would have mounted him and had to kill him after, but he was flaccid, not from lack of will but from lack of blood. That impotence saved him. He was the one. The right person to be my first thrall.

Clawing the shirt from his back, I rolled him over and spat dark red onto golden-brown skin, willing the blood into a tattoo, a badge of words on the back of his neck:

TEAM

GRETA

"I mark thee and bind thee." I said the words of thralldom without officially asking, but his smile let me know there was nothing he wanted more in the entire world than to belong to me. "Master to servant. Servant to master. You are mine until I set you free. You are mine. So mote it be."

Dad had said the experience was pleasurable when he made Rachel his thrall, but with the nameless chupacabra boy, it was more than that. Sparks lit up in my brain, and my legs buckled as I bucked against him, grinding his face into the carpet. All of the pain and confusion washed away on the wave of orgasm and my pants were wet with the scent of blood.

"I'm the boss, Applesauce," I said as I bit through his earlobe and opened wounds in his back with my claws. I watched as the skin flowed back together, then I parted it again, and he bit back a scream. "No!" I shouted, swatting the back of his head hard enough to concuss him. "Scream for me. I command it!" I drove my foreclaws knuckle-deep into his shoulders, and the howl that ripped free of his lungs was a primal thing beyond pain, a letting go of whispers, a surrender to noise. The wounds knit back together quickly, and his eczema was completely gone.

"Me next?" the female chupacabra asked.

"I decide who gets to be my next thrall." My eyes flashed crimson, and she responded to the anger with a smile. My breath no longer came in ragged jags. My lungs were still, my chest quiet. I was centered. Powerful. At peace. My body, once more only an interface.

"I don't understand everything that just happened," Evelyn said from the apartment below, "but can I say that if this is going to happen every time you get horny and frustrated, I'm buying you the biggest damn selection of vibrators and sex toys known to man."

"Why?" I asked, but Evie never answered.

"What's your name?" I asked the chupacabra boy.

"I wouldn't know," he answered. "You haven't named me yet."

Very good. What sort of fruit would fit him? But no, not a fruit. He was nothing like those rejects Apples and Oranges. A noise. A noise that was a triumph over silence . . . What was the name of that Spanish metal band I'd heard Telly listening to from time to time? I remembered.

THE METAL'S GONNA GET YOU

Warcry walked up to the rear of the McDonald's, cutting right through the breakfast drive-through traffic. A padlocked metal grid blocked off the ladder providing rooftop access, but he didn't slow. His body, lean and well maintained, coiled and leaped, easily bringing the lowest exposed rung within reach, the rest accomplished by easy traction from the charcoal FiveFinger TrekSports he wore.

The smells of cooking meat and brewing coffee reached him even on the roof, and I smelled them through him in a dreamlike haze, lying in Fang's trunk, fast asleep and wearing Percy's glasses.

This is how you do it? I asked Percy, envisioning my words as blocks of red text.

I cannot see exactly what you're experiencing, Greta, but I imagine it's similar. How many senses do you get? His answer appeared in the air above Warcry, strokes of a golden pen writing in the air.

Three that I've noticed. I thought back. *Smell, sight, and hearing . . . but no touch or taste.*

Those two are the rarest of all, Percy wrote. *A lost opportunity, perhaps, but the three you have are typical of Vlads.*

Just as well, I thought to myself. *Warcry touches his face so much, it would have given me the creeps to have to feel it all the time.*

Can they hear you? Percy wrote.

No. The admission stirred resentment chased by self-loathing and inadequacy in my belly. Warcry paused, questioning wordlessly. *They seem to pick up on my emotions, but apparently, that's the best I can do when I'm asleep.*

Deciding to keep going with the plan, Warcry settled in next to the edge of the rooftop, mostly out of sight, and pulled out his smartphone, flipping through the photos I'd scanned in from the scrapbooks Evelyn had found.

My three thralls perched on breakfast stops nearest the Void City police station downtown: McDonald's, Krispy Kreme, and Arby's. I could have used a fourth thrall to cover the Waffle House, but I didn't want to enthrall the fat one until he lost weight. The others in the hallway weren't in the running. They hadn't been brave enough to come walking in the door of the Martinezes' apartment, and I couldn't see myself joined to fraidycats.

Moving from one thrall's perceptions to another felt less like changing channels than rolling out of bed early in the morning and hitting the snooze button. It took time, and for random intervals, I dropped contact completely, sleeping the sleep of the dead until another dream cycle got me close enough to consciousness to reconnect.

While Warcry couldn't stop touching the now-smooth skin on his face, Nightwish obsessed over her legs, running her hands over her shins and thighs, then hugging her arms. I hoped she just looked cold to anyone who saw her. No one would be watching her up on the roof of the . . . But she wasn't on the roof.

Nightwish sat bold as brass in the dining area of the Arby's, eating a croissant and sipping at a cola. Two cops walked in through side doors, and she took a long hard look at them as if it were more natural than breathing to notice them and watch them. I couldn't compare them to the pictures from the scrapbook, but she could. Images flipped past on the smartphone's touch display like slides on an auto-advancing carousel, with the plus button stuck.

I watched for hours, sleeping on and off, until, through Chthonic's eyes, I saw Evelyn sit down at the table where Chthonic had made himself comfortable.

"What are you looking for, Greta?" she asked, directing the question half to herself, half to my thrall.

I couldn't answer, but Chthonic did. He passed her his phone.

"What?" She studied them. "These are the pictures from the photo albums I found? They're all cops."

He nodded. "Some. The ones she wants us to examine."

"Why?"

"I don't know."

"Why?" She looked at me, through his eyes, and her mind touched my mind . . . barely. Archives of horror, those things at which other Vlads quake, waited to be shared with her, but not through Chthonic's mind. He might break. I wasn't ready to give up my new toys and throw away the pieces yet. I settled for sending words rather than pictures. Safer.

Speaking, even telepathically, felt like shouting into a bucket of syrup . . . which . . . I've done, actually. My verdict? Sticky and hard to get out of your hair. I finally gave up and used acid.

When Dad was human, after Korea, Marilyn convinced him to try being a cop. They didn't know how the world worked. They didn't know that all the good cops were puppets.

I follow you so far, Evelyn thought back at me.

I . . . Dad's nostalgic. I struggled to remain close to consciousness. *And . . . I was remembering how, when he made his current thralls, some of them got younger, more attractive, even. He . . . deaged them.*

And you—Evelyn chewed her lip—*thought he might have enthralled . . . What? Some of the cops from the old folks' home?*

Yes. Why else would I have smelled his blood in every room?

Blood tattoos? Then why look here?

Breakfast places, I thought. *It's not just doughnuts that cops like.*

Evelyn yawned widely, giving me an excellent shot of her uvula. "Your brain is so slow during the day, it's making me sleepy."

Evie rubbed her eyes and took a sip of Chthonic's Coke.

Caffeine worked on her? That bitch!

"You're pissing her off," Chthonic whispered. "Best get to the point, neh?"

"Oh." She handed the Coke back to Chthonic. "Sorry. Marilyn."

"She feels confused," Chthonic said before I had to try to put it into words.

"Greta, Eric didn't tell you to watch Marilyn," Evelyn said. "You had me tail her the other day, to see where she went and make sure she was okay, but Eric didn't say anything about watching her. If he made a deal with the devil to get her back, do you really think he's going to turn her over to some unknown quantity without keeping a weather eye on the horizon?"

Gears turned and clicked into place. I smiled in my sleep.

"She likes that idea." Chthonic grabbed up his phone and started texting. "Where did this Marilyn get sent?"

"The Iversonian."

"Cool."

An hour later, Team Greta had the Iversonian and his club of the same name under surveillance. By the time the sun set and I woke up for the evening, they'd spotted nine different cops who looked like they might be men from the photo album. Whether doing a drive-by in a VCPD squad car, on foot, or in one case, on mounted patrol, one of the nine passed by the club every ten minutes.

"He's definitely keeping an eye on her," I said, standing next to Nightwish. She rubbed at her elbows, where I'd just fed off her ulnar artery, ignoring the healing wounds at her throat and femoral artery. Thralls heal fast, but she looked weak and pale, which made me want to feed again.

Evelyn saw the look in my eye and touched my shoulder. "Don't you think she's had enough?" She added an emphatic nod as if that would lend weight to her statement. "Give her a rest. You have other thralls."

"I like you, Evie." It was my turn to put a hand on her shoulder. "Do you like me?"

"This isn't a prelude to another weird kiss thing, is it?"

"No."

"Then sure." Her eyes unfocused slightly. "I can't explain it, but I think you're a nice person trapped inside this whole vampire mind trip. I think maybe I understand why . . . a little. Something horrible must have—"

"Don't talk about it unless you want to see it." I looked into her eyes. "Because I can show you, but I don't like it when people talk like they understand me when they don't know shit."

"Right."

"Can I kill you, Nightwish?" I asked the question of my thrall, but my eyes never left Evie. "If I want?"

"Yesss." Nightwish's answer, small and reminiscent of a chupacabra's hiss, hurt Evie more than I could on my own without getting inventive.

"What the hell?" Evie tried to turn to Nightwish, but I held her in place by the shoulder. "Why?"

"Because she's an unwanted thing," I said. "They all are, the chupacabras who want me to lead them. Their parents and fellow uggos probably say they want them around, want them to be happy, but then . . . why make them stay chupacabra? 'Cause that sucks, and Popsie could cure any of them . . . let them go, let them heal, but he doesn't want to. He just wants them to do as they're told and not ask any questions and pretend to be happy."

Nightwish was nodding.

"They say they want noise, but what they want is difference. Change. To feel. And good or bad, I can make them feel something. It's what I do. Dad was lost when he rescued me, but I rescued him, too. Just a little."

Nightwish held her wrist out, and I sank my fangs into the radial artery and let her drop when she fainted. Warcry and Chthonic ran over, each taking a shoulder, and pulled her up.

"Sheriff," Evie said. "Can we not let ourselves get distracted?"

The "Sheriff" got my attention. I like respect.

"I don't want to step out of line, but is showing me how badass you can be really how we want to spend our time?" She nodded at the Iversonian. The club was just now opening. Cars were queuing up, and a redcap in a dirty leather jacket was parking cars. "I've seen all your forms. I know how scary you are, Sheriff. What I don't know is what Eric Courtney is up to, and I thought that was the important thing."

"You're right, Deputy." A squad car with two of the men from the scrapbook pulled around the corner, driving slowly in front of the Iversonian. As it neared us, I let my claws slide out, my eyes go red, and all my vampiric speed come out to play. Daddy said I couldn't kill the VCPD, but he never said I couldn't carjack and waterboard them.

Public Safety Tip #5: I have no accord with Geneva, I've never met anyone named Miranda, and "due process" is a misspelled discussion topic for why grass is wet in the morning.

$\blacklozenge$ **32** $\blacklozenge$

MAYBE THERE'S SOMETHING TO ALL THIS STUFF AFTER ALL

Tending bar takes more skill than some give credit for, and I don't mean that in a Tom-Cruise-in-the-movie-*Cocktail* way. It also kills me that for some people, that reference is to a classic movie from a time gone by. To me, Tom Cruise is just a baby, and that movie was yesterday, but there are kids old enough to drink who come into the Iversonian, and to them, Tom Cruise is a punch line on some cartoon I've never watched.

Worse, to the Iversonian himself, I'm the same way. And for the record, whoever invented the damn apple mojito should be shot in the face twelve times and then run over. In a busy bar, there simply isn't enough time to mix the damn thing. I don't think it's worth the money in the ingredients, either.

"I said, 'Go fuck yourself, blue eyes.'" The twentysomething at the bar I'd convinced the Iversonian to let me open in his upstairs area didn't seem to understand that I wasn't going to fill his drink order.

"I just want an apple mojito," Blue Eyes repeated. "What's the problem?"

"Fine." The three-deep crowd at the bar all wanted my attention. "Twenty bucks, then."

"But they're only ten downstairs."

The urge to throw the guy across the room slid up my spine and sat on my shoulder like a tiny demon urging me to give in. All I had to do was tap in to the ambient life force around me, and I'd have the strength to do it. Knowing how true immortal powers work makes it clear why a guy like the Iversonian would want to run a club. More lives meant more life force, and more life force meant that if I wanted to throw my strength around, I didn't run the risk of killing plants and animals or giving people cancer by drawing too much and confusing their immune system or mutating cells.

His girlfriend cringed apologetically. "Geez, Dylan. Just order something simple, like a lemon drop."

I laughed, one explosive burst of air. Lemon drops are almost as bad, and they leave me with sticky fingers.

"Chelsea," I said to the bartender next to me, "my tips are yours. I'm out."

Chelsea glared at me with purple-accented eyes of pink, and the air around her sparkled. I forget what kind of an elf she is, but she's good at her job and three times as patient as I am. She says the patience comes with age. Ha!

Bass thumped in time to the beat of a song I'd heard, but never with the mix that had been applied to it now. Humans danced with fae and a few vampires, but mainly the fae folk, since most of them could disguise themselves enough to pass for human. Especially with the amount of body modification some of the Iversonian's clientele had undergone.

Headed out? the Iversonian asked telepathically from a spot at his favorite table.

I'll be back for my lesson.

Paying a visit to Greta?

Why do you ask? I thought as I shoved my way between two idiots.

She's outside. He raised his glass at me as I caught a glimpse of him through the crowd. *I thought you might have sensed her. Most true immortals learn to do that eventually, at least with Masters and Vlads: pick up on the energy that lets them sense each other.*

Nope, I thought back.

And now she appears to be stealing a police car.

What? I squinted, and the little blue lines of life force (or soul energy, as the Iversonian liked to call it) popped into view. I drew in little sparks of it to feed my speed and muscles. Stronger and faster, I elbowed my way through a sea of bruises and bumps, then out the front door.

✦ 33 ✦

THE WORLD ACCORDING TO APPLESAUCE

Marilyn charged out the door of the Iversonian wearing a low-cut purple silk top and black leather pants with straps running up the sides. The boots and jacket I recognized, but she wore makeup . . . She never used to wear makeup. Or . . . maybe . . . a little, but not like this. Not since I'd known her. A leather cord dangling around her neck caught my eye, and I thought I saw a hint of gold: a ring through which the cord had been threaded, peeking out between her breasts.

Her engagement ring, I thought, *but are you Mom or an imposter with that makeup and those clothes?*

She waved.

I looked away, punching the cop in the face again and forcing him into the back of his squad car with his buddy. *Screw the not-Mom.*

"Officers Salvadore Donatello and Carl Vicks, you're coming with me." They were a lot quieter unconscious. Bruises turned purple, then yellowish, and started to fade. If they weren't somebody's thralls, they were missing a great opportunity. Either way, they were hiding something, because they looked and smelled like normal humans. I'd made three thralls now, and I thought I should be able to tell if these guys were thralls, but I wasn't getting anything. Maybe I was doing it wrong. Even with Uncle Percy's glasses on my face, I didn't see anything to explain the healing.

His words appeared in a golden script across the lenses. *I'll check again when we have more time, but I don't see any magic.*

"This is so wrong." Evelyn put a hand over her eyes.

"Start the car, Deputy."

"We're not going to kill them, right?" She opened the driver's door. It had slammed shut in the struggle.

"I'm not allowed to kill them." I handcuffed Sal's hands behind his back and slammed the rear door. "Duh!"

"Greta!" Marilyn shouted as she darted across the street between cars. "Greta! Wait!"

"Go on ahead." I shut the passenger door, which hung open, the window shattered where I'd punched through it and dragged Carl out of the vehicle. "Take them to my place. I'll catch up later."

"You're the boss," Evelyn said as she pulled away.

Marilyn met me at the sidewalk. I don't think she noticed Chthonic and Warcry watching her, one from the alley and the other from a nearby parking deck. Nightwish was even harder to spot, mixed in with the hopefuls waiting in line to get into the Iversonian.

"What's going on?" I hugged Marilyn begrudgingly. Mom or not, I still liked her, loved her even, maybe. She was familiar, and a person who'd always tried to be nice to me, cared for me—unless she'd misled me about being Mom.

"Were those cops?" Her eyes searched mine, and I wondered what she hoped or feared to find there. Her eyes widened in an expression of . . . something.

"Maybe."

"Please don't be cute, Greta." What did that look in her eyes mean? I'm better with negative emotions than positive ones, for the most part. Compensation comes in the forms of other people's reactions or by monitoring subtle changes in pulse and pupil dilation. Reading Marilyn should have been easy, but my fundamental confusion about her status and mine added to the existing difficulty in a way I don't think I'd experienced since my first few years of undeath.

"I wasn't." I ran my hand along her throat, closing it just enough to feel her breath and pulse together beneath my palm. "I don't know what they are. They used to be cops, but I don't think they are who they say they are, so I'm going to question them."

"Does Eric know what you're doing?"

"I don't know." My left hand went to my pocket, and I traced the edges of my badge through my jeans as my right hand felt her false mortality. "I'm the sheriff, though. So I can do what I want."

She's learning, Uncle Percy wrote. *I see things hanging in her soul matrix already: weapons, some sort of armor. The Iversonian is keeping his word to your father; he's teaching her. But I don't see a tithing cord or soul tap. It's surprising.*

"Greta . . ." She pulled away from my hand, and I fought the urge to tighten my grip and not let her go, to cling to that illusion of normal life. Hers, I mean. I didn't know how to feel about an i-Mom-mortal.

"Sorry." I jerked my hand away as if I'd been stung by a wasp. "I like to feel your heartbeat and your lungs moving air. I'm glad you're young again. Is the Iversonian nice?" *Are you fucking him?* I shifted to put her upwind of me and sniffed for man smells but found only the scents of sweat and alcohol and cleaning products that I expected if she was being faithful to Dad.

"If you want," she said reproachfully, "we'll go rent a room, and I can strip down so you can get a really thorough whiff."

I would have liked that, but I didn't think it was a real offer, so I apologized again. I still don't like to apologize, but Mom or not, I like Marilyn. She deserves an apology sometimes, too. She understands me better than anybody else.

"You're only looking out for your dad," she acknowledged. "Here, put your head to my chest so you can have a good listen." I did as she asked. "I'm not having sex with anyone, and I'm not dating anyone, and I'm not interested in dating anyone, not even your dad, until I sort some things out."

It was the truth, and it earned her another hug. Maybe she wasn't Mom, but she had so much potential to be Mom again, or still be Mom, that I couldn't hurt her or be too mean to her.

"Okay . . ." I couldn't *call* her Mom, though. It wouldn't come out. "I have to go . . ."

"One thing," Marilyn added. "That other vampire who was with you. That's Evelyn, right?"

"Yes." I clapped my hands, not knowing what else to do with them that didn't involve claws, squeezing, or more hugs. "She's my deputy, and her head comes off and then goes right back on again with no trouble. She's Dad's second cousin a few times removed, so technically, they could fuck and it wouldn't be weird or anything."

"Ha!" Marilyn brayed, then coughed. "They're not, though, right?"

"Nope." This was dangerous territory for me. Like the reason I've been trying to stay out of rooms with Dad and High Society vampires in them. I don't like it when people deny Dad what he wants or what he deserves. My eyes flashed red, and the diamond from Marilyn's engagement ring caught the rays, bent them, and refracted them as dots of red so that it looked like fireworks going off in her décolletage. "He only wants you, and you won't let him have you."

She sighed. "I guess I—"

But I was gone. I couldn't listen to her anymore without wanting to hit her and open her up to see what needed fixing. Why didn't she want Dad? What was wrong with her? Why couldn't I cut it out and feed it to Talbot like a demon?

I met Chthonic, Warcry, and Nightwish three blocks over in front of Query's Quick Pawn, and the three of us climbed into Nightwish's 2000-model Cadillac. Parts of its metal body were rusted through, and the paint job was a muddle of blue and primer gray, but it ran. Nightwish drove while both Chthonic and Warcry squeezed into the back with me.

"I'm cold." At once, they pressed against me, their body heat a shield against the ever-present chill. I excited them, but they didn't have the same effect on me. I wanted to eat them, kill them, tear them apart, but then they wouldn't be able to keep me warm. I've grown up a lot . . . I'm learning to take better care of my things. I will say this, though: Erections make damn good hand warmers.

"Turn on the radio," I said, wanting noise but not conversation. "And stop moving around, you two. If I get anything sticky on my hands, I'm going to wash it off with your blood."

"How can she just do that?" a whiny male voice was saying. "I was just out minding my own business on one of the nights when vampires are allowed to be out, and then the fucking sheriff and her lesbo sidekick are beating the hell out of me and dangling me off a rooftop. This shit never used to happen under Phillip."

"Thanks for your call, Travis." Sly Imp's voice came in a beat later, with Gorillaz bed music playing underneath. Was that "Revolving Doors"? "What do you think, Void City? Does Eric Courtney need to rein in his daughter, our Sheriff of Slaughter? Hello, you're in league with Sly Imp."

"Yeah." The voice sounded young and angry. "What the

hell, man? E'rbody says Er'c is tough an' all, but I ain't seen him do shit that she ain't done her damn self if it need doin'. We only have her word that he saved her at all. I think she killed Lord Fat Ass and gave her pops the credit cuz she got crazy daddy issues. Know what ah'm sayn'?"

Whimpers came to my attention from close by, and when I noticed the sounds were coming from Chthonic and Warcry, I let go, wiping my hands on their pants. "You two are lucky that's blood." Neither thrall spoke, eyes wide, looking straight ahead. For a brief second I played with the notion of resuming my grip and seeing whether their eyes would actually pop out of their heads if I applied more pressure.

Annoyed with them both, I climbed into the passenger seat and got out my cell. Four callers later, I could see my apartment building, and Sly Imp finally gave the number to call in again. While Nightwish pulled in through the automated security gates (using my code and parking pass), I dialed the number.

To my astonishment, Sly Imp himself answered. "You're in league with Sly Imp."

"No." My voice shook. "I'm not."

"Be that way, caller. I—"

"If you hang up on me, I'm killing you and everyone in your building."

Sly Imp laughed nervously. "There are six different radio stations operating out of this one building, caller. And we have excellent guard demons. Gyre, run the mystic ID on this caller and let's—"

Gyre, his sidekick of the airwaves, came on next. "It's Greta Courtney."

"What?"

"It's the sheriff."

Silence.

All of his listeners heard more dead air in that pause than they probably had in the last year of broadcasting.

"So glad to find out you're a fan of the show, Your Slaughterness." I'd shaken him, but his chutzpah was back. Faked or not, I liked the recovery.

"I'm not."

"A new listener, then. I—"

"Find something else to talk about," I said. Nightwish turned off the car and slumped down in the seat. She looked tired. "But stop talking about my dad."

"Sheriff Courtney," Sly Imp began, "surely you must understand the supernatural community's interest in your adopted father."

"Adopted?"

"Well"—Sly Imp was nervous again, clearing his throat—"I . . . assumed. You know what? Forget about that. What my listeners would just love is to hear your side of everything. Tell us your history with Eric Courtney and how you came to be our resident lawperson."

"Do a lot of vampires listen to your show?"

"This is the most popular talk show in the greater Void City area," he said. "I have a huge vampire and demon listenership."

"Good." I got out of the car and cocked my head; I couldn't hear the two cops. "Tell them that my daddy is the biggest, baddest vampire in this town, and he will be treated as such. He will be respected and well treated or the perpetrators will answer to me."

"Up close and personal?"

"Up close and 'Oh no, I hope Greta doesn't know the one secret way to end me forever, oh, fuck, she does. Ack. Thud. Slurp. Poof.'"

The night air picked up, blowing over me, and I luxuriated in it despite the perceived chill. This at least I could do. Dad kept stopping me from killing people I needed to kill, but I could threaten these people and make them respect him or pretend to, and he didn't care about the difference. Dad is all about perception. If they seemed to respect him, that would be good enough for Dad.

"I have a bank full of callers that say otherwise."

"One word," I said, "and I'll be listening for their voices in the night. They may be fine for a while, but eventually, I'll find them or Fang will. Good night, demon." I hung up.

"Caller, you're in league with Sly Imp. Go ahead." Nothing. "Let's try line two, Gyre." Nothing. "And line four?" Nothing there, either.

My smile grew large enough to qualify for lying-Grinch status.

"Sheriff Slaughterhouse has made her point, folks," Sly Imp said. "Enough politics, but don't tune out. Next hour I'll have Rolfindorf Rottingham, the new power forward for the Void City Howlers. He's a Norse werewolf. We'll ask how he thinks the team is shaping up after all the recent changeups, and does the new coach, Carmen Samburro, have what it takes? Can a female hockey coach make it in Void City?"

My smile vanished when I saw Evelyn standing empty-handed in my apartment without the cops.

"I'm sorry, Sheriff." She held out a note. "Captain Marx delivered it herself."

> Dear Greta,
>   Please leave the cops alone. You can help them. You can ask for their help; you may not hurt them. Otherwise, you've been doing a great job.
>
>   Love,
>   Dad

Damn. Thwarted again.

"What do you think?" I asked, aiming the query at both Evelyn and Percy (via his memento mori glasses, which were still on my face).

"I think we'll have to explore another lead," Evelyn said. "We'll need to steer clear of anything involving people who may or may not be his secret thralls. Can you think of anyone or anything else we might try?"

I think you're very close, my dear, Percy penned.

Maybe. I chewed my lip. "We got the names of those cops, though, didn't we?"

"Yes," Evelyn answered. I snapped my fingers, and my three thralls were at my side. "First," I said, "I want you to turn into dogs so I can pet you, because it's just occurred to me that you can. And second, we have the cops' names. Now let's find out who they are and what they mean to Dad."

✦ 34 ✦

ERIC

I NEVER LIE . . . TO HER

"No."

"No?" Talbot held up the newest set of bills, watching me from across my desk. "If you don't do something, she's going to figure it out."

"So what?"

"So what?" Talbot put down the bills and looked at Magbidion, who was sitting in the recliner I'd bought for the office but rarely sat in. Mags looked half asleep. "You've put that one through an awful lot of trouble for 'So what.'"

"That's true."

Magbidion smiled. "I'm okay with whatever, boss." His speech was slurred. "We can rest up and try again or . . . something."

"No." I knew it, and Magbidion knew it, too. This was a one-shot plan. If I screwed the pooch, The Plan or this version of it would never work again.

"You could try ordering her not to interfere." Talbot leaned over the desk and took the checkbook from me. "And writing these checks yourself."

"I think that's the one order I could give her that she wouldn't follow, Talbot."

"I thought she'd do anything for you."

"Anything except let me get hurt." I powered down the computer and leaned back in my desk chair, watching him flawlessly fill out checks in my handwriting. "I could tell her to rob banks, kill women, children, and puppies, or even ask her for sex, and she'd probably go along with it, but can I get Greta to let some demon that I can't fight beat the hell out of me? I don't see that happening."

"True enough." Talbot looked up from signing my name. "I could always—"

"Not this time."

"Mind if I write myself a big fat check while I'm forging sigs?"

"If you think I owe it to you, take it all." Nervous, I got to my feet and started wearing a path in the carpet. My nighttime secret camped at the edges of my memory, messing with my brain. Familiar things woke memories that were prone—if I was too distracted—to turn into full-blown hallucinations.

"A cargo container shipped all the way from France on an otherwise empty sailing vessel, at vampire safety rates," Talbot commented as he wrote a check for a particularly large bill.

"Garnier," I said, using the code name for a being with whom I'd tussled back in Paris on my honeymoon. "Doesn't come cheap. I gotta grab some air."

"Go ahead, old man," Talbot said. "Try not to get lost on the way across the street."

"Yeah, right." I stepped out into the hallway.

"Oh, and watch out for the weregecko assassins in the hall."

"The wha?"

I looked up and marveled at the wonder and complexity

of the universe. I knew there were all kinds of therianthropes, but fucking weregeckos? Six of them clung to the ceiling, bedecked in bandoliers of stakes and throwing stars, each wearing a dark-colored gi. The one closest to me looked for all the world like a giant version of the Geico gecko, but with leopard markings and all ninja'd out, his toes and fingers bending backward at strange angles as he clung to the ceiling in the hall. As he opened his mouth with a hiss, his tongue darted at my head like a thick pink blackjack.

I dodged left as throwing stars rained down from above and the geckos attacked.

"You've got to be shitting me."

♦ 35 ♦

CHASING LEADS

Greta had her own ideas about research, but my methods needed neither thralls nor supernatural abilities. My ways were as simple and old as my mortal profession, even if the tech changed as the news media itself mutated and grew.

Sitting at Eric's desk, I slid open the lap drawer. His passwords were there on a Post-it note, but I could have guessed them easily enough. They weren't quite as bad as "password" or "123456," but they were still things you aren't ever supposed to use: Greta's birthday, Marilyn's birthday, Fang's license plate—which says FANG.

Eric's e-mails didn't tell me much. He'd been corresponding with someone in Europe about demons. How their chains of command worked. How their power levels worked. What was the difference between a Nefario and an Infernatti? Was Magbidion right about someone called Lady Scrytha? There were other questions, too, about things called Soul Bonding and Soul Burn.

I plugged in a thumb drive, set his PC to making an archive copy of his e-mail, and wrote down his settings so I could set up his account as an alternate on my own PC. As much as I liked Greta (despite my better judgment), I wanted to keep the option of killing this guy.

Leaving that process running, I locked the desktop and walked out into the hall. I'd seen Eric head over to the club, even said hello to him, but he wasn't suspicious enough to ask me what I was doing at the Pollux. I was his daughter's deputy, and he took that at face value in a naive way that would have made me feel guilty for sneaking around if he hadn't been the guy who'd torn off my head and thrown it down a manhole.

Padding down the hallway to Eric's bedroom, I heard Erin and Cheryl talking downstairs but couldn't make out what they were saying. To add an extra layer of quiet to my creeping, I let myself drift away from the ground, floating down the hall. His bedroom door stood open, but inside, there wasn't much of interest: clothes, a new television, a refrigerator.

"I wonder how much blood an Emperor keeps on hand," I asked myself as I opened the fridge. The six bags surprised me, but not as much as the leftover steak from Outback, the half-six-pack of Coke in glass bottles, and the Tatsu 7 Go Gurt. And I opened the styrene container and balked: a piece of birthday cake?

Something else weird ran up the side of the fridge interior. Because it was empty, I needed a few moments to identify it, but it was either a very strange beer-bong attachment or a scabbard.

I took a picture with my phone's camera and moved on to the bathroom. Kneeling close to the floor revealed some sort of powdery residue. My senses are better with my head detached, but I went mundane tech first. I pulled a UV penlight out of my bag and, after I flipped off the bathroom lights, let it play across the floor.

The magic circle it revealed got photographed, too. That had to be Magbidion's doing. I didn't know enough about magic to tell what it meant or implied. Like a good reporter, though, I knew who did.

A couple hours later, I was pulling off I-65 in Pelham, Alabama, with huge white natural-gas tanks looming large to my right. I turned right again before Highway 31 and wended my way along the heavily forested back roads so common in Alabama. Five more minutes, and I pulled up to a small square building behind a high chain-link fence. I parked my Harley on the grass next to the fence, not wanting to drive it on the gravel, and flew up and over the fence.

Unlike other vampires, *nukekubi* show up on camera unless our heads are detached (or that's how it works for me), so when the large metal garage-style door rolled up and the men with guns, crossbows, and crosses stepped out, I wasn't surprised.

"I want to talk to Pythagoras."

Wood, a heavyset man with long stringy unwashed hair, headed up the pack. As I settled to the ground, he spat. Wood has never liked or trusted me. "Maybe he doesn't want to talk to you, leech."

"And maybe he does." Pythagoras rolled out of the shadowy recesses of the building, stopping at the concrete edge of the Golden Triangle's safe house. "It all depends on what you have to tell me."

"Call off the ghostbusters here, and I'll be happy to tell you a lot of things."

"Very well." Pythagoras tipped the control of his electric wheelchair back, and I walked in after him.

Pythagoras isn't a magician himself, but he's used mages from time to time to hunt vampires, to level the playing field. When I stepped into the warehouse, for example, I obviously tripped some sort of ward or barrier, because the symbols on my neck lit up, my fangs came out, and my eyes began to glow. Wood and his boys got spooked, but Pythagoras rolled on without comment.

Holy symbols bedecked the interior walls, but aside from that, it looked like I'd walked into a low-tech Batman's version of a weapons locker. Weapons ranging from swords and crossbows to AK-47s and bazookas lined the walls. At the center of the back wall, a Mac and a PC sat side by side. At the back left, on a mat, a one-armed man was demonstrating staking techniques on a high-tech dummy while a real (and totally staked) vampire lay next to it on the mat.

Wood and his buddies rejoined the class as I followed Pythagoras over to the computers.

"How are you getting along with the Courtney family?" he asked.

"It's weird." I set my thumb drive on the computer hutch. "I haven't seen the father make a live kill since I got there—like he's trying to quit—but the daughter kills easy as breathing."

"Breathing is easier for some than it is for others." Pythagoras took the thumb drive and plugged it in. "What am I looking at?"

"Courtney's e-mail archive and some pictures I took while snooping around."

His PC screen filled with thumbnails. He clicked on the black-light mystical symbols, and I caught a twitch at the corner of his mouth. The hint of a smile. "Where did you find this?"

"His bathroom floor."

"I'll send the images to Iso, but this is a multipurpose construction of some kind. It's related to concealment with the power created in the circle but focused through something else—I'd guess the caster, him- or herself—but Iso will know for sure."

"Iso?"

"Isosceles," he said. "He's my contact in the Mages Guild. And that's all you need to know about her."

It's always bugged me, the way Pythagoras swaps gender pronouns when discussing a resource he'd like to keep under wraps, but I let it go.

"What are these?" He clicked on the scanned images of the cops from Marilyn's scrapbooks.

"The sheriff—" Pythagoras started violently when I said the word. "The daughter," I corrected, "has her new chupacabra thralls looking into that."

"Why?"

"One of the clues we followed led us to a home for retired Void City police officers. Courtney had trashed the records, and there was a residual scent of what the daughter seemed certain was Courtney's blood."

"Interesting." He twitched the joystick on the arm of his chair, rotating back for a better view of my face. "What else?"

"Some of the cops we've seen around town." I tapped the screen over one of the faces. "They're these men, and they have quick healing, but—"

"But aren't detectable as thralls?"

"Yes."

"They're thralls," Pythagoras said, "which is curious."

"Why?" I asked.

"Because I have it on good authority that Eric Courtney is no longer as he appears to be."

"What is he?"

"There's one way to find out." Pythagoras waved a hand at one of his troops. "Get her the katana I was prepping for her."

Wood walked over to a sealed case and typed numbers into a keypad. "We only have one more of these, Pyth."

"Thank you for the reminder, Woodroe." He directed the next bit directly to me. "We gave the other one to John Hawkes, and it wound up in Ebon Winter's hands."

A sapphire nimbus clung to the edge of the blade when

Wood drew it. The cloud of magic was slight but obvious.

"What does it do?"

"It's a sword," Wood snapped. "It cuts things." He sheathed it again and handed the sword and scabbard over to me.

"Okay, so how am I going to use it to determine what Eric Courtney is or isn't?"

"You aren't," Pythagoras said. His software ejected my thumb drive. "I just wanted you to have it."

"Unh." I coughed, exasperated. "Then how do I do that?"

He clicked back to the image of the magic circle. "Simple. Courtney is working with a mage. A soulless one, yes?"

I nodded.

"He's the one powering the magic, whatever it is. Kill him." He made an "easy as that" gesture. "Kill him and the spells will drop, then whatever he's hiding will be out in the open. Can you do that?"

"I've never killed a human like that, just murdered—"

"The man sold his soul to a devil, Evelyn." Pythagoras touched my hand. "He doesn't count as human anymore. He abandoned us and sided with the monsters of his own free will."

"Yeah." I nodded, trying to convince myself. "I guess so."

"Know so," Pythagoras said, "and choose your time wisely. Courtney is planning something. Wait until he's at his most exposed, and then kill the mage."

✦ 36 ✦

ERIC

OLD FRIENDS WITH NEW CAUSES

A week after the fight with the weregecko assassins that Winter sent me as an I-still-publicly-hate-you present, I was still in the habit of checking the ceiling when I entered a room. Magbidion lay on my bed again, his face so white, I was afraid things might already have gone too far. My special invisibility-to-demons necklace, the Blind Eye of Scrythax (which I'd gotten back only a week or two before), moved up and down with each ragged breath. Talbot stood over him like one of those cats in old wives' tales who steal the breath of babies.

"How bad?"

"You can't wait any longer," Talbot said.

My cell vibrated.

DAYTIME SUPPORT: *not yet—the plan app* was displayed on the touch screen.

"Give me a timetable," I ordered, as if Talbot had a magic chart of how long Magbidion could continue to maintain all the spells and enchantments I had him running before he finally died of exhaustion. To his credit, Talbot's eyes changed from normal to glowing star emeralds without comment or objection. Maybe he'd become fond of my mage. Or maybe such abject loyalty fascinated him.

"He might make it to morning." Talbot touched Magbidion's forehead, his hand coming away wet with sweat. "He might not. It's a close thing."

"Mags?" I asked. He didn't answer. His lips were moving too soft, slow, and slurred for me to have a chance of reading them. His hands twitched occasionally as if completing portions of a mystic gesture in his semiconscious state . . . still maintaining the spells.

How much longer? I typed into my cell.

DAYTIME SUPPORT: *Rockstar says at least three more days.*

Too long, I typed back. Get everyone into position. I'm calling a friend.

DAYTIME SUPPORT: *Eric, if you do it this early, the Marilyn portion of the plan may fail completely.*

C'est la vie, I typed back. I had hope. Hope would have to be enough.

I closed the app, sent one text, and then walked down to the street. Fang's radio blared 100.6 FM (WVCT—Void City Talk Radio). Sly Imp was interviewing a local demon who claimed to be upset about the exclusivity of Orchard Lake and Sable Oaks, the local werewolf- and vampire-only neighborhoods just outside of Void City proper.

"Just because I'm a demon doesn't mean I don't like to fish and swim or drive a pontoon boat around a lake, but the parasites and the monthlies have all the best lake property sewed up tight."

"Now," Sly Imp cut in, "all that's true, Diaxicrotioush'nar, but can you honestly tell me that part of this, even if it's only a little bit, is not about property rights but about the contract you have on Eric Courtney's thrall Magbidion?"

"I'll admit the little greaser is overdue for collection, but that's a separate topic. I—"

"I hate to cut you off, but Gyre just handed me a note that—well, if it's true, then I expect our fearless fucktard of a vampiric lord and master"—he switched into a Ricky Ricardo impression—"has some 'splaining to do. Caller?"

"Hello, Sly." The lingering trace of hoarseness wasn't enough to obscure the words or disguise him at all. Talbot nodded to me on the way to his motorcycle.

"You certainly sound like the man, but that doesn't mean you're him."

"Some in my place might quote Mark Twain, but I find that cliché." The warmth in Father Ike's voice was a narcotic to some, a balm to others. Hell, even I was glad to hear him speak. "Others might quote Scripture. I can think of several passages that would be easily misused. John 11:25 might be misappropriated to claim biblical power and authority or intervention: 'Jesus said unto to her, I am the resurrection, and the life: he that believeth in me, though he were dead, yet shall he live.' First Corinthians 15:22. 'For as in Adam all die, so also in Christ shall all be made alive.'"

"That definitely sounds like you, Father, but even I can quote Scripture."

"Of course you can, Sly. James 2:19," Ike cited. "'For it is written that demons believe and shudder.' But your listeners don't really want to hear me preach, do they? If so, I have several sermons . . ."

I laughed, and so did Sly Imp. "No, thank you, Father, but if you could do me a favor and pass the Jude test?"

"Come now, Sly," the voice said, so softly that the roar of Talbot's bike almost drowned him out as my favorite mouser shot by on his way to the VCU campus. "'Thou shall not test the Lord thy God.' Faith is not a parlor trick—while I'm afraid my survival very much is. Well, that and a testament to the usefulness of CPR training."

"C'mon, Father. If you're really who I think you are, you can bind a demon like me with one specific quote."

"I know the passage of which you speak, Sly." Ike took a long breath, and I wondered what was going through his mind. This kind of up-front showy thing is something Ike has always disliked. He's more comfortable working with people on a personal level, but with what I offered him to help me after I strangled and resuscitated him . . . let's just say I understand why he was willing to comply. "You want me to bind you, but I think that's foolish. Why would any Christian want to bind a demon on earth?"

"Waitwaitwait—" Sly cut in. I guess he saw what was coming next. You see, vampires tend to steer clear of Ike because merely touching him can set us on fire, but when confronted with demons, if he wants to, if he feels it's the right time, Father Ike can—

"In the name of Christ Jesus, I cast you out."

I guess I'd expected a scream or *kaboom*, but the silence spoke volumes.

Gyre, Sly's sound tech, came over the air next.

"Thanks for the call, Father Ike," he said, "and I hope you don't mind me ending your call, but I don't have any desire to join Sly in the Pit just now." He cleared his throat and stepped up to the plate with a passable imitation of his former boss's jaunty style. "So . . . what do you think, Void City? Father Ike is revealed to be not only among the living but actively casting demonic shock jocks into hell? Who knew priests could pull that shit via telephone? Can all priests do it, or just badass soldiers for the Big Sky Bully, like Father Ike? Call in and speak your piece on the Widening Gyre."

I was tempted to call in myself and take Gyre to task for

stealing the name of his show from the title of a Kevin Smith *Batman* limited series, but there was no time after the moment Father Ike's voice came over Fang's car speakers. The opening volley was out and fired across Scrytha's bow. Father Ike was alive, and boy, was Scrytha going to be pissed. The Plan was in full swing, and the only two people who could make it succeed or fail were the women I loved most.

For once in my life, there was nothing I could do to save myself. The fight was coming, and there was no way on earth I could win it alone.

MARILYN

OLD DOG NEW TRICKS

Void City University abuts the northwest side of the city, its high brick walls drawing a demarcation that says clearly to all: Void City Ends Here. The last time I'd set foot on campus had been for the graduation ceremony of one of Eric's former strippers. Bethany, I think her name was. I can't even remember what degree she was working on, only that she graduated magna cum laude and Eric was so proud that he bought her a car.

I pulled up to the gate on my Harley and waited while the guard walked out. A middle-aged man with balding hair and a paunchy waist, the guard didn't look that threatening unless you happened to see his supernatural side: an anthropomorphized rat clad in black armor dotted with cruel-looking spikes that glimmered with a hint of magic. Maybe it's that I've never liked rats. His security badge said NIMH, and despite my nerves, it gave me a slight chuckle.

"Nimh?" I handed him my student ID.

"S'ironic." He took my badge and gave it a sniff. The accent was one of the British ones, but I didn't know them well enough to tell which.

"Yeah."

On the other side of the iron gates, students went about their business, heading to class or their dorms or wherever. I wasn't sure I belonged with them, but Eric had been right about one thing. There were all kinds of things in this world I wished I knew more about, and wasting the time I had now would be crazy. I'd decided to start with a business degree, because in the back of my head, there was a little dream Eric and I had talked about back when we were engaged: a bar I wanted to open. Not a strip club or a bowling alley but a real . . . joint. No dancing or loud music, just a few pool tables and—

"Mind's a terrible thing," he said, handing me back the ID.

"To waste?" I looked at him.

"That, too." He waved, and the gates opened to let me in.

"How long before I get to use the automated gate?" All the supernatural students had to come in the front gate, past the wererats, but I hoped that wasn't a permanent thing.

"After the appropriate, miss."

"Appropriate what?" I slid my ID back in my leather jacket. "Amount of time?"

"Could be, miss."

Finding a place to park took less time than I'd thought and gave me a chance to wander about campus. The army-surplus duffel on my shoulder weighed me down enough that I decided to carry it up to my dorm room. Dorm room. I sniffed. The very idea of a dorm room still cracked me up, but the Iversonian had insisted. "It will help you remember how young you look on the outside, to remind yourself that you are forever changed."

"'Besides,'" I quoted him under my breath, "'everyone needs a college experience, to be on one's own amongst strangers. Of course, I had mine when we were just inventing the concept. If yours involves a healthy fraction of the sex and vomiting mine did, I shall be impressed . . . and appalled.'"

After dropping things off, I checked my schedule. I didn't know why I'd signed up for a night class. Maybe I hoped there would be more people closer to my real age in it. Ten minutes later, I was seated in Accounting 101, waiting for Professor Duncan to come in and bore me. I had a thin tablet computer with a touch screen that I'd been assured all the kids craved and used for notes, though I'd yet to manage more than buying my textbooks on it. I fumbled with the stylus, trying to get it in a comfortable writing position, then gave up and reached into my messenger bag for the pen and notebook I'd packed just in case.

"You've got to be fucking kidding me," came a voice from the door.

"Hello to you, too, Tabitha." I left the pen and notebook where they were.

Tabitha dressed like some damn sluppie (slut + yuppie), all designer labels and accessories, making me momentarily self-conscious in my white T-shirt and jeans. I'm still getting used to not wearing granny panties and Depends. Given Tabitha's relationship with Eric, I felt particularly self-conscious about the engagement ring that hung on a leather cord around my neck, hiding in my cleavage.

"So?" She sat down next to me.

"So . . . ?"

"Did he give you the same talk he gave me?"

"Given that we're both here, I'd guess there were similarities." *Except he loves me and he doesn't love you.*

"Accounting 101?" Tabitha took a long break before she said that. I didn't know what was going through her head, but I imagined it couldn't have been fun to sit next to the woman whom the man she loved cared for more than he cared for her. It took a lot of guts to sit down next to me and be civil. Then again, Tabitha never lacked guts.

"I know a lot about running a bar, but not all of it comes from the correct way of doing things."

"What? You mean Fang fees and vampires?"

"Yeah." I looked down at my tablet. "I'm not sure I'm going to stay in town, and I don't want there to be any surprises. Plus, I have to admit I like the idea of being able to say I went to college, that I have a degree in something. What about you?"

"Eric gave me a lot of money in the divorce settlement, and I don't want to get screwed out of it or wake up one morning to find I squandered it all without realizing it." She looked at her hands, at some spot of paint on the cream-colored walls, and then at the door. "Are we the only students?"

I checked my watch. "They've still got twenty minutes."

"I guess we are early." Small talk was killing her. Vampires have little tells: Her nails were longer than they had been upon entering the room . . . not claws but longer. Her eyes had brightened in color, not glowing, exactly, but a color shift toward red. Her enunciation was more formal—clipped, preparing to speak around fangs without lisping.

"I can drop the class if you want, Tabitha," I offered.

"No," she said too quickly and too loudly. "It's fine."

It wasn't, but I took her at her word, because going into it further served no purpose other than to increase her discomfort and my own.

"Why—" She cut herself off, touching her hand to her lips, the poster child for Was That My Out-Loud Voice.

"Go ahead." I tapped my tablet and entered the pin. "Ask it."

"It's personal."

"Ha!" My laugh made her blink. "I've fed you blood, seen you naked, and staked you through the heart. Even if I hadn't, your sense of smell is strong enough that you can smell what color my panties are, so personal is fine."

"That last part sounded like Eric."

"We've known each other a long damn time." I flipped through screens until I found the note app I wanted, the one that looked like a yellow legal pad. "How do you know it's not Eric who sounds a lot like me? I'm older than he is."

"You are?"

"Yep." I typed "Acunting 101" at the top of the page, noticed my mistake, and added the missing C and O. "So what's twisted your nipples, honey?"

"Why didn't you let Eric turn you?"

"I was Roger's thrall, Tabitha." Immortal memories can be tricky things. It was as if I were in two places: sitting in the classroom and standing over Eric's grave simultaneously. "When Eric came back, I missed my window of opportunity, just like I did when he was alive. We were always in the wrong place at the wrong time. At first it was that I was older. Then it was Betty Lou. Then the war. The VCPD. Roger. It was such a different time. I don't think you can really even understand how different."

"Like what?"

"Well . . ." I watched her eyes. Did I want to try and explain it to her? I thought about how hard she'd tried to keep Eric, and how much of that was her getting caught up in the mess between Eric and me, and thought, *It's the least I can do.* "Maybe you know it, maybe you don't, but I cheated on Eric with Roger."

She nodded.

"But back then. God. Today you would have called it rape. Eric, Roger, and I were going to a Halloween party, but Eric got called in to work. He insisted Roger and I go on. I was mad at him, and I drank too much at the party, and somewhere between helping me home and making sure I got into the house safely, Roger had me bent over the kitchen counter, telling me how we were meant to be together. How he'd always loved me."

"Shit." Tabitha put her hand on mine, and I couldn't tell if it was sympathy or a vampire's natural urge to be warm.

"After that, I tried to make sure I kept away from him, but whenever Eric was on a late shift, Roger would try to find some reason to come over." My tablet blinked off, and it startled me to suddenly see my very young reflection in the black screen. "Or he'd come out to the bar I was working at, and he'd play nice and respectful, and I'd think everything was fine . . . until the next time. After a while, I almost looked forward to it. I didn't know what they were doing to Eric at work, the magic brainwashing and forgetting and all of that. I just knew that he was changing, becoming more distant and quiet and angry."

"Why didn't you tell Eric?"

"I should have," I said, nodding, "but he didn't have many friends back then. A lot of his old buddies were doing the hippie thing, and they didn't like him anymore because he was patriotic, pro-military, and a policeman. They were trying to speak truth to power. As a result, they hated The Man, and Eric was doing his damnedest to be The Man. When I didn't tell him at first, after a certain point, it was all too late, because Roger would tell him about all the earlier times and—"

"And you thought Eric would blame you?"

"No." I took a breath, waking my tablet and reentering the pin. "I knew he would believe me and forgive me, do his best to understand or forget, but . . . the timing was always wrong. It sounds stupid now, knowing what I know, but I did the same things when Eric rose. I thought everything would be okay, that he'd come back to rescue me. I thought that having returned from the dead, he'd automatically know everything, and it would all be okay, but he didn't remember dying, much less possess some secret knowledge from the grave, and I waited too long. By then I was a thrall. Roger had literally compelled me not to say anything or tell anyone."

"Wow." The voice came from behind us. "That's absolutely tragic."

Talbot perched in the row behind us, his chin resting on his hands.

Tabitha asked, "Talbot, what are you doing here?" at the same time I asked, "What do you want, cat?"

"Just checking in." He rolled his neck, the sound of deep pops clear even to my nonenhanced senses.

"Ha!"

"You wound me deeply, Marilyn." His voice sounded hurt, but his expression colored him amused. "Aren't I allowed to look in on old friends from time to time?"

"You looked in," I said. "Now, unless you're actually taking Accounting 101—"

"Oh, I'm auditing the class," Talbot added quickly. "It seems campus security is so tight all of a sudden that the only way a supernatural can get on campus without fighting a plague of wererats is if he has a valid student ID."

"I wondered what was going on with that," Tabitha said in a voice that suggested: "Look, I have boobies!" Had they slept together, or did she just want to bang the kitty?

"It seems they have a new student whose protection they have been ordered to assure at the peril of total annihilation." He smirked and met my gaze. "Not that anyone here would know anything about that."

"If they ever have a supernatural version of *TMZ*"—I turned back around to face the front of the class and my tablet—"you have a career waiting for you."

"Don't worry," Talbot said. "After she kills him, the new management will leave you to your own devices."

"She?" Tabitha asked (and if she hadn't, I would have, just to be clear).

"Scrytha," Talbot said.

"The demon he made the deal with?" Tabitha asked.

"No shit, Sherlock." I packed my tablet back into my messenger bag and slung it over my shoulder. "When is this happening, Talbot?"

As if on cue (and knowing Talbot, it may well have been), his cell chirped. He flashed it in my direction: 911 was all it said on the text he'd received.

"Now."

"Then get off your ass—" Tabitha started.

"He's not going, or he wouldn't have come," I interrupted. "He's here to make sure I know."

"And not me?" Tabitha got to her feet, claws out.

I didn't have time for her shit. "Why would he want you to know?"

"I can help," Tabitha snarled. "This isn't all about you, Marilyn. You aren't the only woman Eric's ever loved."

"Yeah." I sighed. "I'm pretty sure I am."

"You bitch!" Tabitha coiled to jump.

"This"—I tapped into the surrounding energy, since Talbot was full of it, with extra to spare, and activated my speed—"is not"—in my mind's eye, I could see the things I'd stored in energy form hanging about my person like accessories I could click on or off like a digital paper doll— "about"—I clicked on the loaded crossbow and poured more energy in to make it real again—"you"—and fired, staking her through the heart with a crossbow bolt. "It never was."

I didn't even watch her body thud to the ground. My eyes were on Talbot. "Just say it, cat."

"Say what?" He held up his hands. "Don't shoot?"

"Whatever you came here to say." I stepped over Tabitha's prone form and felt guilty about putting a crossbow bolt through her top. All her clothes were so expensive, there was no telling how much she'd paid for the thing, and it looked like silk.

"Demons can be like vampires." Talbot scratched his nose.

"Different power levels, social responsibilities, even unique kill conditions. Scrytha made the move from Nefario to Infernatti when she signed Eric up and made a deal. Unlike vampiric power levels, though, demonic advancements can be taken away."

"And?"

"Eric called her out. He's not being a good little servant, and she just found out."

"So she has to make an example of him?"

"You could say that."

"Why aren't you helping him?"

"I helped him kill Captain Stacey," Talbot said. "If I help him kill the Infernatti . . . That's two big ones close together. If it comes down to it, I might be willing to incur a longer exile for him, but not if I don't have to. In El Segundo, I was the only one who could help him. I accepted the exile for my actions. But what he needs now, you can do."

"Really? What the hell can I do in a fight that he can't?" I looked at the accessories I'd bonded to my spirit, all items the Iversonian had suggested: a pair of crossbows, three stakes, a long knife, a bastard sword, some body armor, and a change of clothes. "Eric is like Godzilla compared to me."

"Demons tend toward old-fashioned weaknesses. The more powerful the demon, the more old-fashioned the weakness. Almost anything can be killed if I eat it, for mine is the power to devour. Really, though, if anyone can fit the whole being inside herself all at one time, that's the real trick. More to the point, Scrytha's weakness now that she's an Infernatti is based on the virtue she abused to make her first deal."

"Love?" I asked.

"Unconditional love," Talbot clarified.

"But Eric—"

"Eric made the deal," Talbot interrupted. "No matter what he does, he can never win. He can't hurt her. Can't bruise her.

He can't even bloody her nose. Why do you think Magbidion needs Eric to defend him against a demon? Like Eric, he shook a devil's hand. Once you do that to seal a deal, the demon is immune to you forever."

"Where is he?" I asked, running for the door.

"Where do you think?" Talbot asked.

And I knew. So much for my first day of class.

✦ 38 ✦

WHO RUNS BARTER TOWN?

This is Percy," I told Evelyn.

As a sign of trust, I'd let her look inside my closet. I don't think she understood all the chains, the leather straps, or the duct tape. Unlike Uncle Phil, I knew that a stake through Uncle Percy's heart did nothing but suspend his need for blood, kind of putting the vampire side of him on hold and letting the mummy side become dominant. His mummy side didn't need to eat or sleep, and it didn't show up on vampiric mental radar, either.

Uncle Phil had displayed Percy in a glass box in the middle of his living area, like a giant Ken doll with a plaque under him that read: *My dear Percy, who serves as a remembrance to all that I do not bluff, I do not make empty threats, and there are indeed worse fates than death.*

I'd put Percy in a case, too, but mine was made of an airtight box within a box constructed of bulletproof glass and hand-etched with holy symbols by William, the Alpha of the Orchard Lake werewolf pack. Also, as Uncle Phil had before me, I staked him, but unlike my nefarious dead uncle, I'd taken the further precaution of wrapping Percy from head to toe in duct tape, leather, and the Infernal Chains of Sarno Rayus, which had been used on Talbot by Lord Phillip a while back when they tried to steal Dad's soul. Just because Uncle Percy likes our arrangement and agreed to it doesn't mean I trust him during the day, when I'm asleep.

"Is that water between the two layers of glass?" Evelyn asked.

"Holy water," I answered gleefully.

"And those little boxes with the blinking lights at each corner?"

"Blessed shaped charges of C4," I said. "If the glass breaks, Percy go boom. He'd probably survive it. He's an Emperor-level vampire, like Dad, but I'm pretty sure this whole arrangement will decorporealize him long enough for me to feed his memento mori to Fang and get my mummy kit."

"You know how to kill a mummy?"

"Oh." My eyes flashed red, bathing Uncle in the light of my killy-killy gaze. "Given enough time and exposure, I know how to kill anything and anyone. It's my thing. Dad may be the über vamp, but I'm the Omega vamp, the über killer. Anything short of a true immortal, I can end forever."

"Including me?"

"I haven't checked." My eyes closed, and I thought about killing my deputy, wanting her ended. "Keep your head separate from your body for seventy-two hours, then when your body rots, dissolve the remains in holy water. Once that's done, your head will combust in sunlight. Expose it to sunlight, let it burn, then bury the ashes of your head on holy ground, and you'll be dead forever. It's complicated and time-consuming but easily done."

"Oh." Evelyn blanched, taking an unconscious step away from me. "I . . . uh . . . good to know."

"I guess." I closed my closet door. "What I'd like to know is what would happen if we pulled off your head and put it on the body of a decapitated animal. Like, could I put your head on a horse's body and have an Evie-corn? Or would that be an Evie-taur?"

"Can we please never try those things?"

"I guess I can live with the curiosity," I said with a sly smile, "as long as you're a good deputy."

I felt Warcry, Nightwish, and Chthonic trying to tell me something, but I ignored them. My chat with Evie was way more fun. I noticed Nightwish's heartbeat out in the parking lot when she pulled up in her battered old car, and I frowned.

"That's not a bad-deputy smile, is it?" Evie asked.

"Nightwish just pulled up, and her heart is racing."

"You can hear her heart from here?"

"Can't you?" I walked to the front door and opened it.

"Maybe vampire hearing is more acute than *nukekubi* hearing?"

"Duh," I said. "I'm always cuter than you."

Evie froze, trapped by that feeling I get a lot from people who can't tell whether I'm joking or whether I really didn't understand what they said. I could have let her in on the joke, but I like the way it keeps people off balance not to know the whole of me.

"Mistress!" Nightwish shouted when she saw me. "It's all over town. Lord Eric didn't kill Father Ike."

"Duh!" I said again. "I knew that. I was spying on him when he strangled Ike and set the church on fire. I was there even before then, when he fought Winter on the steps of the church. I almost jumped in to kick Winter's ass, but I was afraid it would embarrass Dad."

Nightwish stared at me blankly.

"So?" I wanted her to elaborate.

"The demon," she said, though she was clearly out of breath. "Reviving the priest and hiding it from her . . . It broke your dad's deal with some demon . . . and now she's going to show up in person to punish him."

Oh, please, like Dad and Talbot can't handle a demon.

"She who?"

"The demon."

"Which demon?"

"Someone called Scrytha."

"As long as Talbot's there—"

"But Talbot's not there," Nightwish blurted. "Chthonic tried to tell you mentally, but you were busy. Talbot rode off. Warcry tried to follow him but got stopped by the security guard at the college."

"Do you smell that?" I asked Evelyn.

"No." She sniffed the air. "What am I supposed to be smelling?"

"Dead cat." I thought back to the fight when Dad's sire had come to town, when Talbot left me to be kidnapped and tormented by Uncle Phil. I thought of what Phil would have done to me if my control over the connection to my body hadn't been as strong as it is. My eyes went red again, catching Nightwish in their red light.

"I'm sorry. I'm sorry. I'm sorry." She crumpled under my ire. I stepped over her on my way out the door.

"Wasn't Fang in the parking lot?" I asked.

"Your dad has him," Evelyn answered, keeping step with me.

I broke into a run.

Top vampire speed.

Nobody hurts my dad!

✦ 39 ✦

ERIC

MY COMEUPPANCE

And there she was, Lady Scrytha: ex-Nefario, full Infernatti, and (according to her) the being who writes my honey-do list until the end of time. For once, I'd come face-to-face with my chief irritant while none of my family was being held hostage. My club wasn't torched or rigged to explode, and my movie theater wasn't on fire.

Scrytha looked as alien as her father, plus had an extra set of breasts I didn't think she'd had the last time we met. Precious and semiprecious jewels studded twin pairs of ram's horns jutting from her skull. The jewels sparkled in the greenish light from two sets of eyes (one set normal-sized, the other small and round, like evil doll eyes). Her dress was tanned hide of some kind, though it didn't look like leather to me. It gripped her tightly, dual keyholes highlighting cleavage from both sets of breasts, making me uncomfortable.

"Mr. Courtney, to what are you up?" When she spoke, a spotlight from beyond the sight of us nondemons (or at least me) lit her up, and I couldn't help but notice that the tail snaking its way from beneath the hem of her dress cast three shadows.

"To what am I up?" I climbed out of Fang, leaving the driver's-side door open. The car's metal felt cool under my skin, and I traced the lines of his hood. I stopped when I got to his front bumper and leaned against him, the light from his headlights picking out the edge of my jeans and casting Scrytha's right side in shadow. "Is this English as a second language? Next shall I inform you that I'm a person with whom you ought not fuck?"

"Words are important, Mr. Courtney." Her cloven-hoofed high heels conjured sparks of blue flame from the street as she walked closer.

"So is the right lube," Rachel said as she poofed into existence next to her boss. She'd replaced the blue dress with a rubber bodysuit, thigh-high boots, gloves, and a leather duster. She would have looked great in or out of them, but in them, with her tail curling about, making shadows on the street, and those little red horns, she took on the appearance of danger, too.

"Do we call that a non sexquitur?" I punned.

Rachel smiled. Scrytha did not.

"You're hiding something from me, Mr. Courtney, and I want to know what it is." It's always unnerved me, the way her two sets of teeth move out of sync with each other, the inner set of jagged fangs snapping to a beat of its own.

"No, you don't." I patted Fang's hood, looking down with a half smile on my face, hoping that my visual verification that Fang was parked over the artificial locus point would be interpreted as nostalgia or cockiness.

"And why is that?"

"Because . . ." I let my eyes close, one last check to make sure everyone was ready. "Because"—I opened my eyes again—"you remember what it did to the cat?"

If my vampire hearing had worked properly at night, I might have heard a helicopter taking off from a private hangar at the airport. I might have heard a lot of things. I might have heard squad cars rolling this way, their sirens as silent as my grave in Valhalla Cemetery . . . just as soon as I said the code phrase . . . and I was pretty sure it was . . .

"Of what are you speaking, Mr. Courtney?"

"Curiosity."

"And satisfying mine would be dangerous in some way?" Scrytha examined the lacquered claws on her left hand, eyes cutting down at them and then back at me. "I find that highly doubtful. Now answer my question."

"Curiosity," I said again, louder. That was still the code word, wasn't it? Scrytha snapped her fingers, and six more demons poofed in. Large angry demons, three with black chitinous exoskeletons, each one at least as big as the über vamp, the other three sporting grasping gray tentacles and squidlike heads.

Did we have two code words? I know "curiosity" was the code word when we took out Captain Stacey. I could have sworn it was just the one. *You have an app for that, dumbass,* I thought to myself.

"Give me a second." I reached for my phone only to watch it rise out of my hand and roll into a ruined ball of tech.

"No." Scrytha's left hand was curled into a fist. When she opened it, the dead cell phone fell back into my hand. "Right now, Mr. Courtney."

"Telekinesis, huh? Cute." I let the remains of my cell phone drop into the road. "I bet that comes in handy on long lonely nights."

"Yes." Scrytha smiled, the inner set of fangs clenched tightly, the outer set open. "I imagine you would. Is there any other lewd comment you'd like to make before I have my hounds"—she gestured at the chitin-covered demons—"practice tearing you apart?"

"Um?" I opened my mouth to say something clever, but

instead, a demon hit me in the face. I don't know which one it was, probably one of the chitin-covered ones, but I wouldn't rule out Scrytha as the culprit. As I flew backward into the street, I heard Rachel pay me the best compliment I think she was capable of giving:

"We'd have had so much more fun if we just slept with him."

Under the circumstances, I agreed.

40

GRETA

MIGHTY MOUSE STYLE

D ad. Dad. Dad. Dad. Dad."
The word a mantra on my lips, I announced myself to Void City the way a policeman might call ahead to clear traffic lights in the movies. I wanted all greens, and I was going to get them.

Public Safety Tip #6: "Hot pursuit" means stay out of my way, or you might get dead.

"Greta?" Maybe-Mom's voice touched my mind, but not the kind of contact I could push my will across, that funky thing true immortals do—telepathy.

I dashed in and out amid the traffic, cars swerving and honking. What did my portable version of the Veil of Scrythax make them see? A crazed biker weaving in and out on a Harley? A deer? An escaped animal? I couldn't know. Vampires I passed, Masters and Vlads, bounced against my mind, but I dismissed them without heed.

"Greta?" Marilyn said again.

"I'm busy."

A street back, Evelyn rode down the sidewalk on a

motorcycle I didn't know she owned . . . and maybe she didn't own it. I didn't care about that, either.

"Call Marx and tell her I want every cop in Void City at the Demon Heart and Pollux yesterday!" I shouted over my shoulder.

"What?" she shouted back.

I dropped back, running alongside her bike. She yelped, and I grabbed the handlebars, straightening her up, and repeated myself.

"Okay," she said.

"Then get your ass to—" There was a katana scabbard on her back that I hadn't noticed before. "Where the hell did you get that?"

"I mugged Toshirō Mifune's American like-a-look."

I smiled at the Marx Brothers reference. I like my deputy. I wonder if she knows I LoJacked her.

"I want you cutting up demons with it in front of the Demon Heart ASAP."

Hunger filled my gut like it always does, growing worse with each moment of superspeed, each drawn-out second I wasn't helping Dad.

I took the turn from Second Street onto Fifth Avenue, sideswiping a station wagon, its driver's-side door crumpling under the force of my impact. The driver lost control, rammed a parked car, and shot headfirst through the windshield. A spray of blood and glass exploded next to me—a rain of orderly chaos in predictable patterns I had no time to appreciate or enjoy.

"Dad. Dad. Dad. Dad. Dad. Dad."

I did a forward somersault over a Void City Metro bus crossing Fifth and Midnight. My shoulder clipped the frame, and the bus tipped, following me over onto its side. Screams filled my ears like the roar of a crowd, like twenty dying cheerleaders urging me on. No looking back. Even if it means I miss the blood, fire, and Jell-O.

"Jesus Christ," Evelyn's voice said from far off.

Thuds and impacts from behind stirred me on.

Running down the center lane, white lines blurred into one line of white, a track to lead me straight to Dad.

Marilyn's 1200-cc two-cylinder engine caught my attention a block before she turned onto Fifth Avenue ahead of me on Sixth Street.

Greta, she said in my mind again.

How are you doing that? I thought at her.

Practice, she thought back. *You announcing yourself like your father does makes it pretty easy to connect.*

I'm busy, I thought back. *I have to help Dad.*

Then help me get there, she thought. *I'm the one he needs.*

I stopped dead still in the street, cars zooming past me. Why the hell does she get to be the one he needs?

Why do you get to be the one he needs?

The demon he's fighting, Marilyn thought back. *She can only be defeated by someone who loves Eric unconditionally . . . or something that can ingest her entire being all at once.*

But you don't meet either of those criteria. I sped up, pulling even with Marilyn.

Of course I do!

You can fit the whole demon in your mouth? I asked, running up and over a Datsun that was changing lanes. *Is she a tiny demon?*

"I love your father unconditionally, too!" she shouted.

"Bullshit!" I was right behind her.

"Greta, no!" Marilyn screeched as I grabbed the back of her leather jacket and threw her through the front window of Carl's Diner.

"You cheated." I ran alongside the Harley, quickstepping it to a halt because I knew how I would feel if someone wrecked something Dad gave me as a present. "Dad loves *you* unconditionally." I put the kickstand down and left the bike on the sidewalk. "You're fickle," I shouted back at Marilyn, "just like the rest of them! Just like everyone but me!"

Overhead, a VCPD helicopter cut through the night, circling but doing nothing: a holding pattern. Why was it waiting? Where were my sirens? Why weren't my thralls charging in to help? Where was my army of chupacabra? Okay, most of the chupacabra were too pussy to come charging down to fight a demon, but still, it made me mad.

"Fine," I growled as I passed Thirteenth Street, hitting the three-blocks-from-home demarcation, "I'll do it myself."

41

MAGBIDION'S LAMENT

The shortest distance between two points is a straight line (or . . . okay, technically, in a three-dimensional space, it's a geodesic, but that's pretty much the same thing, and I know that only because of the obnoxious math nerd I interviewed once for an episode of *Good Morning, Void City*). Abandoning the bike, I took to the air, like a busty animé version of *Peter Pan Versus the Vampires*. Flying up over the city, I could see the Pollux in the distance. Heading in a straight-ish line instead of the jagged L Greta's use of the city streets forced her to take, I might get there first.

I dialed the Void City Police Department, so the number would show up in my call log in case I had to prove it to Greta, then hung up before anyone answered. While Greta was wrecking half the city and trashing metro buses, I landed on the parking deck connected to the Pollux and peered over the edge.

On his own, Eric wasn't doing well. Demons with shiny black carapaces took turns holding him and pounding his skull while a female-ish-looking escapee from a *Hellraiser/Aliens* crossover and her smaller, more attractively humanoid counterpart looked on. The big one shouted questions at Eric, but I couldn't make out what she was saying, and if he answered her, that was lost to me as well.

Flying down would have been faster, but I wanted clear of the fight for now. If that was the demon with whom Eric had made a deal, then I saw no better time to end Magbidion, and every instinct told me that the demon, whoever she was, was the one from whom Eric most wanted to hide whatever it was he was hiding.

I flung open the stairwell door, leaping from one concrete landing to the next until I reached the first-floor connection to the Pollux. Two of Eric's thralls watched the fight from the glass double doors, and I slid past them.

"You gonna go help him?" asked the thrall with the purple hair, without even looking my way.

Shit!

"Greta's on her way," I said. *Think. Think. Think!* "We're worried somebody might make a move on Magbidion." The truth.

"Shit!" Cheryl. Her name was Cheryl. She took her eyes off the fight outside. "We left him all alone up there!"

"I've got it," I said, rushing up the stairs. "Keep an eye out for Greta. I called the VCPD for backup but couldn't get through. Can one of you try from the landline?"

I didn't exactly lie. "I've got it" could be taken any which way. Lies have always astonished me, the way the first one comes hard, and then each successive deception falls more easily than the first. They gain momentum like dominoes in a line. A quick run up the marble steps, a dash down the hall, and I was alone with Magbidion. Locking the door behind me, I stalked to the side of the bed.

Eyes closed, chapped lips moving softly, he reeked of sweat and sickness.

"Did he say the code phrase?" Magbidion asked.

His head lay on one of the two pillows on the bed. I grabbed the blue pillow and jerked it off the bed. I'd planned to behead him, but the notion of cutting off someone else's head made me sick to my stomach.

"I know . . . that look." His eyes opened lazily, as if he had all the time in the world to act, not just a few more seconds. "That's death. Wanna hear the story of why I sold my soul to a demon, death lady?"

"Yes." I hesitated.

He drew in a wheezing breath. "Too bad." He closed his eyes, resigned to whatever I decided, so I covered his face with the pillow and watched him stop.

✦ 42 ✦

ERIC

THAT'S NOT GOOD!

Swordfish!" I shouted in desperation.

Scrytha raised a hand, and the two demons holding my arms kept right on holding them, but the four demons who were taking turns pummeling my face let up for a moment.

"Are you ready to explain yourself?" Scrytha loomed over me, drool from her lower lip bridging the space between her flesh and mine.

"Klaatu Barada Nicto?"

"What language is that?" Scrytha sneered.

"Geekanese," I answered.

Rachel giggled. "Oh, baby. Just answer her question."

The bones in my face slid back into place, my vision clearing. Teeth that had been knocked out regrew. "I'll answer a question if she'll answer one of mine."

"Done," Scrytha said. "Name your question."

"Do you speak pig latin?"

"What?"

"Just answer the question."

"I've never even heard of pig latin."

"How can you never have heard of pig latin?"

"Now you answer my question." Lady Scrytha raised me to her eye level (the big ones, not the evil round ones) and snarled.

"Nope." If I could have laughed in pig latin, I would have. "I said that I'd answer a question if you answered mine. I didn't say whose question I'd answer, and you didn't specify, so I pick mine."

Rachel stared at me as if I'd lost my mind. Lady Scrytha slapped me so hard that blood poured out of my mouth, and my eyes crossed.

"Indeed," I said as soon as my mouth would respond properly, "I do speak pig latin."

"You cheat!" Scrytha snapped, and something clicked. That's what this part of The Plan had been all about, or a portion of it. Cheating. The letter of the law versus the spirit of an agreement.

"No." I leered, adrenaline pumping, heat flushing through my body. My heart beat in my ears, and it felt like home. "You're the cheater. You abused the terms of our deal. And I'm gonna call you on it. I—"

Scrytha had stopped listening and began sniffing me like a dog.

"Why are you breathing?" Her forked black tongue lapped at my neck. "Why are you warm?" She slashed my throat clear through my voice box with her claws. Arterial spray splattered her. "What is this? What have you done, Mr. Courtney?"

Oh, fuck! I tried to speak, but it came out as a gurgle. *Magbidion!*

Behind her, I heard a solid thump as Rachel went face-down into the concrete; her attacker had long blond hair and wore a hot-pink baby-doll T-shirt that read, IF IT BLEEDS, I CAN EAT IT. Her low-cut jeans were ripped and torn, her tennis shoes scuffed, abraded, and smoking. Clipped through a belt loop, her sheriff's star dangled at a loose angle. On her face, she wore a pair of sunglasses that looked familiar. Behind the tinted lenses, her eyes were glowing the brightest red I'd ever seen.

"What the fuck do you think you're doing with my daddy?"

✦ 43 ✦

I AM THE LAW

I stomped Rachel's head another good time to make sure she wouldn't be setting fire to me in the near future. I would have ripped off her head, too, but I didn't like the look of the big black rhino-beetle-looking demons (does that make them BBRBDs?) flanking Frankenskank. Lemmy Kilmister's vocal line from "Bye Bye Bitch Bye Bye" blared from Fang's speakers, but the car stayed put, parked directly over the artificial-locus thingy Dad and Auntie Rachel had put in.

I frowned at the Mustang. "You're just going to sit there?"

Fang flashed his high beams twice, as if signaling another car to turn in front of him or merge into his lane.

"Are you sure you aren't an import?" I said, sticking out my tongue in the car's general direction.

Fang revved but stayed put.

Three of the BBRBDs moved to protect Lady Scrytha. The light from the sign of the Pollux competed with the angry light of my eyes for reflective purchase on their shiny chitin.

"Greta." Dad coughed. "Don't."

"Don't what?"

"Don't get involved," Dad said. His heart beat loudly in my

ears. His lungs moved. I closed myself off to other vampires, hiding my presence, then revealed it again, but I got no contact from him. Evelyn was in the Pollux. I sensed her, but not Dad.

"Dad?" I asked.

"It's me," he said. "And I'm telling you—"

"To let these demons beat you up in the middle of Thirteenth Street?"

"Yes. Please."

The big black rhino-beetle-looking demons lined up like Spartans, a wall of chitin-covered abs between me, the Frankenskank, and Dad.

"You'd best listen to your daddy," Frankenskank purred. "This does not concern you. This is between your father and I."

"Me," I said, taking a step forward.

"Excuse me?" Scrytha said.

"'This is between your father and me,' not 'your father and I' . . . object fucking pronoun." I rolled my neck, popping it. My shoulders were next, then my back, as I stretched my muscles.

"And here I thought the proper words were so important to demons," Daddy said.

"English is a changing language." Scrytha scowled. "That's how they say it on television and in the movies."

"You should watch more *Sesame Street*," I said. "Let me tell you how to get there." Most big bruisers expect you to try and go around them when you're smaller. I charged right up the middle because I don't care. Pain doesn't matter. The body is an interface, and I'd bet my interface against any Kafka-style demon. "That's it," I said as my claws raked along the carapace of the middle big black rhino-beetle-looking demon, "we can call you Kafka's Horned Unitards." Two of my claws snapped on its armor. It didn't even react, but one of its buddies clipped me in the shoulder, sending me across the street into the wall. Ow. Kafkas. A much better name than BBRBDs.

I ran down the street, looking for something heavy. The

Kafkas didn't give chase so much as alter direction to keep themselves aimed at me.

Building—too big.

Puppy—too squishy.

Human—too fat and too squishy.

It occurred to me a little too late to grab the tire iron or samurai sword out of Fang's trunk. If I didn't come back with something useful, I'd look stupid in front of Dad.

Fire hydrant . . . metal park bench . . . or big blue mailbox? Hmmm.

Then I had it. Epiphany! The right weapon was obvious and I only had to double back a little bit. I cut right on Seventh Avenue and right again on Fourteenth, approaching the Demon Heart from behind and coming in the back way. When I came out the front, I had a sixteen-pound bowling ball in each hand, and Gladys was queuing more of them up by the front door.

"Hello, roaches!" I said, throwing balls. I caught the first one in the shoulder, overcorrected, and hit the second in the thigh. Shards of carapace and polyurethane punched into the wounds, which leaked a pus-like substance instead of blood.

"I'm not drinking that," I said, on my way back for more bowling balls.

"If you cannot stop your offspring, Mr. Courtney," Scrytha said angrily, "I will."

"You?" I laughed. "I'm not scared of you. Daddy can't hurt you because he made a deal with you, but I didn't."

I landed body shots with two more bowling balls before the other Kafkas could get close enough to touch me, hate filling their beady little insect eyes as their buddies squealed and went down, more pus leaking from the holes my makeshift projectiles had punched in their torsos.

"Idiots," Scrytha shouted. "You are not fast enough. Watch Mr. Courtney." She blurred, and only by moving on instinct did I dodge her first strike. "I will handle the daughter."

◆ 44 ◆

EVELYN

SECOND THOUGHTS ON MURDER

Murdering Magbidion didn't feel like I'd hoped. The instant I did it, I heard Dad's voice in my head quoting *Don Quixote* at me, telling me that I was as bad as the company I kept . . . as bad as Eric or Greta . . . and he was wrong. I was worse. As far as I'd seen, Eric killed out of need. He hunted. Greta, too, in her own twisted way, had a morality. She fed on the people she killed. True, she fed too much and far too capriciously, but I had a theory about that. Suppose she had to sate an Appalachiosaurus-sized appetite? If the size of her largest form tied in to her need for blood, her constant hunger made perfect sense. But I . . . I had no such excuse. I neither needed nor wanted to eat the mage.

"I guess it's my turn to try CPR," I muttered to myself.

"Oh, I wouldn't bother," said a smooth-sounding voice. "I've already come to collect him."

A shadow stepped clear of the bed, as if the shadows gathered there had given birth to a charcoal-colored demon, soot drifting from his skin as he moved, leaving dirty trails along the sheets and floor. Eyes like black pits marked his face, but there seemed to be no mouth. In his right hand, he clutched a semitransparent version of Magbidion, rendered in Force-Ghost blue.

"Jesus." I took a step back. All the demons I'd seen before had at least resembled flesh-and-blood animals.

"Diaxicrotioush'nar," his voice crooned, "but that's a common mistake. I'd lost track of him thanks to that little Blind Eye toy of Courtney's, but the moment his soul left his body," he exulted, "I saw him clear as midnight to the eyes of the blind."

"Let him go." I drew my katana, its edge luminescing.

"But you just killed him." The demon gestured at the body. "Second thoughts? I'll sell him back to you. Regret isn't as impressive as other emotions, but I'm not intent on becoming an Infernatti. I'll leave that to Scrytha. Besides, a Courtney's regret? Your souls are trending hot right now."

"You aren't getting my soul, demon."

"I thought not." The indentation of black that served as his eyes seemed to narrow. "Good evening to you then."

Flowing like cloud, his soot billowed toward the edge of the bed. "But—"

Panic gripped my tongue, stilled it, and filled my mind with everything I'd ever done wrong. Like stage fright. Frozen, I couldn't move, couldn't react. I stared as that demon dragged Magbidion under the bed. *I've got to stop him,* I told myself. *I can't let him under the bed. If he goes under the bed, then he'll be gone to whatever place monsters go to once they've done all their scaring and—*

Dropping my katana, I grabbed the edge of the bed closest to me, trying not to think about the soot and the billowing cloud of demon moving through and around my feet. In one smooth motion, I gripped the bed frame and lifted with all my strength. As the bed tilted up, the soot cloud became demon once more. Magbidion's lifeless body tumbled to the floor.

I had no idea if there was time to save the mage, but I was

sure that if I didn't try something, I'd always regret it. I grabbed my katana and slashed down into the demon.

"Very well," Diaxicrotioush'nar said, re-forming at my feet. "If we must." And then the soot flowed over me, and all I could see was black; the sound of powdery soot whirling through the air replaced all sound, and I was engulfed.

✦ 45 ✦

ERIC

ALL THE SINGLE LADIES

Rumpelstiltskin," I said, still trying to think of the code word. "Wankel rotary engine!"

"Maybe it's not something so obvious," said the Kafkaesque demon holding my right arm.

"Die! Die! The sheriff bids you die!" Greta shouted at Lady Scrytha as they threw down away from me and my retinue of insectoid demon detainers—over closer to the bowling alley. I chuckled. Even in a pitched battle with an Infernatti, Greta was trying to amuse me, this time with old pulp-era references.

Scrytha raked Greta's back with her claws, but Greta left a matching trail of wounds on Scrytha's legs, rolling between them and coming up behind her. A cloud of green vapor sprayed from Scrytha's back, driving Greta away from the demon's exposed posterior.

The fight between Lady Scrytha and Greta seemed to be pretty evenly matched when I could actually see it. They kept moving to one side or the other of my viewing area, which was significantly limited, I should add, by the big black carapaces of Scrytha's demonic henchbugs.

Scrytha swung wide, claws extended. Her center claw nicked Greta as she dodged, and for the first time, I got a good look at the puff of smoke, the sizzle of flesh, that happened when Scrytha wounded Greta. Greta hissed as the wound failed to heal. I'd never seen her affected by a demon before. Demon magic, yes, but not tooth and claw. I guessed Scrytha's Infernatti-ness was enough to put Greta's natural defenses in the same category as Rachel's infernal fire.

Likewise, Scrytha burned where Greta injured her. The wounds didn't seem to be healing quickly for her, either, which I guess must have had something to do with Scrytha's whole special-weakness thing. If the universe ever needs any proof that my girl loves her dad, I offer Scrytha's burn-stained skin as evidence.

"What if it was a poem?" asked the one on my left. "Do you like William Blake?"

The demon on my right tutted. "He prefers Carl Sandburg. You can see it in his aura that's he's a Sandburg type of person."

"That's stupid," said a third demon. "With his memory? With the Alzheimer's and everything? There's no way he'd have memorized a bloody poem."

Greta became momentarily visible above the fight as she flew through the air, hurled by one of Scrytha's tremendous blows. Judging from the smile on her face, despite the burns dotting her cheek, hands, and chest, Greta still enjoyed every moment of it. The horn she'd ripped from the side of Scrytha's head contributed to that glee, I was certain.

"Try closing your eyes and thinking about something else," the one on the right said. "That helps me when I can't remember the current pass phrase in the Pit."

"They have pass phrases in the Pit?" I asked.

"For certain areas," the one on the left said.

"I'm talking with beetle demons," I muttered. "And they're

apparently trying to help. What the hell? Now I don't even remember why it was important that Greta not fight Scrytha." Without my stupid app, I was screwed.

"Fang!" I shouted. "A little help?" But the Mustang didn't budge. Apparently, he knew what he was supposed to be doing, and he was going to stick to the program.

A Harley engine cut through the sound of the fight. Marilyn tore in, holding a sword outstretched and parallel to the ground. It glanced off the carapace of one of my guards, and the jolt sent her struggling with the bike to the sidewalk. She rolled free, pulling off her helmet and throwing it to the ground. When she came up, she was holding the sword again, even though I could have sworn she'd dropped it somewhere in there.

"True immortal mojo," I said once I realized how she'd grabbed it. "I see the Iversonian has been teaching you a few things."

"Oh." Marilyn glared up at me. "Are you here, too? I heard Greta was in trouble and came running."

I laughed. "Don't let me distract you."

"If you'll excuse us," said the two beetle demons who weren't holding me as they moved to intercept Marilyn.

"Leave her alone," I shouted.

"I'm a big girl, dumbass." Marilyn pulsed with blue energy as her biker gear vanished and was replaced with modern combat armor. It wasn't as sexy, but she still looked badass. "I can stomp a few bugs."

"Nobody said you couldn't."

"Ha!" She moved to engage the advancing demons. "You just sit pretty and let the girls who love you do the rescuing."

"Now, don't get riled up and go über vamp on us," said the demon on my left. I don't know why he thought the comment would annoy me. I was overjoyed. Marilyn had come to help, and she was happy to be helping. If she wasn't, there was no way she'd be cracking jokes with me. Wait . . . was that part of the plan?

"Come to think of it," said the one on my right, "I would have expected you to do that already. Why haven't you?"

"This would be a good time, Dad," Greta shouted at me from the other side of the fight.

"Yeah. About that. It's the wrong time of . . ." I realized that I wasn't cold to the touch and remembered Magbidion's enchantment was down, which meant the fact that I'm not a vampire at night anymore was just one perceptive demon away from being public knowledge. ". . . day. Shit!" Thank goodness the beetles were dense.

Marilyn clashed with the demons, her sword glancing off their armor as she rolled and spun to avoid their claws. Each attack she made came from a different angle, with a new attempt at penetrating their carapaces. She needed a better bug squasher.

"Damn it, Fang!" I said.

Marilyn dove under a massive claw from the beetle demon and tried hacking at its joints with her blade. Given time, that might work. I watched as she drew in strands of soul energy and channeled them into her strength and speed. She moved like a whirlwind, her shots to the joints slowly having an effect. Marilyn let loose a "ha" of triumph as she took one down. One bug demon hit the ground, but the other crushed Marilyn's arm with a lucky blow, then pinned her to the ground with the follow-up.

"Mistress," it squeaked as Marilyn kept fighting against it. "Perhaps a few more reinforcements?"

"Of course," Scrytha said. "This fight is no longer as amusing as it once was." She snapped her fingers, and dozens of demons appeared like renegades from a *Star Trek* movie, beaming in to join the away team.

Amid the assortment of Khan Canis demons, beetle

demons, and other more human-looking demons like Rachel, five hooded demons in blue robes manifested in the middle of our brawl.

"Is this level of incursion into the human realms truly justified?" one of them asked.

"Wow, Fair Standards and Equitability," the demon on my right said. "You don't see *them* every day in the mortal realm."

"I'm an Infernatti," Scrytha snarled. "I am well within my rights to have an escort." Greta took the opportunity to get in a claw swipe across Scrytha's chest, opening her top and sending smoke from the lower set of breasts.

"Perhaps we should discuss your definition of an escort," said one of the other blue-cloaked figures. As one, they vanished and reappeared around her, a floating cloud of blue cloaks that reminded me of the ghosts in Pac-Man right after he eats a power pellet.

"Yes," said another as Greta stabbed Scrytha in the shoulder with her own horn. "In fact, if I may be so bold, you are allowed to travel with your Infernal Guard and one lieutenant, but that would be no more than nine demons. This is an entire cohort."

"And," interjected another as Scrytha jerked the horn out of her shoulder while dodging one more flurry of attacks, "though it might be reasonable for you to travel with as many as an entire retinue were you to impress your need to do so," snapped the horn back into place, "in advance upon the Council of Vices, a cohort is out of the question," and sent Greta sideways with a snapkick to the face, "so we must ask you to dismiss all of the current demons in excess of nine immediately or risk sanction by our august body."

That sounded familiar, too.

Something Magbidion had said. It rumbled around in the back of my head, and the memory was there, almost as if I were in two places at once: my room upstairs at the Pollux, talking to Magbidion, Winter, and Talbot, yet also down on the street in front of the building, being held captive by the Kafka twins. True immortal memory. I love it when it works.

Fang's engine revved to life. Clouds of smoke from burning rubber rose off his wheels in thick choking clouds, and his tires spun. Flame details rolled up the side of his body. His headlights filled with purple light. Beneath his undercarriage, the metallic symbol that represented the artificial locus point ripped free of its asphalt home, slamming into Fang's undercarriage with a resounding clang.

Purple smoke and blue sparks shot out of Fang's tailpipe, and the whole world vibrated like a window shaken in its frame by overdone bass on a ridiculously loud stereo system. Scrytha held up her hand to make some sort of gesture, but Greta caught her wrist and snapped it, using the purchase to send them both to the ground in a pile of claws and screaming.

Marilyn's eyes lit up with blue light as soul energy from the resulting explosion supercharged her . . . and me and . . . to be honest . . .

I remembered.

ERIC

LOVE IS PATIENT

My memory of events came back to me all at once, but to tell you exactly what happened, I have to let you in on The Plan. The night I'd forgotten, had known I would undoubtedly forget, had happened months ago, shortly after I made the deal with Scrytha.

I remember Winter was wearing a They Might Be Giants *Mesopotamians* T-shirt paired with salsa pajama bottoms and a pair of Crocs with socks.

"Fashion statement?" I asked.

"Compromise," he said irritably. "The gift of miraculously manifesting new outfits is not one I possess. You'll need both of us for this to work."

His skin went tan, eyes shifting to a preternaturally striking shade of blue, his stance shifting from rock-star swagger to that of a man so comfortable in his own skin, it made me want to smile and shake his hand.

"And I," said John Hawkes, "am not wearing all that crap he wears all the time. It's enough having his beauty products take up all the counter space in the bathroom when I'm trying to get ready for work in the morning."

Don't ask me how that all works. I have my own special brand of how-the-fuck-did-that-happen, so I can't act like weird shit doesn't go down in Void City.

John shook everyone's hand except for Talbot's. Talbot, he hugged.

"You guys know each other?" I asked.

"Hey." Talbot winked. "I get around."

"I don't," Magbidion put in.

"I know you've got the whole demon thing hanging over your head, Mags," I told him, "but don't worry. As soon as this is all done, we'll take care of it. You'll be fine. No worries."

"Okay." Magbidion nodded slowly, crossing his arms. "Okay. No worries. You do realize he's a full Nefario?"

"Big demon thing," I said. "Got it. Talbot, you eat the demon."

"If you can get it all the way here, then I'll do my best," Talbot agreed. "But Nefario can be almost as bad as Infernatti about not spending a lot of time in the mortal world. Now that Scrytha has the bump, she might be a problem, too."

"Bump?" John asked.

"Promotion," Winter clarified, the change so fast it made me blink. "A travesty for which the universe has you to thank."

"Father Ike." Talbot coughed. "Pot meet kettle."

"I recant my complaint," Winter said with a bow. "What *is* the name of the demon with whom you dealt, Magbidion?"

"Diaxicrotioush'nar."

"Shit," Talbot breathed, sucking in air through his teeth.

"The Prince of Shadow and Ash." Winter sounded impressed, going so far as to look Magbidion up and down as if reevaluating him. "You don't do things by half measures, do you?"

"I already had magic and didn't know it," Magbidion said. "It was the wrong kind, though."

"What were you?" Talbot asked.

"Zaomancer," he said softly.

"Those the guys who raise the dead?" I asked.

"Resurrect them," Winter clarified. "You'd have been quite sought after."

"And rich," Talbot said.

"And died very old at a very young age if I hadn't been enslaved, entrapped, or murdered first," Magbidion said. "And I would never have shaped fire with my own magic, or made lightning dance in the sky, or seen—"

"We get it," I said. "You dig your new powers better. So what are we going to do about my shit?"

"You shook her hand to seal the deal?" It felt weird to see Magbidion take the lead, but as far as I knew, he was the only one of us who'd ever sold his soul.

"Yep."

"And you never signed anything?"

"She asked me to when she showed up with Marilyn," I said as Mags sat down in a folding chair we'd hastily dragged into the room, "but we'd already talked, so I told her to go fuck herself."

"Good." Magbidion smiled, and it reminded me of the look Talbot gets when he sees a demon he's going to eat, or a mouse. "That means the deal is bound by exactly what you said."

"I don't remember exactly—"

"Yes, you do," Magbidion cut in. "You shook a devil's hand. You can never forget what you said. It's impossible. A law of magic. If you were brain-dead, you'd repeat the words you said until the day your body died or until someone gagged you or knocked you out, so you couldn't say them anymore, and you'd do it in tongues so that anyone in any language knew what you'd done."

"Shit." I looked at Talbot, and he nodded.

"The serious kind," Talbot said.

"Repeat the words," Winter ordered.

"Try not to think about it," John said. "Just say the first thing that comes to mind, and that will be it."

"'I'll do it,'" I repeated. "'Whatever it is. I'll do it.'"

"And she accepted that?" Magbidion asked.

"Yep."

"Then you have a shot," Magbidion said. "What she should have done was call in Fair Standards and Equitability, and they would have insisted that the contract be clarified. You didn't sign anything, and this is pitifully unclear. She'll wait at least six months to try to get you to do anything."

"Why six months?" I asked.

"Because if she can fly under the FS and E's radar for that long, the deal can't be nullified. Then it would be seen as unfair to her, because you enjoyed the fruits of the deal for six months, and for that, she'd have to be compensated." He chuckled. "And FS and E never want to do the compensating."

"Did anything else happen?" Magbidion asked. "Any other demons?"

"A couple of dudes in robes showed up and asked if I'd made a deal with Scrytha of my own free will, and I said that I had and they could screw off, because I wasn't making any deals with them."

"What color were the robes?"

"Blue," I said.

"They were FS and E, then," Magbidion said. "Probably Evaluators checking in on the validity of her claim to Infernatti status. Did they ask you about the deal?"

"I was uncooperative."

"Which was a good thing for once," Magbidion said. "They can't force you to answer questions unless they decide the deal is invalid, and Scrytha must have been calling in every favor she had to get her status confirmed."

"So what are we going to do to get me out of this?" I asked. "How does any of this help?"

"We aren't," Winter said. "Scrytha is going to tell you that her 'it' is going to be that you become her eternal slave."

I looked at Magbidion.

"But she can't do that," Magbidion said. "Eternal slavery has to be spelled out now. Too many deals have been overturned by vaguely defined terms. You have human lawyers to thank for that. She'll probably send someone she thinks you'd really like to work with, but Scrytha was never human, so she'll send someone you want to sleep with. She used to be a madame over a succubi den, so her thoughts are probably a little hardwired in that regard."

"She'll send Rachel," Winter said.

"How do you know?" Talbot and I asked together.

"You had the Eye of Scrythax that can grant eternal life or transfer power," Winter said. "I have the one that sees the future."

"But Courtneys can change prophecy and—" Talbot began.

"Oh," Winter crowed. "It hasn't been right about a damn thing yet where our Eric is concerned, but I can read him like a book. What the Eye does is give me enough of what might happen for me to deduce the rest."

"You're a creepy bastard," I said.

He took it as a compliment and unlimbered another bow. When he came back up, he was John again.

"He so totally is," said John.

"So why are you willing to help?" I asked John/Winter.

"Isn't it perfectly obvious?" Winter said, looking away, and bared his fangs like some wack-job version of a vampire coquette.

"Not to me."

"Then you didn't read the epilogue of the last book," Talbot said.

"What the fuck are you talking about, cat?" I asked.

Talbot batted his eyes at us all, the perfect picture of innocence. "Winter killed a whole lot of vampires?" He waited to see if that rang a bell. It didn't.

"Why?"

"I hate them," Winter said with a golden laugh. "I only worked with them because I needed you in place to kill Phillip."

"I'm a vampire," I said. "Why work with me?"

"You hate vampires." Winter laughed again. "And you're you, Eric." His tone indicated that was all the explanation I was going to get.

"Right." I looked at Talbot again, and he shrugged as if to say: "He's got you there, boss."

An hour later, we were still talking and working things through. Just before dawn, Magbidion excused himself and came back with two blood bags and chalk, then excused himself to the bathroom and started drawing a magic circle on the floor.

"What's this?" Winter asked.

"You mean Mr. Know-It-All doesn't already know?" I asked. "Magbidion, it looks like your enchantment is working better than we thought."

"What enchantment?" Winter asked again. When dawn came, Mags and I let Talbot and Winter watch me make the change from ever-living to undead, from true immortal with a pulse and a reflection to a bloodsucker with neither. I like to think it was at least half as unpleasant for them as it was for me. Just after sunrise, I walked out of the shower, drying my hair and sucking on a blood bag.

"So . . ."

It was awesome to see Winter at a loss for words.

"So?" I asked.

Magbidion took his turn in the shower, and I kept an ear out. I had to remember to watch him right after. Each time seemed to hit him a little harder, and I didn't want him to slip and break his neck or anything.

"So, during the day?" Winter asked.

"Yup." I flashed him my fangs.

"But at night?"

I shook my head, finished off the first bag, and started on the second. "It's not a problem, but if I'm going to take over control of the vampire population . . ." I let my sentence hang.

"Then they can't know," he said, "not until you are already so entrenched that removing you would be more trouble than it's worth."

"And," I said, lowering the blood bag for a moment, "whatever I do can't mess shit up with Marilyn. I want The Plan to help me win her back, not push her further away."

"That could be problematic," Winter said, "but I'm a sucker for long shots and making them into sure things. Give me a week, and let me involve Melvin. I'll come up with something. In the meantime, I want you to start reaching out to some allies I know you have. Tell them you want to kill an Infernatti. Have that one"—he indicated Magbidion with a tilt of the head—"make sure no one overhears the calls who shouldn't. I'll get you an approximate date by tomorrow night."

"And there's my memory thing," I added. "Whatever we come up with and agree to, I won't be able to remember it. Not for as long as this plan is going to take. I'm pretty sure it really is Alzheimer's. Otherwise, the true immortal mojo should have cleared it up."

"We'll get you a workaround," John said. "Do you have a smartphone?"

"Um . . ." I felt like an idiot. "How smart does it have to be?"

"I'll handle that," Talbot offered.

Over the next three weeks, we worked out The Plan. A month later, John and Melvin delivered the app. After that, all conversation about The Plan was restricted to my bathroom, when I was wearing the Blind Eye of Scrythax, or via The Plan's app.

In one of those last face-to-faces, Winter/John, Magbidion, and I were all crammed into the bathroom at the Pollux. I was sitting in the shower, shirtless in my boxers, wearing the Blind Eye of Scrythax and waiting for my sunset transformation.

"I'm not happy about the thrall thing," I said.

Winter sat on the edge of the bathroom counter, which made it doubly strange when he shifted back and forth to John, since John had a reflection and Winter didn't. Magbidion, as usual, sat on the toilet, lid down, and looked tired.

"Eric," John said. He'd let Winter wear his rock-star clothes, so he seemed self-conscious in leather pants, high-heeled boots, a lacy blue shirt, and funky Goth eye makeup. "Think of it this way. You'll be giving most of these guys a shot at revenge. It's payback big-time for the guys who were on the force with you. And for the new guys, you're saving them a bout with Alzheimer's and a sad lonely end in a damn retirement home where they have nightmares about what sick, twisted vampire freaks made them do and/or cover up, then wiped from their superficial memories. And with you in charge, if they want to quit one day and lead a normal life, you'll let them."

Magbidion tapped the shower-stall glass. "Being your thrall is not a hardship, boss."

"Do it during the day—" Winter instructed.

"No shit, Sherlock."

"—around noon," Winter continued. "I'll warn Melvin, and he'll keep the area clear of thralls." He tapped the Blind Eye of Scrythax. "Wear that."

"What about the Ike thing?"

"I don't like the Ike thing, either, Winter," John put in.

"She's going to order Eric to kill him." Winter rubbed at his temple and frowned when his fingertips came away black. "I'm not picking the target, I'm just telling you whom she's going to pick. By having her first command be something so objectionable to Eric, she will believe he won't even second-guess other commands. She thinks he'll be broken and tractable, and he might be, except he has us. How's the CPR certification coming?"

"Greta was curious about why I had her go drop three thousand dollars on a CPR training doll, but when I let her learn with me, she just took it as a weird father/daughter activity and let it go," I said. "It's fine. Suzie lives every time now."

"Good," John said. "Strangle him, revive him, and get him to my place."

"He'll be wearing that"—Winter tapped the Blind Eye of Scrythax—"before you start CPR. And you won't see it again until he makes the call for us and reveals he's alive—unless Magbidion needs it."

"The Blind Eye will hide the wearer from any demon?" I asked. "Even Scrytha?"

"Any demon," Winter agreed. "Scrythax. His daughter. Even the demons from Fair Standards and Equitability."

"And you think that when everyone knows Father Ike is alive and that I cheated, it will bring Scrytha running?" I asked.

"It will enrage her," Magbidion said. "An Infernatti cannot afford to be embarrassed like that without reacting immediately. By not acting, she'd risk being bumped down to Nefario status, and the FS and E will be watching her like a hawk, waiting for her to screw up so they can demote her."

"That's where the . . . What did you call it?"

"Artificial locus point," Mags and Winter both answered.

"Yeah, that." I nodded, feeling the beginning of my change coming on. "That's where that comes in?"

"Yes," Winter agreed. "You'll need Fang parked directly over it and ready to destroy it."

I flashed out of the memory and smiled, looking at all of the demons around me on the street. It felt good to know The Plan had mostly worked. Greta being here may have screwed up the Marilyn part, but I didn't like manipulating Marilyn with some kind of plan anyway. If I had to win her back without Winter playing Cyrano to my Christian, that was fine.

"Breaking an artificial locus point," I said to myself while I could still remember it, "blows all the natural ones for most of a day." I looked out at Scrytha and her horde of demons, at Fair Standards and Equitability, and realized that they were all trapped in the mortal world. Even a powerful Infernatti like Scrytha couldn't go back and forth, not until the effect wore off or she traveled to a natural locus point far enough away.

I laughed out loud. I was trapped in their trap, and they, in turn, were trapped in mine. But even better than that . . .

"And for my next trick," I said to the demons holding me prisoner, "I will remember the fucking code phrase. I can't believe it didn't come out before now, when I was talking about pig latin. I think I must have almost remembered it." We'd picked something I wasn't likely to forget to say, then put it into pig latin so I wouldn't say it accidentally.

"Hey, Scrytha," I shouted. "Uck-fay ou-yay!"

As soon as the words left my mouth, the world went wild. Sirens pealed as the VCPD SWAT team rolled into action. Spotlights flashed from helicopters overhead; the magic that had been muting the baffle of their rotors surrendered to the noise. From one of them—a large military-style transport with two sets of chopper blades—a giant fucking werewolf the size of a horse plummeted to the sidewalk, forcing the concrete to crack and buckle upon impact.

"Bonjour," said La Bête du Gévaudan, code name Garnier

(I think I'll still call him Megawolf). "Took you long enough."
Back in Paris on my honeymoon, things got really screwed up,
and part of it was indirectly his fault, so when I called in a favor
and asked him to make a little road trip, he'd been very quick
with the "oui."

"I was being all dramatic and shit," I said. "It was a caesura."

"Oh, please." Megawolf turned to fight part of the demonic
horde. "Your language is far from poetry, and if that was any
sort of a purposeful pause, it was Shatnerian at best." He took
one long stride away from me before I realized he was really
going to leave me imprisoned by my buggy captors.

"A little help here, dude?" I shouted.

"Let him go," Megawolf growled, looking back over one
fur-covered shoulder. "That he may go forth and never again
refer to me as 'dude.'"

They let me go.

And I never called him "dude" again.

Well . . . not that I recall.

✦ 47 ✦

EVELYN

LOVE IS KIND

Diaxicrotioush'nar bellowed and collapsed, releasing his grip on Magbidion and on me. Coughing and wiping the soot from my eyes, I was trying to find some explanation for what had happened when I heard sirens and a helicopter.

"What the hell?" I asked.

Magbidion's ghost spoke softly. "Eric just destroyed the artificial locus point. Diaxicrotioush'nar didn't come through to the mortal realm himself; he projected his power. When the gates between worlds slammed shut—"

"He lost control," I said.

"Yes," Magbidion agreed. "Now could you please try to resuscitate me? It might not work, but I'd appreciate the effort."

Sparks and wisps of white popped at the edge of his being. Peering into his soul, I didn't see a monster. I saw a person who could face the woman who murdered him and be hopeful, ask for help with a smile and a kind word. There was no reproach.

"Damn," I said as I rolled his body over and tried to get the soot and ash clear of his airway. "Let's hope I remember how to do this."

✦ 48 ✦

LOVE DOES NOT ENVY

Thanks, guys," Eric said to the beetle demons who'd been holding him hostage. "Have you seen my magic ice sword?"

I'd have felt bad ignoring my own fight to watch him, but the beetle I was fighting had the same idea. I knew what was coming even if the demons didn't. Eric has a swagger unlike any other and a smile that says, "Everything's gonna be all right."

"No," said the demon on his left.

"Sorry," said the demon on his right.

"Never mind," Eric said with his trademark smile. As I watched him reach into the cloud of spiritual energy around him, my mouth dropped open. In the sweet spot between heartbeats, his clothes were replaced by VCPD SWAT gear, and in his hand he held the hilt of a sword whose blade was wrapped in or perhaps composed entirely of ice. "I see it."

You're alive? I thought at him. *Immortal?*

"It's complicated," he said aloud.

Eyes flashing blue as he tapped in to the energy around him, he amped up his strength and speed, and I matched him. Lines of blue flowed through the fight, over and across, between him and me and even the giant wolf thing. Eric stabbed the beetle demon on his right through the center thorax, and it stared down at the wound in shock.

To be truly dashing, I thought at him, one true immortal telepathically to another, *you'd need a flaming sword.*

This can be a flaming sword, he thought back.

Forgetting about me, the demon I'd been fighting turned to attack Eric, but I reminded him of my presence with a stab to the joint where his head met his neck, sinking my blade in as far as it would go, then applying leverage like a crowbar.

Oh, really? I thought back.

Yep. He was too busy smiling at me and acting cool to dodge the attack from the demon on his left. It stabbed its pincer-like claws into his back, blood spattering. Eric laughed, and I couldn't help joining in as I finished off the demon I was fighting, sending his mono-horned head toppling free of his body.

On the Eighth Avenue side of the fight, the VCPD swerved in, blocking off the street with armored cars, cops pouring out like marines, shotguns firing and flamethrowers blazing. On the Seventh Avenue side, Eric's old flames (Tabitha excluded) charged in, claws out and fangs at the ready with a passel of werewolves in tow. Some of the demons tried to take to the air when it burst into flame-licked lightning as representatives of the Mages Guild appeared, manning the roofline.

Fang's tires kept on screeching, and P!nk's rendition of "Bohemian Rhapsody" blared over the din of battle, kick-starting directly into the pseudo-operatic portion of the song.

"This is going to reflect very badly on your review, Daughter of Scrythax," shouted one of the blue robes.

"And you, Eric Courtney," another shouted, "will immediately provide all representatives of Fair Standards and Equitability safe passage from this combat zone or—"

The "or" was as far as he got. Greta came out of nowhere, her skin pockmarked and smoking, covered in smoldering lacerations, and ripped its lower jaw free with a roar. "Watch how you talk to my dad!"

Scrytha rose up over Greta from behind, extra arms sprouting from her sides, claws extending to the size of machetes.

"No!" Eric and I shouted. Eric and I ran toward them, dodging Khan Canis demons and beetles alike. Flame scorched the ground in front of me, and I rolled along the asphalt to avoid it, cuts and abrasions healing as quickly as they opened on my road-rashed skin. For two heartbeats, Scrytha and Greta vanished from my vision. Eric decapitated the flame-breathing thing—a half-naked male with wings and tail (an Incubus, maybe?)—growling as two Khan Canis demons caught him from either side with massive ax blows to the back and shoulders.

I turned to help him, slashing the exposed arm of a Khan Canis.

"No," Eric shouted. "Help Greta!"

"Greta?" When I turned back, it was to the sound of primordial fury, a roar out of time. Where Greta had stood, there was now a dragon or . . . a dinosaur. Its eyes flashed red in the lightning and flame. From one of its claws dangled a scrap of blue hood and an ocher-coated jawbone. It was huge, twenty feet or more, and Greta's sunglasses clung to the end of its snout, while her badge and gris-gris bag hung from a cord pulled tight around its neck.

"Greta?"

✦ 49 ✦

GRETA

LOVE DOES NOT BOAST

Fang played a threatening excerpt from Dr. Horrible's Sing-Along Blog, but no one else cared. Scrytha shouted for her demons to concentrate on me. The blue-hooded demons shouted the same thing. Infernal magic blazed through me, taking chunks out of my thick leathery hide, but that's the thing about being willing to die or be destroyed for something. As long as the goal is within reach, nothing else matters. Being the one to save Dad was all that mattered.

"So you love him," Scrytha shouted. "Unconditionally. So what! Love does not conquer all!"

But I didn't need love to conquer all. I only needed love to conquer her.

A cloud of green vapor rose from Scrytha's back, but I bit down anyway, my maw alive with pain. Marilyn stumbled back. I guess she'd never seen an Appalachiosaurus in person. A clawing, scratching, burning thing, Scrytha went down hard, but I focused through the pain, forcing myself to swallow again and again until my belly was full and sick and quivering.

I'd never eaten a whole demon before, but this just had to be how Talbot managed it.

Dad battled free of the Khan Canis demons that had engaged him. He and Maybe-Mom were fighting their way to my feet.

"Greta?" Maybe-Mom asked.

I nodded as best I could, managing more of a predatory bob as smoke escaped my throat from deep inside. Scrytha burned, but so did I.

It didn't matter who won now. Whether or not Scrytha burned her way out of me before I managed to dissolve her to death, I'd proved who loved Dad more.

Not Maybe-Mom.

Not Tabitha.

Not Talbot.

Me.

Nothing needed to be said.

Actions . . .

Speak . . .

✦ 50 ✦

ERIC

LOVE IS NOT PROUD

Damn it!" Greta (assuming it was Greta who had turned into a relatively obscure dinosaur she'd seen in an Alabama children's museum) sagged to her right, then fell like old timber. I dismissed my ice sword, snatching a combat knife from my gear and slashing open my wrist, spilling the blood onto her prone form.

"Cover me," I yelled to Marilyn, Fang, and any of my crew who could hear. Lisa, her long blond hair tinged with blood, led my offspring to my side to protect Greta. I couldn't help but notice that Lisa wore a flannel shirt cinched up under her breasts and a pair of Bedazzled capris. She was swinging an aluminum baseball bat more often than she used her claws.

"First favor you ever ask me for," Lisa said, "and it's 'Help me fight off a demonic army.' You don't go for in for half measures, do you, Master?"

Nancy didn't say a word. Her chestnut-colored hair up in a bun, she wore a tight-fitting catsuit as if she were in an action movie. She fired round after round from twin MAC-10s, one in each hand.

Irene danced in and around the demons, her pink pixie-cut hair twitching to the left and right across her eyes, telegraphing her motions. She fought with tooth and claw, delivering no single telling blow but a cascade of wounds on multiple opponents, doing damage over time to a group of foes, slowing them down, weakening them.

No one was more shocked than I (with the possible exception of Evelyn herself) when Cousin Evie dashed out of the front doors of the Pollux, katana in hand, and sheared a Khan Canis demon completely in twain from the tip of its Doberman-like snout to the crack in its puppy-dog butt.

"Sorry I'm late," she said. "Magbidion—"

"Nice of you to have second thoughts there," I cut her off. "We'll talk later. Right now I need to get more blood out."

"I—" Evelyn hesitated.

"Irene," I shouted, "you're the fastest; I need you to sever all my major arteries and keep them severed."

"Sire's blood," Irene said as she appeared next to me in a blink of vampiric speed. "What an annoying weakness. Won't you run out?"

"Not tonight."

Leave it to Irene to be the world's most capable vampire when it comes to turning me into a human spigot. With her help, I drenched Appalachiosaurus-Greta in my blood. To the world around us, it must have seemed like an endless supply, but I knew all too well from whence the reserves came. Blue lines of spirit energy flowed to me from all of the living things around me. Bacteria died. Animals beneath the streets and in the walls of the surrounding buildings were diminished, cells breaking down or mutating, the bodies' immune systems overreacting to an attack the body had no hope of fighting.

It hit my thralls as well, sapping them of the edge their thralldom granted them. The werewolves slowed, still fighting, but at a speed equal to rather than in excess of their opponents.

Greta improved, but the belly of the beast twisted and turned as Scrytha fought.

"Help her, Marilyn!" I croaked.

Marilyn dropped back, leaving Nancy and Lisa to take up the slack in our defenses on that side, while Evelyn twisted and whirled with her blade in a whirlwind of death that made me glad I hadn't had to fight her without access to the über vamp.

"Do I just—?" Marilyn plunged her sword into Greta's belly, trying to aim her strikes where the skin pulsed and stretched the most. In the end, even with all the help, I don't think we would have managed it without the chupacabra. Megawolf seemed wholly occupied containing the blue-robed representatives of Fair Standards and Equitability, even though their fight didn't look like much more than the Clydesdale-sized dark-furred wolf pacing around the little demons.

Popsie's spine-backed beasties rushed in just as it looked like the VCPD line might break down. Quills flew, punching through armor and cars and walls, but demons, too, the screams of the dying and damned subsumed by the incessant hiss of the chupacabra.

Acrid fumes escaping Greta's stomach singed my eyes and made me nauseous, but I didn't have Irene stop until I noticed I was sinking. Greta shrank beneath me until I stood astride her human form.

"Enough!" shouted Megawolf and the blue robes in one voice.

More than fifty demons lay dead in the street with more than a few chupacabra and thralls alongside. I turned to thank my girls only to find Lisa lying decapitated on the ground, torn limb from limb. I hadn't even felt it. Marilyn and I recovered faster than the rest, and we wasted no time putting Greta's unconscious body safely in Fang's trunk.

"Is she okay?" Talbot asked.

"Now?" I asked, not sure where he'd come from or when he'd gotten here. "You show up now?"

"Class is over," he said, jacket over one shoulder, revealing the forest-green dress shirt and yellow tie underneath. "I e-mailed you and Tabitha a copy of my notes," he said to Marilyn.

"Ha!"

"She okay?" Talbot asked again.

"I think so," I said, "but I suspect we might not know anything for certain until she rises tomorrow."

"Eric Courtney," one of the blue-robed guys said.

"You have much," added another.

"For which to answer," completed a third.

A thump and a growl from Fang's trunk made the little dudes in robes flinch. The trunk latch popped and, weakly, Greta leaned up. Her eyes failed to glow, and only one fang managed to pop through her gums.

"It's okay, honey," Marilyn said. "We've got him covered. You can rest."

"Fugg'n," Greta mumbled as she slumped back down inside the trunk, "kill all you m'rfuggers. Mess . . . my . . . dad."

"Talbot, can you go check on Magbidion?" I asked. "The Decapa-Muppet thought the middle of the fight would be a great time to strangle and revive him."

"A lot of that going around," Talbot said as he headed to do as I asked.

I left the blue boys and Megawolf standing around and went up to the rooftop to confer with Paula, the pyromantic head of our local Mages Guild. Covered head to toe in sweat, she still had twice the sex appeal of most women twice her size.

"You okay?"

"We'll be okay," she said, "depending on how it goes with those guys." She pointed at the FS&E reps.

"It'll work out," I said. The other mages with her sat or leaned exhaustedly, a few smoking, others tweeting, Facebooking, or catching their breath. Back down on the street, I touched base with Popsie and his crew, who agreed to assist the Mages Guild in their cleanup efforts. I assured Captain Marx that I'd be by the station in the morning to talk to her, compare notes, and fill her in on whatever else went down.

It was strange to see the faces of fellow officers from my era, men I'd rescued from senility and retirement with nothing more than blood, words, and will. We chatted inconsequentially, shook hands, hugged, and eventually, after touching base with the werewolves William had sent and making sure my other thralls were okay and didn't need help, getting the bowling alley and the Pollux secured, I said my thanks to the vampires I'd created and once dated, and told them they were free of me. No need to answer my call should I call again, unless they so desired.

"Okay," I said, walking back over to Marilyn, Megawolf, and the FS&E reps. "Let's take this thing inside."

ERIC

ALL YOU NEED IS LOVE

We adjourned to the Pollux. Ironically, to the theater portion itself—the very stage where I'd made the deal to bring Marilyn back. I also insisted on a shower and change of clothes for both of us. I wasn't going to die all sticky and covered in blood. On the other hand, if I was going to choose a place to die, it would be there, under the mystically simulated stars that displayed the real constellations above our heads, but as they might appear in a world without light pollution. We walked out under the mezzanine, and I stared up at those stars, happy to see them and even more overjoyed to see them with Marilyn at my side, even if it also felt as though we were walking into the principal's office to get spanked.

My Mighty Wurlitzer organ was below stage, and the blue curtain hung closed, the movie screen rolled up to the ceiling. The über vamps depicted on the panels masking the organ pipes were newly cleaned, and the ensconced wall lamps flickered as they had when they were gas lamps, even though they'd long been electric. I sat down in the front row and smiled inside when Marilyn sat next to me and took my hand.

Talbot walked down the aisle and touched me on the shoulder. "Weak," he whispered his report on Magbidion, "but fine. " Paula had taken him to the Mages Guild for treatment, and Talbot had ridden with him. "Evelyn is staying with him until I get back."

Marilyn laughed at that, and so did I. "I guess if she wanted him dead . . ."

"Yeah," Talbot agreed. He took a sidelong glance at the FS&E reps gathering onstage. "Let me know how this turns out?"

"Sure."

Talbot walked back down the aisle. I craned around, looking for La Bête du Gévaudan, but didn't see him.

"He," said one of the demons, "has agreed to."

"Wait outside," completed a second.

"Can I wait outside, too?" I asked. "And can I take Marilyn with me? Can we wait upstairs in my bedroom?"

Marilyn squeezed my hand. Without saying anything, in the middle of the fighting, working together to save Greta, we'd come back to a place long gone. I wasn't sure if we were together yet, but it was a touchstone, a starting point. I could handle that. I didn't need an easy fix. I could put in the time. She was worth it. Always had been. Always would be.

"We must discuss your deal," said all four of them in unison. I clapped one-handed, banging my palm on the cushioned armrest.

"Now sing something," I said, "barbershop-quartet-style. Can you do 'Raise Your Glass' like the Warblers, with all the ching-chikka-ching-chikkas? I know it's old, but I keep meaning to buy it on iTunes."

"No," they said in unison.

"Then hurry it up, assholes, because I'm tired of your demon bullshit."

"That demon 'bullshit,' as you put it," one of them said, "returned your Marilyn to you and—"

"And I paid that debt."

"Almost," said one.

"Nearly," said another.

"On the brink of," said the third.

"Not quite," inserted the fourth.

"It is not your fault that the agreement was not clearly defined," said the first.

"But the same," said the second.

"Good faith," supplied the third.

"That kept Scrytha from forever enslaving you with the deal," the second continued, "forces us to conclude that you dealt . . ."

"Dishonestly," supplied the fourth.

"With Lady Scrytha," continued the first, "when you slew and then revived Father Isaac. It was understood that you should leave him dead."

"Yet you did not," said the third.

"So . . . what?" I asked. "You guys—"

"You expect him to kill Ike again?" Marilyn jumped in. "That's not going to happen. I—"

"No," the fourth interrupted. "To settle this matter."

"And close the books on your deal," continued the second. "We request that you perform a service for us."

I opened my mouth to object.

"That or we will rule you willfully negligent and transfer your deal to another demon," said the first.

"One with whom your relationship might be more strained," said the second.

"Diaxicrotioush'nar, for example," added the fourth.

"Or someone with whom your relationship might become

undesirably personal," said the third, "like the succubus you know as Rachel." Damn. I guess it was too much to hope that she'd died on the ground outside during the fight. Trust her to be the only demon smart enough to slip away unnoticed.

"So, because I obeyed the letter rather than the spirit of the agreement," I said, "you're objecting. I thought that's what demons were all about."

"You're confusing us with lawyers," said the first and third.

"Common mistake," added the second and fourth.

"What do you want me to do?"

"What you've been given," said the first, "the return of your lifelong love as a—"

"True immortal," picked up the fourth, "is very valuable. Your task should have been something equally valuable, not the death of just one."

"But the death of or the responsibility for many," the second chimed in. "Our command is simple, and it is one that many of your supporters already desire for you to perform."

"With the sole exception of yourself, your offspring, and those who expressly submit to your command," all four said in unison, "we order you to *destroy all vampires*."

"What?" Marilyn asked, coming out of her seat. "Destroy all the damn vampires? Why not just tell him to destroy all demons? Or destroy all wereleopards? What the hell? Hasn't he been through enough?"

"And if I say no?" I asked.

"Why would you refuse?" they asked together. "You despise vampires. You have often killed them."

"I'll answer that," I said, "if it fulfills the balance of my deal. Otherwise, you can just wonder."

"Then," said the first one.

"We," said the fourth one.

"Will," said the second one.

"Wonder," completed the third.

"What happens if I refuse?" I asked again. "Is it the weird painful feeling like I got when I was ordered to kill Father Ike? Because that I can deal with. You can't undo the deal and mess with Marilyn, because the time within which you could have done that has elapsed."

All four demons pulled back their hoods, and the robes fell away, revealing a single shape, a wrongness upon which I couldn't properly focus. It was just there. A blot, not black, not visible, but an unseen something that had filled those robes.

"On that subject," answered four voices joined as one, "we are content to let *you* wonder."

✦ 52 ✦

GRETA

SCHRÖDINGER'S VAMPIRE

Mom and I sat in the front row of the mezzanine, waiting for *Mr. Blandings Builds His Dream House* to start. We'd saved a seat for Dad between us (Mom likes to be on the end). Our kitties (both Kit Kat Marx and Talbot) sat across the aisle with some of Dad's police thralls. I guess Talbot wanted to seem all cool by staying in a different aisle. Who knows why cats do stuff?

My best friend sat next to me with her head on my shoulder, though I think she would have preferred if I let her head stay between her shoulders instead of balancing it on my left one. Down on the main floor, Dad's non-police thralls stood in the aisles being good little ushers, except for Cheryl, who'd opted to run the concession stand.

My thralls kept to the very back of the theater, I guess because they thought it was cool. I don't know. The smell of blood hovered over the theater, but that's to be expected when half your moviegoers are Vampire High Society. They'd expressly agreed to submit to his command. He had not ordered them to show up for a movie. I guessed they were attending because they wanted to make sure Dad knew they supported him—so he wouldn't kill them.

We heard the sound of the Mighty Wurlitzer as Dad rose up on it via the special lift built into the stage. After the first sing-along, I let Evelyn have her head back.

"Mom?" I said when Dad descended below the stage. I listened for his footsteps under the stage, up the stairs, around to the lobby, and up to the mezzanine.

"Yes?" Marilyn said.

"Just checking," I said.

"Ha!"

The cartoon started to play. It was one of my favorites, with Bugs Bunny and the Instant Martians. Dad joined us, and I took his hand, still weirded out by his heartbeat and body temperature.

"Dad?" I asked.

He held out his wrist, and I bit into the vein just to check. Yep, he still tasted like Dad. "So, during the day," I said.

"For the hundredth time, Greta," Dad said, "during the day, I'm a vampire."

"And at night?" I asked.

He sighed. "At night I'm a true immortal."

"But when you got stabbed through the heart . . ."

"I guess technically, I'm sort of like Schrödinger's Vampire," he said, clearly trying a new tactic. "If I'm dead, then I'm a vampire. Because I broke the Stone of Aeternum in the middle of Scrythax's trying to turn me into a true immortal, it worked halfway. So, normally, at night I'm a true immortal, but whenever I'm dead, I'm a vampire, even if it happens at night. But a true immortal's body doesn't stay dead long, so as soon as I'm not dead, then I'm a true immortal."

"Why?"

"Because Scrythax is a jackass."

"Shhh," said Mom. "The movie."

I enjoyed it more than I thought I would. Every time Tito Vuolo as Mr. Zucco would say "Yep," Dad would say it, too. After a couple of times, I joined in. After I did it twice, all the other vampires joined in. Evelyn glared at me, but I shook my head. I wouldn't say anything to them now, not in front of Dad—I don't think he noticed, and I didn't want him to—but the next time we had a council meeting, I'd have to address it. It had taken three meetings to get them all to stop reorienting themselves to face me whenever I walked into a room with other High Society vampires and Dad.

After the movie, Evelyn and I stalked my parents as Eric dropped Marilyn back by her dorm. (The wererats pretended to ignore us.) We watched through the window as they kissed on the love seat, and even Uncle Percy, who was watching through the glasses I wore, thought it was sweet when Daddy broke things off before they got too hot and heavy.

"I just don't want to screw things up this time around," he said.

"You won't," Mom said.

It was great just to see them talking. Mom made him coffee, and he drank it without vomiting blood or anything. That part was mildly disturbing, but I was willing to let it go if it meant I had Mom and Dad back and I knew who they were.

Chthonic signaled me, and I answered my cell. "Yeah?"

"They're here," he said.

"We'll be right down. I want to watch them a few more minutes."

"Eric?" Marilyn asked. "You still haven't felt anything strange?"

"Not even a twitch," he answered. "Maybe the demons were bluffing about the whole vampire thing."

"I don't think they were," Mom said. "We should look into it so it doesn't bite us in the ass. Tomorrow."

"Are you going to be with me tomorrow?" he asked.

She kissed him long and deep. I even heard mutual tongue action. *Go, Mom!* "You know I will."

"Then who gives a fuck about anything else?"

Evelyn and I made our way down to our motorcycles (I was trying to let Fang stay with Dad for his protection—he needed the car more than I did) and drove across town to my new offices. Evelyn had helped me pick out the fabric and the chairs to make it all very powerful-seeming, so everyone could tell I was in charge.

"Show them in," I said. Chthonic walked in wearing business-casual attire. With him were two Master-level vampires. I let them sense me, getting a sense of them at the same time. They were old but not that old, barely older than Dad. Both were hardworking, rugged-looking men who'd earned their money via hard labor before they'd become vampires.

The one on the left was Alan. He was in charge. The other was Brody.

I imagined Evelyn and I looked imposing. We'd been wearing jeans, T-shirts, and tennis shoes before, but we'd changed into our working clothes. I wore a custom-made suit in blacks and reds, the dress shirt unbuttoned three buttons, my sheriff star pinned to the breast pocket of my jacket. Evelyn's outfit was similar, but in crimson and white, and her star said "Deputy."

"Sheriff Courtney?" Alan said, offering me his hand. "I've been asked to touch base with your father about the territory renegotiation."

"You're mistaken," I said, ignoring the hand. "There is no negotiation. You're dealing with me, and this is how things are going to work: My dad is the King of the Damned, lord of all the world's vampires, and you either swear loyalty to him or my deputy and I pay you a visit and make an example of your thralls and your businesses."

Evelyn's head detached; her subtle way of grabbing the lip of the desk so her body would lock in place and not fall was getting even better.

"And you," she said, with her hair doing the slow-motion ripple it did when detached, as if she were being filmed underwater, "don't want that, now, do you?"

"I'm afraid that's unacceptable, ma'am," Alan said.

"Then in the name of my father, Eric Courtney, ruler of Void City . . ." My eyes flashed red as the stake I'd been holding darted lightning-fast into his heart and out again as he went poof and exploded into dust. ". . . I destroy you."

Evelyn staked Alan's partner, but he didn't dust, which meant that since he was a Master, we knew to which traditional method of vampire slaying he was immune; conversely, all the others, by definition, would work. Chthonic brought in a body bag, and we loaded Brody into it. "Ship him back to his home territory and let him give them one more chance to capitulate." I leaned menacingly over Brody. "We've got to destroy all the vampires who won't swear allegiance to Dad. They'd better get with the program and get with it fast, or Eric Courtney's little girl is coming for them. Every. Last. Fucking. One!"